A FISTFUL OF FROST

A MADISON FOX ADVENTURE, BOOK 3

REBECCA CHASTAIN

Copyright © 2018 by Rebecca Chastain
A Fistful of Flirtation copyright © 2018 by Rebecca Chastain
Cover design by Yocla Designs

www.rebeccachastain.com

Mind Your Muse Books
PO Box 374
Rocklin, CA 95677

ISBN: 978-0-9992385-7-8

ALSO BY REBECCA CHASTAIN

MADISON FOX ADVENTURES
A Fistful of Evil
A Fistful of Fire
A Fistful of Flirtation (a novelette)
A Fistful of Frost

NOVELS OF TERRA HAVEN
GARGOYLE GUARDIAN CHRONICLES
Magic of the Gargoyles
Curse of the Gargoyles
Secret of the Gargoyles
Lured (a VIP newsletter exclusive)

TERRA HAVEN CHRONICLES
Deadlines & Dryads
Leads & Lynxes (forthcoming)

STAND ALONE
Tiny Glitches

Join Rebecca's VIP List to receive free stories, bonus scenes, and extras, plus information about new releases, giveaways, and more.

Visit rebeccachastain.com.

For Mom,
whose compassion, empathy, and love have shaped my life—none of
my successes would have been possible without you.

ACKNOWLEDGMENTS

Before diving into the book, please note that I've included *A Fistful of Flirtation*, the short story of Madison and Alex's date, at the back of the book. You may want to read it first.

This book has been a long time coming, and while I wrestled with it, I greatly appreciated your gentle but insistent requests for Madison's next adventure. Thank you, dear readers, for caring, for wanting more, and for being persistent and patient!

I am blessed with very thoughtful, perceptive beta readers, who all noted different plot and character inconsistencies I managed to over-look in the umpteen times I wrote, rewrote, and edited this book. For their wisdom and for ultimately strengthening this story, thank you to Sarah Gibson, Renea Kania, Scott Ferguson, Diana Blick, Crystal Jeffs, Pam Morarre, Joanne Rimmer, Liz Perez, Rebecca Moore, and Barbara Hamm.

For the final polish, I am grateful *A Fistful of Frost* passed through the hands of my very talented editing team, Carrie Andrews and Amanda Zeier. No matter how many times I edit a book, they always catch errors I miss.

Thank you, Mom, for all the lunchtime visits and for all the dinners and desserts you provided so I could spend more time writing. You and I both know home-cooked meals are a novelty around here. Anytime you want to become this author's live-in chef, you're more than welcome!

For making sure I have space to write and dream, nature outings to keep me sane, and laughter each and every day, thank you, Cody. With you by my side, I can do anything.

Finally, this book and the entire Madison Fox series would not exist without Zenzo, Dame Zilla's real-life counterpart. Zenzo gave me the original idea for soul-sight, though I developed it into something more. She sprawled across my lap through countless hours of writing and editing, and interrupted just as often with demands for me to turn on the bathtub tap or to play chase up and down the hall. For every novel I've ever written, she has been my companion, but now I have to figure out how to do this without her.

Zenzo, wherever you go in the next life, I hope you know you carry a substantial piece of my heart with you. You will be missed beyond measure.

1

SOMETIMES I QUESTION MY SANITY; SOMETIMES IT REPLIES

Inspector Pamela Hennessey leaned close, shouting to be heard above the enthusiastic marching band pounding its way across the football field. "Remember what I said, Madison: Show me you're in control of the pooka. Take charge. You're not helping Jamie by being soft."

Avoiding her eyes, I nodded, keenly aware of Jamie standing less than three feet from us. With luck, he hadn't heard her over the bleating trumpets.

We stood against a retaining wall on the outer rim of the track wrapping Oakmont High's football field. A flailing, cheering quilt of bundled and blanketed people packed the bleachers, and a steady string of teenagers and their parents filed past on their way to and from the concession stand amidst waves of popcorn and hot dog fumes. Normally Jamie would have been at my elbow, begging for a bowl of nachos, and I would have indulged him, but not with the inspector present. I'd met her less than an hour ago, and I'd already lost track of how many times I'd made a fool of myself in front of her. From here on out, I needed to be a shining example of a perfect pooka-bonded enforcer if I stood a chance of saving face—and saving my region.

Jamie edged closer, his shoulders hunched in a dejected curl, his dichotomous soul churning in agitated waves of black *atrum* and white *lux lucis*. I strangled the impulse to comfort him. Like Pamela said, I needed to be firm. Authoritative.

Even if it was my fault Jamie looked lost.

I flexed frozen fingers, encouraging blood and heat back into the digits. A freak cold snap had struck Roseville, California, plummeting the temperature below freezing, and local meteorologists threatened we'd see snow before morning. The novel phenomenon would have been a lot easier to appreciate if I were holed up inside my apartment like a normal person. *Normal*, however, had hopscotched right over me when I'd been born with the ability to use my soul as a weapon.

A dark shape zipped overhead, and I ducked, my free hand spasming around the clunky necklace resting on my chest. My jerky reaction drew stares, but I pretended not to notice. Quick reflexes could make the difference between living and dying in my line of work. Besides, if the norms could see the swarm of tyv drones buzzing above the stadium, they'd do more than duck; they'd run in terror.

Pretending fear didn't stretch taut across my nerves, I examined the latest enemy to invade my region. The drones bore an uncanny resemblance to mosquitoes—if mosquitoes grew to the size of pterodactyls. They possessed spiky legs, multifaceted ebony eyes wrapped around triangular heads, and two-foot-long, needle-sharp proboscises for mouths. Where mosquitoes drank blood, the drones devoured *lux lucis*, the white energy of good people's souls. This bright, undigested energy in the drones' translucent abdomens made it possible to track the otherwise black creatures against the obsidian sky, and I told myself it was a blessing. But since I was Roseville's illuminant enforcer and the person responsible for defending the citizens inside my small region from pernicious, soul-snacking creatures, each glowing drone served as neon-white proof of all the people I'd failed to protect.

An entire sky lit with evidence of my inadequacies as an enforcer, and me standing next to an inspector here to assess my competence. Could this night get any worse?

Pamela gestured to the other enforcer accompanying us and then pointed toward the stands. "Summer, take point but stay close."

Like a perfect little suck-up, Summer Potts jumped to obey, rushing to kneel in front of the stuffed bleachers, out of sight of the crowds but still able to target the soul-hungry creatures dining on them.

"Here they come. Hold your ground, Madison, and aim for the thorax."

Five drones tore themselves from the smorgasbord and whipped toward us on blurred wings. If it'd been just me and the inspector, I would have said the drones were attracted to the pure white shimmer of our souls. I'd yet to meet an evil creature who could resist our untainted *lux lucis*, not even those smart enough to know they gambled with their lives when they snacked on an enforcer. But with the pooka at my side, his soul surging with restrained power, I might as well have been invisible to the drones.

I reached blindly for Jamie's arm with my left hand, pushing him behind me without taking my eyes off the incoming drones. "Stay close and don't feed them."

Here goes nothing. I yanked my palmquell from my pocket, fumbling with the unfamiliar weapon. Painted in eye-watering shades of mustard, the palmquell resembled a gun, which meant I couldn't use it with impunity. People tended to frown upon guns—real or fake— being brandished at crowded high school events. Improvising, I pretended to blow on my gloves as if to warm my hands, disguising the palmquell in my fists. With luck, holding it closer to my eyes would improve my atrocious aim.

The drones dove for us, dropping into range before I had steeled my nerves. I shoved a dollop of my soul's energy into the palmquell, the transfer of *lux lucis* passing through my wool glove and disappearing into the balsa wood gun's bone chamber. When I jerked the trigger, a bright white slug of *lux lucis* arced through the air . . . missing all five drones by several feet. They didn't slow. I pushed more energy into the gun and fired, missing again. The drones closed the distance between us too fast, and I backed up, jostling Jamie. The urge to flee flooded my body with adrenaline. Giving up on accuracy, I shot nonstop, hoping the sheer quantity of *lux lucis* in the air would deter the drones or—if I was extremely lucky—hit at least one.

The drones dodged around the scatter of bullets.

I sucked in a sharp breath, fear coiling in my chest. They'd *dodged*. Not a lot of evil creatures were smart enough for such a simple act of self-preservation. Imps practically killed themselves. Vervet might taunt me first, but ultimately their appetites ruled their actions, making them easy prey. Hounds couldn't stop themselves from attacking, which made them as predictable as they were dangerous. But drones were the lower caste of a more evolved and terrifying creature called sjel tyver. According to my boss, sjel tyver were the brains of the species, which is why I'd assumed that as their scouts, the drones would fall squarely in the "I think with my stomach, so let me help you kill me" category.

Dodging proved that the drones were not stupid and that they might actually be intelligent.

I expected to hear a buzz when the drones zoomed past, but if their wings made such a prosaic sound, the marching band drowned them out. Without slowing, they swept back over the crowded bleachers, blending in with the rest of the swarm. It should have upset me to watch them revert to attacking defenseless norms; instead, I breathed a sigh of relief for my reprieve.

Stomping my chilly feet in my boots, I shook tension from my limbs and monitored the nearest drones swooping along the rim of the stands. They speared their sharp mouths into people's shoulders, necks, and most disturbingly, their faces, feeding without slowing. With bodies constructed not from sinew and blood but from *atrum*, evil energy coalesced into shape and form, the drones existed exclusively in the metaphysical plane of Primordium. In other words, only people like myself and the inspector could see them. The norms should have been equally oblivious to the sharp jabs of the drones' insubstantial needle snouts, but every single person acted out immediately after being struck: a girl in skintight jeans jumped to her feet and boldly picked her underwear from her crack; an elderly man pelted a woman a few rows in front of him with popcorn, temporarily silencing the woman's obnoxious noisemaker while she looked around for the culprit; a mom in so many layers of coats that she looked like a walking sleeping bag grabbed her purse and shoved toward the aisle, only to stop, confused, on the stairs. It was as if the drones' bites prompted people into action, and the action itself didn't matter.

The deafening performance of the band died for three blissful seconds, and in the relative silence, I heard Jamie laughing. My heart warmed until I realized the source of his humor was the peculiar actions of the helpless victims. Pamela sliced her disapproving glare from Jamie to me, and I flinched, mentally adding another mark against us. Then the band launched into Pharrell Williams's "Happy," and the crowd went wild, drowning out any chance I had of remedying the moment. Pamela's attention jerked to the air above my head, and I spun back toward the stands. A trio of drones had split from the swarm, pulled to us by the siren song of my pooka's soul.

Raising my palmquell, I fired a blast of *lux lucis* bullets into their midst and pivoted to track two that darted in the same direction. The turn faced me toward the field, Jamie, and—

The inspector was missing.

Wild-eyed, I searched for Pamela, finding her hugging the retaining wall more than twenty feet down the track, almost back to the stadium entrance. Without lifting her hand from her hip, she fired on the attacking drones, and her white bullets streaked through the air as if drawn to their targets.

Panic receded and I sucked in a breath. She hadn't abandoned me.

Shame chased the thought. I shouldn't need Pamela to do my job, especially since the inspector hadn't distanced herself to assist me; she'd backed off so she could dissect my skills—or lack thereof—from a better perspective.

Shunting *lux lucis* into the palmquell, I sighted on the zigzagging drones. A detached part of me considered how ridiculous I looked to the norms, seemingly staring into the halogen lights, my gloved hands cupped a few inches from my face and my eyes darting back and forth as I tracked drones they couldn't see. The rest of me didn't care. In Primordium, the blinding light of the halogens didn't exist, and I'd work on my covert drone-killing techniques some other time, when we weren't under attack.

The lead drone faltered—no thanks to any of my shots—and then exploded in a puff of harmless *atrum* glitter that faded to lifeless gray as it settled on the gravel. I squinted at the next-closest drone, pulsing *lux lucis* into the palmquell and firing so rapidly it looked as if a single white beam of light extended from the palmquell's tip.

"Hold still, you stupid inflated mosquito," I growled.

The drone took two shots from Pamela before I aligned on it; it died with the inspector's fourth slug of *lux lucis* before I landed a single hit.

I whirled, hunting for the third drone. It had circled wide, approaching from the hill. I brought my palmquell to bear but hesitated, catching Jamie's rapt expression. The pooka raised a hand to the drone, a hint of a smile tipping the corners of his mouth, his posture completely at odds with the threat.

He looked like a person caught in a spell.

The sounds of the marching band receded. The crowd ceased to exist. My world narrowed to Jamie and the drone. I pumped *lux lucis* through the palmquell, but my shots were too slow, and the slender drone flitted through them untouched. No streaks of white bullets came from Pamela's direction either.

What is she doing? Why did she stop shooting?

The drone bore down on us, zipping wide around my *lux lucis* stream to strike Jamie. *Not going to happen.* I shouldered the pooka out of the way, and the drone's barbed proboscis flicked through my chest as painful as a whip crack. I screamed, short and sharp, clutching my breastbone with my free hand.

Incorporeal creatures weren't supposed to *hurt* when they fed!

The drone spun back toward us, angling for Jamie again. *Screw this.* No way was I going to let a drone inflict that pain on my pooka. I tossed the useless palmquell aside and yanked my pet wood from my pocket. A flick of the wrist extended the telescoping petrified wood weapon into a three-foot wand, every inch of it glistening bright white with as much *lux lucis* as it could hold. Planting my feet, I raised the wand in front of me like a sword.

The drone's skittish flight brought it into range, and I burst into motion. Channeling an extra blast of *lux lucis* down the length of the pet wood, I slashed through the drone's wings and thorax. The drone exploded. Black glitter rained down on Jamie and me, temporarily obscuring the world.

"We're leaving. Now." I grabbed Jamie's hand before he had a chance to adjust his soul, and his *atrum* slid cold across my palm. I slapped it back with *lux lucis*. Jamie flinched and shoved all his soul's *atrum* to the far side of his body.

"Shouldn't we—"

"No. It's too dangerous." So long as Jamie was present, the drones wouldn't stop attacking. Despite looking like a teenage boy, the pooka was still a child, having taken physical form for the first time less than a week ago when he'd imprinted on me, tethering us together for the foreseeable future. He needed protection from so many dangers, not the least of which were evil creatures mesmerized by his power.

I hauled Jamie across the track and shoved through the crowd milling between me and the exit. Jamie stumbled behind me, and I squeezed his hand tighter, afraid I'd lose him. Monitoring the skies for drones, I used the pet wood to poke my way past people who lolly-gagged in front of us.

"Where are you going?" Pamela demanded.

I hadn't heard her approach, and I spun, bringing the wand up between us.

"I'm getting Jamie to safety."

She crossed her arms. "Just Jamie?"

"I can't protect him out in the open like that."

"Interesting."

Between one breath and the next, all the urgency bled from me. I blinked, confused, and frowned at Jamie's hand imprisoned in mine. He'd been in danger. The drone had been about to hurt him, and it'd made sense to get him out of the stadium. But—

But I'd killed the drone, and I should have stayed to kill the rest. Furthermore, Jamie had never been in real danger. As a half-evil creature who possessed a frightening amount of *atrum* himself, the pooka didn't have anything to fear from a drone. Even if it had taken a bite from him, the drone wouldn't have gotten anything for its efforts; unlike me, Jamie could prevent creatures from consuming his soul.

Where had that rationality been a moment ago?

Rubbing my chest where the sting of the drone's bite had already faded, I checked Jamie's expression, surprised to see wariness pinching his brows. His soul's twin energies sloshed with agitation on the far side of his body, but his hand in mine—and his entire arm and side— were draped in safe, white energy.

Oh! I'd used my *lux lucis* against him. I'd *hurt* him.

What the hell was going on?

Scowling, I turned back to Pamela. The shorter woman stood just beyond reach of my—extended! blazing!—wand. It'd been the most natural thing in the world to draw the weapon in front of the entire stadium. I hadn't given one thought to the attention I might attract. And how many people had I stabbed with its sharp tip as I'd fled the stadium?

"The first time is the worst," Pamela said.

"Huh?"

Jamie and I shook the ache from our hands when I released him. I collapsed the pet wood and tucked it into my pocket, dismayed when I realized I'd lost the palmquell. I had a vague memory of chucking it...

Pamela extended her hand, holding my palmquell out to me. Feeling like I was moving in a dream, I accepted it.

"What happened?" I asked.

"Come here. You need to recharge."

Pamela led the way to a clump of pines, and I removed a glove and examined my soul. The *lux lucis* capacity of a palmquell bullet was negligible, but given the quantity of shots I'd fired, it was little wonder my normally cotton-white soul flickered faintly. I planted my hand on the nearest tree, and a cool wash of *lux lucis* flowed into me from the bark as the pine selflessly replenished my reserves.

"Why did I—" I stopped myself, not sure how to complete the question. *Why did I forget all my training? Why did I believe it was imperative to get Jamie away from the drones? Why did I feel like I'd been a different person a few minutes ago?* I settled for repeating my original question. "What happened?"

"Drones feed off pieces of souls *and* inhibitions. They take away your restraint, so whatever it is you want to do in that moment, you do it. The effect tends to last about ten seconds, give or take; then you're back to normal."

The anomalies clicked into place: the woman picking her underwear from her butt, the old man chucking popcorn like a child in a food fight—the drones hadn't evoked action so much as freed people *to* act. Whatever impulse they'd had the moment the drone fed, they'd acted upon it.

When the drone took a bite from my soul, I'd been concerned with protecting Jamie. After it had fed, nothing else had mattered. I hadn't thought about the people watching, about my goal to prove myself to Pamela, or even about securing my weapons. My top priority—my *only* priority—had been Jamie's safety.

Like a person hypnotized, I'd made the decisions and experienced the emotions, but I hadn't been in control. Not fully. Which left me playing catch-up even though I'd lived through the events.

"That last drone, why didn't you shoot it before it struck me?"

"I thought it'd be more informative to see how you reacted."

Of course. What better way to test an enforcer than to have something strip away her inhibitions to see how she reacted? I released a slow, deliberate breath, telling myself it was the inspector's job to evaluate my proficiency. Using the drone to do so had simply been pragmatic.

Nevertheless, irritation sharpened my tone when I asked, "And?"

"You confirmed my earlier assessment. You need serious target practice, and you coddle the pooka when you should lead. The road to hell is paved with good intentions." Behind Jamie's back, she gestured to the dark energy pulsing in his soul, her not-so-subtle use of the cliché coming through loud and clear.

As a newly risen pooka, Jamie's powerful soul encapsulated a fluid, perfect balance of *lux lucis* and *atrum*, but his energies wouldn't stay harmonized for long; he'd gravitate toward one side or the other, and it was my job to ensure Jamie made the kinds of decisions that would transform him into a pure *lux lucis* creature like myself—only vastly more powerful.

If I failed, he'd turn dark, and because of the bond linking us, I'd be altered in the process, too.

I couldn't afford to ignore Pamela's advice.

Still . . .

"Protecting Jamie from harm is not coddling."

"Between the two of you, you need protection more than the pooka."

"The drones wouldn't hurt me," Jamie said softly.

"Wouldn't the drone have taken away your inhibitions?" Surely Pamela would agree that an inhibition-free pooka should be avoided.

Jamie shrugged. "I'm not human."

Pamela gave me a pointed look.

"Well, good." I sounded petulant even to myself. *The drones can't hurt Jamie, so why aren't I ecstatic?*

"Indeed," Pamela agreed. "With the drones drawn to him, we can use the pooka to lure them away from the crowds."

Bingo. "You want to use Jamie as bait?"

"Is there a problem?"

I held my body stiff, wanting to look away from the challenge in the inspector's eyes, wanting to check Jamie's face. Hell yes, there was a problem. Jamie was my pooka, bonded to me and under my protection, even if he claimed he didn't need it. The idea of using him made my stomach knot. But Pamela was an inspector. She outranked me *and* my boss. More important, she had actual experience in dealing with pookas. If she said I needed to be firmer with Jamie, then I needed to stiffen my backbone. I couldn't let the bond manipulate me into spoiling him.

"No, no problem here."

How had this evening gone to Sucksville so fast?

2

EVERYONE COMPLAINS ABOUT THE WEATHER, BUT NO ONE WANTS TO SACRIFICE A VIRGIN

An hour earlier, I'd parked next to my boss's orange Fiat at the nether reaches of the Oakmont High School parking lot, a familiar buzz of prehunt anticipation tingling through my limbs. Two days off, even if they had been mandated for recovery, had gone a long way toward restoring my enthusiasm for my job. Squeezing in a much-delayed date with Alex Love last night had done the rest.

I'd had a crush on Alex since the first time I'd shown up at his veterinary clinic with my cat, Mr. Bond, when he was still a kitten. It'd taken a few visits, spaced across a few years, before Alex had asked me out, and then I'd had to postpone. Twice. My reasons had been valid—I'd been a teensy bit busy being bonded by the most powerful pooka born in the last decade and stopping a megalomaniac from setting fire to my entire region—but to Alex, who knew nothing about enforcers and my ongoing battle against evil creatures he couldn't perceive, I'd simply looked flaky. Fortunately, he'd stuck around. Even better, we'd both agreed the date had been worth the wait.

Mmm, so worth the wait. That man could kiss!

"Are you hungry?" Jamie peered at me from the passenger seat.

"What?"

"You made a nummy noise."

"Oh. Ah, no. Just thinking." I deliberately closed the door on the memories of Alex's firm lips and focused on the here and now.

The final gloomy rays of the sun had disappeared behind the cloud-choked horizon, and the gray sky bled to a starless black. I'd thought that after revealing the neighboring warden Isabel to be a vengeful rogue and facilitating her removal, my region would thrive and I'd be able to coast for a few weeks. After all, Isabel had been behind most of the evil I'd fought since I'd become Roseville's enforcer, and with her gone, it stood to reason my workload would be lighter. Even factoring in the temporary expansion of my region to include a third of Isabel's old territory, I'd expected to be done with today's work by noon.

I should have known better. Isabel's actions had warped my region, leaving it primed for a whole new evil creature to invade: sjel tyver. If that wasn't bad enough—and from everything I'd learned about sjel tyver, it was pretty bad—the higher-ups in the Collaborative Illumination Alliance had decided to send an inspector to monitor the situation. A pooka, a rogue warden, and now sjel tyver proved to be too much unusual activity for the CIA to ignore.

I rolled my shoulders, the creep of nerves tightening my muscles. An inspector outranked my boss, and she would be scrutinizing my every move while in town, including my interactions with Jamie. The pooka's dual nature had everyone on edge, and they wanted reassurances that I had him under control. Which I did.

Mostly.

Maybe.

I shook my head and shoved from the dim interior of the car, squinting against the harsh blue LED lights illuminating the parking lot. An icy breeze cut through my jacket, and I zipped it closed beneath my chin, fluffing my scarf around my neck for good measure. If I wanted something to worry about, I should start with my boss's plan for me to fix Roseville's new arctic environment. Though we hadn't discussed how yet, he literally expected me to raise the temperature of our slice of the planet.

If it didn't kill me first, this job was going to give me a major superiority complex.

Bundled in a black leather coat, plaid wool scarf, and dark jeans, Brad Pitt leaned against his pocket-size car. Not *the* Brad Pitt; Warden Brad Pitt, my boss. Squat, with a balding round head and puffy frog lips, he more resembled Danny DeVito than the hunky actor whose name he shared. If he ever resented the inevitable unflattering comparison, Brad never mentioned it and I never asked.

Jamie bounced from the car, a family-size bag of potato chips in hand, his head whipping back and forth to take in the rapidly filling parking lot and the stream of people trekking to the stadium. He might appear old enough to be a recent Oakmont High alumnus, but my pooka had less experience in the world than a toddler, and everything fascinated him, including the yellow school buses strung in a line along the front of the school, each swarmed by teens in letterman jackets weighed down with instruments. I narrowed my eyes at the scene, groaning when I spotted the bright sign above the entrance.

"What?" Jamie asked, tugging his beanie low over his ears.

"It's not a football game. It's a marching band competition."

"What's a marching band?"

"A lot more fun when there's a volume knob included."

"What?"

"You'll see."

I greeted Brad, then popped open the back door of the Civic to retrieve a pair of wool gloves. Since *cold* in Roseville usually meant temperatures in the high forties, Jamie and I hadn't been equipped for a night out in subfreezing elements, and nearly everything we wore had been purchased today. It'd taken three stores to find gloves made from natural fibers rather than synthetic, but wool would conduct *lux lucis* without adding any resistance, so it'd been worth the hunt. We'd also picked up matching black coats, black beanies, black scarves, and dark jeans. In the flat lamplight, even our hair color looked like it matched, though mine was several shades lighter than Jamie's onyx locks. With our identical height, strangers probably mistook us for siblings.

If only they could see the difference between our souls.

Underneath our outer layers, we both wore black zip-up sweaters, dark shirts, and long johns—mine neon green because they were cheap, Jamie's gray because men didn't get color choices. Short of waterproof pants, we were ready to walk through a blizzard.

"We don't have much time before the inspector arrives," Brad said as he scurried around the hood of his car. "Hold out your hands."

I did, and he dumped an item in each cupped palm.

"The soul breaker goes around your neck. Don't take it off until you've chased the sjel tyver out of our territory."

I examined the two items. One masqueraded as a mustard-orange glue gun, but its balsa wood frame and straight nozzle said otherwise. Process of elimination made the other item the soul breaker. By weight and appearance, I would have guessed it to be a replica of a barbaric Celtic necklace or perhaps a Southwestern saddle adornment. A sturdy leather cord coiled in my palm, the ends sewn to a band of stiff leather from which hung a curved chunk of bamboo as thick as a roll of quarters through the middle and tapered up the arms. If it'd been a smidgen larger, it could have passed for connected cow horns. As it was, I could slide my fist through the arms of bamboo with room to spare. Bold black Celtic knots adorned both the leather and the apex of the knocker. The whole soul breaker could be summed up in one word: hideous.

Reluctantly, I slid the leather cord over my head and settled the soul breaker against my chest. Hoping it'd look more attractive on a different visual spectrum, I blinked to Primordium. Color siphoned from the world, redefining it in a deceptively simplistic black and white. Everything inanimate—from my green Civic to the churned mud at the edge of the lot to the beige stucco school buildings—became the same shade of charcoal. Electric lights didn't register in this spectrum, but an ambient illumination prevented the landscape from being washed flat, casting enough shadows to provide definition to objects without ever creating true black. Only two things registered as black in Primordium: evil, or *atrum*, and the vast nothingness of the sky.

Earth's atmosphere didn't register in Primordium, and while the void of space wasn't filled with *atrum*, it simply wasn't occupied by anything. I'd worked hard to ignore the insignificant-speck sensation that wormed through my gut whenever I stood beneath the ebony dome, and I'd been so intent on ignoring the sky that it hadn't occurred to me until now to wonder: How was I supposed to track a flying *atrum*-bodied creature against a black backdrop?

"Are you sure there aren't any sjel tyver here?" I asked.

"Positive. Drones are nearby but not tyver."

"Nearby? Where?" I spun in a tight circle, scanning the skies.

Brad pointed to the stadium. "At the buffet."

Crass, but he had a point. Why would a creature that ate people's souls linger over the slim pickings of the parking lot when it could feast from a congregation?

"I don't see them," I said.

"You can't from here. Focus, Madison. We've got a lot of information to cover before the inspector gets here."

"Are you sure we shouldn't head in? Letting the drones feed on all those people can't be good."

"A few unprotected minutes isn't going to hurt them much. But if you go charging in there without knowing how to defend yourself, and a tyv shows up, you're as good as dead."

"Right. Val made that abundantly clear."

Val was an often irritable, usually sarcastic, undeniably insecure sentient leather-bound enforcer manual Brad had saddled me with when it became obvious I wasn't learning fast enough. I wore Val against my hip on a leather strap that draped across my chest. This enabled the handbook to "see," which went a long way toward improving his general mood. It also ensured he experienced everything I did, which gave him a stake in my survival. I'd put up with hip bruises and occasional strap snags if it meant Val gave me sound, life-saving advice.

Along with telling me that sjel tyver meant *soul thieves* in Norwegian and providing a picture of a tyv—which resembled a human-size mosquito—Val had informed me that tyver were "mortally perilous." After reading that bone-chilling phrase, it was little wonder Val's entry on sjel tyver was burned into my brain:

When sjel tyver feed off normal humans, they steal memories along with pieces of their victims' souls. However, the fluid nature of an enforcer's soul makes it vulnerable, and when a tyv feeds off an enforcer, it can steal the entirety of that person's soul, leaving her little more than a mindless husk. If the enforcer survives the attack, she will be as good as dead, her body permanently comatose.

Drones, the lower scout caste of the tyv species, looked similar to tyver but had been classified by Val as "mostly harmless" for norms *and* enforcers. They merely stole scraps of souls when they fed, but if they collected enough soul fragments, they could metamorphose into full tyver.

My job was to make sure none consumed enough soul bits to evolve.

"Is there ever going to be a time when our region isn't facing a catastrophic threat?" The question blurted out unbidden, whine and all. I'd been an enforcer for less than a month, and I'd been running nonstop since day one, tackling everything from a lusty demon to rampaging, fire-breathing salamanders. Now we had an unprecedented swarm of sjel tyver bearing down on us. Not to sound too juvenile, but . . . it wasn't fair!

Brad swept a hand across his bald crown. "Eventually, yes. You might even get a chance to become bored. Or fully trained." He sighed. "I wish I had more time to prepare you. You're too green to be going up against a creature as strong as a tyv."

"What else is new?"

Jamie finished shaking the crumbs from the bottom of the chip bag into his mouth and joined us. "What's this?" he asked, poking the soul breaker.

"The only weapon proven to be effective against tyver," Brad said.

Jamie gave the bamboo knocker a skeptical eyebrow waggle.

Reminded of the reason I'd blinked to Primordium in the first place, I lifted the soul breaker from my chest to examine it. Nope. It hadn't transformed into something pretty. I pushed a tendril of *lux lucis* through my fingers into the bamboo. The light ran up the gray curves and under the connecting leather bar, leaving a faint white glow. The clinging energy didn't surprise me: Previously living objects like bamboo held and conducted *lux lucis*; I'd expected nothing less from an enforcer weapon. I pushed more energy into the soul breaker, and *lux lucis* rushed up the bamboo, across the engraved leather, and over-flowed to coat the cord around my neck.

Upside down like this, the necklace resembled an Egyptian ankh. If crosses could ward off vampires, maybe this ugly amulet could ward off sjel tyver. Of course, vampires weren't real, but the legend had to have started somewhere.

"Is it a talisman?" I asked, twisting the soul breaker back and forth.

Brad scoffed. Wrapping his fist around the bamboo U, he gave it a sharp tug. The bamboo separated from the leather with a soft *snick*. He held the soul breaker in front of my face, giving me a good look at the exposed tips. Each ended in a razor-sharp hook that glistened white with my residual *lux lucis*.

"You're an enforcer, not a priest," Brad said.

He handed the soul breaker to me, and I took it daintily, feeling like an idiot. A tentative test confirmed the hooks were as sharp as they looked, the sides gritty to the touch. When I curled my hand around the apex of the U, the bamboo arms wrapped around the sides of my fist and the hooks extended a few inches past my knuckles. According to

Val's sketch of a tyv, I'd have to be standing inside the circle of the evil insect's legs to have a chance of killing it with this.

"Are you sure my pet wood wouldn't be better?" At least it'd give me three feet of reach.

"Even if it were sharp enough, it's not coated with the necessary ground seal bone to incapacitate a tyv."

I scrunched up my face. That explained the gritty feel of the soul breaker's tips. "If tyver are so dangerous, why is the best weapon we've got to fight them a horseshoe tipped with fishing hooks? Why not something longer?"

"Because precision matters. The soul breaker's name is literal: it breaks a tyv's hold on your soul, and it's the only thing that will work. If you're snared by a tyv, the time it takes for your *lux lucis* to reach the hooks could mean the difference between your survival and your future as a vegetable. You want the hooks to be as short as possible."

What lovely, nightmare-inducing logic.

"How does it work?" I asked.

"Fill it with *lux lucis* and stab. Aim for the thorax—the part of the body behind the head. Don't overthink it."

I punched the air with the soul breaker.

"Yep. That's it. Now put it away," Brad said.

I examined the necklace, or rather the sheath, to determine how the soul breaker reattached. The engraved square of leather parted along the bottom seam to form an upside-down pocket. When I slid the soul breaker tips back into the sheath, magnets glued on the inside of the leather clicked closed, safely encasing the wicked hooks. I jiggled the cord, and the soul breaker swayed, but it didn't show any signs of falling out.

I clutched the soul breaker and drew it, satisfied when it sprang free in my grip. The thick bamboo fit comfortably in my fist. It might be ugly, but it felt solid. I'd take a well-designed weapon over an attractive, useless one any day.

"What about for the drones?" I asked.

"You won't need it for the drones. For them, you have the palmquell."

"The pom-what?"

"Never mind that. We need to teach you how to net— Gummy worms! She's early." A cordial smile completely at odds with his words and tone transformed Brad's face into a beatific mask. I recoiled but he had aimed the expression beyond me. A compact car pulled into the space on the other side of Brad's Fiat, and I caught a glimpse of two people inside, both with white souls, before they were blocked from view.

"Okay, listen up." Brad turned his back on the newcomers, dropping his voice to a hiss. All traces of his serene smile vanished. "The inspector holds the fate of both our careers in her hands. She's the arbitrator of Isabel's unclaimed region, and she can pass it to whoever she sees fit. By every right, it should go to us." The feral gleam in his eyes made me want to back up. "Opportunities like this don't come often, and she's going to make us prove we're worthy. I need you on your best behavior, Madison. You and Jamie both. Until I say otherwise, do exactly what Pamela says. Impress her. Knock her socks off. Failing that, don't embarrass me."

"I've got this," I promised. I crossed my fingers behind my back and prayed I wasn't lying.

3

SPEAK TRUTH TO POWER

I expected the inspector to look like an Army Ranger, tall, muscular, and radiating an "I could kill you if I wanted to" vibe. The woman who stepped from the car shattered my assumptions. Midfifties, petite, and pale, with a slash of bright auburn in her chin-length white-blond hair, Inspector Pamela Hennessey didn't look authoritative until her assessing gaze landed on me. Then I fought not to squirm.

"Madison Fox and the pooka Jamie," she said, not quite a greeting and not a question. It would have sounded rude if not delivered in her posh British accent. "I've heard a lot about you."

"All good, I hope," I quipped.

She eyed me up and down, giving me a noncommittal, "Mmm."

My smile froze at the corners.

Rose climbed from the driver's seat and shut the car door with more force than necessary. The Latina empath gave me a curt nod, as if we were strangers and not coworkers and friends. *What the hell?* I stopped pretending to smile. Jamie shifted closer, brushing his gloved hand against mine, worry crinkling his eyebrows as he read the tension of the group. I gave him a shoulder bump to reassure him, pretending to be relaxed. Pamela's gaze snapped from our touching hands to our shoulders to our faces, and I fought the urge to leap away from Jamie as if I were doing something wrong.

"Give me a net and let's get your purity test out of the way, Madison," the inspector said.

"Pardon me?" Wasn't a purity test a medieval way to judge a woman's virginity? Not only had that ship long since sailed, but I also didn't see how it would be relevant—or anyone's business. I checked Brad's neutral expression. Did details about my sex life fall under the *impress her* or *don't embarrass me* category?

The inspector rounded on Brad, wispy-fine hair flaring on either side of her pink headband earmuffs. "She doesn't know what a purity test is? You haven't tested her once in the last five days?"

"Madison's purity has never been in question."

A warning frizzled down my spine at Brad's bland tone. She'd put him on the defense. I glanced to Rose for a clue, but she only grimaced and looked away.

"Don't let your recent victories make you arrogant, Brad," Pamela said. "Of course her purity is in question. She's bonded to a pooka."

Aha! This wasn't about virginity; this was about Jamie's dual nature and the metaphysical bond connecting us. I'd been warned—repeatedly—to be careful of Jamie's darker half; more than one bonded enforcer had been corrupted by a pooka's morally ambiguous influence. No one had mentioned purity tests.

"This is to see if Jamie has . . . changed me?" I asked, choosing my words carefully in deference to Jamie. Nothing in his expression said he took offense to the insinuation that our link might have tainted me. He saw nothing wrong with wielding *atrum* as readily as *lux lucis*, and if I failed a purity test, it'd probably make him happy.

"Changed you?" Pamela echoed. "No. I need to know if the pooka's bond has sullied you."

So much for being tactful. I peeked sideways at Jamie, but he hadn't reacted, his gaze focused beyond Pamela on the people walking by.

"Is there a problem?" the inspector asked.

"No. Of course not, but, Inspector Hennessey—" I shot Brad a desperate look.

"Call me Pamela. Never Pam."

"Got it. Um, Pamela—"

"She doesn't know how to make a net," Brad said for me.

"Why not?" Pamela demanded, spinning to confront my boss

again, the hem of her wool coat flaring to reveal the calves of her pale leather boots.

"I haven't had the luxury of instituting a methodical training regimen with Madison."

"Mmm," Pamela said.

I was starting to hate that noise.

"And if she encountered a frost moth?" she asked.

"She has a lighter."

One I'd purchased this afternoon at Brad's insistence. Shaped like a small blowtorch, with a trigger to ignite the flame, it was the fanciest lighter I'd ever owned. It also had the distinction of being the only lighter I'd ever purchased with the intention of using as a weapon—or at least I thought that was the plan. I pressed my lips together. Now wouldn't be a good time to confess that after reading Val's entry on sjel tyver, I'd completely forgotten to ask about frost moths—what they looked like, where to find them, or how to kill them.

"I can instruct Madison on nets now," Brad offered.

The inspector shook her head. "Let's get the inquisition out of the way."

The what?

Pamela pulled her shoulders back and crossed her arms, squaring off in front of me. "Pursuant to the rights granted me as an inspector of the Collaborative Illumination Alliance, I declare my intent to a formal field inquisition of Madison Fox."

"Acknowledged," Rose said.

I darted a look from Rose to my boss. Why did Rose appear to be working for Pamela and not Brad? More important: "Did I do something wrong?"

"That's what I'm about to find out," Pamela said.

"Pamela is questioning everyone in connection with Isabel," Brad explained. "A warden going rogue is incredibly rare, and the Triumvirate want to understand how it could have happened and ensure no other rogues are lurking in our midst."

I let out a breath, trying not to show my relief. *Not everything is about me and Jamie,* I reminded myself.

"A field inquisition is recognized the same as a trial in front of the Triumvirate," Brad continued. "Rose will act in the capacity of Truth Seer, and she will judge your responses for honesty."

Truth Seer seemed an appropriate title for Rose. As an empath, she could sense others' emotions as if they were her own, which made lying to her impossible. Now that I thought about it, her unwilling participation in everyone else's emotions could also explain her tense posture. Heck, if she were picking up only my discomfort, it'd be enough to put that scowl on her face.

We all turned when an SUV parked next to my Civic, disgorging distracted parents and disengaged children with noses pressed to phone screens. No one paid attention to our group clustered in the muddy strip between our cars' bumpers and the fence. Nevertheless, Pamela waited until they walked away before turning back to me. At some invisible signal, Rose stepped forward, expression neutral, and the inquisition began.

"Did you ever work with Isabel?" Pamela asked.

"With? No. I worked in her region at the mall, cleaning up citos for several days."

"Truth," Rose intoned.

I twitched and shot Rose a questioning look. She stared into the space between us, her face the mask of a stranger. I curled my toes inside my boots, resisting the impulse to fidget. I'd done nothing wrong. I had no reason to be nervous.

Sure. Nothing bad ever happens to innocent people during inquisitions.

"Have you ever committed an act that caused *atrum* to accrue on your soul?" Pamela asked.

"On purpose? No." I ran my fingers down the outside seam of my pants, not quite meeting the inspector's eyes. "I've been fed on by imps and vervet. And a demon . . ." I trailed off, deciding it wasn't crucial to list every creature that had tainted me with *atrum*.

Jamie shifted, turning to watch a gangly girl lug a tuba case out of a minivan across the aisle. The pooka's indifference to the proceedings siphoned some of my nerves, and I took a deep breath and stilled my fingers.

"Listen closely," the inspector said when my gaze resettled on hers. "Have you ever *used atrum*?"

"Oh. No."

"Truth."

"Do you think you can handle your region without the assistance of Niko?"

The question caught me off guard. As optivus aegis, Niko

Demitrius assisted in exterminating the most dangerous and deadly evil creatures throughout Northern California. He had frequented my region several times since I'd been hired, but each time the threat level had warranted his elite-enforcer expertise. With Isabel out of the picture, he wouldn't need to drop in quite so often.

"Yes, I can do this alone."

"Truth."

Pamela arched a brow at Rose.

"She believes she can," Rose said.

"Well, that's something." Pamela turned back to me. "To your knowledge, has Brad ever used *atrum*?"

I frowned. "No."

"Truth."

"What do you think of Brad as a warden?"

I crossed my arms. What kind of a question was that with Brad standing right beside me? "He's the best warden I've ever worked with."

"Truth," Rose said on top of Pamela's snort. Brad was the *only* warden I'd ever worked with, and we all knew it.

"Are you in control of your pooka?"

I double-checked Jamie's location. He hadn't moved from my side, but all his attention had pivoted to the inspector.

"Yes."

Rose took her time before saying, "Truth."

"Do you feel a desire to do evil things?"

"No." I bit off the word.

"Truth."

"Does your bond with the pooka influence your actions?"

I huffed out a breath, uncrossing my arms. Jamie had inflated in my periphery, somehow looming even though we were the same height. I needed to calm down before he decided to step in and "save me" from the inspector.

"Of course the bond affects me. That's the point of it. But it doesn't make my decisions for me, if that's what you're getting at."

"Truth."

"Would you pass the pooka's bond to another if you had the opportunity?"

"Never!"

"Truth."

I balled my fists in my pockets and strove to school my expression. I couldn't decide which was worse: the thought of handing Jamie to another person as if he were an object and not a person, or the fact that Pamela had forced the question on me while Jamie could hear the answer. If I'd had any hesitancy, Rose would have seen through it, and it would have ruined my relationship with Jamie.

"What would make you a better enforcer?"

"Training and experience," I snarled.

"Truth."

Pamela gave me her first genuine smile, one I wasn't feeling charitable enough to return. "The trial is complete. Madison Fox, you are free to carry out your duties as an enforcer, barring, of course, passing a purity test."

"Great." The moment she looked away, I shook out my hands, trying to dispel my lingering defensiveness. Jamie studied Pamela with the full weight of his power sitting in his eyes, turning away only when a gaggle of teen boys ran past, laughing and shouting at each other.

Brad checked his phone and announced, "Niko's five minutes out."

My stomach flipped and my heart rate spiked. I tried to pretend my reaction was rooted in dismay. Niko's presence meant the sjel tyver were as awful as Val made them out to be, and the optivus aegis thought his substantial skills would be needed to defeat them. Maybe I should have been grateful, but so long as Niko was hanging around, he would be undermining Pamela's perception of my ability to handle my region.

All those thoughts zipped through my head, nice and logical, but the visceral response of my hormones had little to do with such trivial matters as my safety or my career ambitions. Brad had said *Niko* and my endocrine system heard *sex*.

Pamela checked the clock on her phone, then turned to Jamie. "Pooka, I formally request a prophecy."

"A what?" I asked.

Jamie blinked at the inspector, a slow smile spreading across his face.

"In private," Pamela added when he opened his mouth. "Come with me." She strode down the line of parked cars in the opposite direction of the stadium, and Jamie trotted after her without a second glance in my direction.

I took a half step after them, but Brad laid a hand on my arm. "Prophecies are confidential."

Pamela didn't stop walking until they reached the end of the row and were almost hidden from sight by the line of vehicles. I leaned to see them better and knocked my head against the chain-link fence.

"Since when is Jamie a fortune-teller?"

"Since birth. He's a pooka," Brad said. "Didn't the handbook inform you about pookas and prophecies?"

"Um, maybe?" I tried to remember Val's exact wording.

"Check it again." He turned to Rose, dismissing me. "Did she—"

"Pamela hasn't allocated any portion of Isabel's region to anyone," Rose said.

"Who did you put to inquisition today?"

"Who *didn't* we?" Rose tugged her pea coat tighter around her ample frame, popping the collar to shield her neck from a sharp breeze. Fanning silver nails through her long black hair, she pulled the thick mass over her shoulder to drape down her chest like a scarf.

"Did you get any strong impression from her reactions?" Brad asked.

"She liked a few people better than others, but I couldn't tell if she's planning on setting anyone up as a new warden."

"What'd she feel about me during my inquisition?"

Rose stopped fussing with her coat and pinned my boss with a reproving stare. Brad flushed and grimaced.

"Never mind," he said.

Rose nodded, as if he'd apologized. When they looked my way, I busied myself pulling Val from his strap and opening him across my palm.

In normal sight, every page in the handbook looked blank, like a journal waiting to be filled. Val's true, quasi-animate nature only became apparent when viewed in Primordium. There, he glowed as bright as I did, his text as dark as normal ink. Black on a living creature meant *atrum* in every other instance, but on Val, it just made it easier to read his words. I wasn't sure how that worked, but after I had accepted that a book could be sentient and talk—or write—for itself, I'd stopped worrying too much about the *how*.

"Hey, Val."

Four words blasted across the page in an excited scrawl: *THAT WAS PAMELA HENNESSEY!*

"You know her?"

We met once. It was years ago, when she was a mere enforcer, and she told me a story about another handbook she'd known in England. She looks amazing now. Still sharp as a paper cut and strong enough in lux lucis *to match even your pooka.*

Having seen how much power Jamie could wield, I doubted it, but I didn't contradict Val. I also didn't correct his use of "your pooka" rather than Jamie's name. The relationship between Val and Jamie existed only because both were tied to me. Otherwise my pure *lux lucis* handbook would never have deigned to associate with a half-*atrum* pooka.

Words continued to scrawl across Val's page. *Did you know Pamela's worked on every continent but Antarctica? She speaks three languages and can read hieroglyphics. I think she's the only person alive to have talked to every handbook.*

I eyed the flourishes and curlicues on the fading text. "Does someone have a crush on our inspector?"

Grow up. It's called respect.

Respect. Right.

I checked on Jamie, a trickle of unease ruining the delight I took in teasing Val. How long was the inspector going to keep Jamie sequestered down there? Would she put him to an inquisition? If she signaled Rose to join them, I vowed to tag along, too, no matter what Brad said.

I monitored Jamie long enough to be reassured by his calm energy; if he'd been upset, I'd have seen it in the fluid *lux lucis* and *atrum* lines of his soul.

"What can you tell me about pooka prophecies?" I asked Val.

Check under "pooka."

Great, I'd tweaked his pride.

Hoping he wouldn't pout too long, I flipped through his pages. While most remained blank even in Primordium—to be revealed as Val deemed me worthy of the information—a few held text and sketches. I skimmed past facts on citos, hounds, and imps, stopping when I reached the entry on pookas and rereading the last paragraph:

Pookas are always born in November. In some cultures, they are revered for their ability to bestow prophecies upon others regarding the next year's events. Other cultures kill them outright.

The first time I'd read the entry, I'd been in shock, overwhelmed by witnessing the birth of a literally magical creature, and I'd skimmed right past Val's information on prophecies. By the time I'd wrapped my head around Jamie's ability to transform—at his discretion and seemingly without effort—from a mammoth to a Great Dane to human, I'd completely forgotten the sentence about prophecies. Rereading it now, I found myself less awed than puzzled: How did his ability to shift shapes relate to precognition? Those seemed like two separate types of magic.

I flipped back to Val's first page.

"What sort of prophecies?"

The kind that foretell the future.

"But why can pookas see the future at all?" I asked, ignoring his sarcasm.

It has to do with their dual natures. Your pooka won't always have the gift of foresight, but while he's essentially balanced between good and evil, he's tuned in to some of the turning points of the future. Val's uptight handwriting loosened, the spacing between the words increasing. *Not a lot is known about* how *a pooka can see the future, though. Maybe you should ask him about it.*

Translation: Val wanted to know, but he didn't want to talk to Jamie.

"Stay sharp," Brad barked. "There's a frost moth headed this way."

Rose squeezed into the narrow space between me and Brad, eyes darting. "Where? How close? Is it on me?"

"You're safe," Brad said, patting Rose awkwardly on the arm. Despite working for the CIA alongside us, her skills as an empath made Rose no more able than a norm to see in Primordium.

"Maybe I should wait in the car."

"You're fine. Madison and I both have lighters. We won't let it feed off you—or us."

"I'd be more reassured if Madison looked prepared to do more than catch flies."

I snapped my mouth shut, but I couldn't tear my gaze from the approaching frost moth. With clumsy gloved fingers, I fumbled in my pocket for the lighter.

"It's . . . blue," I said. "Really, really blue." In the monochromatic spectrum of Primordium, the frost moth's ten-inch ice-blue wings glowed like twin neon signs as it coasted above a truck five cars away.

I'd seen color in Primordium before. I'd spent a good portion of last week stuck at the mall killing red and green emotion-manipulating spiderlike citos that existed exclusively in Primordium. However, every other creature I had encountered had been black, white, or a mottled combination thereof. I'd assumed citos were the singular exception.

I needed to stop making assumptions about Primordium.

"I don't care what color it is," Rose said. "You need to kill it dead before it touches me. Or you." She prodded me in the ribs.

"That little creature is responsible for freezing Roseville?" I asked, batting her hand aside.

"That one, plus a couple thousand others," Brad said.

"There are thousands? Where did they come from?"

"Empath hell," Rose grumbled, rubbing her arms.

"They were already here," Brad said. "As caterpillars, they burrow into the soil and trees where they're undetectable to you and me. They can live for decades, maybe centuries in their cocoons, dormant until fire triggers their metamorphosis."

"The salamanders did this?" We'd had a rash of blazes ignite across our region and the neighboring territories when Isabel had disseminated fire-breathing salamanders among our allies as part of her deranged master plan. They'd burned parkland and a Christmas tree stand in Roseville, and the blazes had escalated to wildfires in the foothills.

Brad nodded, his mouth twisting. "In a typical year, we'll see a few dozen come out of firewood, and those die quickly once the temperature rises above forty degrees or so. With all the recent fires, we're up to our fruity gumballs in frost moths, and they've shackled us with this fudgesicle weather just in time for an inspection." He gave the hem of his coat a vicious yank but otherwise kept his expression serene and his tone mild.

It was unnerving, to say the least.

The moth fluttered its wings, twining upward before drifting back down in a lazy circle that carried it away from us.

"I think we're safe," I said for Rose's benefit.

Shuddering, she muttered, "Damn it, Niko. Hurry your scrumptious butt up."

Brad coughed.

"You said there are thousands. Where are the rest?" If any other neon-winged moths lurked among the cars, they would have been impossible to miss.

"They're everywhere it's cold, from the Sierra Nevada to Sacramento and all across our region." Brad took in my distraught expression and added, "I don't expect you to kill them all—just enough to warm up our region a few degrees."

Well, so long as he wasn't asking for the impossible. I eyed the miniature blowtorch in my palm. "If flames cause them to hatch, how is a lighter supposed to kill them? Won't it make them stronger?"

"It's the heat that kills them," Pamela said, coming up behind us. "That's why you have to net a moth."

I did a double take on the inspector. Her soul didn't fit within the confines of her body, like mine, and it didn't have a shape, like a warden's—her steely white energy bulged from her body in ill-defined protrusions. Beside her, Brad's angular soul looked crisp and neat. Like all wardens' souls, his jutted from his body in distinct angles, outlining the precise shape of his region. I noted the extra chunk of land we received when I had bonded Jamie, and the much larger projection of territory temporarily bequeathed to us until Pamela decided how to officially allocate Isabel's old region. The entirety of Brad's wonky soul glowed strong and steady, reassuring me that he'd fully acclimated to our larger territory.

In comparison, Pamela's robust soul looked uncomfortable and lumpy. Maybe she simply had too much power to contain within the confines of her body.

Jamie squeezed in next to me, looking no worse for our separation. We shared reassuring smiles, though mine slid off my face under Pamela's scrutiny. I tried to read her, but if she'd gotten good or bad news from Jamie, I couldn't tell.

"Niko's here," Brad announced.

"He hasn't left your region much in the last few weeks," Pamela said.

I couldn't help but read censure in her statement. Tucking my hands in my pockets, I shrugged deeper into my coat, sneaking a peek at Brad. The criticism slid right off my boss's smooth composure, and when Pamela gave him a pointed look, he simply smiled and said, "Mmm," the sound a perfect imitation of the inspector.

Pamela narrowed her eyes at him, but Brad's poker face remained unchanged. Smiling to myself, I turned away.

The optivus aegis was easy to pick out among the gray cars, his soul gleaming pure white—and completely contained within the confines of his body, like mine and every other enforcer's. He veered toward the frost moth when it descended on two teen girls loitering next to a sedan. Coasting on silent icy wings, the moth landed on the taller of the two girls and began to feed, its wings growing incrementally larger with each swallow.

Niko brushed past the girls, his hand darting out and capturing the moth in a maneuver blocked from sight by the car. When he stepped into the aisle, the moth had disappeared, dispatched out of sight.

Dang it.

Looking no worse for being fed upon, the girl turned to her companion, pulling her into a lusty kiss. The shorter teen returned her affection with equal passion, wrapping the taller woman in her arms. Both were oblivious to Niko.

"It's been years," Pamela said, offering Niko her hand when he reached us.

"It's good to see you again, Inspector."

Niko greeted the rest of us, his sharp eyes lingering on Jamie in an obvious assessment of the pooka's soul. I received a far more impartial glance, and I strove to project an air of nonchalance, pretending my entire body hadn't gone on high alert at first sight of him. Over six feet of sculpted, lean muscle tempered by confidence born of years of experience, Niko looked every inch an elite enforcer.

Not that I'd seen every inch of him.

Not that I would say no if he offered.

I shook my head, slamming the door on my imagination, which filled in pictures of his smooth naked chest, the rolling lines of his six-pack abs, the defined obliques guiding the eye straight down to his—

Gnaaah! Get ahold of yourself, Dice! The flush I'd been fighting crested my cheeks, and when I jerked my eyes from the fly of Niko's jeans, my gaze collided with Rose's. She grinned at me, fanning her face. I blushed all the harder, knowing she'd felt every nuance of my lust.

"You won't be joining us, will you?" Pamela asked Niko, her tone indicating his answer better be no.

"You shouldn't have tyver this low tonight. I'm on my way to Pollock Pines."

"Good. Both of us in the same small region would be redundant." She smiled, but it didn't reach her eyes. "Ah, here's Summer."

Summer Potts, my counterpart in the neighboring region to the south, stood at my elbow, close enough to pinch me, and it took all my self-control not to jump. With my attention laser-locked on Niko, I hadn't noticed her approach, and Summer's smirk told me she knew it.

"Madison doesn't know how to make a *lux lucis* net. Will you teach her, Summer?" Not waiting for a response, Pamela turned to the others. "Let's give them space."

Niko, Rose, Brad, and Pamela tromped down the muddy strip a few feet to give us the illusion of privacy. Shoulders tight, Summer clamped her mouth shut and pivoted to face me. Anger lent definition to her prominent cheekbones, giving her naturally tan skin an attractive glow. Of course it did. Summer was everything I wasn't, including vastly more experienced as an enforcer; why shouldn't she also be beautiful when irritated? I'd once harbored a hope of becoming friends with her, but Summer's expression said she'd rather crush me beneath her heel than talk to me.

Unfortunately, that had been my doing.

4

NO GOOD DEED GOES UNPUNISHED

"I feel really bad about the way it fell out last week," I said, guilt worming through my gut at the memory. There hadn't been time to apologize earlier, and I hoped it wasn't too late. "I never intended to—"

"Save it, Madison."

"I was trying to prevent the wardens from—"

"Don't. Don't make excuses. You gouged as much as you could from my region and my paycheck. Don't try to sugarcoat it."

From her paycheck? Had her warden docked her pay in some form of petty retribution? If so, that was between her and her boss.

"I'm sorry. I wasn't—" I cut myself off this time, stopping before I said, *I wasn't thinking about you.* Those weren't the words of an apology, even if they were true. It'd been at my urging that Brad and I had expanded our region into Summer's. At the time, I'd been too wrapped up in defending my position, my region, and my boss from the greedy manipulations of Summer's warden to consider her reaction or her feelings.

Meeting her hard stare, I realized I would do it again, and the rest of my apology died on my tongue.

Summer tossed her long, ebony braid over her shoulder and grimaced. "Right. That's what I thought. Take off your glove and hold out your hand." She did as she instructed, extending her arm toward me, palm up.

Blinking to Primordium, I mirrored her, the cold air licking around my fingers and stealing their warmth. Summer flinched when Jamie copied us but kept her eyes fastened on me.

"When you're first learning, it's easiest to make a net in your hand. Focus on your palm and push *lux lucis* straight up, but not so hard that it loses its sticky."

"Loses its sticky?" I echoed.

Without acknowledging she'd heard me, Summer gathered *lux lucis* in her hand until it flared twice as bright as the rest of her soul. Then a small bubble formed in the energy, lifting from her palm until it looked like she cloaked a tennis ball beneath her soul.

"*Lux lucis* wants to cling to your body or be released; it doesn't want to be in limbo. The key is to use enough force to push the *lux lucis* away from your body while staying relaxed enough to keep it attached to you. The bubble shape happens naturally."

Okay. Seemed simple enough.

I collected *lux lucis* in my raised palm, then projected it toward the sky. My hand flared like a miniature white sun, but the energy remained glued to my body.

"You have to use control," Summer admonished. "Watch Niko."

Surprised, I pivoted toward the other group. They stood in a loose square, Pamela facing Niko. Abruptly, Niko's soul bubbled over his chest, swelling above his puffy coat in a uniform dome. My jaw dropped when Pamela raised her hands and thrust them *into* Niko's soul.

In Primordium, both Niko and Pamela glowed with equal brightness. Yet the weird laws of this spectrum made it easy to distinguish the shape of Pamela's small, ivory hands inside the white net protruding from Niko's chest. Niko stood immobile, not even breathing his gaze focused over the inspector's head, at the fence. When she cycled *lux lucis* around the misshapen outline of her soul, then up her right arm and into Niko, his jaw clenched, but otherwise he didn't react. *Lux lucis* flowed down Pamela's left arm, swirling around her soul again. I rubbed my breastbone to soothe a sympathetic unease, and the thick leather cord of the soul breaker tangled in my fingers.

The inspector stepped back, brushed her hands together, and

declared Niko to be clean. He took a deep breath, his stiff expression slow to relax.

"What was that all about?" I whispered.

"That was a purity test. Brad should have taught you a net days ago and tested you."

"But Niko isn't bonded to a pooka. Why did Pamela test his purity?"

"Doesn't Brad tell you *anything*? Everyone who came in contact with Isabel is undergoing a purity test and inquisition." Summer tapped my outstretched palm. "Try again."

Pamela recited her inquisition speech and began interrogating Niko, her crisp words carrying across the intervening distance. "Have you ever assisted anyone or any creature in moving, using, growing, or cultivating *atrum* of any kind in your life?"

"Never," Niko answered.

"Truth," Rose said.

I tuned them out and pushed *lux lucis* from my palm, succeeding in amassing an extreme amount of energy in my hand but not in creating a net.

Summer crossed her arms. "You can't bulldoze your way through everything, Madison. This takes finesse. Cut back on the amount of energy and try again."

Restricting the *lux lucis* in my hand, I nudged it toward the sky. A tiny fountain erupted from my palm, spewing bright white light a few inches into the air before the *lux lucis* fell back into my soul. The droplets tingled upon reentry. I repeated the move on purpose, because I hadn't known it was possible. I'd always directed *lux lucis* at or into something, never into empty air.

"You're pushing too hard," Summer said.

I shook out my hand and tried again, refining my control. My soul bulged—

"Do you think Madison Fox is capable of handling her region at its temporarily inflated size?"

My concentration shattered, and the energy in my hand snapped back into place, my palm flaring bright. Summer and I both turned to hear Niko's answer.

Did Pamela get sadistic pleasure out of potentially driving wedges into people's relationships? Why else did she demand our candid assessments of each other when the recipients of our opinions were within hearing range? I hadn't appreciated it when I'd been interrogated, and I didn't appreciate it from my position in the audience either.

I appreciated it even less when Niko took his time responding.

It's an easy question. Come on, Niko. Can I handle my region or not?

"Yes," Niko finally said.

"Truth."

"Do you think Madison's lack of experience presents a drain on your time or resources?"

Wow. Way to pull your punches, Pamela.

"No."

"Truth."

I wished Niko would elaborate. If he told the inspector I was an exceptional enforcer, it'd go a long way toward meeting Brad's goal of impressing Pamela. Of course, if I were an exceptional enforcer, I wouldn't need to rely on Niko's praise to influence Pamela's opinion.

"Why do you think you didn't know Isabel was spreading evil?" Pamela asked.

The rumble of a car driving by drowned out his response. Summer blinked and refocused on me.

"Concentrate," she ordered, as if she hadn't been eavesdropping, too.

Sparing her a glare, I gave the *lux lucis* in my hand another push, not too hard, finding the balance. It reminded me of learning how to blow a bubble in gum, ferreting out the amount of pressure I could exert before it ripped. An infinitesimal gap lifted between the outline of my soul and my hand. Air wafted through it, tangible and startling, and my soul snapped back to my body.

Summer gasped, and I looked up with a grin, half expecting praise, only to follow her wide-eyed gaze to Jamie. The pooka balanced a net the size of a beach ball on his right palm. *Atrum* and *lux lucis* swirled across the surface like a black-and-white rainbow on the outside of a soap bubble; then the *atrum* slid down the sides, leaving a net of solid *lux lucis*.

"Show-off," I said, more for Summer's benefit than Jamie's. I'd seen him cast a much larger net of *atrum* before, though at the time I hadn't known the correct terminology. He'd used it to sully a teacup Yorkie, turning her into the world's smallest hound. I'd convinced

Jamie to eradicate the *atrum* he'd forced on the dog, which he'd done with equal ease.

Beaming at me, Jamie brought his left hand up to cup the bulging *lux lucis* between his palms. When he pulled his hands apart, a separate net wreathed each palm, one black, one white.

"Now you're just trying to make me look bad," I said, watching Summer backpedal in my periphery. "Any tips?"

Jamie shrugged. "It's like starting to shift but stopping partway."

"Since I've only got the one form, that's not terribly helpful."

"Maybe relax?"

Jamie spread his arms wide and inflated his nets until they touched. The amount of *atrum* contained in the far one would be enough to seriously harm Summer or me, yet he didn't show any strain. I should have been alarmed, but I knew Jamie was just playing around.

Summer stumbled against the bumper behind her, the pop of plastic loud in the silence. All conversation in the other group had ceased, and Niko loomed in front of Brad and Rose, Pamela right beside him, both locked on Jamie with equal intensity. The optivus aegis probably had a dozen weapons hidden on his person and the reflexes to use them against the pooka before I could intervene. Who knew what Pamela could do.

"Can you put those away? They make it hard to concentrate." I heard the strain in my voice and cleared my throat.

Jamie reined in his soul, unaware of his audience. "Your first try wasn't completely pathetic," he said.

"Thank you. That's very gracious." Sarcasm helped steady me. I lifted my palm for another attempt at a normal-size net, monitoring Pamela and Niko through my lashes. I couldn't cobble together my concentration until their conversation resumed.

Summer remained as far away from us as the cars allowed.

I coaxed a net into existence, this one the size of a tangerine. Pleased, I drew my hand to my face and examined the gap between my skin and the dome of my soul. It wasn't empty, like I had expected. *Lux lucis* swirled inside the bubble like a metaphysical snow globe.

Rose's stiletto boots clacked like castanets across the pavement, pulling my attention from my soul gazing. She yanked open her car door and jumped in. The door hadn't closed behind her before the engine turned over and she backed out, pulling her seat belt on as she drove away.

"Is everything okay?" I asked Brad as he, Niko, and Pamela rejoined us.

"She's had a long day," Brad said.

Pamela pointed to my hand, where a tiny net still bulged from my palm. "Now do that over your heart."

I fumbled through a half dozen attempts, clumsy under the scrutiny of Niko, Brad, and Pamela, keenly aware of the gap between my actions and the desired goal of impressing her. Only Jamie appeared uninterested. He rummaged through the bag in the backseat of the Civic, pulling out a granola bar and opening it with a crinkle. Perversely, his distracting sounds helped me forget about Pamela and Niko judging me. My soul swelled a few inches above my breastbone.

"Hold it." Pamela stepped into my personal space and placed her hands on my chest.

I barely had time to brace for the intrusion of a stranger's palms on the upper swell of my breasts, let alone the greater intimacy of her touching my soul, before her hands slid inside my net. Dizziness spiraled through my chest at her there/not-there touch. Clinging to the net, I focused on Pamela's stern mouth, her subtle crow's-feet, her pencil-darkened brows, and fought against the urge to jerk clear of her touch.

Then Pamela pulsed *lux lucis* through her hands, and my awareness imploded, following the path of her energy as it invaded my skin, muscles, nerves, and cells. The next pulse collected bits of *lux lucis* from me, sampling and recycling them. Rifling through bits and pieces of *me*.

My soul crawled beneath my skin.

When Pamela withdrew her hands, my net snapped back to my body, and I stumbled against the chain-link fence.

"Easy there." Pamela steadied me with a hand on my arm. "You're clean."

Rose's hasty departure made sense now: Shadowing Pamela all day had forced her to endure not only a procession of uncomfortable inquisitions but also the emotional distress of dozens of purity tests; I'd have run to escape the nauseating ordeal of another one, too.

Half-eaten granola bar forgotten, Jamie pushed to my side, and Pamela backed up so smoothly it didn't look like a retreat. Inky swirls of *atrum* curled over skittering waves of *lux lucis* within the confines of the pooka's body, telegraphing Jamie's agitation. I reached for his bare hand, and the moment we touched, he altered his soul so I made contact with *lux lucis*. He smiled and I returned it without holding his gaze. In Primordium, his eyes whirled in hypnotic spirals of black and white, and staring too long made me dizzy.

I gave his fingers a squeeze, then released them; holding hands in front of the inspector wouldn't project confidence or authority. However, the brief contact did the trick, and his soul's energies calmed. Touching had helped steady me, too, and I savored the return of my equilibrium as I tugged on the glove I'd removed for Summer's lesson.

"Okay, we've got drones to kill and—"

My phone blasted Shakira's "Ready for the Good Times" from my pocket, interrupting the inspector. *Bridget.*

Normally I would have let my best friend's call go to voice mail, but Bridget lived in my region, and this job cultivated paranoia. Yesterday we'd made a pact to dissect my date with Alex, and a low-level worry had settled in my gut when I hadn't been able to reach her earlier.

"Sorry. I need to take this," I said, stepping away from the group. Jamie trailed after me, crunching his way through the granola bar. Brad scowled, his fingers strangling each other, but he smoothed his expression when Pamela turned toward him.

"Hello, this is Madison," I said, unnecessarily formal and hushed. No need to project the nature of my call to the inspector.

"Dice! I'm so glad you answered. Today's been hell. Some first-year got caught in the supply closet with an intern's face up her skirt, and the partners decided to punish us all with a mandatory five-hour sexual harassment and office etiquette training session today, *on a Saturday.* The only thing that got me through those horrid videos from the nineties was looking forward to hearing about your date with the *luv* doctor."

"'Face up her skirt'?" Jamie parroted loud enough to turn Summer's head.

My eyes bulged. Thumbing the volume down on my cell, I put my finger to my lips, my relief to discover Bridget safe and sound swallowed by a flush of mortification. Jamie and I *so* weren't ready for a conversation about oral sex.

"Hello? Are you there?"

"I'm here."

"Oh crap. The date wasn't *terrible*, was it?"

I glanced over my shoulder. Brad's glare should have drilled a hole through my forehead. "Uh, no. I would give the experience high marks."

"Is something evil gnawing on you?" Bridget asked, her tone caught between alarm and disapproval.

I snorted. "Not at the moment." Unlike my family or most of my friends, Bridget knew every detail of my crazy life, up to and including my ability to use *lux lucis* to kill evil creatures she couldn't see. The most amazing part was she believed me.

"I thought humans didn't sniff each other's crotches," Jamie said.

"They don't," I hissed, covering the phone's receiver with one hand.

"Did I just hear a man?" Bridget asked.

Scratch that. Bridget knew *almost* every detail of my crazy life. I hadn't, however, had time yet to explain a shape-shifting pooka to her, let alone the bond connecting Jamie and me. I didn't want to do it over the phone, either, especially not with my boss, my boss's boss, and my boss-mentor Niko a few feet away.

"Then why else would someone have their head up—"

I snatched the last bite of granola from Jamie's hand and stuffed it into his mouth, then hunched over my phone, cupping my hand around the receiver for privacy.

"Do you remember the inspector I told you was coming? I'm training with her tonight. Like right now."

"Shoot! Why didn't you say so? I'll let you go—"

"Wait. Do me a favor. Stay indoors tonight."

"What type of evil creature is it this time?"

This was why I adored Bridget: It didn't matter how insane I sounded; she took it in stride.

"Something called a soul thief. I'll explain tomorrow."

Niko strode past me, a reproving look accompanying his nod farewell. A cold ping of guilt zipped through my body, blossoming to alarm when I checked on the others and found them all waiting on me.

"And tell me about your date? Over lunch?" Bridget asked.

"Deal. Gotta go."

"Who's Bridget?" Jamie asked when I hung up.

"My best friend from college." I squeezed past him, eager to get back to the others before Brad burst a blood vessel. "I'll introduce you tomorrow. I think you'll like her."

Jamie grinned and bounced after me. Tomorrow would be interesting, especially for Bridget.

"Keep me apprised of any changes," Pamela said to Brad as I rejoined them.

"Of course." Dismissed, he departed with one last bug-eyed look for me and a mouthed *"Impress her."*

Without waiting, Pamela marched toward the stadium, and Summer, Jamie, and I rushed to catch up. The inspector took a winding route, detouring to intercept a wayward frost moth that had homed in on a group of teens clustered at the rear of a minivan. The matching lines of their clothing and the blocky letter *V* sewn into their jackets proclaimed them all to be members of the Oakmont High Vikings band. Oblivious to everything except each other, they squealed and yelled and jostled, making a general ruckus for ruckus's sake.

Jamie slowed, enticed by their chaotic camaraderie. Glancing between him and the high schoolers, I realized the pooka would have no trouble fitting in with them. Full of energy, half evil, and more than a little reckless, Jamie embodied the spirit of a teenager.

It made me feel old.

Telling myself it wasn't a bad thing—that with age came maturity and freedom—I examined the teens' souls. Every one of them exhibited a classic norm soul, their accumulated immoral actions splashed in stagnant shades of gray and black across otherwise pristine white *lux lucis*. Humans—normal humans, not enforcers and wardens and people who worked for the CIA—always had patchwork souls. I'd never met a norm over the age of ten who didn't have some gray on her soul, and by the time most people reached their fifties, usually their entire souls were pewter. Or darker.

I'd learned not to judge gray. Gray was the human equivalent of Jamie—some good, some bad. Absolute black *atrum* was another matter, and I steered wide around the one teen with ebony veins running up her knuckles to her elbows.

Grabbing Jamie's arm, I urged him to catch up with the others. The moth followed, drawn by the lure of three pure white souls and one mesmerizing pooka.

"Summer, why don't you show Madison how to exterminate a frost moth," Pamela said, stopping several car lengths from the boisterous band members. The moth ghosted closer on silent, intangible wings, and Summer jostled me aside to put herself in its path.

"How evil are they?" I asked. From afar, the moth had appeared solid blue, but now I could see its body hung *atrum*-black between its radiant wings.

"Mostly harmless," Pamela said. "It would take a long feeding or an absurd number of frost moths to taint a norm, but it could happen. In an average winter, they might not even warrant your attention. Can you see what she's doing?"

I stepped to the side for a better angle. Summer formed a softball-size net in her palm and swept her hand through the moth, miring it inside the energy of her soul. I cringed. Allowing Pamela's *lux lucis* inside mine had been awful; the thought of trapping living *atrum* in such an intimate cage made my stomach twist.

Lowering her arm, Summer turned to face us and drew a lighter from her pocket. The moth dipped its dark head and fastened its tiny mouth on Summer's soul just above her wrist. As it fed, its wings fanned in lazy beats, generating an icy draft that stirred my hair and chilled my cheeks.

Impossible. The frost moth existed solely in Primordium. I could pass my hand right through it. It shouldn't have been able to affect the physical world. And yet . . .

And yet, how else would the moths have lowered the entire region's temperature?

"Even the cooling weather wouldn't be a problem if not for the timing." Pamela's tone took on a lecturing quality. "But combined with the sjel tyver migration, it's disastrous. The tyver will push as far south as feasible, which means they'll be crawling over this region in no time. Normally tyver will migrate no lower than the high Sierras, and the regions up there have measures in place to protect their inhabitants. Down here, the best you guys have is the moderate help of a tragically thinned prajurit population and your palmquells. With all these frost moths bringing record lows to Roseville and more people than ever using their fireplaces, it's going to be a tough fight."

Her comment about fireplaces seemed random until I remembered Val's explanation about tyv reproduction. According to the handbook, tyver had evolved alongside humans, adopting our survival techniques for their gain, most blatantly by co-opting our fires as spawning grounds for their young. Tyv larvae required a cycling hot-and-cold environment for metamorphosis, which made our fireplaces their preferred hatching grounds. Extending their migration as far south as possible proved another tried and true tyv survival tactic; the farther south a tyv drone hatched, the more opportunities it had to feed on human souls during its inaugural migration back to the arctic tundra.

Summer clicked the button on her lighter. Nothing appeared to happen; like other natural forms of light, fire wasn't visible in Primordium, though a quick blink to normal sight confirmed a cone of blue-red flame extended from the lighter's nozzle. Without being able to see the snared frost moth, it looked as if Summer were posing for *Pyro Magazine*, her "empty" hand cupped beneath the slender black lighter, her upper hand holding the flame steady.

I blinked to Primordium to check the frost moth's reaction. The evil insect fluttered its wings, but trapped in Summer's net, it couldn't escape. As fast as a snowflake would melt against a flame, the moth shrank until its entire dark body disappeared inside the bubble of Summer's soul. Summer collapsed the net, and like a magic trick, the frost moth vanished.

"Whoa!" Jamie brushed past me, his hand reaching for the air beneath the disintegrated frost moth.

I blinked to normal sight and gawked at the flurry of white powder drifting from Summer's hand. Jamie caught a piece on his glove, drawing it to his face. I leaned close to examine it with him. It wasn't *lux lucis* made visible in the normal spectrum, as I'd first assumed. It was snow.

Before I could stop him, Jamie lifted his glove to his mouth and touched his tongue to the flake. It melted upon contact.

"Wicked cool," he exclaimed.

My mouth curled in horror. Consuming the remains of an evil creature couldn't be healthy. It definitely wasn't hygienic.

Glancing around to see Pamela's reaction, my gaze snagged on Summer. She watched Jamie, or rather, she watched Jamie's lips, and the intensity of her stare didn't look like a woman grossed out by seeing him eat flakes of a frost moth's carcass *or* like an enforcer suspicious of all things pooka. She looked . . . hungry.

Summer stalked toward Jamie, smooth as a mountain lion after prey. Alarm bells clanged in my head. I stepped forward, breaking her fixation on the pooka. Pinning me with a venomous glare, she curled her fingers into a fist around her lighter and cocked back her arm.

"What are you doing?" I asked.

"I'm going to—"

Pamela slid between us and laid a gentle hand on Summer's elbow, turning her toward the stadium. "Lead the way."

Something hot flared in Summer's eyes, then died. She gave herself a shake, and when she glanced over her shoulder at Jamie, mistrust tightened her expression once more. Whatever had been going through her head a moment ago, she'd safely tucked it out of sight.

"Keep up, Madison," Pamela said before falling into step with Summer.

Frowning, I trailed after them, nudging Jamie to get him moving when a costumed mascot running down the next aisle distracted him.

"What the hell just happened?" I whispered to Val, discreetly tugging him from his strap and opening him.

Nothing. Just like nothing happened the minute before that and the minute before that and the minute before that and the—

I gave him a shake. "Val, come on. Right now, something happened with Summer."

Sure. Probably.

"Val . . ."

How hard is it for you to hand me to Pamela?

"It's proving very difficult since you won't tell me anything I want to know," I hissed, holding the spine of the book against my lips so he could hear my teeth grit.

If I tell you, you'll let me talk to her?

"Yes."

Frost moth.

I waited for more words to appear, feet dragging to allow the gap to widen between me and the inspector. "Val . . ."

Frost moth. Frost moth. Frost moth. Flip the page already.

Oh. I thumbed ahead to his entry on frost moths. Next to a black-and-white sketch of a moth sat a succinct paragraph. I skimmed over the description to the heart of the short entry:

Frost moths consume cooler emotions as they feed. This drain on a person's calming sentiments, such as logic and patience, creates an emotional vacuum—one that is typically filled with a person's hotter emotions until she stabilizes.

"The moth made her angry?" I asked, remembering Summer's clenched fist.

Yes.

Anger hadn't been her emotion when she'd looked at Jamie, though.

Pamela. Now. You promised.

"Yes, Master," I said, sure Val would miss my sarcasm.

Picking up my pace, I joined Summer and Pamela at the back of the ticket line and waited until their conversation came to a natural lull.

"Pamela, do you have a moment to speak with Val?"

"Who?"

I held the handbook up. "Valentine, er, Valentinus Aurelius." He'd introduced himself as such, though I suspected he'd made up the pompous name to make himself sound important. Fortunately, he'd been pleased at being given a nickname, and I'd been calling him Val since.

"Ah. I remember this book." Pamela took Val from me and ran her gloved fingertips over the colorful ribbons on his cover. "It's looking much healthier than the last time I saw it. Kudos to you, Madison."

"Thank you. He's been eager to be reacquainted with you." I crossed my fingers that Val would play it cool.

She opened him and a flurry of words flowed across his page, but the angle prevented me from reading it. Whatever he said made Pamela chuckle and Summer glare at me.

"That's incredibly flattering," Pamela said, speaking to Val. "And what is your assessment of Madison?"

Of course she would ask that first. Val's response was much shorter this time, and Summer laughed, covering it with a cough when Pamela shot her a look. I crossed my arms and pretended I wasn't straining to read Val's text. I should have reminded him we were supposed to be impressing the inspector, not airing grouchy opinions.

"I meant as a companion for you," Pamela said, and the mirth in her voice stiffened my spine.

A trio of trumpet-toting teens pushed the wrong way through the line, jostling me against Jamie and ruining my chance to eavesdrop on Val and Pamela's conversation. Settling back on my heels, I surveyed the crowd. Swap out the Vikings insignia on the stadium walls with Berkeley yellow jackets and add in another thousand people, and this could have been a commonplace scene from my high school days. Jamie, however, bounced on his toes, enthralled by the crisp winter air scented with competing aromas of caramel corn and nachos, the band's music thumping through the stadium, and the jazzed-up crowd singing along.

A group of girls slowed to give Jamie a frank appraisal—which he completely missed, just as they appeared oblivious to my glare. I recognized Jamie qualified as "hot" by most women's standards. I wasn't blind. His striking golden eyes shadowed by thick, dark lashes were enough to turn heads, but combined with the kind of square jawline cartoonists loved to exaggerate and a devil-may-care smile, and he earned a phenomenal number of second glances. But when I looked at him, I saw a five-day-old pooka who needed protection. Even from horny teenage girls.

Dang it; I was back to feeling old.

I shoved my hands into my pockets, fighting the urge to whisk Jamie back to the car. I recognized the bond's manipulation in the extreme reaction. Jamie wasn't in danger here. If anything, he represented a threat to everyone else.

"Interesting," Pamela said, openly talking to the handbook and managing not to look crazy in the process. "I would love to learn what you've been up to since we last talked, but right now, we've got work to do." Pamela handed Val back to me with a rueful shake of her head. "I do so love the ones that still have their personalities."

We reached the front of the line, and Summer stepped forward to pay the ticket taker. I used the opportunity to peek inside Val. His comments about me or anything else he and Pamela had discussed were gone. In their place were three exuberant words.

She remembered me!

"You're hard to forget," I grumbled before sliding him back into his strap. I'd ferret out what he said about me later. Forking over a twenty to the teen behind the booth, I accepted two tickets and handed the extra to Jamie.

"We should get food," Jamie decided, eyeing the concession stand. If he'd been in his Great Dane form, his tail would have wagged right off his body.

I tugged him after Pamela. "Maybe later. Right now, we need to focus on impressing the inspector."

"I could impress her with how much I can eat."

"I don't think that's what Brad had in mind," I said, but the idea made me grin.

A dozen frost moths fluttered around the outskirts of the crowd at the concession stand. They lit upon people walking alone or in pairs, feeding for a few seconds at a time before flapping to the next person. Each time they ate, their wings grew, and more than one frost moth flew on wings larger than hubcaps.

Pamela ignored them, weaving through the milling people until she reached a pocket of empty space at the edge of the stadium. Steep bleachers lined one side of the football field, the aluminum benches packed with patchwork-norm souls. A marching band danced across the field, a hundred teens playing at earsplitting volume. Without walls and people in the way, the brassy notes of Beyoncé's latest hit bombarded my eardrums. Baton twirlers and flag wavers circled the band in nonstop, spinning accompaniment, but their energetic antics couldn't compete with the acrobatic feats of the tyv drones above the stands.

My fingers tightened on Jamie's arm. Seeing the sketches of drones in Val hadn't prepared me for the real deal. With wingspans as wide as my stretched arms and two-foot-long barbs projecting from their triangular heads, the drones looked like cartoon monsters come to life as they skimmed through the stands, striking victim after victim, their translucent abdomens swelling bright with *lux lucis*.

Jamie tugged at my fingers, and I released my death grip with a distracted apology. Summer said something, but her words were lost under the concussive beat of the drum section. Pamela pointed to her ear and shook her head, then gestured for us to circle behind the stadium.

I hesitated before following her. I didn't want to turn my back on the drones—or all the innocent victims—but I also didn't have a clue how to proceed.

"How can they hold that much *lux lucis* without dying?" I asked. Some of the drones' bloated abdomens looked close to bursting. Consuming such large quantities of *lux lucis* should have countered their body's *atrum* and killed them.

Pamela didn't answer until the concrete wall of the restroom building stood between us and the band. "The sac in their abdomen allows them to metabolize the *lux lucis* at a manageable rate. Plus, the energy they steal is more than the surface *lux lucis* an imp or the like might take from a person. Tyver and drones cut deeper. That's why a tyv can steal the entirety of your soul or whole memories from a norm.

Drones are weaker, so they take only inhib—" Pamela cut herself off, her whole body tensing.

I spun, expecting a Kamikaze drone. Instead, I saw Jamie. He'd roamed a few yards away to a cluster of granite boulders edging a landscaped flower bed, and he jumped along the rocks with the enthusiasm of a goat, testing out his new hiking boots. Despite the crowds, no one paid him much attention. I suspected he wasn't the first person to climb over those rocks, probably not even the first person tonight.

He was, however, the first pooka to do so, and imps came out of the metaphysical woodwork when they spotted him.

Shaped like sable chinchillas with bodies of coalesced *atrum* and very little brain matter, imps were the least threatening evil creature in existence. Discounting their disproportionately large mouths filled with rows of sharp teeth and their propensity to view me as a snack, imps were actually cute. Jamie thought so, too, which was the problem. Letting him play fun uncle with a herd of imps was exactly the sort of display Brad had warned me to avoid in front of the inspector.

Crap. I should have anticipated this. Crowds attracted *atrum* creatures, and *atrum* creatures couldn't resist Jamie, imps least of all.

A handful of imps bounced up the boulders and leapt for Jamie's legs, climbing his body like squirrels up a tree. Each sank their teeth into him as often as claws, but Jamie didn't allow them to feed off his soul. He even went so far as to restructure his energy so *atrum* coated him from head to toe, hiding all his *lux lucis* beneath it. I had seen this transformation before, but it always stole my breath. Standing atop the boulder, his body a dark silhouette of pure *atrum*, Jamie looked as sinister as a demon and twice as powerful.

The first of the imps reached Jamie's shoulders, and he sent them tumbling down his arms to his hands, where he windmilled them and launched them into the sky. The imps flew through the air, mouths open in unmistakable glee. Before they'd begun to fall back to earth, Jamie launched another handful.

Menacing, my pooka was not.

Smiling, I turned to explain his actions to the inspector, but my words died in my throat. Pamela's tense posture hadn't changed, but while I'd been distracted, she'd materialized a vicious hunting knife from somewhere on her person. Even more terrifying, she looked prepared to use it—on Jamie.

5

I LICKED IT, SO IT'S MINE

I lurched in front of Pamela, breaking her line of sight on Jamie. Behind her, Summer clutched her sheathed soul breaker, her expression equally menacing.

"Hang on, let me explain," I said, raising pacifying hands in front of both women.

Pamela shifted to the side, never looking away from the pooka. "You're not going to let him—"

"Of course not." Abandoning diplomacy, I scurried up the boulder to Jamie's side before the inspector decided to intervene. With a knife.

My screwed-up pooka-bonded instincts clamored for me to keep Pamela in my sight, but I forced myself to turn my back on her. She wasn't a threat. Not to me, and not to Jamie. Not really. He was my responsibility, and she wasn't going to kill him over playing with a few imps.

Nevertheless, I positioned myself between Jamie and the blade-wielding stranger—

Aargh! She's an ally! I insisted, wrangling my thoughts clear of the bond's distortion.

Arguing with myself only partially worked. My shoulder blades tingled in response to the perceived threat of the inspector—or maybe from the force of her stare—but shielding Jamie with my body soothed my protective instinct enough to focus on the problem. Flooding a hand with *lux lucis* until it glowed five times as bright as the rest of my body, I held it between myself and Jamie.

The imps plunged from him to me, drawn like moths to the brightness of my soul. Jaws agape, they snapped rows of razor-sharp teeth into my hand, arm, and torso. Unlike Jamie, I couldn't prevent them from feeding on me, but I didn't want to. One by one, I pumped their tiny bodies full of *lux lucis*, overloading their simplistic systems. If allowed to eat at their own pace, imps could nibble their way through the entirety of my *lux lucis*, but forcing energy into them faster than they could handle caused them to explode into harmless puffs of *atrum*. The black dust fell to the rocks, fading to inert charcoal before it settled.

After the last imp died, Jamie dropped his arms to his sides and relaxed his soul. *Atrum* and *lux lucis* swirled under his skin, the white energy twisting vines around his black limbs. I read his unhappiness in those snarls of energy as much as I did on his face, but our imp rule was simple: As long as they remained on him, I wouldn't touch them, but the moment they took a bite out of my soul, they died.

He understood I couldn't let any creature of *atrum* feed on my soul, and I understood he saw the imps as harmless and fun. I used to take delight in killing imps. They were brainless and evil, with voracious appetites. They were also easy targets, and wiping them out served as a quick way to feel accomplished.

That was before I'd seen delight on an imp's face—and before each imp's death stole another piece of my pooka's happiness.

Jamie gave me a sad smile that I returned.

"Come on." I hopped to the ground and Jamie followed.

"Does that happen often?" Pamela asked.

I checked her hands, relieved to see them empty.

"No." I'd seen Jamie play with imps on other occasions, but he hadn't been alive long enough to do anything *often*. So what if I was splitting hairs?

Jamie stepped around us and reached for a frost moth gliding above our heads. It flapped higher, then circled back, angling to land on Jamie.

"Get that away from him *now*," Pamela barked.

"Uh, let me . . ." I pushed *lux lucis* from my palm, and my hand flared bright; then the *lux lucis* splattered skyward. "Just a moment..."

Another moth joined the first, followed by a third and a fourth.

Summer competently formed a net and captured the moth nearest her, bringing her lighter to bear. *Show-off.*

"Concentrate, Madison. You can't let any moths feed off your pooka."

The urgency in her tone alarmed me. "Why not? What will happen to Jamie?"

"Nothing," Jamie said.

"It won't be pretty. Hurry," Pamela ordered, overriding him.

Eyes darting between them, I gave my *lux lucis* another push, clinging to it at the same time, and an infinitesimal net lifted from my palm. Rushing to Jamie, I swiped my hand through the frost moth, and the net caught around the moth's back legs, snaring it before it could land on the pooka. I spun, carrying the frost moth with me and away from Jamie—and I would have tipped right over if Pamela hadn't caught my shoulders.

Dizziness swirled from my hand to my head, the intangible moth body displacing the *lux lucis* in my net. When the moth's little legs wriggled, vibrations jittered through my soul and up my arm, and the familiar icy touch of *atrum*—one I'd experienced hundreds of times from imp and vervet bites—pervaded my hand, then faded.

This close, I could see the facets of the moth's glossy eyes; its slender, delicate antennae; and the soft, downy fur that coated its black body. Its blue wings, so thin they all but disappeared when viewed head-on, stretched and retracted, gently fanning my face with bitter-cold air. I lifted my hand, entranced. The wings resembled the most complex snowflakes ever formed, twin sheets of ice-crystal fractals spiraling outward from the moth's body to prism-spiked tips.

I held the push-pull balance of *lux lucis* with all my concentration and watched helplessly as the moth closed its tiny mouth on my wrist. Goose bumps rushed up my arm, and I shuddered at the renewed chill. As if to compensate for the cold generated by the moth, my body temperature flared. I reached for the zipper of my jacket. The moth flapped, passing its wing through my forearm, and I gasped at the bone-deep freeze that swept my hand and wrist.

Jamie stretched over my shoulder with *atrum*-coated fingers and trailed them along one wing. The moth's antennae wriggled and it stilled, no doubt enjoying the pooka's touch.

"You can't let him do that," Pamela said, her voice jolting me.

I glared at her over the back of the moth. What did she know about what I could and couldn't let Jamie do?

"Get out your lighter and kill it already, Madison. You're taking too long."

"I'm working on it. Back off." Did Pamela expect me to be perfect on my first try?

I rummaged in my pocket with glove-thickened fingers, pulling out my lighter as the moth began to struggle. I clicked the trigger on the lighter, thankful Brad had instructed me to get one that worked easily with gloves, and held it in the vicinity of the moth. Its wings flapped harder, generating a gust of cold air and magnifying the dizzy, disconnected sensation between my head and hand; then its wings shrank and its escape efforts slowed. The inky body dwindled against my hand until it nestled in my palm. Experimentally, I pulsed *lux lucis* into it the same way I had the imps, and the moth puffed to glitter. In normal sight, a confetti of snow blew from my palm.

Pamela grabbed my hand holding the lighter, sparing me from setting my sleeve on fire in the two-inch flame. I jerked away from her, embarrassed and irritated. Squinting, I examined the side of the lighter in the glare of the halogen lights, finding a slider switch to decrease the length of the flame. By the time I looked for the next frost moth, Summer had already dispatched them all.

"Took her long enough," Summer said, speaking to Pamela as if I didn't exist. She glanced at Jamie, then away, but not fast enough to hide the telling dilation of her pupils and the hunger I'd witnessed earlier. This time I recognized it.

Would you look at that? Summer is attracted to Jamie. I widened my stance, prepared to tackle the other woman.

"Are you sure it's safe for her to be out here? For her and us?" Summer asked.

My spine stiffened. I couldn't stop Summer from being angry with me—maybe I even deserved her hostility—but I drew the line at letting her badmouth me to the inspector. "I got the job done, didn't I?"

"Madison will be fine," Pamela said.

"Look at her. One spark and she'd go up." Summer whipped her hand into my face, snapping her fingers.

I jerked and slapped her hand away, but she'd already danced back. Flushing, I balled my hands into fists.

"She's not ready for this, any of it," Summer said, her gesture incorporating the drones in the stadium and Jamie in one sweep. "She should never—"

"Never what, Summer?" *Go ahead. Say it so I have a reason to slap you.*

The thought jolted through my rage, shattering it. Blinking, I crossed my arms and tried to make sense of my wild emotions.

"She's a power-grubbing, half-fledged enforcer who's weaseled—"

"Enough!" Pamela didn't raise her voice, but her tone cut through Summer's diatribe as if she had shouted. "That's the frost moths talking, and you should know better."

That's right: The frost moth's bite stole rationality and patience and similar cool-headed emotions. I hadn't expected it to affect me so quickly, and my combustible reaction didn't bode well for the rest of the night. Nor did Summer's.

She met the inspector's steely gaze with a hot glare, then spun on her heel and stalked away. Planting her hands on her thighs, she stared at the ground, her long braid hanging over her shoulder. Her lips moved, but I couldn't hear what she said. Probably just as well.

"That was enlightening," Pamela said to no one in particular.

"Was Jamie in danger?" I demanded.

"From an *atrum* creature? You're asking the wrong question, Madison. A frost moth can't hurt a pooka, but a pooka who's not in control of his emotions would be a danger to us all." She had the gall to look Jamie in the eye when she spoke.

The pooka's expression flattened. The shifting energies of his soul remained calm, but his eyes held a maturity not usually present. It reminded me that even though he'd risen from the ground only five days ago, he had been incubating for decades, aware of the world above him long before he'd become a part of it.

Then the moment passed, and he was just Jamie again, just my pooka. Mine to protect and guide.

"I see," I said, because Pamela seemed to be waiting for a response.

"I hope so."

She turned away, calling to Summer, and I took the moment to squeeze Jamie's hand. His lips curled in a faint smile that barely formed before dissolving.

"I don't know what you two have between you, and I don't care," Pamela said as Summer rejoined us. "I expect you both to act like professionals, frost moths or no frost moths. Am I clear?"

"Yes, Pamela," Summer and I said in unison. For the first time since I'd arrived on the high school grounds, I felt like a child again, and I didn't like it one bit.

"Good. The drones don't appear to be going anywhere, so let's take out as many frost moths as we can in the next ten minutes; then we'll head into the stadium."

Pamela tasked me with the stragglers around the restroom while she and Summer took on the bulk of the frost moths circling the crowds. When Pamela drew close to the concession stand line, where a handful of frost moths fed, she flared a *lux lucis* net two feet around her hand, swept it in a wave, and captured three moths at once. Lighter at the ready, she shrank all three in half the time it'd taken me to kill one. She even managed to turn her body so her torso hid the frosty explosion of their deaths from the majority of nearby norms.

She did it all without breaking her stride.

Val was right: Pamela was a badass. She might even be as strong as he had claimed. Summer wasn't too shabby either, though she had to stop to make each kill.

When Pamela turned to check on me, I jumped and jogged toward the nearest frost moth, Jamie trailing behind me. Creating a *lux lucis* net proved much easier with practice—and with no one watching.

"Cute," Jamie said when I proudly displayed the grapefruit-size net I'd made on my first attempt.

"Cute? Way to take the wind out of a girl's sails."

He grinned.

Two frost moths spotted Jamie at the same time and coasted in on snowflake wings. I swiped for both, catching one.

The world tilted toward my palm as my brain tried to compensate for the sensation of a foreign body squirming inside my soul. When the moth sank fangs into me, a wave of toasty warmth chased the initial chill. Bringing the lighter to bear, I shrank the moth before it could mess with my emotions. The wings and body decreased to the size of true snowflakes and I pulsed *lux lucis* through the moth's *atrum* body, exploding it.

Ha! Take that, Summer. I might be the newest enforcer on the block, but I learned fast.

"Is it getting hot?" Jamie asked.

I whirled toward the pooka. The second frost moth clung to his forehead like a mutant horn, and the flap of its growing wings blew strands of my hair into my open mouth.

"Shoo! Get away!" I batted my hand at the moth—*through* the moth. I forgot to form a net. I forgot the moth wasn't solid and wouldn't be scared of my flapping arms. I panicked.

Jamie giggled and feathered his fingers along the moth's wings.

"Scare it off, Jamie. We can't let it feed on you."

"I only let it have a few bites. Just nibbles. To warm up. But now I'm hot. I think I should change. I've got on too many layers."

"No! Give me a minute." I fumbled to create a net, spewing energy and turning my hand into a strobe light in my haste. Both caused Jamie to giggle harder.

"You could help," I said.

He tilted his head, his whirling eyes peering through a crystalline wing. "You should see the world like this. It's psychedelic."

My brain finally kicked in, and I lifted the lighter toward the frost moth. The lure of a pooka's tasty soul couldn't compete with the threat of heat, and it fluttered skyward. I was ready when it swooped back for a second feeding, having finally managed a moderate net, and I swiped the moth from the air as Jamie reached for it. The world spun on the fulcrum of my arm, and Jamie and I collided. I closed my eyes, swallowing hard to quell a burst of nausea. The frost moth sank tiny teeth into my forearm, and heat banished fledgling goose bumps.

I opened my eyes, surprised to find myself propped against Jamie, and shifted the trapped moth away from him. Raising my lighter, I— My gloved fingers clutched nothing but air.

Searching the ground, I spotted the slender weapon several feet away. When I took a step toward it, Jamie stumbled with me, wrapping an arm around my shoulders.

"Jamie?"

"I really glad I bonded with you," he said from too close, his grin sloppy.

"Me too."

The moth fed. Despite holding my arm stiff in front of me, its large snowflake wings slid icy fingers through my head and shoulders each time it flapped. The alternating heat of the furnace warming inside me and the intense cold of the wings made my head swim.

"Let go, Jamie. I need to get the lighter." I pumped *lux lucis* into the moth to slow its growth. It didn't work. Until I could shrink it, pure *lux lucis* wouldn't affect it.

Jamie wobbled on unsteady legs, but I didn't have time to spare for his aberrant balance issues. Dragging him with me, I staggered toward the lighter.

"No, I'm really, really glad I picked you. You're, like, the best. You're *nice*."

I twisted to look at Jamie and his goofy grin. What had gotten into him? He had allowed the moth to feed, but he looked happier than ever, not angry.

When I bent to pick up the lighter, Jamie slid off my shoulder and collapsed to the ground beside me, rolling slowly onto his back, his movements hindered by his breathless giggles. I clicked the trigger of the lighter and shoved it at the frost moth, locking my legs so I didn't land on my butt next to Jamie. The moth quivered in my trap but continued to feed even as its wings shrank.

"I should change." Jamie unwound the scarf from his neck and discarded it on the pavement, then dropped his beanie on top of it.

"Hang on. That's a bad idea." Distracted by my own wooziness, I tried to form a logical argument, incredibly proud when I came up with, "You'd freeze."

"But that bush wants me to pee on it."

I snorted, then giggled. Picturing the shrub pleading to be urinated on sent me over the edge, and I laughed so hard my knees buckled. Crumpling next to Jamie, I remembered at the last second to keep the lighter away from my arm. Just because I couldn't see the flame in Primordium didn't mean it wouldn't burn me.

Come on, moth, die already. Its wings shrank to saucers, then smaller, and I shoved a hearty wallop of *lux lucis* through the tiny moth body, exploding it and setting my hand glowing like a flare.

Leaning back, I stowed the lighter in my pocket and wiggled my fingers, admiring the strength of my *lux lucis*. Jamie pressed his gloved hand to mine, palm to palm, fingers to fingers. It didn't surprise me that our hands were the same size; I half suspected Jamie had modeled his human dimensions after mine.

Warm affection swelled within me, filling my chest and making it hard to breathe.

"Thank you for picking me, Jamie," I said.

"You're the best."

I bumped his shoulder affectionately, surprised when the motion set off fresh dizziness. Twisting, I scanned my body for frost moths before remembering it had been the netted moth, not a moth's bite, that had made me dizzy. I examined my palm, but the net had collapsed with the moth's death. I checked my other palm just to be sure it hadn't formed a net while I wasn't looking, and the thought set off a fresh wave of giggles.

"Can I change now?" Jamie asked, unzipping his jacket.

I put a hand on his arm to stop him, catching myself against the pavement with the other when I misjudged and tipped too far. Straightening, I frowned as my befuddled brain made a long-overdue connection: I felt drunk.

Which made no sense, not even when factoring in a frost moth. Experimentally, I performed the Madison Fox Sobriety Test: Planting a hand beside either hip, I shook my head swiftly back and forth like a woman in extreme denial. I tipped into Jamie, dizzy and giddy.

Oh yeah, I was drunk.

Jamie repeated my sobriety test, knocking himself over. Laughing, he straightened and did it again.

Check that: *We* were drunk.

The effect must have been wearing off, too, because I started to make more connections. Since I'd never seen Jamie behave like this before, it had to be related to the frost moth. Letting it feed on him hadn't made Jamie angry or out of control; it'd given him a buzz. And somehow, through the bond, his buzz had passed to me.

I grabbed the pooka's arm to get his attention.

"How do you feel?" I asked.

"Warm. No, hot. Hungry."

We had fallen near the back side of the bathroom, but plenty of people were in sight, and more than a few watched us. I'd have kept a wary eye on us, too; we probably looked high or crazy. Likely both.

"Do you still need to pee?"

"Yeah!" He scrambled to his hands and knees, his soul fluctuating.

Audience be damned, I tackled him. Looking crazy was better than people witnessing Jamie's transmogrification into a dog.

Jamie made a strange sound, half bark, half yelp, and we fell in an uncoordinated tangle. His noise and the absurdity of the situation spurred fresh laughter, sapping the strength from my limbs, and I collapsed on top of him. Jamie shook beneath me, his weird sounds worrying until I realized he was laughing too hard to get a full breath. I cobbled together the strength to roll onto my back, and Jamie flopped over next to me on the dirty pavement. Swiping tears from my cheeks, I blinked to clear my vision—and my stomach sank to my toes.

Pamela stood at our feet, arms crossed, expression sour.

6

LED ASTRAY BY GOOD INTENTIONS

y eyes darted to Jamie, and my heart started beating again when I confirmed he was still human.

"What is going on here?" Pamela demanded.

"We were, ah . . ." I fumbled for an explanation, my thoughts logjammed behind a wall of inappropriate amusement and alarm. "A frost moth . . . I killed it, but not before it had a tiny snack on Jamie."

"I see." Her tone should have frozen me to the pavement.

"I need to pee," Jamie said.

"Right. Okay. See that sign of the person with straight legs. That's the men's restroom. Don't go in the one with the person wearing the triangular cape. That's the women's restroom." I was babbling, but it was better than looking at Pamela. After scrambling to my feet, I helped Jamie to his, then sent him on his way with a nudge to his back.

"You are dangerously close to your pooka, and too lenient," Pamela said the moment he scampered out of earshot. "Form a net over your heart."

I straightened from brushing grit off my jeans, trying not to show my dismay. "You want to do another purity test? Here?" Glancing around, I saw we were essentially alone, the few nearby people preoccupied with each other and their phones.

"Now."

It took four tries before I formed a net over my heart, and the moment I did, Pamela shoved her hands into it. I locked my knees, flinching with each pulse of the inspector's *lux lucis* sifting through me. After an unbearable thirteen seconds, she snapped her hands free of my net and clapped them.

"You're clean. For now. But you're on a slippery slope. As far as I can tell, you haven't a thimble of control over the pooka. If you keep to your current course, you'll lose him, and you'll lose yourself right along with him."

"I'm doing my best—"

"You're floundering."

The truth silenced me. I understood my responsibility to Jamie—to teach him to be solidly good, purely *lux lucis*—but reaching that goal was akin to driving blindfolded. I didn't know which route or actions led toward my goal and which led to disaster. The only thing I'd decided on was not to rush.

"The pooka is part of why the triumvirate chose me for this assignment. I once worked a region alongside a bonded enforcer."

"You did?" Surprise added volume to my voice.

"I was an enforcer at the time and was transferred to the territory to assist while the resident enforcer brought his pooka in line. I spent a lot of time with those two, and I can tell you with absolute certainty that you're doing everything wrong."

I swallowed my knee-jerk denial.

"You need to be *much* firmer with your pooka. They respond to authority, not coddling. If you don't take charge, that pooka will to go dark, and he'll drag you down with him. The only way he's going to learn what's right is if you train him."

"That's what I'm doing." I checked the restroom, thankful Jamie wasn't close enough to hear this.

"It looked to me like you were rolling around, playing hanky-panky with him."

Hanky-panky? With Jamie? Gross. "That's not at all—"

"And what are you calling that spectacle with the imps?"

"I took care of them."

"That's right: *You* took care of the imps. *You*, not him. He should be protecting you, not buddying up to evil creatures. More to the point, he should *never* use *atrum*. If unexercised, his *atrum* will atrophy, just as the more he uses *lux lucis*, the stronger his good side will become. Ultimately, that's the only way to change him into a creature of good. But that will happen only if you set him on the proper course—starting with no longer allowing him to use *atrum*." Pamela placed a hand on each of my shoulders, her expression earnest. "I'm worried for you, Madison. I don't want you or the pooka to turn to *atrum*. I've seen it happen, and it's not pretty."

She released me, studying my face. "You're making a mistake, seeing him as human. Jamie is not like you or me. He doesn't need a peer or a friend. He needs you to lead, to command. From where I'm standing, it looks like he's calling the shots. That's a recipe for disaster."

I swallowed hard. Pamela was wrong: I didn't see Jamie as a human; he was so much more, including a friend. Despite all the warnings I'd been given about not getting too close to him, in less than a week Jamie had wormed his way into my heart. I'd sworn I wouldn't let it affect the way I interacted with him, but of course it had. Dismay hollowed my stomach at the realization I might be wrecking Jamie's chance to evolve into a good pooka.

"So I need to be stricter?"

"Set rules and boundaries. He's too powerful to run as wild as he does."

"Okay." *Command? Train?* I mentally recoiled from the harsh words. I'd hesitated to demand Jamie cut out *atrum* partially because I didn't want him to think I didn't love him for who he was, *atrum* and all, and partially because I had no means to reinforce such an order. But Pamela said my strategy of leading by example was taking us both down the wrong path. If anyone would know, it was the inspector.

Or maybe she was exaggerating to scare me.

Jamie scurried out of the bathroom with his gloves between his teeth, shaking his wet hands wildly.

"I think there's a frost moth in the sink pipes," he announced after taking his gloves from his mouth.

I mimed blotting his hands on his legs, and he chose to misinterpret my gesture as an invitation to dry his hands on my pants. Disapproval radiated off Pamela, but rather than confronting Jamie about such a trivial matter, I scooped up his discarded scarf and beanie, giving both a shake to remove the dirt. Jamie shoved his fingers into his gloves and the beanie on his head, then wrapped the scarf into a misshapen knot. My fingers twitched to help him, but I stopped myself, sensitive to Pamela's scrutiny. She'd probably misconstrue the gesture as coddling.

"We should find another moth so we can warm up," Jamie said.

I mentally dropped my head in my hands and forced myself to admit maybe Pamela was right; maybe I had no control over Jamie. But even without her warning, I wouldn't have said yes to the frost moth. I had no desire for another drunken interlude.

"It's not true warmth. The moth tricks your brain," I said. Channeling my dad, I added, "Jump around a little and you'll warm up."

"You don't have to give reasons, Madison. Give orders," Pamela said as she watched Jamie bounce beside me.

"Should we go kill drones?"

The inspector's arched eyebrow said she saw my question for what it was—the most blatant diversionary tactic ever—but she let it go without comment. She signaled to Summer, and we regrouped in a quiet patch of ivory lawn behind the stadium, out of sight of most of the norms.

"Before we go out there, I want to see what we're working with," Pamela said. She drew a palmquell from her pocket, gesturing for us to do the same. I retrieved my balsa wood gun, simultaneously checking the others', pleased to find them as hideous as mine—Summer's in shades of pink and Pamela's an eye-watering teal and yellow.

"Nothing attracts the attention of norms quite like waving around a gun, so keep your palmquell hidden in your hand and do your best to disguise your shooting. You don't want to alarm the public, for their sake and because we don't have time to waste persuading the police that we're harmless."

Aha. That answered the question about the palmquells' hideous colors. With its mustard-yellow tones, norms were far less likely to mistake my weapon for a real gun.

"You're going to need to hit a drone's thorax to do any good. Let's see your aim. Show me how close you can get to my target." Pamela discreetly shot a *lux lucis* bullet into a boulder fifteen feet away.

Summer aimed, sighting down the barrel of the palmquell. It looked like she was pointing, which, although rude, wasn't typically frightening. When she fired, a *lux lucis* splat landed a few feet from Pamela's.

"I'm a little rusty," she said.

"Have you fought tyver before?" Pamela asked.

Summer shook her head. "I did some training in Truckee two winters ago, but we only encountered drones."

I examined my palmquell, looking for a port for ammunition and not finding one. Brad hadn't given me any bullets, either, which meant the gun must work similarly to my other weapons. In other words, I was the ammo.

Wary of burning out the palmquell, I eased *lux lucis* into it. The white energy sank from my hand into the balsa wood, collecting inside.

"Any day now," Summer said.

Pressure built inside the palmquell until it held almost as much *lux lucis* as my pet wood could, and a subtle pushback of resistance warned me its internal chamber was nearing full. Satisfied, I lifted the gun, aimed, and fired. A beam of white light like a colorless burst from a laser gun in a sci-fi TV show streaked through the air and hit the ground ten feet to the right of the target.

"Try again," Pamela said.

My next shot landed eight feet to the left. My heart sank, my hopes of being a natural markswoman dying before they'd fully formed.

"My goodness," Pamela said.

"I've never shot a—" I glanced around and lowered my voice. "I've never shot a gun, palmquell or otherwise. I'll get better with practice." I would have to. I couldn't get much worse.

Pamela gave me two minutes to practice, and I peppered the ground around the boulder in a flurry of *lux lucis* splatter, only a handful of lucky shots landing closer than five feet of the target. After the first few misfires, Summer proved a natural, stacking shot after shot atop each other.

As far as olive branches went, I hoped the humility of my pathetic performance might start mending the rift between us, and I asked Summer for shooting pointers.

"Try harder," she snapped.

Pamela stared at the sky, tracking two new drones incoming from the north. "We can't wait any longer. Let's head in. Remember: aim for the thorax. Just do your best, Madison, and try not to get zapped."

Jamie jogged to the boulder we'd used for target practice and swept away the *lux lucis* with a fan of *atrum*. Summer and Pamela froze. I sucked in a sharp breath.

"Jamie! Leave it!" I ordered as he stepped to the side to clean away the last traces of my wild shots.

"But this is inanimate," he said, perplexed.

Our first day together, when I'd been laying out my ground rules, I'd explained that since *lux lucis* and *atrum* didn't exist in inanimate objects, part of my job involved wiping out all residual *atrum* left behind by evil creatures. Jamie had agreed with my reasoning, and using the same logic, had started removing *lux lucis* from inanimate surfaces, too. I hadn't pushed the issue since doing so would have undercut my own argument. I had hoped over time, Jamie would see merit in leaving *lux lucis* untouched, where it had the potential to positively influence whoever came in contact with it. It had been part of my drip campaign to bring Jamie around to my way of thinking, but Pamela had scared me. If she was right, taking it slow could actually hurt him.

"Today we're leaving *lux lucis* where it lies."

"But why?"

I glanced at Pamela. She expected me to assert my authority and prove I was in control—and an enforcer in control of her pooka didn't offer reasons.

"Because I said so." *This is me, putting my foot down, hoping I'm not trampling Jamie's trust in the process.*

I tried to take comfort in Pamela's approving nod, but all I saw was Jamie's bewilderment.

Pamela marched for the stadium, Summer at her side. Like a good enforcer, I fell into step behind them. I didn't let the slumped slope of Jamie's shoulders or his betrayed expression pierce my resolve.

"Come on, Jamie," I said, jaw locked so tight it was hard to push the words out. After a hesitation, Jamie trotted after us, and by the time he caught up, the noise of the crowd made it plausible for me to pretend not to hear him whisper my name like a question.

Twenty minutes later, I reentered the stadium with Jamie and Pamela after my drone-prompted dash out, fighting the urge to slouch. First, I couldn't control Jamie. Now I couldn't control myself. One strike from a drone, and I'd fled.

Way to be impressive, Dice.

"We've left Summer alone far too long," Pamela said, picking up the pace. "The drones are getting stronger. We need to take them out while they're still relatively weak—and before they return to feed the tyv controlling them."

The band on the field finished in the formation of OHV as we crested the walkway at the front of the bleachers. The crowd went wild before the last note died, half the stadium leaping to their feet to celebrate the home team, and the drones flitted in a frenzy above them, eating with abandon.

"Bloody hell," Pamela cursed.

Summer was missing.

Pamela shoved through the throng of people milling at the railing and squeezed up the stadium steps. Jamie and I pressed into the gap behind her. When it came to spotting people in crowds, my eyes tended to blur all the faces together, and I had to concentrate to see individuals. I'd make a dreadful FBI agent. Fortunately, I was an enforcer, and I had the advantage of Primordium.

In a sea of gray faces and blotchy norms, Summer's bright white enforcer soul shone like a beacon. Legs braced for balance, arms extended above her head, she stood atop a bleacher seat halfway up the stands and shot straight up into the drones. Her proximity meant she hit more than she missed, and fierce glee pulled her features tight. To the casual observer, she looked like one of the cheering throng, even if she didn't always face the field.

Pamela slowed when she spotted Summer, and she pulled me close so I could hear her above the cheering.

"This is why enforcers always work tyver in pairs. If one of you gets struck, the other protects until they recover."

"She looks fine to me," I groused under my breath.

Summer's hands fell to her sides and she blinked at her surroundings like a woman waking in the middle of a sleepwalking episode. She gave her shoulders a shake and checked the sky for nearby drones, then eased from her perch.

Great. Summer had been struck by a drone, and she'd charged deeper into their midst. She'd been so focused on killing them, she'd put herself right in the heart of where they were feeding. Whereas when I'd been struck, I'd fled the stadium.

I wished I could blame Summer for making me look bad, but I was handling that just fine on my own.

"The moment they notice you, start walking," Pamela ordered

Jamie. She pointed to the far side of the stadium. "Head that way, and don't stop until you're in the baseball field."

Beyond the track encasing the football field, a carpet of white lawn bulged into a vague square configuration defined by four charcoal baseball diamonds at the outer points. A quick, blinding blink to normal sight confirmed the stadium's halogen lights didn't illuminate the far field.

"You want me to lead the drones out there so you can kill them?" Jamie asked.

"Of course," Pamela said, shooting me another of those pointed looks. She trotted down the steps to meet Summer at the railing without looking back.

The crowd quieted as the next band took the field, and a handful of people rustled in the stands, collecting items and pushing toward the exit. I allowed an elderly couple to precede me, intentionally distancing myself from the inspector before turning to Jamie. Pamela's instructions be damned, Jamie deserved an explanation.

"These people are innocent and can't do anything to defend themselves. It's up to us to protect them."

"Why? The drones don't hurt them."

"How do you know? They hurt me." I rubbed my chest, remembering the sharp pain.

"All it does is free them."

"Free them? The drones take away their self-control. They make people do things they don't want to."

Jamie flinched. "So earlier, you didn't want to save me?"

The soft question tore my heartstrings.

"Of course I did. That's *all* I wanted to do, because I was afraid you were in danger." I reached for his hand, giving it a shake to make him look at me fully. "But you said the drones aren't a threat to you, so now you can help me. I need to save all these people. They can't fight back, and they don't deserve to have pieces of themselves stripped away."

Jamie roved indifferent eyes over the norms, unconvinced.

"Drones exist to feed and protect tyver, right?" I asked, trying a different tack. "Tyver that would happily steal my soul and leave me brain-dead. If we kill the drones now, it increases my chances of survival." My words chased a shiver down my spine.

Jamie took a deep breath and let it out before he turned back to me and nodded.

"Let's go." Elbowing my way through a knot of teens, I hustled to the inspector's side as a pair of drones darted toward us.

"They've spotted the pooka," Pamela said, tracking the drones but not shooting. "Keep going, Jamie. We'll follow from a distance."

Jamie glanced to me for confirmation.

"Come on," I said, leading the way.

Pamela clamped a hand on my bicep. "No, Madison. Jamie goes ahead alone. We need room to work without getting zapped by those suckers."

"If I'm beside him, I could use my pet wood again." Which would increase my chances of killing a drone by one hundred percent.

"No. You need to learn how to take them out before they're close enough to touch. Go on, Jamie."

Jamie took in the inspector's grip on my arm, then my face. I nodded, trying to look encouraging while grinding my teeth. Shoulders hunched, Jamie threaded around a couple carrying nacho platters and trudged toward the far end of the stadium.

Pamela released me and gave me a pat on the back, as if to say, *See, that's how you give orders.*

Jamie's dejected posture grated, and it took all my self-control not to race after him. I blamed the bond for making me so sensitive to his emotions. After all, I hadn't asked him to do something painful or wrong. All he had to do was walk a few yards ahead of us . . . luring creatures he saw as harmless to their deaths.

It's for his own good, I told myself.

The first drone buzzed Jamie. I raised my palmquell and fired a shot that, unsurprisingly, landed nowhere close to the drone's slender body. Pamela pushed my hands down before I could take a second shot.

"We don't want to scare them off. Wait until more gather. With luck, the pooka will make this easy for us."

I squirmed, fighting to obey the inspector when every instinct clamored for me to protect Jamie. Only his reassurance that the drone couldn't hurt him enabled me to master my body and stand idle while the drone's needle proboscis sliced through his arm.

The pooka turned toward the drone, lifting a hand to pet its leg. He didn't look in pain. I let out a gusty sigh of relief, which Pamela echoed a moment later when the drone flew away unchanged, proving he hadn't allowed it to feed from his soul.

Hunkering deeper into his scarf, Jamie resumed his plod toward the baseball fields, but not before I caught sight of his sorrowful expression. My heart constricted.

This is for his own good, I repeated to myself, but the hollow words provided no solace.

I'M LIKE A CANDY BAR: HALF SWEET, HALF NUTS

amela didn't let me move until Jamie was more than halfway to the other side of the stands, and even then, she insisted on going first, setting a much slower pace than I would have. I bounced behind her, a squirmy, sharp sensation tugging me back to Jamie. Our bond prevented us from getting too far apart, but I couldn't blame the distance for this compulsion. This had everything to do with the slump of Jamie's shoulders and the downward curve of his mouth. The bond was manipulating me. If Jamie had been happily frolicking with the drones, I wouldn't have suffered this compulsion to rush to him, which was probably why Jamie and I had been able to separate much farther last night without a problem. Last night had been all about fun: Jamie had gone out with Sam, his only normal friend—or at least his only friend who was also a norm—and I'd gone on my date with Alex.

In the freezing cold, squeezing through a throng of strangers, with the marching band blasting Queen's "We Will Rock You" and drones bombarding us from above, I suffered a pang of jealousy for my past self. Dinner last night with Alex felt as if it had happened to another person in another lifetime. I tried to recall the nuances of our toe-curling farewell kiss, hoping to siphon a fragment of joy from the memory, but Jamie's despondent plod smothered the reminiscence with guilt.

What I wouldn't give to be out with Alex again tonight instead of here!

"Look out." Summer's monotone caution came a second before pain punctured my shoulder. Too late, I flinched and jerked aside. The drone blasted past, sweeping up the bleachers, snacking as it retreated. I gave myself a quick pat-down, finding my phone in my jacket's left pocket.

"What are you doing?" Summer asked. White bullets danced from the tip of her palmquell, and she crowded me, pushing me toward the railing as if herding me.

Using my teeth, I pulled off a glove and thumbed through my contacts. "I'm calling Alex."

"Alex? Who's that?"

"He's hot stuff," I said, listening to the phone ring. *And if I play this right, I can ditch this miserable event and spend a much more pleasurable night with him.*

"*That's* what you were thinking about? A guy?" Summer removed her hand from my arm, a wicked smile curving her lips. "This should be good."

The phone rang three times. Alex answered just as my reasoning brain kicked back online, and my stomach dove to my toes.

"Hello?"

"Uh." I jerked the phone from my ear and stared at it. I should hang up.

"Madison?" Alex's voice sounded tinny and small.

I smacked the phone back to my ear. "Alex! Hey. I hope it's not too late to call."

"How old do you think I am? It's barely seven."

"Oh, right." I banged my forehead against my palmquell, hoping I'd shake loose something witty.

Summer brushed past me, her ugly chuckle audible between drumbeats. "Real professional, idiot."

She caught up with Pamela in a few strides. Scowling, I ducked behind two rail-thin teens before the inspector turned and caught me on the phone. My stealth was likely pointless. Summer had probably already ratted me out.

Every instrument in the marching band bleated and banged at once, kicking off a tune I didn't recognize and all but drowning out Alex's next words.

"Where are you? Are you at a concert?"

"I wish. It's actually a high school marching band competition. Some, um, friends invited me." I pressed the palmquell to my free ear, using the weapon as a clumsy noise blocker. Halfway across the stadium, drones circled Jamie like hyperactive vultures, but Pamela and Summer ignored them to pick off those that remained above the crowds. Peeved, I sighted over their heads, aiming for the drones closest to Jamie. My white bullet ripped through the tip of a drone's wing. Success! Sort of. The drone didn't slow or even acknowledge the hit, but having the palmquell pressed to my skull improved my aim.

Realizing I'd been silent too long, I blurted out, "I, ah, just wanted to call and tell you what a good time I had last night." When my words registered in my brain, I squeezed my eyes shut and willed the concrete beneath my feet to open up and swallow me. Seriously? I couldn't have sounded more corny if I'd tried.

"I had a good time, too."

My eyes sprang open. "Yeah?"

"I'm glad you called. We haven't set up our next date yet."

"No, we haven't." Grinning this hard made talking difficult.

"I'm busy tomorrow, but would you be up for meeting me for lunch on Monday?"

"Monday?" I fired another dozen shots, each one almost on target. *Take that, Summer. You can shove your professionalism comment where the sun doesn't—*

My gaze collided with Pamela's and my whole body froze. I hadn't realized a person could pack such wilting disapproval into a single look.

"Unless that's too soon. Or you don't get a lunch break," Alex added.

"Um." Chatting on the job didn't even fall close to the goal of impressing Pamela. How much more could I lower her opinion of me?

"Or you don't eat lunch . . ."

I forced a laugh, cringing at the fake sound. I needed to get off this call, but I couldn't just hang up on Alex, and Pamela's censorious gaze sapped my brain cells. Staring at my feet helped.

"I was trying to picture my schedule on Monday. Lunch sounds great." If tyver were our priority, and they hunted at night, I should be free for a midday date.

"What time works for you?" Alex asked.

I pretended to have the same lunch hour as him, leaving it as a happy coincidence and not explaining my open-structured job, since that would lead to too many unanswerable questions.

"I should get back to my friends," I said after we made plans to meet at a restaurant near his practice.

"Right. Have a good time. And thanks for giving me something to look forward to."

"My pleasure."

My smile died the moment the call ended and I caught sight of Jamie. Plagued by a scourge of drones, he descended the stadium's far stairs toward the baseball fields, his posture more appropriate for a man walking to the gallows. I pulled the lead out of my feet and rushed after him, but Pamela stepped into my path, stopping me short.

"Was that Brad on the phone?"

"Uh—"

"A personal call?"

"Yes."

"That you initiated?"

"The drone . . . I wasn't thinking—"

"That's why you don't let your focus drift while hunting drones." Pamela pinned me with a stare, waiting.

"It won't happen again," I promised.

Jamie's pooka magnetism had drawn all but two drones from the smorgasbord of norms, and Pamela picked those off with rapid-fire accuracy. I took the opportunity to passcode lock my phone, turn it off, and stuff it in the inner zipper pocket of my coat, in case I got another uncontrollable urge to call someone. I pretended not to notice Summer's smirk.

When we exited the stands, Pamela kept our pace slow, gesturing for Jamie to hustle ahead. He plodded deep into the baseball fields, turning at Pamela's order toward the darkest corner. Only then did she let him stop.

"Hold them," Pamela instructed.

Jamie's eyes sought mine, and I read his anger loud and clear across the twenty feet separating us. Shards of *lux lucis* and *atrum* collided in his soul, piercing each other again and again. When I didn't countermand the inspector's order, he folded his arms over his chest and tipped his head back to watch the drones. They milled in the air above him, fifteen or twenty swooping and diving around him, probing him with their sharp proboscises.

"Their fascination won't last," Pamela said. "Take them out quickly."

As if her words were their cue, a handful of drones split from Jamie, most angling for us and a few zipping back toward the crowd. Counting on the shadows to hide me from the norms, I planted my feet and extended the palmquell in a thoroughly conspicuous manner, determined to improve my aim.

And relative to my atrocious beginnings, I did. Over the next hour and a half, I hit my targets a total of eleven times. However, those shots were scattered among several drones, and my kill total remained unchanged at one—the drone I'd slain with my pet wood.

Having witnessed Pamela's shooting prowess in the stadium, I had no doubt she could have wiped out the entire horde of drones herself. Instead, she worked on the fringes, killing those that angled back toward the stadium and leaving the rest to Summer and me, including all newcomers trickling in from the northern horizon. Like everything else with the inspector, the drones were a test.

Summer passed. I didn't.

I got struck five times for every drone hit Summer took, her superior marksmanship saving her from all but the most devious attacks. The first three times a drone stole my inhibitions, I ran straight to Jamie, apology on my lips. Each time my head cleared before I reached him, and I retreated to my inspector-designated distance, apology unvoiced, telling myself I was doing the right thing. I needed to wrestle control of the bond before it ruled me. I needed to harden my heart against Jamie's sunken posture and mutinous expression. I needed to do what was right for the both of us, and according to Pamela, coddling him would cost us both our lives—or at least our lives as good people.

I pictured forming a shield around my heart to protect it, but the defensive walls only succeeded in amplifying my guilt back to me.

Kill the drones. Kill the drones. Killthedrones.

Chanting helped me focus, as did locking my vision on the sky so I couldn't see Jamie. Freed of one emotional distraction, I acted out in different idiotic ways when drones sucked away pieces of my soul— like chucking my palmquell in fit of rage and collapsing to my knees, screaming my frustration and pounding my fists into the frost-tipped grass, or chasing after drones, jumping and leaping like a demented terrier, trying to catch them with my bare hands.

Pamela observed it all, judging and finding me lacking.

With a steady stream of new drones replacing those we killed, the fight might have continued all night if the drones hadn't abandoned the field. In eerie synchronization, the scattering of remaining drones lifted straight into the air, their spindly legs flopping loosely beneath them like jagged kite strings. Pamela cursed and fired a blur of *lux lucis*, downing three in quick succession and proving my theory correct: She'd been holding back to observe our aptitude. But even the esteemed inspector's palmquell had a limited range, and two extra-strong drones zoomed over the high school toward the northern horizon.

Pamela had her phone to her ear before they'd disappeared from view.

"Brad, it's Pamela. Where are the drones headed?" she demanded. Then, after the barest pause, "Already? Any others?"

Tugging off my soggy glove, I bent to trail my left hand through the trampled grass and absorb its *lux lucis*. Ideally I would have recharged on larger, stronger plants. As a rule, I tried not to take too much energy from any one plant. They all sacrificed their *lux lucis* unreservedly; it seemed poor repayment to kill them for their generosity. A dozen darkened circles around the field already stood testament to the *lux lucis* I'd absorbed and the lawn I'd killed during my tantrums, but I couldn't muster empathy for the fragile blades dying beneath my fingertips as I walked to Jamie.

"Thank you, Jamie. You did a great job." Far better than I had done, even if he'd only had to stand there.

His hateful glare speared through my heart; then he turned away, staring after the drones.

I sucked in a deep breath and let it out slowly. Pamela was an inspector with decades of experience. She'd witnessed successful pooka-enforcer interactions. I'd be a fool to ignore her advice. Jamie and I would get through this adjustment period and all would be okay again.

The rationalization didn't make me feel better.

I swiped my wet fingers on my jeans, adding a thimbleful of moisture to pants already soaked from my knees down. A breeze skimmed the field, sinking glacial thorns straight through my saturated jeans and thermals to my icy legs. Uncurling the fingers of my right hand from the palmquell took concentration, the numbed digits slow to respond. I thrust the weapon into my jacket pocket, stowed my wet gloves on the opposite side, and chafed my hands together. When I'd kindled a faint heat, I stuffed my hands in my armpits. Despite all my layers, the cold imprint of my fingers chased goose bumps down my ribs.

"Let's go," Pamela said. She angled for the far exit, circling behind the stadium. Summer trotted obediently after her, irritatingly perky. She didn't have a drop of moisture on her pants.

"Good job tonight," Pamela said when Summer caught up to her.

"Good job tonight," I mimicked in a snotty voice, careful to keep it a whisper. Jamie might have smiled. Or it might have been my imagination.

"Come on. We don't want to fall behind Ms. Perfect."

Glaring holes in Summer's back, I stomped after them. Twin blisters on my heels brought me up short, and I adjusted my gait to an ungraceful hobble. I'd purchased the boots this morning, and there hadn't been time to break them in properly. Fortunately, Jamie appeared fine in his equally new boots. He tagged along, keeping five feet between us. The pointed separation rubbed more painfully than the blisters.

Couldn't this night be over already?

"We've got tyver incoming and Madison can't hit the broadside of a lorry," Pamela said, phone once again pressed to her ear. "Do you have time to do some training?"

I strained to hear the other end of the conversation or even the tenor of the other person's voice, but between the echoes of the marching band bouncing off the brick walls of the classrooms on our left and the clomp of our footsteps on the concrete path, I had to settle for eavesdropping on only the inspector.

Crossing my fingers, I sent up a small prayer. *Please let her be talking to Niko.*

"Exactly. Have you given any thought to my offer?" The crowd's cheers drowned out Pamela's soft laugh. "That's precisely why I need you. How about I pretend you haven't answered, and you take another night to think on it."

Pamela ended the call but made me wait until we reached the parking lot before she filled me in.

"You've got marksmanship training with Doris tomorrow."

Of course. I should have expected it would be Doris. My first night on the job, she had taught me the basics of how to use *lux lucis*. The retired enforcer seemed to be the local go-to choice for training incompetent new hires.

"She'll pick you up tomorrow morning at seven."

"Thanks," I forced myself to say, nixing my fantasy of sleeping in. Doris was the only octogenarian I knew with more energy than the average toddler. She'd probably show up early.

"Any sign of sjel tyver?" Summer asked.

"Last sighting was near Dutch Flat. They'll likely be here tomorrow or the next night," Pamela said.

I needed more time. One day of target practice—two, if I was lucky—wasn't going to cut it. Unfortunately, I didn't have a say in the matter.

"Where to next?" I asked.

"We're done for tonight. The drones fled this region, but they'll be back tomorrow."

I didn't hear much past *we're done*, her words eclipsed by the gratitude and dread seesawing in my empty stomach. Considering the imminent tyv invasion, spending more time training tonight would have been prudent. However, between the strain on the bond and my battered confidence, I welcomed a reprieve.

Pamela added a few admonishing words of caution and several pointed looks I guessed to be about Jamie before she and Summer slid into Summer's sedan. The moment her door whooshed shut, a weight fell off my shoulders.

Jamie and I continued down the row to my Civic and crawled inside. I turned the heater on full blast and celebrated the view of Summer's car departing the lot. Tipping my head back, I closed my eyes and welcomed the ringing in my ears, which almost drowned out the muted, incessant pounding of the current marching band. Jamie shifted beside me, his jacket rustling against the seat, and I cracked an eye to check on him. He stared out the side window, as if pretending we weren't close enough to brush elbows. In Primordium, I couldn't see his reflection in the glass, but the sloshing lines of his soul signified a lessening of tension in him, too.

I closed my eyes again. The serenity pervading my thoughts had all the signs of the bond manipulating me, but I already knew it fostered a desire for proximity with my pooka, and this was the closest we'd been in over an hour. If it also helped lift Jamie's mood, so much the better. I couldn't stand it if he remained mad at me.

When the vents began to fan lukewarm air against my cheeks, I stirred myself into action. Stripping off my beanie and scarf, I tossed them into the backseat and blinked to normal sight. I tugged my seat belt on and waited for Jamie to follow suit before I put the car in gear.

I didn't attempt to breach the silence. I didn't know what to say. But I had to fix the rift between us. If nothing else, I wanted to see a smile on Jamie's face before the end of the night, which is why instead of heading straight home, I detoured to Dairy Queen.

I hadn't had time yet to introduce Jamie to many of the best things in life, but I had made sure he knew the pleasure of brand-new socks, soft blankets, and ice cream. Of the three, ice cream ranked highest on Jamie's list of favorite things, which was why when the drive-through cashier handed over two Blizzards—both half Oreo, half M&M's, one small, one large—he perked up enough to turn toward me and snatch the large from my hand. His eyes flicked to my face and away so fast I wasn't sure he saw my smile. I set the small in the cup holder and scooped a spoonful before easing out into traffic.

Jamie ate in silence, pausing every so often to clutch his forehead to soothe a brain freeze, but otherwise not slowing until he scraped the bottom of the paper cup. After his fifth wistful glance at my barely touched ice cream, I licked my spoon clean, set it in the center console, and handed him my Blizzard.

"Go ahead," I said when he hesitated.

With more dignity this time, he accepted the offered dessert. If I hadn't been watching so closely for it, I would have missed the faint curve of his lips.

Finally.

When I pulled into my parking space in front of the three-story apartment complex we called home, Jamie bounced out of the car, racing toward the stairs before I'd swung my feet to the pavement.

"Jamie, hang on."

With obvious reluctance, he stopped on the walkway.

"You're going to need these." I tossed him the keys. My blistered feet weren't up for a sprint up two flights of stairs, and I didn't want to make him wait.

Jamie caught the keys and took off. I draped my scarf across my shoulders, stuffed my beanie in my pocket, and retrieved my purse from under the driver's seat. Doing my best not to aggravate my raw heels, I hobbled up the long walkway to the stairs.

Tranquility cocooned the complex despite it being a Saturday night. A few days into December, we were in the sacred window between Thanksgiving and Christmas house guests and family gatherings, when everyone either hunkered inside, recuperating and practicing calming mantras for the stresses yet to come, or fled to the bars and the embrace of liquid freedom. Next weekend would be soon enough to panic over last-minute Christmas shopping and meal planning.

A ping of alarm jolted through me when I contemplated my holiday plans. As always, they included packing up Mr. Bond and driving thirty minutes to Lincoln City to spend Christmas with my parents. Adding our new kitten, Dame Zilla, to the mix would fall under "the more, the merrier." But I hadn't considered how Jamie would fit in. He would come with me, of course, but how was I going to explain a shape-shifting pooka to my parents? Not by telling the truth, that was certain.

My parents didn't know anything about the crazy my life had turned into. To them, I was squandering my potential at yet another temporary job, this one a sales rep for a bumper sticker company. I'd never had specific career ambitions, as evident in the revolving doors of my employers. When I took this job, I'd gotten my first taste of what people meant when they talked about finding their calling. Being an enforcer gave me a true sense of purpose—despite the dangers, weird hours, secrecy, bizarre coworkers, and daily run-ins with evil. However, considering my parents would commit me to the nearest psychiatric facility if I told them I could not only see souls but could also use mine as a weapon against evil creatures they couldn't perceive, I shouldered their quiet disappointment without complaint.

My mind drew a blank on a reason my parents would find credible for me to be living with a teenage-looking male roommate. Maybe I could take him to Christmas as a Great Dane.

The thought arrested me, one foot raised above the first stair, disaster after imaginary disaster unfolding in my mind's eye. My parents' strong belief in spaying and neutering all pets would be the first catastrophe, especially if Jamie understood what they'd propose to do to him. How would they react when Jamie wanted to eat at the table with us? If I had to insist Jamie eat on the floor, how would *he* react? At the very least, my parents' house wasn't Great Dane–tail proofed.

Oh God. Dad's model train sets. No. Jamie had to come as a human, and I had to think of a plausible explanation.

Later. I had enough on my plate now.

Fully aware I was stalling, I slid Val from his strap and opened him to his first page. Rushing up to the apartment so I could force Jamie to talk to me, and likely start an argument, would be foolish. Plus, if I gave Jamie a little space and time with the cats, maybe he'd forget about being angry at me.

Cowardly? Possibly. Prudent? Definitely.

"How'd you hold up in our first foray with drones?" I asked Val.

I thought the goal was to impress Pamela, not to impress upon her how unsuited you are for the job.

"Says the book who trash-talked me to the inspector."

You didn't expect me to lie to Pamela, did you? She would have seen right through that. I mean, she's AMAZING! Did you see the way she took out those drones? What about how big her nets were? She's strong and fast and smart and so talented! She didn't even need you or Summer there.

"Yeah, I got that impression, too." My stomach churned and I blamed it on the ice cream. I couldn't be jealous of my handbook's infatuation with another person, could I?

"Why do so many evil creatures prey on emotions?" I asked before Val could compose a ballad in Pamela's honor. "Last week, the citos were amping up everyone at the mall; now we're plagued by frost moths. Even the drones mess with emotions in their own way." The question had been knocking around in my head all night, but I hadn't wanted to voice it in front of Pamela. I didn't want to leave myself open to potentially looking like an idiot. Or rather, *more* like an idiot.

Technically, citos aren't evil; they only make it easier for humans to do evil.

"I don't want to argue semantics, Val. You know what I mean."

Fine. Imagine if you had no physical form. How would you feed?

"On something equally intangible?"

Precisely. If you think about it, all atrum *creatures feed on emotions. The only constant among humans is your propensity to allow your emotions to dictate your actions. Imps and vervet drain* lux lucis, *which weakens a victim's sense of morality and makes him or her more likely to succumb to baser desires, or rather, baser emotions. The person then willfully accumulates* atrum, *making it a by-product of their own emotions.*

"That seems like a stretch."

If you need another example, there's the demon that turned you into a lust machine . . .

"Okay, you made your point." He knew about the demon? Someone must have blabbed to him, because that incident had happened before we'd been paired up.

A bitter wind gusted through the open stairwell, solidifying ice crystals in my wet jeans. The heated apartment beckoned, and I mulled over this new perspective as I climbed the stairs.

Sometimes emotion-manipulating creatures aren't a bad thing. Take the frost moths. They only recently evolved to feed in a way that's truly evil.

"What prompted the change? Was it Isabel?"

Ha! Oh, wait; you're serious. I always forget what small increments humans measure time in. No. The frost moths evolved to host and spread atrum *in the last 10,000 years or so.*

"So, by *recently*, you meant sometime before the last ice age, give or take a handful of millennia?"

Exactly, Val said, missing—or ignoring—my sarcasm.

"How were they ever helpful?"

Moths have a symbiotic relationship with humans. During the darkest, coldest months of the year, they encourage warmth.

"You mean anger," I said, thinking of how quickly the argument between Summer and I had escalated.

Sure, they can get your blood pumping. With frost moths around, your ancestors worked through their disagreements quicker.

By ancestors, he probably meant the Neanderthals.

But I meant warmth as in affection. Frost moths enhanced warmer emotions, pulling tribes together, ensuring the renewal of the species.

"Are you talking about sex?" I blurted out, belatedly checking my surroundings. I stood alone on the second-floor landing, talking to a book. Conscious of the peepholes on the apartment doors and my budding reputation as the weirdo neighbor, I shuffled up the next flight.

Until the last couple of generations, infant mortality rates were drastically higher. Procreation was imperative for you guys to survive. Frost moths singling out a village was a sign of good fortune.

I remembered Summer's hungry perusal of Jamie and my instant aggression. Val had the benefit of an archaeologist's detachment, not to mention the sexual experience of a leather-bound book. I, on the other hand, had a hard time imagining those ancestral villagers appreciating the interference of another species in their relationships or their love lives.

Since humans were transitioning to living indoors and always around a heat source, Val continued, *only the frost moths that could double feed*—lux lucis *and emotions—survived.*

"Thank you for explaining," I said, forestalling a full-blown lecture. Three more steps and I could remove these boots and see if my heels were a solid mass of blood and blister or if the pain only made it feel that way. "Any chance you'll tell me what you said about me to Pamela?"

Nothing worse than you proved tonight.

I grimaced and closed the book. I allowed myself one last self-pitying sigh before straightening my shoulders and lifting my chin high.

It was time to face Jamie's wrath.

8

HAPPINESS IS A GREAT DANE

A welcome blast of heat stung my chilled cheeks when I shoved open the front door. Peeling off my coat and scarf, I draped them over the half wall to the right of the door, laying Val on top. Jamie's apparel littered the front room, and I blinked to normal vision to skim the piles of garments, determining from the lack of underwear and long johns that he was still human. A second later, I heard him in the bedroom.

"Ow, no, Dame Zilla! My fingers are not the toy!" Jamie darted out of the bedroom and down the hall toward me, a long string dangling from his hand. His pounding feet rattled the bookcases against the walls, but I couldn't bring myself to admonish him, not with that ear-to-ear grin.

A tiny tabby kitten ripped around the corner, claws digging into the carpet, front feet flying high in clumsy pounces. Mr. Bond, my over-weight adult Siamese, trotted after them, eyes locked on the kitten. Jamie thundered around the single chair in the front room, and Dame Zilla leapt through the air, claws splayed, mouth agape. All five-point-six pounds of her landed on the string, and Jamie let it drop as if she'd yanked it from his hands.

Mr. Bond spotted me and his tail lifted. Chirping, he trotted to me.

I wasn't the only one who'd had her life upended in the last few weeks. Mr. Bond had gone from being an only and much spoiled cat to sharing a house with a man who turned into a Great Dane, and last night we'd added a kitten to the mix. He'd handled it all with an aplomb I was both proud and jealous of.

I bent to pet Mr. Bond as he stropped my ankles. He paused mid-rub to sniff all the scents on my boots, then flopped atop my toes and swam across the damp leather. Dame Zilla tore past us in pursuit of a foam ball, pointy tail wagging as happily as a dog's.

Contentment washed through me, sapping the last of my tension.

I looked up, meeting Jamie's golden eyes across the room. His easy smile slid off his face, and he sat, drawing his knees to his chest. His long johns rode up his calves, exposing the tops of his wool socks. Mr. Bond's purr filled the room, punctuated by muted thumps of Dame Zilla's ball chase through the bathroom.

"I'm sorry," I said, holding Jamie's gaze. "Tonight sucked."

Jamie blinked but said nothing, and the silence wedged between us.

"We needed to impress Pamela, for Brad and for me. She's smart and knows a hell of a lot more than me." Especially about pooka rearing. "With tyver coming, I need to learn everything I can as fast as I can, because I don't want to be turned into a vegetable."

"A tyv wouldn't hurt you. I'd make sure of it."

The statement would have made Pamela happy.

"You shouldn't have to. I should be able to defend myself." *And you.* If I were a better enforcer, I wouldn't have had to let Jamie be used as bait. I could have shot the drones from the sky before they got close to him, and I could have done it while standing right beside him.

Mr. Bond wrapped his claws around my ankle, his enthusiastic cheek rubs bordering on an attack, and I shooed him away. He rushed to the carpeted cat tree, sharpening his claws with a gusto that quivered the heavy frame.

"Why wouldn't you let me clean up the *lux lucis* on the ground?" Jamie asked.

I considered lying but didn't see the point. "Pamela says it's better if you don't use *atrum*." Seeing his frown, I added, "Especially not on something so trivial."

"But you wouldn't have let *atrum* remain on the ground."

"No." I maintained eye contact with difficulty, feeling like a hypocrite for changing the rules. Neither energy belonged on inanimate objects, but only *atrum* would cause harm if left in place.

"Because *lux lucis* is better than *atrum*?" he asked.

"Because *lux lucis* never steered a person toward malicious actions." I chose my words carefully. I believed with all my heart in *lux lucis*'s superiority over *atrum*, but I wasn't going to say as much to my half-*atrum* pooka.

"Who determines what is good and what is evil?" he asked.

"You do. I do. The easiest way is to check your heart. Does whatever you're doing feel right? If you put yourself on the other side of the equation, would you still think it's right? If not, it's probably evil."

"If an imp killed you, it'd be evil, so how is it not evil when you kill imps?" He made the logic leap so fast he must have had some version of the question already prepared. Standing as bait in the field had given him plenty of time to think.

"It's not evil because I'm protecting myself. Allowing an imp to chew on my soul and slowly convert my *lux lucis* to *atrum* wouldn't be good, either. Imps make the choice to harm me. Defending myself isn't evil. If I sought out someone harmless and tried to hurt or kill them, that'd be evil."

Jamie mulled over my answer, and I tensed for his next question.

"Can I take the first shower?"

"Uh, sure." Hiding my relief, I bent and unzipped my boots. I had little doubt we'd return to this topic, but I was grateful to let the conversation go for now.

While Jamie trotted off toward the bathroom, I finally eased free of my torturous shoes. Peeling my socks down, I examined my heels. Neither looked half as bad as they felt.

Dame Zilla burst from the bedroom, tripping Jamie, and tore down the hall. At the last second, she puffed staticky hair, arched her back, and bounced sideways at Mr. Bond where he stood beside the cat tree. Two of her tiny paws could fit in a single print of Mr. Bond's and her arched back barely came up to his breastbone, but she didn't let their vast size difference intimidate her. Ears canted sideways in obvious befuddlement, Mr. Bond sat back on his haunches, but when Dame Zilla reared up and swiped at him, he batted her aside. Undeterred, she launched for his shoulder. Mr. Bond pinned her to the carpet with a single paw to her head. Twisting free, the kitten darted away. Mr. Bond's plaintive meow made me laugh.

❄

I didn't feel completely human until I stepped from the shower, warm and clean. The yellowing splotches on my forearms from last week's battles had almost faded, but I'd added fresh purple to my knees tonight. I should have expected as much. Since I'd become an enforcer, I hadn't enjoyed a single bruise-free day, which said more about my ineptitude than it did about the job.

Stretching biceps sore from tonight's unaccustomed use, I towel-dried my hair, then eased my feet into my softest socks and dressed in worn yellow polka-dot flannel pajamas adorned with pink bunnies. Per his request, I'd purchased Jamie an identical outfit. He wore the pastel pajamas with unabashed happiness tonight as he cavorted on the floor with the cats, using a wand with a long feathery string to drive Dame Zilla nuts and occasionally entice a pounce out of Mr. Bond. Predictably, when I headed for the kitchen, Mr. Bond and Jamie came running.

Ignoring my first instinct to root through the drawer of takeout menus, I opened the pantry cupboard instead. I typically viewed cooking with the same enthusiasm as dusting—something to be done once every two to three months—but my budget didn't have the wiggle room to accommodate a roommate who ate enough for three people. Home-cooked meals were the heinous solution, and Jamie and I had spent yesterday wending up and down the grocery aisles to stock the refrigerator and cabinets.

Bridget was going to laugh until she passed out when I told her my credit card company's fraud department had contacted me after that abnormally astronomical grocery bill.

I put Jamie in charge of feeding the cats, and as the new, proud pet parent of Dame Zilla, he leapt at the opportunity to win her affection. Mr. Bond got dry kibble in his bowl in the dining room; Dame Zilla feasted on special kitten food atop the cat tree, out of Mr. Bond's gluttonous reach.

I'd rescued Dame Zilla and her siblings from ignorantly neglectful teens two weeks ago, and the kittens had been in the care of Alex and his staff since. The others had adopted out quickly, but for reasons I couldn't fathom, no one had swooped Dame Zilla up. With the tiniest nudge from Alex and his assurance that the company of a kitten would be beneficial for Mr. Bond, I'd adopted her. Bringing home a kitten last night after a remarkable first date with the hot veterinarian who'd nursed her back to health ranked high on my all-time best moments.

Seeing Jamie's face when I'd explained she was his pet came a close second.

The pooka took care with his soul, always presenting a solid shell of *lux lucis* when near Mr. Bond and Dame Zilla. In return, they adored him. If he let his soul relax to its usual chaotic mix, the cats shied away. I considered using the cats' reactions in my argument for *lux lucis*, but remembering how much Jamie enjoyed the affection of imps who approached him when he cloaked his soul with *atrum*, I kept my mouth shut. His dual nature provided him optimum opportunities to interact with all the creatures he loved. Why would he want to give up one for the other?

Mood souring, I filled a pot with water, another with a jar of marinara sauce, and set both on burners I hadn't used since Bridget had insisted we make s'mores last winter. I rummaged through the cupboard for noodles, jumping when my cell rattled out "Hail to the Chief."

"Here, Jamie. When the water boils, pour these in and turn the burner down to medium," I said, thrusting the box of noodles into his hand and rushing across the room to my coat. Rifling through the pockets, I tugged free my bright green phone. I'd named it Medusa and it held the honor of being my first-ever cell phone. My initial enthusiasm had waned substantially in the weeks since I'd purchased Medusa; the cell phone meant I never had an excuse for being out of reach.

"Hello, Brad." I plopped down at the dining table, where I could keep an eye on Jamie in the kitchen.

"How'd your training with Pamela go?"

"Didn't she tell you?"

"I'd rather hear it in your words."

Atrocious summed it up. So did *catastrophic, deplorable,* and *depressing.* "It could have been better."

Brad grunted. "Any flaws in the palmquell?"

"Other than user error? No. It's the perfect size for me. The soul breaker is . . . nice, too. Thank you. You have an eye for weapons." After my disastrous performance tonight, I wasn't above softening Brad up with flattery.

"I'm glad you think so, because you're paying for them out of your next paycheck."

I jerked straight, fingers tightening around the phone. Enforcer weapons weren't cheap. They weren't even reasonably priced.

"Hang on. How much did they cost? Am I going to have any money left in my check?" I still had rent to pay and my car payment, not to mention a pooka literally eating through my savings.

"You will if we get to permanently expand our region. More region equals more pay."

"It does?" Summer's comment about me gouging her paycheck snapped to the front of my thoughts before Brad responded. If more region equaled more pay, the opposite had to be true. When Brad and I had taken control of a slice of her region, she had taken a pay cut. No wonder she harbored a grudge against me.

The region we stood to assimilate if Pamela granted us a permanent expansion was more than triple the amount we'd gained from Summer. My next question came out fast and hopeful: "How much more?"

"Enough to cover your expenses. But this is about more than a raise. I don't think you grasp how unique this opportunity is. Regional boundaries rarely shift. Having our borders expand twice in one week is about as likely as you bonding two pookas in the same amount of time."

I glanced at Jamie. He'd opened the box of noodles and cracked three into his mouth, chewing loud enough to hear over Mr. Bond crunching through his kibble. Contentedness radiated through the bond, but this evening's turmoil lurked fresh in my thoughts. Being pulled around by one pooka, teaching him right from wrong, was a full-time job. Two pookas at once would be insanity.

"We need this, Madison. We need to keep as much territory as the inspector permits, because we're not ever going to get another chance like this."

Brad sounded earnest, and he'd never struck me as greedy, but I wished we were having this conversation in person so I could read his expression.

"Aside from money, what would more region mean for us?"

"You'll gain experience faster, and it'll add weight to your résumé when you transfer."

You'll gain experience faster was code for *you'll have more work.* It wouldn't simply be a matter of more square miles to cover, either. If we kept our part of Isabel's territory, we'd gain responsibility for a mall and a jail—two labor-intensive, high-risk locations. I'd spent the morning cleaning up the flotsam of *atrum* around the jail, and I didn't relish retaining permanent rights to protecting that particular piece of land. Nor did padding my résumé in preparation for a transfer add any appeal. Most of my friends and my parents lived within a short drive of my apartment, and I liked Roseville. I didn't see myself wanting to move anytime soon.

All in all, money looked like the *only* incentive.

"What's in it for you?" I asked.

"Respect." His sigh gusted harsh across the phone receiver. When he spoke again, his voice escalated in volume, and I held the phone from my ear to spare my eardrum. "If I had a bigger region, people might stop stuffing their heads up their own Jolly Ranchers when I enter the room. Do you think I like working out of taffy turd offices like our new headquarters? Having every acquisition request denied by rote? I swear the CIA has a butterscotch-blasted 'denied' stamp with my name on it. I'm sick and tired of it." He paused, then added, softer, "I've been living under the shadow of my past long enough."

A week ago, Brad wouldn't have been this forthright with me, but that was before I'd saved his life and our region. I'd earned the right to his trust, which included being told the truth about his past. At one time, Brad had been in charge of the largest, most coveted region in California, but when one of his enforcers had gone rogue and another died, he'd been demoted to our scrap of a region in Roseville. From what I'd seen from his interactions with his peers, his reputation had taken an even larger hit.

Maybe his fall from grace should have alarmed me, but in the short time I'd worked for Brad, I'd come to trust him with my life. He'd hired me, a completely inexperienced enforcer, gotten me training, risked what remaining credibility he possessed to support me, and had done everything within his power to keep me safe. He'd never been anything but honest with me—often frustrated and overprotective and short-tempered, but always honest. He had recognized the evil in Isabel when no one else did. He had good instincts and the best interest of his region at heart.

I sighed, realizing I would have done everything in my power to make sure he got the regional expansion he wanted, raise or no raise. It was the least I could do.

"Are you sure impressing Pamela is our only option? What about being judged on past accomplishments?"

"This isn't the time for jokes, Madison."

"You haven't seen me with a palmquell."

"That was before you were properly motivated. Soul breakers aren't cheap."

"How not cheap are we talking?"

The sum he quoted dropped my jaw. "Are you going to spread that across three paychecks or four?"

"Two, if we keep this region."

I did quick mental math of my potential new salary, and my mouth gaped again.

Not privy to my imitation of a dying fish, Brad drilled on. "Pay close attention to Doris tomorrow. Show Pamela you've got the drive and skills it takes to handle this region. Anything less, and we don't stand a chance."

No pressure.

I stumbled from bed the next morning, bleary-eyed and clumsy, almost trampling Jamie. Nothing about my apartment qualified as "spacious," least of all the bedroom. I'd squeezed a full-size bed, narrow dresser, and tiny desk into its confines, along with enough plants to replenish my *lux lucis* twice over. Jamie's circular, cushioned doggy bed took up the remaining space.

As was his habit, Jamie had transformed into a Great Dane before bedding down last night, and I'd tucked a fuzzy plaid blanket around him. He'd kicked the blanket off at some point, and he greeted the morning sprawled on his back, his hind legs braced against the side of my bed, his front curled against his chest. Ebony fur coated him from nose to tail, accentuating the fluffy gray-and-white ball of Dame Zilla curled against his neck.

Mr. Bond jumped from the bed, landed beside Jamie, pausing long enough to yowl in his face. Then he hopped over the pooka's deep chest and trotted out the door, meowing louder than the beeps of the alarm clock. Dame Zilla's head popped up and she chirped, stretched, and cantered after him. Jamie grinned, adding a soft *whuff* to the animal chorus.

Thus begins another day at the Fox household zoo.

"Put on some underwear before you come out," I reminded him, heading for the bathroom.

After dressing in yesterday's clothes straight from the dryer, we fed the cats, and Jamie got his first taste of the darker side of pet ownership when I designated him collector of litter box offerings. By the time he returned from the Dumpster, I had breakfast on the table: Greek yogurt, granola, and fresh berries—honest to goodness grown-up food. Too bad it didn't taste like donuts.

I ate yogurt by the vat these days. Absorbing *lux lucis* from plants replenished any I expended, but consuming *lux lucis* increased my base level of power faster, or so Niko claimed. For food to retain its *lux lucis*, it had to be a raw plant or still living when it passed down my throat, like the probiotics in yogurt. I supposed any fermented food would work just as well, but I'd take yogurt over kimchi or sauerkraut any day.

I'd yet to see any results from my new and improved diet, but I could get behind a meal plan that didn't require cooking.

Jamie pounced on his food with an enthusiasm I suspected he'd learned from Mr. Bond. The least picky eater I'd ever encountered, the pooka would consume dog food kibble and Brussels sprouts with equal delight, no matter what his current shape. The first time I'd witnessed him shoveling kibble into his human mouth with a spoon, I'd gagged and instituted a strict rule: People ate people food; dogs ate dog food. Jamie found my squeamishness perplexing but funny.

We ate in silence, accompanied by the crunching sounds of Mr. Bond and the rustle of Dame Zilla stalking through the jungle of plants crammed into my front room. I'd barely polished off my bowl of yogurt—and Jamie hadn't finished inhaling his third helping—before a pounding rattled the front door. Padding across the carpet, I peered through the peephole. A black sleeping bag with arms and a white-haired perm bounced on my doorstep. I checked the microwave clock: 6:56. Early, as expected.

Snapping back the dead bolt, I opened the door. Frigid air swirled around my feet as Doris trotted in, and I slammed the door behind her.

"Well I'll be damned. It's true," Doris said, staring at Jamie.

Jamie stared back, his hand hovering over his bowl, yogurt clinging to the fingers he'd been using to scoop out the remnants. At least he didn't have his face in the bowl.

Doris whirled and slapped my arm hard enough to sting. "I leave for a few weeks and you get yourself bound to a pooka? You do move fast, girl. I thought for sure Brad was pulling my leg."

Rubbing the pain from my bicep, I blinked to Primordium, relieved to see Jamie's soul twirled with peaceful braids of *lux lucis* and *atrum*. So far, the only person to rile Jamie by sight alone had been Sharon, the creepy receptionist at our headquarters, which I secretly thought proved Jamie had good instincts.

"Hi, I'm Doris." The retired enforcer strode to the table and extended her hand to Jamie. She didn't exhibit fear or suspicion, which placed her a step above Summer and Pamela.

Jamie eyed the yogurt on his fingers, then made a *lux lucis*–coated fist and offered it to Doris. They bumped knuckles.

"I'm Jamie," he said.

"I'm a simple woman, Jamie, so here's the deal: If you don't mess with me, I won't mess with you, and we'll get along great."

"Deal," Jamie said, showing off the granola in his teeth when he grinned.

Seeing they were capable of playing nice, I hustled to the bedroom to collect Val and our coats. The handbook spent his nights tucked safely away in the closet, well out of reach of Mr. Bond. Something about Val's nature hit Mr. Bond's senses like crack-laced catnip, and he would fixate on Val unless the handbook was out of sight. Dame Zilla wasn't immune, either.

Sliding the closet door aside, I hit pause on the audiobook running on my laptop and lifted the earbuds from Val's cover. After his initial hesitation to explore fiction, Val had developed a passion for fantasy and science fiction, and I had spent over a hundred dollars in audio-books for him in the last few days. As soon as I got a chance, we were headed to the library, but in the meantime, providing the handbook with entertainment during the lonely nights seemed the least I could do for him. Plus, it had the added benefit of improving the grumpy book's mood.

When I returned to the front room, Doris had her coat unzipped and spread wide, flashing Jamie.

"Have you ever seen anything cuter?" she asked.

"Yep." Jamie darted around the table and scooped Dame Zilla from behind the TV. "This is my kitten," he announced with the pride of a new father.

"She's yours?" Doris stroked her fingers through Dame Zilla's fur, earning an immediate purr.

"Madison got her for me."

Doris arched a gray brow at me. "Okay, hot stuff, you be the judge. Which is cuter, the kitten or my great-granddaughter?"

Doris pulled the edges of her knee-length puffy coat aside. A thick pink sweater engulfed her from neck to midthigh, a giant rectangular photo of an infant in a panda onesie printed across her chest and stomach. Jamie lifted Dame Zilla up, and she kneaded the air, her purr revving louder.

Apparently, I was the hot-stuff judge. "Oh, ah, it's too close to tell." Doris snorted.

"You're the cutest, aren't you?" Jamie murmured, snuggling the kitten to his chest and carrying her to the top perch of the cat tree. He'd spoken in the exact tone I used with Mr. Bond.

"Not a sight I ever thought I'd see," Doris whispered to me, watching the pooka and kitten interact. Never shy, Mr. Bond threaded through her legs, rubbing on the shifting hem of her coat and meowing for attention. Doris gave herself a shake, clapped her hands, and announced, "I hear we've got a lot of work ahead of us. Chop-chop."

After saying our good-byes to the cats, I locked up and we clattered down the stairs to my Civic. Doris called shotgun, then had to explain what that meant to Jamie. While they talked, I set the defroster to full blast, our body heat having instantly fogged the windshield. The temperatures had sunken to record lows last night, and frost coated the grassy hill in front of my parking space, turning the green blades a crystalline gray in the lamplight. If not for the awning above the car, I would have been scraping ice off the windshield. Eliminating the frost moths last night obviously hadn't been enough to restore Roseville's typical balmy winter weather.

"Is that a handbook?" Doris asked when she saw me adjust Val's strap to get my seat belt situated.

"His name is Val."

Doris released a low whistle. "Brad must really like you to spring for one of those. Hand it over."

I unhooked Val and passed him to Doris. She ran her fingers gently over his cover before opening him. "Hi, Val. I'm Doris."

Text scrawled across Val's page, unreadable from my angle. When Doris thumbed through him, black writing coated every single page.

Val had a firm policy of showing only the entries he felt the enforcer reading him was ready for, which meant more than ninety percent of the book remained blank for me.

Sparing a glare for my traitorous handbook, I checked Jamie in the rearview mirror to make sure he'd latched his seat belt, then backed out of my spot.

"Where to?"

"The Quarry Ponds center," Doris said.

"Where the Christmas tree stand burned down?" The stand had been a casualty of Isabel's strategic destruction of my region, all the fresh-cut trees fodder for one voracious pyro salamander. I'd cleaned the residual *atrum* from the site Thanksgiving morning, and Brad hadn't mentioned it as a problem area since.

"That's the place. It's guaranteed to have frost moths."

"I don't need to practice killing moths. I need to work on my aim for taking out drones."

"It's called multitasking, and with tyver coming, you can't afford not to."

The Quarry Ponds shopping center squatted beside Douglas Boulevard, squeezed between a dated feed and tack store on the right and protected marshlands wrapping around the left side and back. Across the cattail-studded water behind the complex towered multimillion-dollar homes on manicured lots larger than the average Walmart. The architects of Quarry Ponds had attempted to capture the same grandeur in the center's stone facade and tiered fountains, falling short. At best, they'd succeeded in creating an illusion of tranquility, making the most of a deep parking lot and plenty of trees to separate shoppers from the Douglas traffic hurtling by at freeway speeds. On a Sunday morning at sunrise, we had the lot to ourselves.

I parked near the feed store. Beyond it, a forest of pines stood in unnatural clumps, corralled into rows by festive red and green rope. The burned-down Christmas tree stand had been restocked the next day, the charred rubble of the old stand removed and the ash-matted dirt converted to a makeshift parking lot. Electric-blue frost moths drifted over the tree stand and through the parking lot like ghostly butterflies. I gave up counting them when I reached twenty-five. No wonder the dozen we'd killed last night hadn't made a difference. Three times as many moths sullied this tiny center. How many more were spread throughout my region?

"Hang on," I said when Jamie reached for the door handle. "You know the rules, right?"

He met my gaze in the rearview mirror, his expression guarded.

"Today's like last night: Only use *lux lucis*. No *atrum*," I said, just to make it clear. "And don't—"

"Feed anything. I know." Anger sparked in Jamie's eyes before he shoved from the car and slammed the door behind him.

I flinched and clicked my teeth shut. Our fragile truce hadn't lasted past sunrise. It'd been foolish to think a single apology and some fun time with the cats would be enough to bring Jamie around. Getting him to accept Pamela's new, stricter rules would take time.

"He's testing your authority," Doris said.

"Is that what Pamela told you?"

"No, that's what my eyes told me. Pamela said he's calling the shots."

I swallowed my protest. Arguing about my relationship with Jamie wouldn't change Doris's—or Pamela's—mind.

"Whoa! Does he do that often?"

I whirled around in time to see Jamie finish stripping down to his birthday suit. Fortunately, the car door shielded his lower half, sparing me the need to poke out my own eyes. I scrambled for my door handle. I had to stop him before—

Jamie's soul flexed and bubbled in a complex net; then his human shape melted into an enormous Great Dane. The fluid transformation took less than five seconds.

"Doesn't that beat all," Doris whispered on an exhale.

I agreed. I'd seen Jamie shift between his human and dog form a dozen times, and it still took my breath away.

I finally found the handle and popped the door open. Bitter cold air slapped my cheeks, sliding icy fingers down my neck as I exited the car. Scanning the lot, I confirmed we were alone and no one had witnessed Jamie's metamorphosis. We had a rule against changing in public. Technically, he hadn't broken it, but his transformation had been an obvious act of defiance.

I tightened my scarf and tugged on my beanie, silently arguing the merits of scolding him. Deciding my words would not only fall on deaf ears, but also make me look weak in front of Doris, I pinched my lips together and marched around the car to collect the pile of clothes Jamie had abandoned on the pavement.

Doris straightened from the car, Val open across her palm. "It's a bit like one child leading another, isn't it?" she asked him as she watched Jamie trot to the nearest tree, lift his leg, and mark his territory.

Only scarier, Val agreed in font large enough for me to read.

Lovely. Today's training would be accompanied by heckling from the peanut gallery. Why had I gotten up early for this?

9

ONLY LEFT-HANDED PEOPLE ARE IN
THEIR RIGHT MINDS

Gritting my teeth, I stuffed Jamie's clothes into the backseat and his boots onto the floorboard. After mentally shoving my anger after them, I slammed the door shut.

"Is he bigger as a dog?" Doris asked.

"Than as a human? I think he weighs about the same."

Muscled through the shoulders and chest, sleek everywhere else, and tall enough to ride, Jamie's Great Dane form stretched from door to door when he lay in the backseat of the Civic, and if we were standing side by side, he wouldn't have to stretch far to stick his nose in my armpit. Despite his impressive doggy form, his short dark fur wouldn't provide much insulation from the freezing morning air.

"Jamie, come put on your sweater before you catch a cold," I called. Hearing my words, I snorted. I sounded like my mother.

The pooka took his time, detouring on his way back to the car to sniff various patches of ground. I pretended not to notice his subtle rebellion and instead walked to the trunk to retrieve a giant canine sweater we'd picked out together at an overpriced pet store—the only place we could find a garment for a dog his size.

When I straightened from the trunk, Jamie sat beside me, a tongue-lolling grin on his face. My irritation fizzled out, and I swiped a hand across his *lux lucis*-coated forehead. He leaned into my touch, and the bond threaded thicker between us, losing its brittle edges. I let out a soft sigh, keeping my back to Doris. I couldn't explain the importance of being in sync with my pooka without it sounding like I was under his thrall, so I preferred to avoid the topic altogether.

I suspected getting the sweater on a normal dog would take a great deal of wrestling or a very patient dog. Jamie made it easy, thrusting his head through the neck hole and standing for me to connect the Velcro strap under his stomach. I stood back to admire the outfit on him. With bunched cotton riding up his neck to his floppy ears and thick fleece draping his back and flanks, Jamie looked every part the hipster dog.

He twisted back and forth, checking himself out, and whined at me.

"You look quite dapper," I assured him.

"That look is all the rage in LA," Doris said.

Jamie perked up and wagged his tail.

"Does it pinch anywhere?" I asked.

He barked and shook his head.

"Okay. Stay close, please." I gave him another stroke across his wide forehead, then patted his rear to signal he was free to go.

He barked again and trotted off to explore the landscaped planters.

Doris's face twisted through a series of emotions. She didn't give voice to any of them, but I got the gist. I'd just petted Jamie. I knew he wasn't a dog. If he were in his human form, I wouldn't be okay with running my hands over him. Patting his naked human rear was out of the question. But when he wore the guise of a Great Dane, he was as much dog as pooka, and he seemed to enjoy the different style of affection. When human, we occasionally held hands when he needed comfort. Petting him when he was a dog was little different.

I hoped my logic was my own, not the bond's manipulations.

Doris gave herself a shake. "Let's get started. Pull out your palmquell and take a shot."

My stomach churned, last night's failures gelling into a knot of dread when I grasped the palmquell. "At what?"

"Anything you think you can hit."

As tempting as it was to shoot the Civic—only two feet behind me, it was a sure hit—I fixed my sights on the nearest frost moth. If any part of the moth had possessed true mass, the entire creature would have crumpled, but in the metaphysical realm of Primordium, its black cylindrical body floated effortlessly on fragile wings of lacy ice tipped with dendrite crystals. Giving a lackadaisical flap, the moth coasted in a smooth arc. Hitting it should be easy.

I fired a bolt of *lux lucis*. It streaked across the black sky and splatted to the pavement.

"What were you aiming for?" Doris asked.

I pointed at the moth. Doris walked up to my shoulder and squinted. The white energy smeared the charcoal pavement at least seven feet to the right of where I'd aimed.

"Annie Oakley you are not. What was with your stance? You're not a gunslinger at the O.K. Corral. Don't shoot from the hip. Lift your gun and aim using the front sight."

"The what?"

"The little thing sticking up at the tip of the palmquell. Center your target on that. Pamela didn't teach you any of this last night?"

"We were at a high school. She didn't want us to draw attention."

"Oh. I see her point. People are real jumpy about guns in schools."

"People are jumpy about guns anywhere. What if someone sees me?"

"Now?" Doris glanced around the empty parking lot. Every few minutes a clot of cars gusted past on the boulevard, but the well-placed trees did a good job of screening us from them.

"Not now. When I'm out at night. Shouldn't I learn how to shoot discreetly?"

"First you have to be able to hit something; then we'll work on discretion."

The frost moth landed on my forearm and sank tiny inky teeth into my soul. A trickle of heat slid through me. I shoved the palmquell into my pocket, retrieved my lighter, and bubbled my soul around the moth's tiny legs, making a *lux lucis* net on my first try.

"Don't kill it," Doris said, showing a complete lack of appreciation for my new skill. "Scare it off a ways and try again."

Irritated, I collapsed the net and flamed the moth. It launched into a tight, skyward spiral. Swapping the lighter for my palmquell, I held the gun at arm's length, sighted down the top of the barrel, and fired. Nothing hit the moth until it spread its wings and settled into a slow, lazy loop above my head. When I finally nailed a wing with a splotch of *lux lucis*, the moth didn't react, its bright blue appendage impervious to the energy.

"I did it!"

"As long as the drones come at you in slow motion, you'll be fine," Doris said, cutting off my celebration before it began. Her gaze slid past me, and her hand dropped to a single, extra-large knitting needle protruding from her coat pocket. "What happens if a moth feeds on Jamie?"

"Nothing bad." He'd said he wouldn't feed anything, but given his rebellious impulses this morning, wariness compelled me to pivot and check on him.

Two frost moths, both with wings as large as my steering wheel, coasted to Jamie and settled on his back. Without looking up from the bush he had his head buried in, Jamie pulsed *atrum* down his body. The evil energy flowed like wet paint from his spine to his toes, saturating him in absolute blackness as dark as the empty sky above us. The frost moths fluttered away. I expected them to circle back for a second attempt at feeding, but they drifted higher, dismissing him.

I performed my patented head-shake sobriety test, reassured by my lack of dizziness. Jamie had followed through on his promise.

"See? Nothing." I checked Doris's expression. Her hand clutched the knitting needle in a death grip. "No need to poke anyone." I kept my eye roll to myself.

"I'd do a lot worse than poke him." Doris whipped the wooden instrument from her pocket. Ending in a blunt tip coated with a coarse substance like a match, it resembled an obese drumstick until she snapped it in half vertically. The tip split into two sharp hooks and the long length became two arms connected at the base by a hidden rivet.

"Is that a soul breaker?" I couldn't take my eyes off Doris, not while she brandished the weapon like a knife. Not when she'd said she'd do a lot worse than poke *him*. Hooks that sharp would pierce a pooka as easily as a tyv. If she made a move toward Jamie—

"Yep. I designed it myself." She smiled, a bare twitch of her mouth. Tension tightened her body, and her grip on the soul breaker never slackened. "You do realize that if you shoot me, it won't do anything to me, right?"

I stared in shock at my arms held rigid in front of me, pointing the palmquell at Doris's chest. *Oh crap!* Dropping my arms, I took firm rein on my emotions. Jamie wasn't in danger. Doris wasn't a threat. And a palmquell wasn't a real gun.

Thank God.

"I, ah . . ." Another purity test loomed in my future when Doris reported this incident to Pamela.

"You're jumpy." Doris snapped the soul breaker back into a single stick and slid it into her coat pocket. "Use those reflexes on the frost moths, and we won't have a problem."

I nodded, my head bobbing too many times, but I couldn't make it stop. Sucking in air through my nose, I forced my feet to turn away from Doris. Oblivious to my turmoil, Jamie trotted to the next planter box, nosing through the bushes and startling a pair of towhee into flight.

Stupid pooka bond. It made me crazy while Jamie got to coast along, feeling nothing.

Three moths approached on lazy spirals and I channeled my frustration into the palmquell, firing *lux lucis* in a steady stream. One in a dozen shots hit a target.

"Whoa, there, Rambo. Spraying the whole sky will only wear you out. Slow down, aim, and fire with purpose."

I took a deep breath, closed one eye, sighted down the barrel, and fired. The shot went wide. With the same aggravating care, I prepped and fired another shot. Doris jogged around me so she could study my face during the next near miss.

"Aha! There's your problem. You're left-eye dominant and right handed. Close your left eye and try again."

I did and put two successive shots through a frost moth's wings as it plummeted toward me.

"Did you see that?" A kernel of hope took root in my chest. Maybe I had a chance of defending my region and myself against the drones after all.

"It's a start. And Val's right. You should kill that moth," Doris said, waving the open handbook in my direction. "There's plenty more. With the next one, try to shoot it when it's more than four feet away."

I didn't duplicate the same success with the next moth, but I missed less often. Squeezing my left eye closed caused my cheek to cramp, but when I opened both eyes, my shots became erratic. On a whim, I swapped the palmquell to my left hand, closed my right eye, and fired. My shot hit a frost moth five parking spaces away. It flapped and twisted up an invisible air current, and I chased it with seven more shots, every other bolt of *lux lucis* hitting a wing.

Doris cheered. "Now we're getting somewhere!"

Over the next half hour, my skills improved until I could reliably hit a slow-flying creature the size of a turkey from less than ten feet away. I wouldn't win any prizes with my marksmanship, but I savored my accomplishment nevertheless.

As a reward for my improvement, Doris increased the difficulty, insisting I walk in between shots, pacing back and forth across the parking lot and stopping only when a moth flew into range. When I got the hang of that, she made me run circles around her, staying close enough to rescue her from frost moths.

"Any chance you're going to help?" I asked as I wiped out my twelfth and thirteenth—or was it my thirteenth and fourteenth?— moths. Doris stood useless next to me, too busy chatting with Val to form a net or even to hold out her lighter and melt the buggers faster.

"You need the practice more than I do." Doris took in my glower and gave me a sweet smile. "Besides, learning to deal with the emotional backlash of a moth is part of the training."

How much was Brad paying her for this lesson? Maybe I should let him know she didn't do anything but stand there with her thumb up her—

I drew a deep breath of cold air into my lungs and squelched my unjustified, moth-fueled anger.

"Maybe you could"—*make yourself useful and*—"answer a question for me. When I trap a moth in a net, it doesn't feel wrong. If you took away its emotional exploitation, it'd be less intrusive than an imp. But when Pamela put her hands in my soul for the purity tests, it felt like . . ."

"Like a metaphysical Pap smear by an indifferent doctor?"

I cringed at the analogy but nodded.

"It's a bit logical, a bit woo-woo," Doris said. "You're built to take out evil creatures, so using your *lux lucis* to trap a frost moth is natural, and killing it feels right. Having a stranger feel up your soul doesn't. Or I should say, having this *particular* stranger feel up your soul rubs you the wrong way. Oh, pipe down, Val. I'm not disrespecting Pamela. I'm saying she and Madison aren't compatible." Doris rolled her eyes and tilted Val so we couldn't see his protests. "That's the woo-woo part. With the right person, combining souls doesn't feel wrong at all." Doris's exaggerated wink lent the weight of an innuendo to her words.

Her phone chirped in her pocket, and she pulled it out to read a text, walking away as she did so and cutting short the start of an interesting conversation. I took the opportunity to massage my burning shoulder and bicep. The palmquell weighed less than a pound, but I wasn't used to holding my arm extended and steady for minutes, let alone hours.

I tugged my phone from my pocket and stared at the display. Make that *hour*, singular. At this rate, my arm would fall off before tonight's drone hunt, saving me another embarrassing evening with the inspector.

Sacrificing an arm was almost worth it.

Doris took pity on me. "Let's take a break from the palmquell and get you proficient at netting while moving."

"Why?"

"The idea is to hone your muscle memory. Building a net while your brain is partially occupied with keeping you from falling on your face will speed up the process. Do you remember the first thing I ever taught you?"

"How to kill an imp? Yeah." Duh.

"Not that; what I told you about *lux lucis*."

I thought back to our first training session. It'd been only a few weeks earlier, but with everything that had transpired since, it felt like half a lifetime ago. "You said to use it every chance I get."

"Exactly. I meant it, too. You've had a busy start to your career, and it's kept you on your toes, but that's not enough. If you're going to stay on top of your region, you have a lot of catching up to do as an enforcer. Most people in your position have had years to perfect their skills, and their use of *lux lucis* is automatic. You're going to have to work harder to get there faster. So let's see you jog and net. And be careful not to light yourself on fire."

Words to live by.

I trotted around the parking lot, floundering to make a net, my steps clumsy and my *lux lucis* pulsing with frustrating erraticism in my palm. Jamie chased me for a while before loping off, tongue lolling. At least one of us was enjoying themselves.

By the time I had control of a peach-size net, I had a stitch in my side and sweat beading my upper lip. Snaring a moth, I slowed to a walk to kill it before looking for my next victim. If I'd known I was going to be running a marathon, I would have worn sneakers. At least my thick socks prevented fresh blisters from forming on my heels.

"Most of the moths are in the back now," I said, returning to where Doris sat on a bench.

"Why don't you do laps?" She looped her finger through the air to indicate the entire center.

Scowling, I shoved back into a jog and angled through the wintry center courtyard separating the two halves of the complex, exiting onto the back patio rather than taking the long way around. Frog croaks and red-winged blackbird warbles cut short at the sound of my pounding steps, and at least twenty moths, each as large as a hawk, fluttered from the frost-limned marsh grasses.

Turning right without slowing, I bubbled a net on my palm on my sixth attempt, just in time to snare three moths at once. A surge of heat flared through me as three mouths fastened on my soul, and my eyes watered from the bluster of cold air stirred by their wings. Whipping the lighter back and forth through their bodies, I urged them toward a faster death, then blinked away tears and examined my surroundings. The other moths stalked me, coasting closer on silent wings.

Jamie rounded the corner, an imp riding his shoulders. Tiny dark claws pierced the pooka's hide, and the imp's round face lifted to the sky as if it could feel wind through its dense *atrum* body. I pulsed *lux lucis* into my palm, meaning to brighten my hand, but a net swelled instead. Jamie veered wide, but the imp couldn't resist the glowing ball of light, and it leapt onto my palm, disappearing into the net. Startled, I released the *lux lucis*. Part of me expected to see the imp sitting in my hand, but my palm was empty. The imp had vanished without even a trace of explosive glitter.

I double-checked the remaining moths, flashing the lighter's flame at the closest to scare them off before turning to Jamie. "Where did the imp come from? Show me."

Tail drooping, Jamie led the way to the opposite end of the patio. A smear of *atrum* spilled from a bar's fenced-in patio outward, the puddle roughly the size of two tables. Whatever had left the evil stain had long since moved on. Given the location, I suspected the source had been the predictable combination of alcohol and humans. A fight, physical or verbal, might have been enough to produce this *atrum*.

"Please clean it up." I'd seen Jamie clear three times as much *atrum* with a single paw's blast of *lux lucis*. Trying to sound casual, I added, "Go ahead and wipe out any other traces of *atrum* you encounter, too."

Jamie glanced from the *atrum* to me, then back the way we'd come.

He wouldn't.

"Jamie." I sank a warning into the two syllables.

His ears twitched, but he didn't look back at me. Slowly, he turned and walked away.

"Jamie!"

Soul spiking with aggravation, Jamie tucked his tail and loped out of sight around the corner.

I took two steps after him, then jerked to a stop. Even if I could catch up to a Great Dane on foot—and I couldn't—then what? Grab him by his vest and drag him back here? Rub his pooka nose in the *atrum*? I couldn't force him to clean it if he didn't want to. Strong-arming him would accomplish nothing but pissing us both off.

This was the crux of the problem with my responsibilities as a pooka rearer: I couldn't enforce anything. In every form, Jamie equaled or outstripped me in mass, and he possessed enough *atrum* to win a head-to-head fight against three of me. He was smart and naïve, powerful and impressionable. I'd fractured the delicate framework of my authority last night, or so it seemed, but according to Pamela, it'd been built on quicksand anyway. Jamie's rebellion stemmed directly from my leniency.

Now what? Where was Pamela and her advice when I really needed it?

Squatting, I rolled *lux lucis* off my fingertips. The white energy ate through a swath of *atrum*, leaving behind clean charcoal-colored concrete. Shifting, I repeated the maneuver twice more to erase the *atrum* completely, then walked to the marsh's edge and recharged from the sturdy trunk of a cottonwood.

I forgot about the frost moths until frozen wings raked through my chest and stomach, constricting the air in my lungs. Heat blossomed in its wake, overpowered by ice again when a second, then a third, fourth, and fifth moth landed on my head and shoulders. More swarmed, diving to land on my thighs and ankles, tiny mouths fastening on my soul. Sweat broke across my back and scalp, and I formed a hasty net, swiping it down my body and capturing four moths before scaring off the rest with the lighter.

Melting four moths at once took time, and I paced the patio to evade the others, arguing with Jamie in my head. By the time the moths puffed to snow, my hands were sweating inside my gloves and I'd verbally eviscerated Jamie fifteen different ways.

"Who wants to die next?" I asked the moths, raising my arms wide.

The drove of moths descended.

Wiping out the entire flock kept me occupied for twenty minutes, but did Doris come check to make sure I hadn't fallen in the marsh and drowned? No. Did she worry I might need help? Of course not. She languished on her sun-warmed bench with her new best friend, Val. Two useless lumps. They were perfect for each other, swapping old war stories and getting off on dragging the new girl through ridiculous, pointless tests. Training should involve instruction. If all Doris wanted to do was sit on her ass soaking up the morning sun, she could have at least let me sleep in.

When the last frost moth died, I stomped across the patio hard enough to knock mud from my boots, kicking a bolted-down metal table in passing for the hell of it. Jamie hadn't shown his face again, either, which was just as well. I'd rather wait until he resumed human form and I had him somewhere captive, like in the car, before giving him the reaming he deserved.

With my left hand clenched around the palmquell tight enough to make the balsa wood creak, and the lighter crushed in my right fist, I barreled through the shopping center courtyard, intent on giving Doris a piece of my mind.

The retired enforcer stood at the other end of the opening, deep in conversation with a man whose soul shone like a god's.

Niko.

10

DIGNITY? I GAVE THAT UP YEARS AGO

The clear, vibrant texture of Niko's soul hit my retinas and flash-fried all rational thoughts. My footsteps accelerated. Undeniably the most perfect man I'd ever seen in Primordium, Niko radiated purity and strength like visible pheromones, and every cell in my body stood at attention.

My knee clipped the edge of a low planter box, and the sharp pain burst across my senses, pulling me up short. I bent to rub my knee, breaking my line of sight on Niko. *Had I been about to run to him?*

Blinking to normal sight, I took another peek at Niko.

He stood in a weak sunbeam, the pale light playing across the smooth curve of his shaved head, adding a glint to his dark eyes and accentuating his firm lips. I hadn't realized skin that dark could glow.

Even relaxed, Niko radiated power, as if he were always a breath away from exploding into action. Nothing fazed him. If he'd found himself Jamie's keeper, he would have had the pooka wrapped around his pinkie by now. If he were enforcer of this region, tyver wouldn't dare set proboscis or wing inside the borders. The man exuded confidence—all earned—and my libido lapped it up.

Niko's gaze collided with mine, and molten heat coursed through my body, weighting my breasts and tightening my nipples before settling lower. I held my breath. It was that or pant, and I retained enough sanity to spare myself that embarrassment.

What the hell was wrong with me? The man might be sexy enough to melt butter in a meat locker, but usually I had better control—

The frost moths.

Doris motioned me over to them. I shook my head and raised a hand to ward them off. Curling my toes inside my boots, I fought my body's compulsion to launch myself at Niko. Mimicking Doris's gesture, Niko said something to me. The thundering of blood in my ears drowned out his words, but the crook of his lips tugged me off balance.

Biting the inside of my cheek, I tore my gaze from Niko and spun on my heel. I didn't have the control for a dignified retreat, so I bolted, sprinting around the corner and throwing myself against the cold stucco wall. On a normal day, Niko fused my synapses; Niko plus the consuming heat of frost moths melted my brain.

Dropping my hands to my knees, I gulped icy air, not straightening until my head cleared.

Doris rounded the corner at a jog, spotted me, and shooed Niko away, assuring him I was fine.

"What happened?" she asked me.

I blinked to Primordium, surveying the marsh and homes beyond it. The landscape stretched in a gray-and-white calico as far as the eye could see. I'd lost track of how many frost moths I'd killed. Apparently all of them.

"Frost moths happened," I said.

"Ah."

I heard her laughter in the short sound.

"Did you know he was coming?" I asked, biting off each word.

"Yep. Got his text a bit ago."

"A heads-up would have been nice."

Doris grinned. "And miss your expression? Niko should be hormonal goo on the pavement back there. Or you should be, the way you were looking at him."

I stuffed my weapons into my pockets and dropped my head in my hands. My cool gloves felt divine on my flaming face.

"Then you got all constipated-looking," Doris continued, "and I thought maybe you were having a heart attack, so I came to check on you."

"You're not being even remotely helpful."

"Oh, don't scowl. It's not like I planned to have him show up when you were hopped up on frost moth fumes."

I took a deep breath and let it out slowly. "Is he still here?"

"Yep, still here," Niko said from just out of sight.

I closed my eyes and prayed for a lightning bolt to strike me dead. When nothing happened, I pushed away from the wall, straightened my coat, and yanked my beanie tighter to my scalp.

Just pretend like it never happened. I'm a professional. He's a professional. There's no need to make the situation more awkward. As if that were possible.

I strode around the corner in time to see Jamie pee on the back tire of Niko's BMW.

"Are you okay?" Niko asked, his voice neutral.

I jerked my gaze to his before he followed my line of sight and caught my pooka in the act of vandalizing his car. "Mmm-hmm. Peachy."

Laughter danced in his eyes, the bastard.

Jamie trotted away from the BMW. Since the coast was clear, I stalked past Niko toward the parking lot. With any luck, a change of scenery would erase the whole embarrassing ordeal from everyone's minds—or at least disrupt the loop playing on repeat in my head.

"What's the emergency?" I asked. Niko hadn't shown up just to humiliate me. That had been a bonus.

"No emergency. A change of plans," he said, falling in step with me. "We're making a last-ditch effort to cut the tyver off at a higher elevation. If we can raise the temperature up the hill, they'll never make it to Roseville."

"Okay." I waited for the part that involved me.

"There were, what, four forest fires in the foothills this year?" Doris asked.

"Seven."

"That's a boatload of frost moths."

I glanced around the empty lot. The tree stand covered less than a quarter acre and it'd spawned close to fifty moths when it had been torched. How many hundreds of acres had burned in the forest fires? The hills must be overrun with frost moths.

"We're calling in every enforcer who can be spared, including you, Madison."

"Brad said it was okay for me to go? Pamela, too?"

"If Doris will fill in for you." Niko turned to Doris. "Brad said you'd be well compensated."

Jamie spotted us and circled closer, checking my expression. I strove for neutral, still unsure how to respond to his rebellion. The soft wag of his drooped tail halted when he caught Niko watching our exchange. Niko didn't miss much.

"Freelance is good for the body and for the bank account," Doris said with a shrug. "Besides, you never fully retire from being an enforcer, at least not until you die, and even then, I bet somebody in the afterlife will have work for us."

"You're not looking for anything more permanent?" Niko asked.

"Than death?"

"Than freelance," Niko corrected.

Doris gave him an unfriendly look. I stepped out from between them, coincidentally putting myself between Jamie and Niko. Sure. Coincidence. Not the blasted bond prompting my actions.

"Don't you start," Doris said, waggling a finger at Niko. Next to him, she looked like a child, but I had no doubt she could back him into a corner with that sharp digit alone. "Pamela already tried to stick me with Isabel's old region. What about me gives off the vibe that I want to be turned into an office drone?"

"I think it's your sneakers," Niko said.

They both examined Doris's lime and purple tennis shoes.

"She offered you the whole region?" I blurted out.

"Yep. One fool or another has been trying to stuff me into a warden straitjacket since I got my first gray hair. Do yourself a favor, Madison: Dye your hair. Especially if you go gray early, like I did. It'll save you a lot of pointless conversations."

Jamie crept closer and put his cold nose against my wrist between the gap of my coat sleeve and glove. I rubbed my thumb down the bridge of his muzzle.

Yes, I still love you, you obstinate pooka.

"Jamie, I request a prophecy," Niko said.

That's right! Between the frost moths, drones, and emotional turmoil of last night, I'd forgotten to ask Jamie about his strange ability, but it wouldn't slip my mind again.

The Great Dane nodded and stretched his legs in a telltale fashion.

"Wait!" I clamped my hands to his sides. "Change next to the car, please."

I went with Jamie to help him out of the vest. Opening the back door of the Civic, I tossed it onto the seat and leaned in for Jamie's boots.

"Wait until I've got—"

"Burr!" Jamie exclaimed.

Two white human feet danced on the freezing pavement behind mine. I gave myself whiplash when I jerked my head forward before I caught sight of any other bouncing bits of him.

"Here, let me get out of your way." I bumped into Jamie when I backed up, but I didn't look to see which part of him I'd hit. Thrusting his boxers in his general direction, I hustled around the car and out of view.

"He doesn't understand modesty," I explained to Doris and Niko.

"Val says you're too uptight about nudity," Doris said.

She and Niko turned curious faces to me. My cheeks flamed. "He's one to talk. He's always wearing a thick leather jacket."

"She's got you there, Val," Doris said.

Niko chuckled and strode off with a fully clothed Jamie at his side. They didn't start talking until they were out of earshot. I'd never wished for the skill to read lips more than I did in that moment.

"Do you know if Pamela has anyone else lined up for the position?" I asked, hoping I could pass along useful information to Brad.

"Why? Looking for a career change already? I think you've got your hands full learning everything you need for . . ." She trailed off, eyes narrowing. "It's Brad, isn't it? He wants the region."

"Not Isabel's entire region. Just what we hold now."

"How much land did he nab?"

I outlined our new boundaries, and Doris released a low whistle. "That's quite an upgrade for you both."

"Brad said region boundaries rarely change . . ."

"That's an understatement."

"Do you think we have a chance at keeping any of Isabel's territory?"

Doris tapped her fingers against the soul breaker protruding from her pocket. "It's beyond time for the CIA to restore some of Brad's dignity, but Isabel going rogue really stirred the hornet's nest. From what I understand, the higher-ups just realized they're not as omnipotent as they thought they were. I expect they'll err on the side of ultra-conservatism when picking Isabel's replacement."

In other words, they weren't going to pick the tarnished warden and his know-nothing enforcer.

"Don't look so glum. Ultimately, it's up to Pamela."

Brad might as well throw in the towel now.

Jamie finished prophesizing, and as the two men walked back to us, I scrutinized Niko's face, but he gave no indication of his thoughts.

"Are you going to ask for a prophecy?" I asked Doris. Maybe she'd let me listen in.

She scoffed. "I don't need a foretelling mucking up my thoughts."

Jamie ducked into the Civic, rubbing his arms with his hands, his teeth audibly chattering. Niko walked around to the driver's side of his BMW but didn't make a move to get in.

"Doris, I feel obliged to ask one more time: Are you sure you want to stick around? You're retired. You don't need to chance an encounter with sjel tyver. You could take a trip, head south."

Doris gave him a scandalized look. "You're still young and all your parts are still eager to perk up, but have you seen how old the men I date are? I'd be a fool to miss out on this windfall of frost moths. I've already lined up three outdoor dates this week."

"Three?" I echoed, impressed.

Doris's smile straddled the line between demure and smug. "Would have been four, but Harold broke his hip."

Three dates with three *different* men? Cotton-topped, great-granddaughter-picture-adorned, eighty-something Doris was a player.

"Glad to see you've got your priorities," Niko said.

"Damn straight."

Still grinning, Niko shifted his attention to me. "You and I are paired up to clear a remote location outside of Colfax, so I think it's best we carpool. Meet me at the park and ride off Sierra College in half an hour."

"Okay," I squeaked. Me, an unprecedented number of frost moths, and Niko. What could go wrong?

Doris chuckled under her breath as we got into the car. I snapped out of my daze and pointed a finger at her. "No comments."

We made the drive back to my apartment in silence, which freed my mind up to replay over and over again my appalling reaction to seeing Niko and imagine even worse embarrassments in my near future.

"What's your motto today?" Doris asked when I dropped her beside her Miata in the overflow lot near my apartment building.

I stared at her blankly. Don't maul Niko? Keep my pants on?

"Regarding *lux lucis*," she prompted.

Oh. Right. "Use it all the time."

"And in your case, shoot everything in sight. It's the only way you're going to improve fast enough to be a lick of good against the drones."

With that confidence booster, she handed back Val, hopped into her toy car, and tore from the lot.

"Want to come up front?" I asked Jamie.

"I need to pee."

I turned off the car. "Grab some snacks while you're up there. Don't take too long."

He snatched the keys from my hands and bolted from the Civic. With envious ease, he sprinted up the walkway, taking the stairs two at a time, and he'd unlocked the apartment before I remembered he'd spent the entire time we were at Quarry Ponds peeing on everything in sight.

"What are you up to, pooka?" I shoved from the car, ready to chase after Jamie, but stopped when I caught sight of him in the front room's sliding glass door. He snuggled Dame Zilla to his chest, head bent to touch noses with her. With a sigh, I relaxed against the door of the Civic. Getting the kitten for him might have been a stroke of genius. Unlike the imps, she was a creature he could play with that I wouldn't have to kill. Plus, his desire to spend time with a pure *lux lucis* creature had to work in my favor, right?

The clouds played peekaboo with the sun, and the breeze whisked away what little warmth the flickering rays provided. I slid back into the driver's seat and shut in the remaining heat, checking the clock on the dash. I'd give Jamie five minutes before I retrieved him.

"Sweet Home Alabama" jingled from my pocket. I pulled out Medusa and stared at a picture of my mom's face. Better to answer now than have her keep calling while I was out with Niko.

I chose to ignore how the phrase *out with Niko* added an erratic skip to my heartbeat. He was just a coworker.

A smoking-hot, extremely talented coworker.

"Hi, Mom."

"Madison, do you have a minute?"

"I have exactly four," I said, eyes on the clock. "I'm about to leave for, um, a hike with a few friends." I wasn't the most inventive liar, but I was proud of the plausibility of my outing and how closely it mirrored the truth—minus, of course, all the details that would have sent Mom into a panic.

"A hike sounds lovely if the weather holds. You'll take your rain gear?"

I glanced down at my arctic-chic outfit. "Yep. I'm prepared for anything."

"Good. Okay, I won't keep you. I just wanted to let you know your dad and I have tickets for the Sierra Scenic Train tomorrow."

She paused like I had a clue what she was talking about. "The what?"

"It's a train that goes from Roseville to Reno through the snow."

"It's very romantic," Dad shouted in the background.

Right. Romantic. My dad loved all things trains. It'd be a miracle if he remembered Mom existed once he caught sight of the first engine.

"What's in this for you?" I asked Mom.

"It's Johnny Cash themed. Carol went last week and said they've got an impersonator who looks like Johnny in his prime."

I rolled my eyes. "So up and back in a day. Are you prepared for twelve hours of fanatical foaming from Dad?"

"Oh, no, we don't come back until Tuesday."

Alarm bells rang in my head. They'd be in overt tyv territory overnight? "How long is this train ride? Will you be in Reno by dark?"

"I hope not. I want to see the snowcapped Sierras at sunset."

"You'll stay inside the train at all times?"

"It's going to be ten below over the summit. Of course we'll be inside, won't we, Oscar?"

"I make no promises," my dad shouted.

I dropped my forehead to the steering wheel and focused on keeping my breathing even. The odds of tyver or drones attacking a lone train were slim. "When you get to Reno, you'll stay indoors, right?"

"Well, I had plans to skinny-dip in the Truckee River . . ."

"Mom! I'm serious."

"What's gotten into you?"

"Nothing. I just worry about your health." *And your memories and your inhibitions.* Oh holy hell. Drones and casinos? If ever there was a place where one needed to have full control over their faculties, it was at a casino. As long as they stayed inside, they'd be safe, though. They were norms. They wouldn't have their souls ripped from their bodies, only their memories.

This pep talk wasn't helping.

"How was your date?" Mom asked.

No segue. No lead-in. No time for me to collect my breath. A click announced my dad picking up the other extension in their house. I banged my head against the steering wheel.

"It was nice."

"Mmm-hmm," Mom prompted.

"Alex is very nice." *And a great kisser and handsome and so wonderfully normal.* "You'd like him."

"Does that mean we get to meet him?" Dad asked.

I rolled right past the question and gave them superficial details of the date, like the restaurant we ate at and a brief background on Alex: He grew up in Newcastle, a twenty-minute drive up the freeway; he had two older siblings, a sister who worked as a lawyer in San Diego and a brother who lived in LA working as a physical trainer for celebrities I'd actually heard of. His parents were divorced, and his dad had kept the house in Newcastle while his mother had landed in San Diego near the sole grandson.

When I'd prattled on long enough to give the illusion of having told them all the interesting facts, I decided to have a little fun with them.

"Then the date ended in the most spectacular way you can imagine," I said, infusing innuendo into my voice.

"Whoa! La-la-la-la," Dad said, and hung up.

"Madison, don't be crass," Mom chastised.

"Ew! I'm not the one with my mind in the gutter," I said with false innocence. "I adopted a kitten from Alex's clinic."

"You got a kitten? Oscar, she wasn't talking about S-E-X."

She spelled it out. I'm twenty-five years old, and she spelled it out.

"What's it like?" Mom asked as Dad clicked back onto the line.

"Her name is Dame Zilla, she's a tabby, and she's rambunctious and adorable."

"How's Mr. Bond taking it?" Dad asked.

"Really well. I think they'll be good for each other."

"Too bad you won't be home today, or we'd pop over to meet her," Mom said.

"We'll have to meet her when we get back," Dad said.

"Okay. We'll chat then." My words came out strangled, but I managed to get them off the phone without making any official plans.

Crap. So much for waiting until Christmas to figure out how to explain Jamie's presence in my life—and my apartment. Maybe something brilliant would occur to me in the next two days.

I stared at the phone until the screen went dark, but when no inspiration struck, I turned it back on and texted Bridget that something had come up at work. Our plans for lunch would have to wait. I held back mentioning Niko—she'd demand details and I didn't feel like typing them out. Bridget texted back immediately, understanding that work came first. There were benefits to having a workaholic friend.

Wait. I was the one working on a Sunday. Was *I* the workaholic friend? When had that happened?

Right about when my job and my survival became interwoven. Nothing motivated me to work overtime quite like trying to save my own skin.

I shoved from the car. Jamie's five minutes were up five minutes ago. I made it halfway up the walkway when I heard Jamie lock the front door and pound down the steps. He carried a grocery bag loaded to the brim, colorful cellophane chip bags protruding from the top.

"I said to grab a snack." *Not to pack for a weekend in the woods.*

"Oh, did you want me to get some stuff for you, too?" Jamie started to turn around.

I shook my head. "Come on. We're going to be late."

No one mentioned if all pookas had the metabolism of hummingbirds or if it was just mine. Given the state of my savings account, it seemed like an important detail to not overlook. Maybe I could get a clause put in the enforcer contract stating the CIA had to immediately issue a Costco membership and small farm in the event of bonding a pooka. It was too late for me, but future enforcers would thank me.

While Jamie munched his way through a bag of Doritos, I powered over a gauntlet of speed bumps before turning onto Sierra College Boulevard and kicking it up to fifty-five, speeding to make up for lost time. Playing with Dame Zilla had soothed the kinks from the dual energies of Jamie's soul, leaving him as relaxed as a lava lamp. If I brought up his earlier refusal to clean up the *atrum* puddle at the shopping center, and worse, to follow my order, I'd ruin his mood. I took the coward's way out, telling myself my reprimand would carry more weight if I waited until he acted out again.

"So, you can tell prophecies," I said, relaxing into the calm energy seeping through the bond.

"Yep."

"Can you tell me what you told Niko?"

"Nope."

I hadn't thought so, but it didn't hurt to ask. "What about me? Do you have a prophecy for me?"

Jamie set his bag of chips in his lap and squinted at me. "Sometimes."

"What does that mean?"

"Our lives are so connected it makes your future fuzzy to me. But every once in a while you do something that makes a future moment clearer or erases it."

"Oh." I didn't know if I should be disappointed or relieved. "What about right now?"

"Fuzzy."

I let that absorb, changing lanes to pass a slow SUV. "How does it work with other people?"

"Sometimes when I look at people, their energy creates bubbles, and those show me the future."

"Bubbles? Like the bulges in a warden's soul?"

Jamie scrunched his face and shook his head. "Have you ever had a soda?"

I nodded, guessing he'd been introduced to the sugary carbonated beverage when he'd been out with his friend and I'd been on my date.

"It's like that. The bubbles are *inside* people's souls, floating around. When they rise to the surface, I can see pictures inside them. It's usually a cluster of images, not what *will* happen, but pictures of what *could* happen. When I give a prophecy, I describe the pictures."

I tried to imagine it and failed. The world must look drastically different through pooka eyes.

"If you only tell people about possible futures, how is that helpful?"

I glanced at Jamie to make sure he hadn't taken offense to my poorly worded question.

He shrugged. "They want to prevent the bad stuff from happening."

"Can they?"

Jamie shrugged again.

Maybe Doris had the right idea. What good was a prophecy if a person couldn't act upon the information and change things for the better?

Niko's car sat alone in the carpool parking lot, and I pulled into the space next to him, shrugging out of my coat, scarf, and beanie before getting into his car. I still wore a sweater and a long-sleeve shirt, but the act of stripping anything in Niko's presence made me self-conscious. I piled my garments on the seat behind Niko, and Jamie added his outerwear, making a huge mound on the leather seat. Tugging a hair tie from my pocket, I pulled my long dark hair into a snarled ponytail as I walked back around to the passenger side. I'd seen snow bunnies make this layered, mussed style look sexy, but I suspected the best I attained was the ever-cringe-worthy "cute."

Jamie transferred his bag of snacks to the seat beside him, then climbed into the back. Niko's eyes tracked him in the rearview mirror. If he had a problem with being in a confined space with the pooka, Niko's face didn't show it.

I buckled myself into the front seat, settled Val on my lap and my purse at my feet, and did my best not to take obvious deep breaths. Niko's intoxicating scent, a subtle combination of roasted cinnamon, coffee, and heat, swirled through the cabin of the car, mingling with the aroma of rich leather and, even fainter, vanilla.

My heartbeat kicked up, every nerve in my body sensitizing to Niko's presence.

Zero frost moths in the vicinity, and I was primed to jump the man because he smelled so good.

I cracked my window and prayed for a miracle: *Please don't let me make a complete fool of myself today.*

11

I DON'T HAVE A DIRTY MIND; I HAVE A SEXY IMAGINATION

"Are there going to be a lot of enforcers meeting us?" I asked, hoping I could put a buffer of strangers between myself and Niko.

"We mustered fourteen from nearby regions. The wardens made a grid of the affected land, and you and I are taking one of the larger areas."

"Just us?"

"Even with the extra hands, there's too much ground to cover to have enforcers overlap."

Then why not spread the two of us out to different sectors as well? Why was I the only enforcer being escorted by the optivus aegis?

Because I'm the only enforcer whose competence is in question. As Pamela had noted, Niko had spent a lot of time in my region. In the last few weeks, he'd trained me on how to net a hound, backed me when I bonded Jamie, and he'd been instrumental in thwarting Isabel's most diabolical plans. If I'd been a full-fledged, experienced enforcer, I wouldn't have needed his assistance at all. In reality, I'd be dead several times over without his intervention. Niko more than anyone else understood the limits of my proficiency.

My propensity to behave like a lust-crazed fool in his presence likely hadn't done much to raise his opinion of my capabilities, either. I wished I could say this morning's humiliating performance had been unique, but it merely ranked top of the Madison's Most Embarrassing Reactions to Niko list.

I sneaked a peek at Niko through my lashes, waiting for him to comment on my earlier foolishness. He merged onto the freeway and we blew past Loomis, then Penryn without him so much as parting his lips.

"Whoa! Look," Jamie said, his voice full of wonder.

I twisted in my seat. Jamie had abandoned his bag of snacks and faced backward, his body contorted around his seat belt so he could stare out the back window. The freeway climbed into the foothills in a long, straight line, and at the peak of a hill, the view stretched behind us to the high-rises of downtown Sacramento and beyond.

"It's so big," Jamie breathed.

"What is?"

"The world."

Guilt stabbed me. All I'd shown him since he'd risen was my tiny sliver of a region. Aside from a smattering of shopping trips and one short outing during my date, we'd spent all our time running from one emergency to the next. Even his first venture outside Roseville wasn't for fun.

I shifted to face forward again, fresh insight dawning. "Was a stipulation of my involvement in today's efforts that you kept an eye on"—I pointed to Jamie but said—"us?" Wardens were all about reducing the level of evil inside their borders, and bringing a pooka through their territory increased the odds of an escalation of *atrum*. No one would be throwing out the welcome mat for me and Jamie until I'd convinced him to embrace *lux lucis*.

Niko flicked his eyes to mine, then back to the road. "I suggested you come."

"Thank you. He needed this," I whispered, too soft for Jamie to hear.

"You both did."

Not sure what he meant by that, I let my eyes drop. Niko had pushed the sleeves of his sweater up, revealing smooth, muscled forearms. The tendons in his right arm flexed as he changed his grip on the steering wheel, then adjusted the vents. When I realized I was contemplating the texture of his skin—would it feel as silky as it looked?—I gave my head a little shake of admonishment and turned to stare out my window.

Silence thickened in the car, and my thoughts spiraled outward, latching on to the most pressing worry. "My parents are going to Reno tomorrow. Are they going to be in danger? Should I make them cancel their trip?"

"What are they doing in Reno?" Niko asked.

"I don't know. Gambling, I think. Maybe seeing a show. They're taking the train, so they won't have a car."

"They should be fine. It's probably safer in the mountains than in the valley right now. Reno and all the regions in the Sierra Nevada have defenses in place for tyver."

"Really? Then why don't we have those, too?"

"Because most of the defenses are built into the architecture. I could tell you all about county building codes and regulatory hoops the CIA had to jump through to make sure our safety measures were included in general construction laws for chimneys of homes above a certain elevation and how all this was accomplished without tipping off the norms, but I don't want to fall asleep while driving."

I'd forgotten the tyver laid their eggs in chimneys.

"Why weren't those laws used in Roseville?"

"It would have been an unnecessary pain in the ass. The lower elevations rarely maintain the arctic temperatures tyver require. Occasionally an enterprising sjel tyv dips down into undefended territory, but the weather usually chases it back up the mountains before it can do much damage. With all the frost moths turning the foothills into an ice box, we can't count on the weather to help out this time."

"Unless we can kill enough today."

Niko shook his head. "Probably not even then. At best, we'll prevent the freezing from spreading farther. When the tyver come, we want to narrow their options as much as possible."

I slumped in my seat. I hadn't realized how much I'd gotten my hopes up. So long as the drones were around, I didn't stand a chance of impressing Pamela. Plus, I wasn't looking forward to pitting myself against a creature that could steal my entire soul.

"There are going to be some confused meteorologists trying to explain the cold pockets around here over the next few days." Niko grinned, perfect white teeth flashing. He sobered when he saw my glum expression. "Your parents are going to be fine. You don't find a lot of chimneys at casinos. They're also norms, right?"

"Yes."

"Even if a sjel tyv does get them, they won't lose their souls. Right now, your parents have far less to fear than we do."

Such backhanded comfort.

Niko pulled off the freeway in Auburn, parking in front of a small deli. Jamie ordered three sandwiches, proving that despite his sheltered life, he knew his way around a restaurant menu. I picked a veggie-loaded—and therefore a *lux lucis*-loaded—sandwich, hoping it'd get me brownie points with Niko, and I insisted on paying for everyone since Jamie's selection had tripled the bill. The pooka polished off a sandwich before we reached the car. The rest got packed into an ice chest in the trunk to be saved for a later lunch.

Niko merged back onto the freeway. Hills and trees streamed past, blanketed by high, rolling clouds. After minutes of silence, in which Niko exhibited no inclination to burst into a lecture, I relaxed into my seat. My worries quieted, soothed as much by Niko's calming presence as by my proximity to Jamie. I practiced forming nets in my palms, but the pooka's innocent wonder and enthusiastic reactions to the most ordinary of sights became a fun distraction. I pointed out hawks and buzzards, deer grazing in a meadow, water reservoirs tucked into a hillside, and homes nestled among the trees, and Jamie gawked at them all like a child who'd grown up in a hole in the ground. Go figure.

"If there's all this space, why don't the people in Roseville spread out?" Jamie asked.

"Some people like to live closer to conveniences like restaurants and shops. And some people prefer to live way out here and drive to the city when they need something."

"There aren't any restaurants out here?" Jamie asked, appalled.

That's my pooka. "A couple, but not like in Roseville."

Colfax raced by, a series of car dealerships, building supply companies, and chain restaurants plastered to the edge of the freeway, with promises of a historic downtown hidden behind the hills. The freeway had long since narrowed to two lanes, and as we left behind civilization, the median shrank on either side of the freeway until a concrete barrier hugged the fast lane and trees crowded the slow lane.

We drove for miles without spotting a single home, road, or off-ramp, rapidly ascending in elevation, and just when I was getting ready to ask Niko where he was taking us, an exit appeared around a wide corner and we coasted off the freeway. Ten minutes of weaving along a twisted frontage road dumped us onto a narrow paved lane barely wide enough for two cars to pass. A few homes huddled next to the road, windows lit and chimneys smoking, and even more gravel driveways disappeared into the thick forest of pines and oaks. The pavement gave way to a one-lane chip-and-seal road, and Niko braked to accommodate a flock of quail darting across the bend in front of us. I'd lost all sense of direction, but Niko didn't hesitate at each fork in the road, not even when it transitioned to a muddy path with a spare foot of clearance between his car's glossy body and the overgrown, sharp manzanita branches on either side.

Occasionally, a house peeked through the foliage, the thick forest disguising all but the brightest windows. I blinked to Primordium and gasped. The road twined like a charcoal ribbon through a riot of pristine white *lux lucis* that shimmered with varying degrees of understated and ancient strength. Above us, the lace of barren white oak limbs and sprays of white pine needles overlaid the black sky. I pressed to the window, soaking in the beauty. When I turned to check on Jamie, I found him in an identical position, and we shared a grin.

"We have to walk from here," Niko said, easing his car into the weeds of a narrow turnout and cutting the engine.

I snapped the locks shut before Jamie could leap from the car. Unhooking my seat belt, I twisted in my seat to face him.

"Do you want to be a human or a dog?" I asked. Even if no witnesses were close enough to view his transformation once we got out, the terrain was too muddy for him to switch back and forth, and I had no desire to hike around carrying his clothes if he suddenly decided he wanted to be a Great Dane.

Jamie cracked his window, sniffing the air. "Dog. Definitely dog."

"Okay. When we get out, you have to stay in sight the entire time. It'd be too easy to get lost if we were separated. Do you promise?"

"I promise." He tugged on the door handle, but it didn't budge.

"Do you have enough room to change back there? I don't want your clothes to get wet."

Jamie yanked his sweater over his head, taking the long-sleeve shirt underneath with it. I popped my door open and jumped out as he reached for the button of his jeans. Niko stepped out, too, but he observed Jamie's transformation through the window.

Crisp air slid into my lungs, soaked with a woodsy pine aroma and spiked with the tangy notes of the forest undergrowth crushed beneath the BMW's tires. I breathed deep. Department stores attempted to mimic this clean scent every Christmas, but the bitter, cloying candles and perfume-doused pine cones never came close.

The car's warmth dissipated, a soft breeze cutting through my sweater and slithering across my naked neck. Tucking my hands into my pockets, I waited until Jamie barked before I turned around and opened the back door. An enormous Great Dane sprang free, gave himself a full-body shake, and shoved his nose to the mud to track unfamiliar scents.

"Hang on, Jamie. Let's get your vest."

I'd packed it with the rest of our cold-weather gear and retrieved it after shrugging into my coat. Jamie circled me, rubbing his tall shoulder against my hip, mouth open in delight. I swallowed a laugh when he started to sit, only to spring up when the cold ground met his bare tush.

"Remember, no feeding the frost moths or anything else we encounter," I said, sliding the vest over his neck. He puffed air, blowing out his cheeks and flapping his lips. "I'll take that to be your full consent." Squeezing my arms around him, I smoothed the Velcro closed around his torso. "Too tight?"

He shook his head, hot salami-scented breath fanning my face. I gave his side a pat and prayed he'd behave.

Niko stood by the open trunk, snapping into waterproof pants, his dark eyes missing nothing of our exchange. I donned my scarf, beanie, and gloves, repositioning my soul breaker on top of my coat, in easy reach. Then I ran inventory. Knife at the small of my back: check. Pet wood in an easy-access pocket: check. Val against my hip: check. Palmquell in my left hand, lighter in my right: check and check.

Niko pulled a small ice chest from the trunk and slung a backpack over his shoulders. He'd finished his ensemble with a black lightweight jacket zipped to his chin and black beanie pulled down low over his forehead and ears. Like me, he had selected clothing to blend in at night. Or maybe he'd picked his outfit because it accentuated his badass vibe. Decked out in a similar amount of black, I achieved, at best, a stark, washed-out look that might make people hesitate.

"It's this way." Niko led us up a gravel driveway. "Stick close when we pass the house, Jamie. People around here tend to shoot loose dogs."

"What?" I grabbed Niko's sleeve to pull him to a halt. "Why didn't you—"

Niko's subtle head shake dried up my protest. Oh.

"Jamie, come here," I said to capitalize on Niko's ploy to prevent Jamie from roaming too far.

Tail tucked, Jamie trotted to my side. I rested a hand on his shoulders and we walked close enough to trip each other. The pooka kept *lux lucis* spread along his shoulder and back, and his head swung to and fro, likely looking for snipers in the trees.

We climbed the long driveway cut into the side of a hill, rounded the corner—and the enchanted white forest vanished. Bland gray rolled across the hillside, punctured by ragged gray trunks against the black backdrop of the sky. I blinked to normal sight, and the hill splashed black with soot, the charred trunks all that remained of a once-thriving forest.

Niko selected a bulldozed path off the driveway, avoiding the cottage set atop the hill. Five glorious oaks stood like sentries around it, guarding the home from complete desolation. The warm glow of the windows attested to occupants who'd come within feet of losing their most prized possessions.

"Isabel did this?" I asked, my breath frosting in the air. My boots sank an inch into the mud with each step, and Jamie's toes made soft suction sounds beside me.

"She claimed these fires were accidents, started by salamanders that escaped during transport. It's a little too convenient how they wiped out the homes of the most prominent prajurit clans in the area, though."

"Please tell me Isabel spends her days somewhere damp and cold, forced to listen to nonstop Red Hot Chili Peppers on full blast while being repeatedly inflicted with paper cuts."

"That's very specific," Niko said.

"It's the worst I can think of at the moment."

All thoughts of revenge vanished at the next bend in the path. The hillside dropped into a steep descent a mile or more into the canyon, opening the view all the way down to the American River and miles in every direction. Greenery poked through the decimated hillside to the north, where the remains of the fire met a wall of living forest. Snow dusted the next closest ridge, and the peaks beyond were coated white. To the south, endless blackened hills rolled toward the horizon, fog forming and dissipating in hypnotic twists above the wasteland. The river roared through the canyon, the sound muted by distance and the foaming torrents a mere sparkle among the shadows. Across the gap, a lush forest climbed the opposite hillside.

Unimpeded, a blast of arctic wind buffeted the hillside, stinging my eyes. I tucked my chin into my scarf and blinked to Primordium.

My heels dug into the mud and I clutched Jamie's vest. Flurries of ice-blue moths swirled across the ruined landscape and ghosted in blizzards of frosted wings on the drafts swirling through the canyon. Like mutant spores or a grotesque fungus, they clustered on burnt trees, adding bright splotches to the lifeless gray husks or coating the entire column, their wings so dense as to appear a single, fluttering entity.

"There must be a hundred of them. Thousands," I breathed. If a handful in Roseville could keep the temperatures near freezing, this many could incite a blizzard on a cloudless day. I glanced skyward, but in Primordium, I couldn't see the clouds thickening above us. I crossed my fingers that they'd hold tight and save their snow for the mountains.

"Come on," Niko said.

We forged our own trail along the edge of the burned forest, angling away from the cottage toward the next ridge and the *lux lucis*-filled trees at the peak. Jamie swung his head back and forth, then bolted down the hill.

"Jamie!" The canyon swallowed my cry.

The pooka glanced over his shoulder, his tongue flapping from his mouth as he ran. Then he stuck his nose to the ground and wound through the blackened stumps. I should have been more specific when I'd made him promise to stay within sight. I hadn't planned on having acres of open space. If he ranged too far, I wouldn't be able to reach him in time if he got in trouble.

"Is there really any danger of homeowners shooting him?"

Niko tracked Jamie with narrowed eyes, his expression closed. "It's unlikely. Most of what's burned is federal land. He should be fine." Selecting a moderately clean, flat boulder, he deposited the ice chest and his backpack.

"Stay near the tree line where you can refuel," he instructed. "I'll go this way; you go that way. Stay in sight, but let's put some distance between us."

His smile, there and gone almost too fast to see, ignited a stinging blush in my cheeks. He wanted space between us so I wouldn't tackle him if the frost moths fed on me.

"Don't flatter yourself."

Niko widened his eyes in an attempt at innocence that fell flat on his masculine face.

I spun on a heel and marched away. Slick mud tried to toss me on my butt, and I stumbled through several sliding steps before catching my footing again. Tugging my coat straight, I lifted my chin and pretended I couldn't hear Niko's chuckles.

The moths lifted from their dead perches, fluttering to feast on our souls. I caught the first four before they landed on me, snatching them from the air in a net and melting them before they took more than a mouthful of *lux lucis*. The next three slurped from my soul as they died, pulsing warmth through my limbs. Then they came too fast to count.

Their sheer numbers robbed me of any chance of finesse. I abandoned my target-practice plans; the moths didn't permit a spare second between attacks to allow me to aim. As it was, I couldn't prevent being fed upon by those I netted; I could only limit my exposure to the moths' mood-modifying bites, and I alternated between melting trapped moths and chasing the rest from my body. To avoid being mobbed, I zigzagged across the slippery hillside, staggering into the gritty masts of dead pines and churning ash and charred bark into the mud. The frost moths pursued me with methodical relentlessness, never permitting me a breather.

I existed in a state of irritation. Since my evasive maneuvers inevitably carried me downhill and all the living trees stood at the hill's crest, every refueling required an arduous hike. By the end of the first hour, my boots pinched, my head hurt, my thighs burned, and my fingers had cramped around the lighter.

When my body's pains weren't consuming my thoughts, I ranted about Jamie's behavior. I concocted a laundry list of punishments for his increasing disregard of my authority. I drafted manifestos of rules and regulations. I relished in shouting matches with him, all in the confines of my head. Keeping my mouth shut, holding my anger in, took all my strength, especially when Jamie galloped past, tirelessly exploring the burned acres as if he had damned wings on his feet while mine were weighted by rings of leaden mud.

But the worst was when I'd catch sight of Niko. One glimpse of his blazing soul and muscular grace, and all the frustration or fury burning my insides sparked against my attraction to him, igniting a hormonal bonfire that seared through reason. I lost track of the number of times I caught myself undressing Niko with my eyes, mentally choreographing graphic sexual fantasies, eyes glazed over, only to start back to reality with him watching me, his grin infuriatingly knowing. After a while, I started making faces at him—and widened the distance between us so he couldn't see my blushes.

Niko earned his fair share of curses for dragging me into this torturous cleanup project, as did my parents for passing along a genetic cocktail that obligated me to fight *atrum*. For good measure, I lumped in the CIA for ever forming to put people like me into the line of fire. Let the norms deal with this mess. Can't see the creatures attacking you? Tough. I couldn't see germs, but I'd learned to wash my hands. The resilient would survive. Meanwhile, I could go back to a peaceful life somewhere safe and warm.

Why wouldn't this moth in my net melt?

I pushed the flame closer. No corresponding warmth heated my glove.

Blinking to normal vision, I examined the minuscule flame flickering from the head of the lighter. According to the clear fuel gauge on the side, only droplets remained. Crap.

Collapsing the net, I chased the frost moth away with the pathetic flame. At least twenty more circled above me, snowy vultures that wouldn't wait until I died to feed. Jamie trotted along the curve of the ridge at least a half mile away, too distant to assist me—if he would even bother to come when called. I had balked at testing his obedience because, despite my ridiculous moth-fueled fantasies, I hadn't determined a punishment he couldn't simply disregard. Balling my fists in annoyance, I searched the hillside, using my peripheral vision to locate Niko without allowing myself to really look at him. If anyone came prepared with extra lighters, it would be Mr. Controlled and Competent himself.

I broke into a weary jog, eyes on the moths. When one swooped close, I flicked the lighter on and scared it back, but otherwise I conserved my meager reserves. I'd never live down what I might do if I were overwhelmed by frost moths and Niko had to come to my rescue.

My stumbling pace gave my head time to clear before I reached him, and I studiously ignored memories of the lascivious ogling and wanton body language I'd exhibited in the last hour. Just a professional enforcer here. Nothing else to see.

A deaf man would have heard my graceless approach, but Niko took his time dispatching a handful of moths before turning to me.

I raised my lighter and gave it a shake. "I'm almost empty. Do you have a spare?"

Niko's eyes landed on my breasts, then traveled up my chest to my lips. Heat smoldered in his gaze, pinging through me, rooting me in place. I swallowed hard. Lust, pure and unadulterated by moths, unfurled deep inside me, pulsing with an electric current that polarized my nerve endings when Niko's lips parted and his tongue grazed his bottom lip. Guilt followed, wearing Alex's face.

When it came to dating, I wasn't a sophisticated twenty-first-century woman. I didn't have the emotional bandwidth to juggle men. Entertaining lustful thoughts about Niko while under the influence of frost moths fell under the heading Work-Related Stress and could be dismissed as the passing fancy it was. My body's instant response to Niko's blatant appraisal flirted with a line I wasn't comfortable crossing. Alex was the real deal—kind, handsome, available, and, most important, genuinely into me. Niko suffered from too much frost moth heat.

I jerked away from the kiss I'd been leaning forward in preparation for—*when had that happened?*—and backpedaled up the hill. Niko prowled after me.

Oh God.

My heart bumped into my throat and my feet stopped moving. I licked dry lips, and Niko's gaze zeroed in on my mouth again. One kiss wouldn't be so bad, would it?

Niko closed the distance between us, stopping when mere inches separated us. The warmth of his breath fanned across my parted lips and he leaned in—

He pulled himself up short, spinning to present his back to me, his hands bunching into fists. I let out a shaky breath. Right. Don't take advantage of a man under the influence. Bad Madison.

I sidestepped my disappointment, bundled it up with misplaced guilt, and buried it with the countless embarrassing moments I'd added to the tally for today.

"Sorry about that," Niko said without turning.

"For what?" I cleared my throat when my voice cracked. "My ego needed a pick-me-up."

That earned me a tight smile aimed in my general vicinity.

"I've got lighter fluid in my pack," he said.

"What about a large paper bag?"

Niko frowned. "For what?"

"To wear over your head. It would save me a lot of future embarrassment."

Niko's shoulders relaxed. "I'll see what I can do."

We trudged up the hill together, using our lighters to fend off moths rather than kill them. We'd roamed farther from our supplies than I realized, and by the time we got back to the ice chest, my stomach grumbled like distant thunder.

"Let's break for lunch," Niko suggested as he refilled my lighter.

I rubbed my stomach. "It's that or I start gnawing on my own limbs."

Jamie flew across the hillside, leaping fallen oaks and bounding up the steep slope to flop at my feet.

"I take it you're ready for lunch, too?"

He nodded enthusiastically, arcing a string of drool through the air.

We sat on the flat boulder. Cold seeped through my jeans to chill my backside, but I didn't care; being off my feet was worth it. After checking the sky to confirm the nominal warmth on my face was indeed sunshine breaking through the clouds, I freed Val and used my palmquell and a clean rock to anchor him open next to me. Niko glanced at the book and raised his eyebrows in a silent question.

"I thought Val might be tired of being cooped up."

This view is amazing, Val said. *Too bad the sun isn't stronger. My pages could use a little natural bleaching.*

"Remind me the next time the sun is out."

I unwrapped Jamie's sandwiches, laid the paper flat on the ground, and set the sandwiches on top. Jamie engulfed the first sandwich in a single bite.

"Try chewing," I suggested. "I don't know how to do the Heimlich on a dog."

He gave the second sandwich a perfunctory chew before tossing it to the back of his throat and swallowing.

Unwrapping my sandwich, I focused on eating every last crumb, using my lighter to scare off persistent frost moths between bites.

Wind sighed through the trees behind us, the peaceful sound punctuated by the crinkle of paper and the piercing cry of a red-tailed hawk hunting over the canyon. I soaked in the absence of city sounds, soothed by the wild, bright lines of the forest across the canyon and on the distant hills. The vastness of the view settled into my body, the raw presence of nature knitting mental stress fractures. A calm I hadn't experienced since before Pamela arrived—since before I'd accepted the enforcer position—grounded me, and I stopped stuffing my face to breathe it in.

"Better?" Niko asked.

"Yes." I tilted my head back and closed my eyes. Good company, food, and the lassitude in my limbs melted away the last of my tension.

After a while, I opened my eyes and took another bite of my sandwich, openly studying Niko. He slouched on the rock, one elbow resting on a raised knee. The intimidating elite-enforcer vibe that usually encased him had fallen away. Maybe it'd all been a figment of my insecurities, and the rare slip in his control that proved he wasn't perfect had changed my perception, or maybe he'd let his guard down. Either way, sitting next to him in the sun, Val and Jamie beside us, stirred a fond sense of companionship inside me. Niko was still too sexy for his own good, but it didn't mess with my head like normal.

"Why did you bring me today?" I asked.

Niko wiped mustard from the corner of his mouth with the back of his hand, finishing his bite before responding. "You don't know differently, but the amount of conflict in your region has been highly irregular. Isabel was to blame, and everything would have slowed down after her arrest, but you bonded a pooka."

Jamie licked up sandwich crumbs, then nosed the ice chest. I opened the single-serving potato chip bag and angled to pour them onto the paper, but Jamie stuffed his muzzle under the bag, so I dumped the chips into his mouth. The second bag's contents went on the paper to force him to eat slower.

"We expected frost moths after the salamanders, but not like this," Niko continued after pausing to watch the potato-chip-gargling spectacle. "Not enough to draw tyver down to Roseville."

"Yeah, it's been intense," I said, prompting him to get to the point.

"You're on a fast track to burnout."

Surprised, I turned from Jamie to face Niko. "I think I've done a good job handling everything."

"You have. In a few weeks, you've gone from knowing nothing and being squeamish about killing imps to ferreting out a rogue warden. You enforce Northern California's most dangerous region, and you're doing it with a powerful pooka tugging on loyalties so fresh the paint hasn't dried on them."

"Are you suspecting my purity now, too?" I checked for frost moths before claiming my rising anger as justifiably mine.

Niko raised a placating hand. "I'm saying you've had a lot thrown at you, and I don't want to see you get crushed by it. I thought a day away from the demands of your region and the inspector might do you good. Helping out here and getting practice with frost moths is a bonus."

I polished off my sandwich while mulling over his words. "Don't take this the wrong way, but don't you have better things to do?"

"Healthy, well-balanced enforcers make my job significantly easier."

"Mmm. I bet experienced ones are even better."

"You've done fine so far."

Such faint praise, yet my chest swelled with pride. Good thing I had reality to deflate me before I popped. "Pamela hasn't been impressed. I don't think she's going to let Brad and me expand our region."

"Do you want to?"

"Honestly?" I peeked at him. "I don't know. I don't want to take on more than I can handle. And no wisecracks about it being too late already."

"That's not what I was going to say."

I've already covered that topic extensively, Val said.

"Pipe down," I admonished without putting any heat into my tone.

Jamie folded his bulk into an awkward hunch, lowering his massive head to my thigh with a heavy sigh. *Lux lucis* sheathed him to his shoulders, *atrum* painted his back half, and the two energies met in an unwavering, straight line around his rib cage as if two different dogs had been sewn together. Content, I stroked Jamie's forehead, letting my fingers trace the growth patterns in his soft coat. Something dark slid across Niko's expression, there and gone too fast to identify.

"Go ahead," I said. "Lay some of your optivus aegis wisdom on me."

"I was going to say it doesn't matter what you want."

"Oookay. That's not what I expected."

"You can't control how the regional boundaries fall. All you can do is protect the people in your region—and your pooka—as best you can. Focus on that, and let the politics sort themselves out."

I cocked my head, contemplating him. "Not bad advice."

"Have I ever led you astray?"

A pinprick of ice grazed my cheek. I checked for frost moths, but the closest one fluttered a handful of yards above us.

SNOW! The bold word covered the entirety of Val's page, the equivalent of him screaming.

Another tiny flake, barely larger than a grape seed, brushed my nose. Jamie lifted his head, scenting the air. I brushed a flake off Val before it could melt against his pages.

Close me, quick! Don't let me get wet!

"Under the coat or out where you can see?" I asked him.

Under. No, where I can see. But under if it gets bad.

"Okay. I'll keep you safe." I closed Val and slid him back into the strap against my hip, his spine facing the sky so the snow would slide off him.

"Let's see what we can accomplish with a few more hours," Niko said.

Groaning, I stood, stretching to warm my cold joints before helping Niko pack.

The next hour passed in an endless repetition of the morning's frost moth exterminations, only this time I slogged around the muddy slope on a full stomach. When a band of seven bright white prajurit darted along the ridge, flying in tight formation, I stumbled to a halt to watch them, as eager for a distraction as I was to witness our fascinating allies in their element. Zipping around the frost moths as if the insects were frozen in the sky, the prajurit paused near Jamie, the leader dipping to land on his wide *lux lucis*–coated nose. A moment later, Jamie pointed his muzzle toward me, and the prajurit buzzed up the slope—two women, five men, all of them proportionate dolls with enormous eyes, round wings, and bee abdomens. They stopped to hover two feet in front of me.

I blinked to normal sight, marveling that these fairy-size creatures existed for norms to see, but they somehow remained hidden from detection nonetheless. They each wore outfits in various eye-popping hues, from teal to fuchsia to mint, their short coats and calf-length trousers embroidered with silver designs too fine for me to discern. Woolen wraps circled their lower legs, ankles, and arches, leaving their toes and heels exposed to the elements. I shivered in sympathy, though the cold didn't seem to affect them. All seven prajurit carried twin blades strapped to their hips. The micro swords looked like flashy adornments for expensive cocktails, but I'd seen prajurit in action, and the tiny blades were lethal to *atrum* creatures three times their size— and to humans who pissed them off.

A raven-haired woman who levitated herself slightly ahead of the others offered me a shallow bow.

"Madison Fox, we have heard tales of your battles," she said, her voice high-pitched but melodic. "*Suku Ek Emas* welcomes you to our territory."

They'd heard of me? Way up here? "Uh, thank you." I returned her bow clumsily.

"Sunan Wulan appreciates your service."

Sunan was a title of respect for the clan's queen and ruler. Since I hadn't yet learned the proper protocol for interactions with tiny royalty, I relied on what I recalled from period-piece British movies when I crafted my response.

"Please tell Sunan Wulan it is my pleasure, but not mine alone. I came with Optivus Aegis Niko Demetrius."

The leader gave a signal and three prajurit peeled away from the cluster and beelined for Niko's bright figure just visible around the bend of the hill.

"Our faith in the Collaborative Illumination Alliance has been sorely tested," the small woman said. "The dispute between your wardens spilled blood on our lands and destroyed our homes. These are not the actions of allies."

"I agree." What else could I say? *Sorry* didn't cut it.

"We have spoken with the local warden, who promises us retribution and compensation." From the grins on her companions' faces, whatever deal they'd struck had been good for them. "We hope to rebuild our trust in the CIA by strengthening ties with you, Madison Fox."

"With me?" Personally? Didn't they realize I was a nobody in the CIA?

"You destroyed the poisoned titan arum." The prajurit rubbed their wings together, creating a sour noise that bit at my eardrums.

The titan arum had been Isabel's most atrocious crime. Held sacred by the prajurit, the towering tropical plant's death-scented blooms were irresistible to the prajurit. Armed with this knowledge, Isabel had slathered a blooming titan arum with poison, luring entire clans to their deaths. All because prajurit were the natural predators of salamanders, and Isabel had wanted to use the fire-breathing creatures to make Brad look incompetent. What a waste.

"Your spirit is that of a prajurit," the tiny woman continued, and her tone implied I'd been given the highest compliment possible. The remaining prajurit hovering behind her bowed, the blur of their wings never faltering. "We would be honored to send a contingent of *Ek Emas* to build a base in your region."

"I look forward to working with them." I wasn't sure in what capacity, but having more bodies in my region combating evil would be welcome.

Satisfaction suffused her tiny features. "May the light shine on your hunt."

Her words sounded formal, and I scrambled for a proper response. "On yours as well."

With a satisfied nod, she darted away and the others followed. They converged on Niko, hung in the air long enough for a brief conversation, then soared into the surviving forest, disappearing among the branches.

Huh. I was famous among the prajurit. If I could figure out a way to work that into a conversation with Pamela, maybe she'd be impressed.

12

YOUR JEALOUSY GIVES ME ENERGY

We may not have eliminated enough moths to restore normal temperatures, but we had made commendable progress by the time Niko drove Jamie and me back to my car. I tried to accept it as a win and not fret about the approaching night of drone hunting. At least it wouldn't be as humiliating as the first night. It couldn't be.

Don't jinx yourself, I thought.

Jamie crawled into the Civic, pausing long enough for me to lay down a blanket in the hopes of saving my cloth seats from the ash-mud slurry coating him from nose to tail. I hadn't fared any better, and when I'd tried to wipe the grime from my jeans and coat, it'd only ground the mud deeper into the fabric. Niko had insisted I change into a spare pair of his pants he'd materialized from the BMW's trunk. They sat loose at my waist and baggy around my thighs, and I had to roll them up an inch at the cuffs so they didn't drag the ground, but otherwise they fit.

I did my best not to think about Niko in these same pants, just his underwear separating him from the inside of these jeans. Unless he went commando.

"Keep your soul breaker on," Niko said as he handed me a bag stuffed with my dirty pants and muddy coat.

"Where I go, it goes," I promised. I hiked his pants back up and slid into my car. Niko waited until I turned the Civic's ignition; then he pulled out of the lot. I watched his black car disappear down the on-ramp to the freeway.

Brad had texted earlier with instructions to be at his office at seven thirty, which left me time to kill. I should have gone home and squeezed in a quick nap, but with anticipatory dread squirming in my stomach, I knew I wouldn't be able to relax. Instead, I called Bridget.

"Are you still up for a visit, even if I'm too dirty to come inside?" I asked when she picked up.

"Are you too dirty for the patio?"

I smiled and backed out of the parking spot. Bridget was the best. "Turn on the heat lamps; we're coming over."

"We?"

"I've got a surprise for you."

Jamie slept through the short drive to Bridget's house and woke as I parked in the driveway. I twisted in my seat to look at him.

"Bridget is a norm. She knows all about what I do, but I don't know if she's prepared to see you change shapes. Do you promise to stay in dog form?"

Jamie's jaw cracked in a huge yawn, his tongue curling toward the roof of his mouth, but he still managed to nod. Yawning in return, I swung out of the car and opened the back door. Jamie slid forward until his front feet hit the pavement, then hopped to get all four feet on the ground, dragging the blanket with him.

Bridget burst from her house. Dressed in faded jeans with legitimate holes worn through at the sides of the knees and an oversize UC Davis hoodie, she looked more like a college student than a successful lawyer. The French cottage behind her fit the lawyer image better, with its rock facade and white shutters, all of it encased in shrubbery pruned to geometrical perfection.

"Hello there. Who's this?" Bridget bent to catch Jamie's head in her hands, her fingers curling into the soft hair behind his ears and expertly scratching. Her voice spiraled higher as she addressed Jamie. "Aren't you a cutie? So big, too!"

Jamie thumped his butt to the cobblestone driveway and wagged his tail, leaning into her hands. Maybe my decision to delay telling her about his ability to transform into a human hadn't been as well thought through as I'd believed.

"Look at your boots," Bridget exclaimed, catching sight of a gritty leather toe peeking out from the hem of Niko's pants.

"You should see the rest of my clothes."

She gave me a once-over. "So?"

"Oh, these are Niko's. Here are mine." I popped the trunk and showed her the bag of folded mud that was Jamie's sweater and my pants and jacket.

"Niko's, huh?"

Bridget had met Niko once, but she'd been fall-down drunk at the time, and she didn't remember the encounter. Since it had also included a traumatic hostage situation with a demon, I hadn't made an effort to help her recover the memory. She did, however, know Niko was the optivus aegis and sexy enough to fry brain cells. She must have been dying with curiosity, but instead of peppering me with questions while we stood in the driveway, as I would have done, she let us into the garage and threw my grubby clothing into the washer with a heap of detergent. Jamie tagged along, leaning into Bridget for pets she happily supplied.

"Wait here, I'll be right back," she said, after directing us to a weathered wooden table situated in the middle of a paving-stone patio in her backyard. She hustled into the kitchen through the sliding glass door.

If the meticulously groomed front yard conformed to every home-owner association guideline, the backyard was a study in rebellion. A jungle of low-water plants cloaked the fence on three sides, circling the flaky trunk of a thick myrtle. Ceramic pots of all sizes squatted in every available free space, overflowing with a riot of greenery and flowers. With two heat lamps chasing away the chill, the patio sat in the middle of the oasis, and a long pergola strung with zigzagging lights bathed the yard in an intimate glow. Bridget knew how to turn a small space into a retreat.

I blinked to Primordium, checking for frost moths. If any were in the neighborhood, none dared encroach upon the warm yard.

I adjusted the far lamp, lowering it to accommodate Jamie. Bridget emerged from the house with a thick picnic blanket, and we arranged it next to the table. Jamie flopped onto it, laid his head on his paws, and closed his eyes. He'd altered his soul, coating the outer layer with *lux lucis*, and I rubbed his forehead. If only all our moments together could be this uncomplicated and peaceful.

Bridget disappeared back inside. I unhooked Val from his strap and laid him on the table. I'd stuffed my palmquell into my purse when I'd taken off my filthy coat, and I pulled it out now, lining it up next to the handbook. The pet wood and lighter came next, followed by the knife, which I unhooked from my belt so I could lean back without the sheath jabbing me.

Bridget paused in the act of carrying a tray filled with teacups, a steaming teapot, and snacks back to the table.

"Should I be worried?"

"About?"

She nudged her chin toward the lineup of weapons. "Are we in danger?"

"We should be fine." I scanned the skies. The sun had set, but if Brad had felt drones in the area, he would have called.

"We need to work on your reassuring skills." Bridget set the tray on the table, went back inside, and returned with slippers and a towel. "For your boots," she said.

"You're the best." I tugged off the boots, slid my feet into the world's fluffiest slippers, and sat with a groan.

"Okay, start at the beginning. Where did you get Jamie?"

"First I'd like to introduce you to Val." Seeing Val chatting with Doris this morning had made me conscious of his inherent isolation. Unless I opened him, he didn't get a chance to participate in the world around him. I'd be a grumpy beast, too, if I were forced into his passive role. Since he'd seemed to appreciate getting to be a part of my lunch with Niko, I thought maybe he'd enjoy this, too.

"Who's Val?" With complete naïveté, Bridget picked up the handbook and thumbed through his pages, all of which would look blank to her. She ran her fingers over his cover, then used the towel to clean off dried mud. "This is beautiful. The detail on this cover, the way these ribbons of color flow through the leather. This isn't some knock-off journal. Where did you get it?"

"From Brad. That's Val, the book."

Bridget's fingers stilled.

"In Primordium, those pages are full," I said. "He speaks, or writes, on the first page."

"Are you telling me this book thinks?" She closed Val and hugged him to her chest.

I rolled my eyes. I should have expected her to react like this. I loved a good fiction novel, but Bridget loved *all* books. She couldn't pass a garage sale, used bookstore, or Barnes & Noble without buying at least one book.

"He thinks, has opinions, cracks jokes, gets mad—and he observes from somewhere on that leather jacket you're smooshing against your breasts, which is why I carry him around in this strap." I pointed to the leather strap I'd left dangling across my chest.

"A sentient book. That's got to be the coolest thing I've ever heard of."

"He has his moments." Val also had a lot of moments in which I'd wished he had a neck I could strangle, but I left that unvoiced.

When Bridget finally relinquished him, I opened Val to his first page and set him between us.

She's a norm! Val's observation filled the entire page.

"But a very cool one. She's a lawyer."

"What? What's he saying?" Bridget asked.

Right. Including Val had been easy with Niko and Doris, because they could read what he said, too. Being an interpreter wasn't going to be as much fun.

"He's surprised I'm chatting with him in front of you, a norm."

"This is surreal," Bridget said.

A lawyer? I bet she knows some amazing librarians.

I translated, and Bridget laughed.

"Now I know for a fact that you're not teasing me, because you'd never say that." She petted Val's open page with obvious yearning. "Dice, your life is crazy."

"Absolutely."

Bridget poured hot tea for each of us, then thrummed her fingers on the table while I took a sip.

"Okay, enough with the torture! Where did you get a Great Dane? Why are you in Niko's pants? What about poor Dr. Love?"

"It's not like that." But I couldn't help replaying the heat in Niko's eyes as he'd leaned in to kiss me. Why had I backed up? Alex and I had been on only one date. Taking a once-in-a-lifetime opportunity to kiss Niko wouldn't have made me a horrible person.

Just a skeevy person, taking advantage of a frost moth–induced moment that would have made our interactions afterward even more awkward. As flattering as it was to know Niko found me attractive, he'd never once showed any interest in me when in full control of his emotions. I'd be a fool to read too much into that almost-kiss.

"Oh, it's not?" Bridget asked, and I realized I'd paused too long.

"I got dirty while *working* with Niko. You saw my pants."

"Uh-huh. And he was like, 'Why don't I help you take those off?' And you demurred, professing, 'Oh, you can't! If you do, you'll set my panties on fire.'" She gave Niko a growly voice and me a falsetto that probably carried through the neighborhood.

"I did not come over here to be laughed at."

"There's nothing funny about third-degree burns on your vagi—"

"Bridget!"

"At least tell me: Did he strip out of these and hand them to you or did you help him undress?"

"They were a spare from the trunk of his car. I fell in mud and used the towel I was supposed to sit on to wipe down Jamie, and Niko insisted I wear his *spare* pants so he didn't have to get his car detailed when I got out. *And* he sat in the car while I changed."

"That's boring. I'm going to pretend you got to see him strip."

We both paused to savor that mental image. I wasn't sure how Bridget pictured Niko, but so long as she imagined male perfection, she was close.

The washer beeped, and we both jumped, which made us laugh. Bridget insisted on switching my clothes to the dryer herself, and since I had melted into the chair and the pulsing in my feet promised pain if I put my boots back on, I didn't protest.

"So, our region is in trouble?" Bridget asked when she returned.

It was sweet of her to say *our region* when she just lived here and taking care of it was my responsibility.

While snacking on crackers and hummus, I explained the frost moth phenomenon. Once I started talking, I couldn't stop. I prattled on about my day in the foothills with Niko—glossing over all the embarrassing parts—about our goal to reduce the moth population enough to raise temperatures again, the proactive measures she should take to protect herself, and what it felt like to hold a moth with a net formed from my soul.

In my haste to show off my expertise, I'd explained the tyver and their drones and all the dangers they presented before I realized I should have kept the information to myself. Bridget couldn't see drones, she couldn't detect when they fed on her, and she couldn't do anything about it even if she found herself unexpectedly acting on her impulses. Seeing the fear grow behind her big green eyes choked off my words. I reached across the table to grab her hand.

"I'll do everything in my power to make sure you're safe," I promised her.

"I know. But what about you? These tyver can *steal your soul*." She shuddered. "That's crazy dangerous. Like, life-and-death dangerous."

Leaning back, I gripped the handle of the soul breaker, which rested against my chest. "I'm not wearing this gaudy necklace for my health. Oh, wait. Yes, I am." I gave the handle a tug, revealing the wicked hooks on the tips of the weapon. "If any tyv gets close to me, I'll skewer it." Through force of will, I sank enough confidence into my words to fool my best friend.

"That's my girl. Give 'em hell."

Jamie stretched, then released a long sigh in his sleep. Bridget and I glanced down at him, and I used the moment to segue into explaining his presence. I kept the details brief—he was a pooka who had bonded with me and it was my job to convince him to transform his half-and-half soul into a shining beacon of pure *lux lucis*. I skipped over mentioning his ability to change shapes or that he'd risen straight from the soil beneath the under-construction parking garage at the mall. I also avoided mentioning my complete failure in controlling him. I'd scared Bridget enough for one evening.

She sat back, staring into space, her pointer finger tapping her lips. I waited quietly, letting her absorb the thousand and one bizarre details I'd unloaded on her. If our roles were reversed, I wondered if I'd have believed her. My world sounded almost too fantastical even for me to believe, and I lived it.

Bridget gave herself a shake. "You sound like a total pro. Look how much you've accomplished. You've got a slew of weapons, a talking book, and a pooka. It's like you've been an enforcer your whole life."

"It feels like a lifetime since I was hired." I scooped hummus onto the last cracker and slumped back in my seat. As much as I would have loved to do nothing other than chat with Bridget for the rest of the evening, my time was fast running out. With a sigh, I bent and picked up the towel and one muddy boot and started cleaning away the grime.

"With all that's happened, it's no wonder you're not bursting to tell me about your date," Bridget said.

Mmm, Alex. Maybe tomorrow's lunch date would include a quick make-out session. I didn't relish blatant public displays of affection, but if I lured him back to my car . . .

"You can't smile like that and say nothing. I want details," Bridget demanded.

"Should I start with how wonderful Alex is? I wish you could see his soul; it gives yours a run for its money."

"Clean soul, check," Bridget said.

"He was on time, dressed sublimely, courteous, a good driver, a real gentleman—"

"Yadda, yadda. Get to the good stuff already. How real is this? Are you going to tell him about being an enforcer?"

I started shaking my head before she finished the question. "I like him, so, no. It's way too soon to dump the whole 'I see souls' bit on him. Plus, I like that I get to be normal with him. After all the madness with the salamanders and Isabel, spending time with him was like a vacation."

"Okay." Bridget traced the rim of her mug with a finger, then crooked an eyebrow at me. "Are you sure he can kiss? You sounded so hesitant on the phone yesterday . . ."

"Oh boy, he can kiss! Just the right amount of tongue and heat and, you'll laugh, but my toes actually curled and— Dame Zilla!"

Bridget fell back in her chair, laughing. "Is that what the kids are saying these days?"

"No, it's our new kitten." I pulled my phone out of my pocket. Large numerals announced the time as 7:14, sending a spark of adrenaline through me. "Shoot! I've got to get going. Here." I thrust the phone into Bridget's hands and stood. My thigh muscles protested; my calves chimed in. "Check out the pictures. Dame Zilla is the most adorable kitten ever. She's one of the ones I rescued. Alex and I picked her up from his clinic after our date."

We'd also made out in his empty reception room, but I forced myself to set the memories aside and keep moving. While Bridget cooed over all our pictures, I stuffed my feet back into my boots, clipped the knife to my belt, shoved the pet wood and lighter into my back pockets, crammed the palmquell into my purse, and secured Val in his strap. After the initial introductions, Val had been suspiciously quiet, but finding out what had prompted his shyness would have to wait.

Jamie roused, stood, and shook, looking a great deal more refreshed. As wonderful as the food and tea had been, and as great as it was to chat with Bridget, I couldn't help being jealous of his power nap.

"Who's this guy in your apartment?" Bridget asked, holding the phone up for me to see. On the screen, human Jamie lay on his back, Dame Zilla sprawled across his stomach.

"*That's* an explanation for another day." I couldn't drop that bombshell and walk away.

Bridget's pale eyebrows lifted to her coppery hairline. She zoomed in on Jamie's laughing face. "You had a male model in your apartment and you're going to make me wait for an explanation."

Jamie barked.

"No," I told him, in case he'd offered to transform.

"Okay, explain," Bridget said.

"I was talking to Jamie. The answer for you is still that you have to wait. I am a woman of mystery. You must allow me to keep a bit of my mystique."

"Madison Amelia Fox!"

I darted around Bridget when she tried to block my path and ran to the garage.

"Thanks for doing my laundry." I stripped out of Niko's jeans and into my toasty pair straight from the dryer. The metal button seared my stomach, and I danced in place until I got my shirt tucked in.

"You're impossible! At least tell me if he has a girlfriend. Has anyone called dibs on him yet?"

"Bridget! He's years too young for you!" I yanked on my jacket and held out Jamie's vest to him. He trotted over and slid his head through the neck hole.

"Pay no attention to Bridget. She doesn't know what she's talking about," I whispered to him.

"Too young? He's what, twenty-two? Four years' difference is nothing."

Twenty-two? I took the phone back from Bridget. She was right: In the angle and lighting of the picture, he looked like a college kid.

"I'm going to be late," I said, urging Jamie toward the car.

"I know where you live, Dice. I'll get an explanation out of you!"

❄

I braced a gloved hand against the fence for balance and stretched one leg, then the other, savoring the rush of blood to my toes as the balls of my feet throbbed in relief. My thighs were so tired. My feet ached. Why had I agreed to run around a mountainside with Niko today, knowing I'd be hunting drones all night? Summer and I hadn't been out here more than an hour, but I was past ready to head home—as soon as I caught my breath. I should find a nice dry place to sit.

I scanned the neighborhood, disgusted to discover not a single home had a traditional porch, let alone a friendly rocking chair where the resident enforcer could put her feet up for a spell.

Put her feet up for a spell? When had my brain been overtaken by a Southern woman? Why was I squatting? Ah, yes, because a drone had freed me to take uninhibited action—or in my case, uninhibited *in*action.

I shook off the cotton fuzzing my thoughts and took stock. Jamie trotted across the street several houses away, ignoring me as he had been since he climbed from the car. A single drone buzzed past him on its way back for another bite out of my soul. Growing bored with Jamie's slow pace, the imps joyriding on his long Great Dane back leapt after the drone and bounded toward me. Chilly moisture soaked through the fingers of my glove on my right hand, but I still had my palmquell clutched in my left. Summer stood beside me, long hair flowing free below the hem of her beanie, palmquell raised to sight on the drone. From this angle, she was all legs and arms and steely strength, like a Native American cover model for a sci-fi novel, her posture radiating *badass*. All she needed was a spaceship behind her or maybe the colorful flare of a sun going supernova. Meanwhile, I cowered at her feet, lost in daydreams of rocking chairs.

I swept my pet wood through the incoming imps, killing them, and stood in time to watch the drone explode into glitter ten feet from us. Summer could have killed it just as easily on its first pass, *before* it took a bite out of my soul, but where was the fun in that? I glared at her back as she stalked away.

"Stay behind me," Summer said. "We wouldn't want you to get hurt."

I caught up with her in three strides. "You do remember I was there when you told Pamela you've never fought a tyv, right? You're hardly more experienced in this instance than I am."

"I'm more experienced than you in *every* way. You may have other people fooled and you may be milking your circumstances for all they're worth"—her gaze flicked to Jamie, and I bristled at the implication I'd use my bond with the pooka to advance my career—"but your Brave Little Naïve Madison act won't work on me this time."

This time? "What—"

"Poor, helpless Madison," Summer taunted. "She constipated her own powers for years, but now she's glommed together some courage. While she blunders around, figuring out the difference between her ass and *atrum*, she needs protection. Just watch your back, because she'll steal your region the first chance she gets."

My mouth hung open. Summer's resentment went far deeper than a cut to her paycheck. She thought I'd duped her. I strangled my frustration and tried to form a logical argument.

"I never pretended to be anything other than what I am: a new enforcer," I said.

"You shouldn't even be an enforcer. You know *nothing*. You should be working under someone, but instead I get to hold your hand. Your incompetence is a menace."

My control snapped and I laughed, a bitter, harsh sound. "Right. People love throwing that word in my face. But you had a decade to figure out Isabel was rogue, and it took me only two weeks. If I hadn't been busy killing a demon my first week on the job, I might have figured it out sooner. If that's incompetent, then what does it make you? Pathetic?"

I couldn't decide if it was a good or bad thing that other duties had prevented Pamela from chaperoning us. Brad had seemed confident we didn't need her help, and I appreciated not having her present to witness Jamie's flagrant disobedience, but it also meant I got Summer's cheerful disposition all to myself.

"Are you trying to brag?" Summer tilted her head back to track a trio of drones as they buzzed high above the houses, ignoring us. "You have no command over your pooka. You can't handle your region. You can barely control your *lux lucis*. You're a disgrace to the job."

"Are you sure you're not projecting? It must stink to think so little of me and have the inspector see us as equals."

If I hadn't been glaring into her face, I would have missed her flinch. I'd struck a nerve, and I let her see my gloating smile.

"I'm here because Pamela instructed me to be your babysitter," Summer spat back.

Her words speared straight through my flimsy self-confidence, and my smile slid off my face. More than once, Brad had sent me out with a babysitter. Niko's role in today's outing fell under that heading, too, even if he'd dressed it up in other terms. Having someone else with more experience accompany me made sense. I needed training. But entertaining the thought of Summer as my babysitter rankled. Plus she was wrong. No enforcer went solo against drones or tyver. It was the rule.

Before I formulated a properly scathing comeback, my phone rattled out "Hail to the Chief." Peeling off a glove, I unzipped my coat and dug into my sweater's pocket, pulling out my cell phone and putting it on speakerphone as I answered. Arms crossed, Summer waited at my side.

"A tyv just breached the northern border less than a mile from you," Brad announced.

Adrenaline jolted through me, spiking my heart rate, and I choked down a knot of panic.

13

WHERE AM I GOING AND WHY AM I IN THIS HANDBASKET?

"The tyv will come at you if you drop your guard," Brad said. "Don't. Don't even get close to her. The tyv is too strong—for either of you."

I caught the slight emphasis on *either*. *Take that, Summer.*

"Focus on picking off drones. There'll be plenty with the tyv. Whittle down her strength by whittling down their numbers."

Brad had already gone over our strategy when we met at the office. Drones served as slaves for tyver: They scouted for chimneys suitable for hatching grounds, provided tyver with food, and administered protection and support. Brad likened drones to the supply line of an army, without which tyver would falter before they even got to the battle. Since the battle was over my region or possibly my soul—I'd gotten confused in the analogy—I liked the sound of our guerrilla tactics. It beat charging into a head-on fight I might not survive.

"*Suku Hujan Gembira* has been notified. They'll be on site in twenty minutes or less," Brad continued. The closest prajurit clan, the *Hujan Gembira* had been on standby since yesterday. It'd be up to them to kill any eggs the tyv laid while we dispatched drones. "Be careful, and call me if you need anything."

I returned the phone to the pocket of my sweater and zipped my coat closed over it. With more drones on the way, I couldn't chance leaving myself easy access to the cell. One rash call to Alex last night had been more than enough.

Shivering, I tugged my damp glove back on and burrowed my fingers into my armpits.

"Don't get in my way, and don't slow me down again," Summer said, and broke into a sprint.

I rolled my eyes and rushed after her. Jamie spotted us coming his direction and spun to run with us, tearing his way across lawns and leaping hedges. I wanted to yell at him to use the sidewalk and stop destroying people's yards, but I saved my breath.

Following Summer irritated me on principle. I wanted to know where we were going, but I forced myself to keep up as we pounded down Nebula Court and across Orion Way before veering left on Galaxy Lane. This hilltop happened to be the tallest in the greater Roseville area, but whoever named these streets had still been ambitious.

At nine o'clock on a Sunday night, a hush enshrouded the neighborhood street. In normal sight, inviting golden light spilled from windows, competing with the cool blue flickers of TVs and computers. Yellow streetlamps and porch lights watched over well-manicured lawns and driveways crowded with shiny sedans and minivans. In Primordium, the subdivision looked the same as it would have in daylight—white lawns rolling to the sidewalk, bright trees stretching bare limbs toward the black sky, and a faint glow of people with mishmash souls moving inside their homes, all of it illuminated in the never-changing, ambient glow.

I hadn't seen a norm outside in the last half hour. Even the late-evening dog walkers were snuggled in their cozy homes, enjoying their central heating.

Lucky norms.

I banished my budding resentment. I should have been grateful. The cold weather made it possible for sjel tyver and their drones to invade my region, but it also made it easier for me to hunt them without a norm interfering. Tucked inside, people remained as oblivious to the unleashed Great Dane dashing through their yards as they did to the two gun-waving women, who up until Brad's phone call, had been darting spastically through front yards, firing imperceptible bullets at invisible creatures.

Summer passed our cars and kept going, her effortless steps

taunting me. My feet hit the pavement with heavy thuds that jarred from my soles to my eye sockets. I bet she felt like she was running on cotton candy.

Jamie raced ahead of us, pausing to sniff fences and bushes and bumpers, but always leaving several car lengths between us. Smart pooka. If he came close enough to grab, I'd latch on to his sweater and not let go until we headed home.

The wide paved road fed into a narrow chip-and-seal driveway that predated the subdivision. A sturdy wooden fence stretched from sidewalk to sidewalk, delineating the private property from the public, and a heavy chain served as the gate. Summer hurdled the chain like an Olympic athlete. I slowed, jogging up the sidewalk and into the mud to go around the fence.

Beyond the gate, the driveway wound down the side of a precipitous slope to a home out of sight behind a cluster of oaks. Summer stopped before the drop-off and scanned the northern horizon. I fell in beside her, grasping my side and breathing louder than a racehorse at the finish line. Jamie roamed down the hill, rustling through dried grasses.

The steepest part of the hillside had been spared the advance of urbanization, and thick white trunks of native oaks traipsed down the incline, their roots carpeted with last season's weeds. At the base of the hill, the open space ran up against the rigid lines of another subdivision. From our vantage point, I could peer into the backyards of two rows of homes below us before the rest of the valley condensed into a sea of rooftops. Beyond them, the junior college's stubby buildings defined the northern edge of my region's border.

A seething beast of legs and wings and patchwork black-and-white segments oozed over the rooftops. We'd found the sjel tyv.

"Shouldn't we get down there?" It seemed like the appropriate question, though keeping my distance had far greater appeal.

"By the time we get to our cars, the tyv will be here. Get ready to run."

I hoped she meant run away.

The colossal tyv surged into the air, skimming the barren oak canopies and climbing faster than her cumbersome bulk should have allowed.

"Come on." Summer sprinted back toward the gate and the subdivision beyond it.

I shoved my burning thighs into motion. Right. Run *toward* the evil creature that would enjoy ripping my soul from my body. This job fuzzed the line between stupidity and bravery more every day.

Once I had the smooth pavement of Galaxy Lane beneath my boots, I ran with my face upturned to the sky, heart thumping in anticipation of the sjel tyv cresting the rooftops. Drones streamed overhead in a strung-out procession, too high for my palmquell and too fast for my aim. Wings blurring, they disappeared southward, swarming deeper into my region.

Nails scrabbling on the asphalt, Jamie blasted past me and Summer in an impressive display of speed I could never hope to match. His marble soul drew swaths of drones in his wake, and he darted in circles, playing with them with the same enthusiasm he exhibited with imps. Even distracted, he kept his distance, his antics enticing the drones away from us, and I suspected he wasn't motivated by a desire to protect *me*.

Summer flung herself behind an oversize pickup parked at the curb and I slammed into the panel beside her as the sjel tyv billowed over the rooftop two houses ahead of us. I gulped air, trying to quiet my ragged breathing. Together we crept down the length of the truck, peeking over the high bed at the monstrosity crawling across the tile roof. I kept a death grip on the handle of my soul breaker.

Val's illustration had failed to capture the horror of a living tyv. Shaped like a drone on steroids, her massive abdomen stretched five feet long, all of it bloated thicker than I could circle with my arms— if I were feeling suicidal enough to try. Six long, segmented legs, each as thick as my own and coated with wicked black barbs, jutted from the sides of a fuzzy thorax so full of *lux lucis* it looked milky. Huge mesh eyes coated her triangular head, which tilted back and forth, her overgrown antennae sampling the air. Like the drones, she had a proboscis instead of a mouth, and hers was as long as a narwhal tusk and just as sharp. Her wings fanned out to either side, two enormous black-veined sails she used for balance. For flight, she had drones.

They teemed beneath her, their smaller bodies so thick I mistook them for deformed appendages at first. She crawled over them, pivoting to dip her hind end into the closest chimney. The sides of her abdomen flexed, and an egg dropped down the flue. A flurry of drones beat their wings beneath her, those at the front stretching forward in a linked line like so many mutant flying reindeer. Straining, the roiling mass carted the tyv to the next house.

Rooftop visits during the wintry nights, eggs deposited down the chimneys, a sleigh of bodies beneath her—give the sjel tyv a red coat and call her anti-Santa. Naughty? You're safe. Nice? Step right up; she'll eat your soul.

If fear didn't have me trembling in my boots, I'm sure I would have laughed.

I tried to count the drones ferrying her, but their densely packed bodies made it impossible. Not that the specific numbers mattered. A solid estimate put their numbers above forty, and more ranged in a loose swarm around the tyv. If they all turned on us at once, Summer and I would be toast.

I hadn't fully grasped what it meant for the tyv to control drones through a hive mind until I saw them in action. The drones beneath the tyv served as an extension of her massive body, lifting and turning in maneuvers so coordinated they appeared choreographed. The fluid harmony of the drones and their ability to anticipate the tyv's needs went beyond training or practice; the drones were so eerily synchronized they had to be acting on the impulse of a single brain.

When the whole hideous affair achieved liftoff again, I crept forward. Summer threw an arm in front of me.

"No closer," she said. Raising her palmquell, she fired on the stragglers recovering on the first roof. A contingent of fresh drones broke away from the tyv and rushed us.

"Split up!"

I raced across the street, sliding as I rounded the bumper of a sedan. Summer charged around the truck and up a driveway to put a garage door at her back. The drones divided and attacked. I fired over the roof of the sedan, and with the drones in a tight cluster, I landed several hits before sprinting out of their path. Miraculously, they swept past me.

I spun, spotting the reason for my reprieve: Jamie. The drones converged on him, cloaking him from sight. Taking advantage of their preoccupation, I hammered them with *lux lucis*. When a puff of *atrum* glitter exploded over Jamie, I remembered to muffle my whoop of victory before it woke the neighborhood.

Jamie growled and tore off. The remaining drones followed, gliding above his back as if tied to him.

Summer sauntered down the sidewalk. All four drones that had attacked her were gone, likely all dead. I scanned the rooftops. The tyv hadn't slowed or even appeared to notice our skirmish. She dropped an egg down a chimney six houses up the street and rode her slaves to the next house. Swiping a fat drone from the air with a barbed foot, she rammed her proboscis into its abdomen, cannibalizing its milky *lux lucis*. When she released it, the drone flopped to the roof, its emaciated black body twitching helplessly.

"Stick close," Summer said, breaking my horrified trance.

We marched after the giant tyv, pausing to fire on drones at the outskirts of the flock. When the first bright white bullet streaked through their midst, a pack separated from the main group and dove toward us. I planted my feet and fired, exploding the first drone. Summer killed two more as we sprinted in opposite directions, and the drones scattered to follow us. I fired as I ran, missing more often than hitting, ducking and weaving around the street until I eliminated the last drone chasing me.

"Fall in," Summer barked.

I jerked around, surprised by the half-block gap between us. I'd been so focused on the drones, I hadn't paid attention to Summer's location, or my own. Holding my cramping side, I trotted to Summer. She didn't give me a chance to catch my breath; the moment I caught up with her, she broke into a jog toward the tyv that now hunkered atop a house at the far end of the block.

The drones were ready for us this time, and a tight contingent attacked before we got close to the tyv. Summer stood her ground, firing in short, efficient bursts. I tried to mimic her but had to duck aside to avoid being struck. The drones chased me. As tempting as it was to run and shoot willy-nilly again, I kept Summer in my sights and studied the drones' attack strategy between evasive sprints. It didn't take long to verify my suspicion: They weren't acting randomly. They herded me away from Summer, and divided, we made easier targets.

Determined to thwart the drones, I zigzagged back toward Summer. Pain lanced through my spine. I gave up attempting to avoid drones and sprinted for the other enforcer, ignoring the second and third whip of pain through my body. I had to get to her side. I had to plant myself next to her and not move.

Black glitter fogged the air above Summer, and I dove through it, shoving against her left side as if I could graft us together.

"Watch it," Summer growled.

A drone darted in from the right, jabbing Summer's shoulder before I could bring my palmquell up. The light in her soul fluctuated, dimming and flaring in a lightning-fast pop. The drone levitated, a blur of *lux lucis* sliding visibly up its proboscis, through its thorax, and into its abdomen. If I'd blinked twice, I would have missed the whole thing.

Summer swiveled toward the tyv and charged.

"Summer! Wait!"

I surged after her. She ignored the drones tearing bites from her soul, concentrating a stream of *lux lucis* in the tyv's direction, even though the energy arced in a useless stream that splattered the pavement well short of the tyv. I ignored the drones, too. Nothing mattered except sticking with Summer and *not moving*.

If she hadn't tripped over the base of a mobile basketball hoop left at the curb, I wouldn't have caught her. She fell forward, bracing a palm against the pavement to catch her balance, and I snaked my hand around her belt. Oblivious, Summer launched forward again. My arm jerked in its socket and I flew through the air, coming down almost on top of her.

"Stay still," I ordered, tightening my grip and hunkering into a wide-legged stance. She strained toward the tyv, but this time I only rocked in place.

Good. We were together and stationary.

Pain in my strained shoulder socket overtook the urgency to hold my ground next to Summer, and I blinked, befuddled, at the woman flailing against my grip on her belt, her whole body straining to get closer to the tyv. Comprehension came on a surge of righteousness. *Ha!* My drone-zapped impulse had saved the day. Any minute now, Summer would realize it, too, and I looked forward to rubbing her face in it.

"Let me go," Summer demanded, running in place. Her soul dimmed alarmingly, her mindless stream of *lux lucis* spilling her reserves in a widening pool twenty feet in front of her. "I'll kill her. I'll show Pamela I've got what it takes."

Drones lifted the tyv to the next rooftop. Summer yanked her soul breaker free and jabbed the air in front of her, heedless of the hundred-yard gap between her weapon and her target. I sidled around behind her to stay out of her way, never breaking my grip on her belt.

The drones grew bolder, recognizing weakness in their prey. I used my signature spray-as-much-*lux-lucis*-into-the-air-as-possible tactic to drive them back. If any drones died in the process, so much the better, but protecting Summer was my top priority. In her current state, if I lost my grip, she'd charge to her death.

Jamie loped around us, and the drones flocked to his irresistible energy, trailing after him when he tore away from us toward the tyv. Frowning, I contemplated his retreat. Had he done that to help me or to save the drones?

Summer backpedaled, knocking me down. Pain blossomed across my kneecap and flared up my leg, chased by the icy chill of water soaking into my jeans. I used my grip on Summer's belt to hoist myself back to my feet, almost toppling her.

"Enough already," she groused, tapping my arm with her palmquell.

Seeing sanity had returned to her eyes again, I uncurled stiff fingers from her belt and rubbed my palm down my leg, chafing blood back into my cramped digits.

"Oh holy crap, she's coming this way."

Summer scooped an arm under my elbow, spun me, and ran, towing me beside her. I glanced over my shoulder in time to see the tyv float across the street in our direction like a grotesque parade-day balloon suspended on the bodies of her slaves. Whipping my head back around, I ignored the pulsing pain in my knee and sprinted for all I was worth.

A flurry of drones descended on us, and without slowing or unlinking my right arm from Summer's left, I fired into their midst. Summer tugged us across a soggy lawn and slammed us into the base of a thick maple. In tandem, we smacked our free hands to the bark, sucking down the tree's *lux lucis*. Energy gushed back into my limbs, and I downed three drones to Summer's five before the skies around us cleared. The tyv had disappeared.

"Where'd she go?" Summer darted to the sidewalk, scanning the sky.

"There." I pointed to the tail end of the tyv's posse gliding over the back fence of a two-story house across the street. The mass of drones and tyv settled on the far roof, inaccessible from our current location. To catch up, we'd have to circle the block.

Jamie had already come to the same conclusion, and he galloped down the opposite sidewalk. I started to rush after him, but Summer grabbed my arm.

"Slow down. You'll wear yourself out if you race around like that."

Jamie careened around the corner and disappeared down the side street. With him out of sight, urgency nipped at my steps, but my thighs agreed with Summer, and I slowed to a manageable jog.

"Is it your years of training that made you go Kamikaze back there?" I asked. "If so, I'm impressed. I mean, just think about how fast you would have died without my *incompetent* help." I should have held my tongue, but I couldn't resist getting in the jab.

"At least I didn't give up."

"Because rushing to your death is so much better than taking a breather." Would it hurt her to say *thank you* for saving her life?

We made a right at the corner and jogged down the sidewalk, feet hitting the concrete in tandem.

"*Suku Hujan Gembira* have arrived!" cried a high-pitched voice near my ear.

I swerved and ducked. A bright white prajurit body zoomed around my head twice before hovering in front of me. The tiny man brandished two naked swords in an artful flourish that tipped him head over feet. Round beelike wings carried him back up to my eye level, and he saluted before zipping in front of Summer. She slowed, and I caught up with her again. The prajurit had no problem keeping pace while flying backward.

"Gusti! This is not a race. Conserve your strength," scolded a female prajurit, dropping from above and startling me yet again.

"Yes, Asih," Gusti grumbled.

Summer's crimped expression tried to convey a statement; it was either "See? I told you" or "You look like an idiot every time you're frightened by a prajurit." Probably both.

"And sheath your weapons," Asih ordered. "These are our allies."

Gusti sheepishly tucked his swords back into the twin sheaths on his hips.

"Is this all of you?" I asked, twisting to look around and jostling Summer in the process. She elbowed me back to my side of the sidewalk.

"We're the forerunners." Asih's tone told me I'd asked a stupid question.

"Madison's pitifully ignorant," Summer said, and she had the nerve not to sound out of breath. "She doesn't know how clans work."

"Madison? You're Madison Fox?" Gusti's wings buzzed in excitement.

"Of course she is Madison Fox. She's the watcher of this territory," Asih said.

"I am honored to be your forerunner." Gusti bowed, and I had to slow to prevent a collision.

"Your clan brings much needed support to us, Asih," Summer said. "Your bravery and honor in working outside your territory will be remembered."

"You are a wise human, Summer Potts," Asih said.

It didn't surprise me that they knew who Summer was, too, only that her name elicited no reaction from Gusti. Summer deserved far more awe than I did, but she wouldn't hear it from me.

We rounded the corner into a long cul-de-sac at a fast walk, and I finally spotted Jamie. Wreathed in drones, he wove among the parked cars half a block away from us, keeping pace with the tyv as drones carted her from one rooftop to the next.

"The pooka has turned?" Asih asked. Her tiny body lifted in alarm, and her swords leapt to her hands. Beside her, Gusti mirrored her defensive position.

"Of course not!"

Neither prajurit looked reassured. I didn't blame them. With his entourage of drones and his soul cloaked with *atrum*, Jamie looked pure evil.

"He's just testing his boundaries," I said.

"That's what you're calling it," Summer murmured.

I gritted my teeth.

"I will inform the Sunan," Asih said. Keeping a suspicious eye on Jamie, she continued. "Gusti, standard cloak and tag. Vary at your discretion. Report in twenty."

Gusti crossed his swords in front of his chest in a salute. Asih buzzed over our heads and disappeared in the direction we'd come from. Gusti waved to Summer and me, then ducked under the eaves of the nearest house, following the underside of the slope toward the peak of the roof. Fast as a hummingbird, he darted to the chimney, paused to do something I couldn't make out from the ground, then dropped back beneath the eaves and beelined for the next house. I lost track of his small form among the branches of a sycamore.

By unspoken consent, Summer and I drifted into the middle of the street where we'd have more maneuverability. A sharp breeze cut across my cheeks, doing nothing to cool the sweat accumulated on my scalp beneath my beanie. A scattering of frost moths coasted through the neighborhood, but I ignored them. They weren't fast enough to catch us while we were chasing drones, and Brad had made it clear not to expend our *lux lucis* on moths tonight. All our efforts were to be focused on killing drones.

The rasp of frigid air on my esophagus quieted as I caught my breath. I tried to keep my thoughts away from visions of home and my bed. Running for my car if I was struck by a drone would be a waste of energy, and it would fuel Summer's prejudicial opinion of me.

Four houses from the tyv, we stopped. My hand strayed toward the soul breaker at my neck. Summer's did the same, but when she caught me looking, she dropped her hand.

"Stay close," she ordered.

"Back atcha." I deflected her disdainful glare with a saccharine smile.

Side by side, we strode for the nearest drone outliers. Seven peeled away from the tyv and bore down on us, agile and hungry. I sighted and fired, exterminating the lead drone before ducking behind a Prius. Summer dodged in the opposite direction, and we circled back together at the front bumper, streaks of white bullets fanning across the dark sky. The drones died. More replaced them.

The individual skirmishes ran together, but no matter how many drones we killed, we made no tangible dent in the invading mass. A steady trickle of dark drones departed from the tyv's escort party, most ignoring Summer, me, and even Jamie in favor of the wide-open expanses of my region. For every drone that left, another replaced it, most approaching from the north, but more than a few returned from deeper in my region, no doubt reporting about the cornucopia of unprotected chimneys ripe for the taking. The incoming drones always glowed bright, their thoraxes and abdomens full of pieces of soul fragments stolen from my norms.

The tyv migrated without rhyme or reason. She laid eggs all the way down one street, skipped the next, hit every chimney but two on the following street, then hopscotched up the adjacent row of houses. Her pattern wasn't that of a creature attempting to flee or even evade us. If she'd felt threatened, she could easily have flown out of our range, or she could have banded all the drones against us. In a singular, focused attack, the drones could have easily overwhelmed a dozen Nikos and Pamelas; two enforcers at a perpetual state of half energy wouldn't have stood a chance. Yet, the tyv deployed just enough drones to hassle us and keep us occupied. Whatever the tyv's intelligence, it didn't extend to strategies of annihilation. Or maybe giving birth to fifty eggs an hour and coordinating the minds of another fifty living drones took up most of her attention.

Not having wings, Summer and I had to cover twice as much ground to follow the tyv's erratic path, and every street seemed to slant uphill. Given the tyv's size and the sheer number of drones orbiting her, it should have been impossible for her to fly out of sight in the scant minutes it took us to wipe out a handful of drones, but she did it more than once. Fortunately, we had Gusti, our own aerial scout, to point the way.

Other members of the *Hujan Gembira* clan flitted from chimney to chimney, dropping blazing white beads into the infected fireplaces. During one respite, while I leaned against a sturdy oak absorbing much-needed *lux lucis*, I asked Val about their activities and learned the beads were a sticky concoction of sap and sage leaves coated with *lux lucis*-rich hellebore pollen, all handmade by the prajurit. The strong *lux lucis* in the pollen countered the tyv eggs' *atrum*, the sage served as a fire retardant to deprive the eggs of the heat they needed for metamorphosis while the pollen worked, and the sap acted as the glue to hold everything together and was an additional form of fire suppressant. The prajurit could carry only so many beads at a time, and despite how fast they worked, they fell behind until only Gusti remained close, scouting and marking the tainted chimneys.

My thoughts spiraled toward self-pity as the night wore on. I wanted a smaller region, maybe one limited to just this hilltop, just these three hundred or so people. Then I'd stand a chance at saving my region from the tyv, or at the very least, after tonight, she'd move on to the next region and I could be done with her entirely. Instead, I'd be out again in the dark and cold tomorrow, whittling away at a never-ending army of drones, chasing a giant bug that could kill me if she ever looked up from laying eggs. More than once I wished the tyv would attack so I could kill her and go home and sleep. Then I'd remember I wasn't suicidal and I'd wrangle my thoughts back to the safer *kill drones, kill drones* mantra.

I should have felt a sense of pride in my work. I was keeping up with Summer, an experienced enforcer. I was chipping away at evil, defending my region as best I could. I'd killed more drones than I could count, which vindicated my poor performance the night before. In every way, I exemplified an enforcer in charge of her region . . . except when it came to control over Jamie.

He ran wild, and after hours of denial, I forced myself to admit he'd gone beyond testing his boundaries to openly helping drones, repeatedly enticing them out of range of our palmquells. He didn't seem to care that whenever the drones grew bored with him, they struck at me or that they fed the tyv looming above us, the same tyv that would happily consume my soul and turn my body into a brainless husk.

His ambivalence to the pain the drones inflicted on me and the danger they presented hurt and infuriated me. We were supposed to be a team, tethered together by the bond *he* initiated.

"Pamela was right. You're not in charge of the pooka. I don't think he even respects you," Summer said as Jamie galloped away for the umpteenth time, drones merrily strafing him.

I hated that I agreed with her. Whatever part of our bond that had kept Jamie in line and listening to me had worn thin. This was the dangerous pooka everyone had warned me about, and a squirming feeling in my gut told me his actions were only going to get worse.

Yet Pamela expects me to assert dominance? How?

At least when Summer reported my failures to the inspector, she wouldn't be able to relay the suffocating betrayal I endured every time Jamie chose a drone over me. That pain I locked down tight beneath layers of anger.

Eventually even the bitterness numbed, frozen by the temperature and my exhaustion. My world narrowed to Summer and the drones, keeping up with one, shooting the other, and doing my best not to confuse the two. When the latest batch of drones harassing us turned tail and tightened around the tyv, I slumped forward to brace my hands on my thighs, and not even my curiosity perked up. Earlier in the evening, Summer would have harried the retreating drones, but the hours had stripped away her initiative, and she slouched beside me. The drones clustered in a familiar formation, preparing to lift the tyv a greater distance than a single house. The preponderance of dark limbs and soul-rich bodies of well-fed drones heaved its combined bulk into the sky and swept away from us straight down the street along the ridgeline of the homes. Summer and I stayed put, waiting to see which direction they'd veer. If they went right, we would follow; if they went left, we had to backtrack to circle the block.

The tyv and her sleigh of slaves didn't slow. I squinted dry eyes, my vision blurry with fatigue, but it wasn't an illusion. The tyv surpassed the final house in the subdivision, and at her current rate, she and her convoy would be over the freeway a few miles to the west before I could pinpoint the direction of my car.

"Crap. Now what?" I asked.

14

I DON'T HAVE A SHORT TEMPER, I HAVE A PROMPT REACTION TO BS

A tiny speck of white raced through the sky, bobbing and weaving like a sparkler held by a running child. The light coalesced into the shape of a prajurit as Gusti back-winged in front of us.

"She's out of my range," he said.

"Call Brad. See if we need to relocate." Weariness stripped Summer's voice of its usual derision.

I tugged off my glove and fumbled under my jacket, fingers clumsy from the cold. The clock on the display read 3:13 a.m. No wonder gravity felt extra strong—I'd been up almost twenty-four hours, nearly all of it on my feet.

Brad answered on the second ring, his voice loud against my ear.

"She's going to ground," he said, skipping a greeting.

"Where?"

"Hard to say. It's one of those fizzle stick aspects of tyver. How did you do tonight?"

"I have no idea." It sounded better than telling my boss I thought events would have unfolded exactly the same if I hadn't been present. No need to advertise my uselessness.

"Get some sleep. See you at the office tomorrow afternoon."

I hung up. "We're done for the night."

"I heard," Summer said.

Gusti saluted and zoomed off to find his clan. I watched him go, envious of his perennial energy. Summer trudged toward the nearest cross street. Jamie and I followed. No imps rode him; no drones drafted off him. His tongue drooped from his mouth, and he walked with his head and tail down, not deviating to sniff anything. He'd finally run out of energy. We paused together on the corner of Sandhurst Court and Yarrow Way. Sandhurst ended in a cul-de-sac behind us, but Yarrow curved out of sight in both directions.

I pulled my phone back out of my pocket, blinked to normal sight, and opened a map app. When I plugged in our location and Galaxy Lane, a little blue line zigzagged across the screen and the bottom of the picture said we were over a mile from our cars. If Summer hadn't been looking, I might have cried. My legs didn't feel like they had another mile in them.

"This way." I pointed, willing my feet to budge. We both stared down Yarrow. Fog cocooned the street and houses, muffling the rest of the world. A light dusting of snow blanketed the asphalt, tiny ridges of powder outlining the cracks, and the only tracks marring it were our own. No one moved inside the homes, all the windows dark and still, all the inhabitants asleep and blissfully unaware of giant flying soul thieves or eggs incubating in their banked fireplaces. Nothing left to do but head home.

My feet remained rooted in place. The little map on my phone mocked me.

I pictured my bed.

My foot lifted.

Nothing looked familiar on the trek back to our cars, but then again, I hadn't been paying attention to the scenery before. Summer and I split the street, trailing our fingers along the plants near the sidewalks to recharge our *lux lucis*. With how much energy I'd expended tonight, I suspected I'd need a solid meal—or a tub of yogurt—before mine stabilized.

When our cars came into view, Summer kicked in a reserve of energy I didn't possess, climbing into her car and pulling from the curb before I got the passenger door of the Civic open for Jamie. She didn't say good-bye or even toss me a wave. I expected nothing less.

I fell into the driver's seat and forced myself to immediately turn the key and put the car in gear. If I paused to savor the sensation of being off my feet, I wouldn't start moving again. The air gusting out of the vents felt warm against my face, though it had to be as cold as the car. Adjusting the heater to low so I wouldn't lull myself to sleep, I widened my bleary eyes and drove home. Jamie panted quietly in the seat behind me.

Not even the cats cheered our collective mood. Mr. Bond must have assumed we'd abandoned him to starve to death, his dinner having been delayed by almost seven hours. He greeted us with piercing yowls and twined between my legs until I dumped a cup a dry food into his dish. Dame Zilla blinked sleepily from her perch atop the cat tree, and when I deposited her food bowl next to her, she scarfed down the wet food, purring between each bite.

I sent Jamie to shower first and braced myself against the kitchen counter while I shoveled yogurt into my mouth. My stomach cramped and gurgled, unused to dinner at four a.m. The pooka emerged in human form, dressed in sweatpants and a T-shirt, his face drawn in unhappy lines. I tried not to read anything into his decision not to wear the pajama set that matched mine. Dame Zilla tore through the house, hopping and leaping down the hallway after a fake mouse. Jamie's morose expression didn't alter as he watched her.

I ignored the bond's pressure to cheer him up. If Dame Zilla in all her adorable kitten glory couldn't get a smile out of the pooka, I didn't stand a chance. Especially since I didn't care that he was upset. I didn't want to see him smile. I wanted an apology. He should have been the one trying to cheer me up.

I opened my mouth to say as much, then shoved another bite of yogurt into it instead. If I started talking to Jamie, it would devolve into a fight, and I didn't have the strength for it. Pushing from the counter, I set the half-empty tub of yogurt in front of Jamie and headed to the shower. When I emerged, warm for the first time in what felt like years, I circled the house, turning off lights and setting the wards. Jamie slumped in the middle of his bed, still in human form, and I ignored him, clicking off the bedside lamp and sinking the room in darkness.

Just how he should like it.

The rustle of clothing informed me Jamie had changed into a Great Dane. Exhaustion swamped my bitterness, and I dropped off to sleep before Jamie finished circling on his bed.

❄

When I climbed out of the Civic and opened the passenger door for Jamie the next day, the sharp rays of sunlight cutting through the puffy clouds insisted it was almost eleven, but my brain wasn't convinced. Six hours of sleep had been just enough time to petrify every muscle in my body without giving me any sense of rejuvenation. It had also unleashed a string of nightmares from my subconscious, in which Jamie in Great Dane form flew among the drones, morphing into a tyv and stealing my soul. I'd begged and pleaded with him to spare me while he'd jabbed a sharp proboscis into my abdomen again and again. Waking to Mr. Bond tromping on my stomach hadn't helped.

Jamie dropped to the pavement beside me, his black coat glossy in the sunlight. He squeezed between the parked cars and stopped at the bumper, his back to me. Our interactions this morning had been stilted, made more so by the deadline of my lunch date with Alex.

"You can accompany me as a human or a dog," I'd informed Jamie twenty minutes ago in our front room.

"I don't want to go. I'll stay here."

I'd been tempted, so very, very tempted. The restaurant sat within the tether range of the bond, so it could have worked. Pretending to be normal around Alex would be so much easier without Jamie present. But I didn't trust the pooka to be on his best behavior, especially not alone. I might return to find Mr. Bond and Dame Zilla turned evil and the place overrun by imps and vervet. Or worse, I might return and find Jamie gone.

"Where I go, you go," I said.

"Then let's both not go. It's not like you have to. It's not work." He didn't bother to look at me when he spoke, staring sullenly at the string he twitched for Dame Zilla.

"I want to go. I like Alex. I want to see him again."

"Fine. I'll go as a dog."

"Then you'll have to wear a collar and a leash. You have to look like a normal dog."

"Whatever."

Now, holding the collar out for Jamie to put his head through, I thought his *whatever* was going to backfire. He tilted his wide head back and forth, dark nose lifted to breathe in the scents of the parking lot, and he took a step toward the nearest tree, ignoring me.

"You agreed to this," I said.

Jamie swiveled to pin me with hard golden eyes, his lips closed tight. I couldn't read his Great Dane expressions as well as his human ones, but his hostility came through loud and clear. Keeping my reciprocal irritation from my face took effort, and I didn't break eye contact as I held the collar at arms' length. We hadn't had time to stop by a pet store for a real collar, so I'd improvised, knotting together the ends of a white cloth belt I'd found in the back of my closet. At last, Jamie slid his head into the loop and the dangling ends of the belt hung across his chest like a crude, limp bow tie.

I picked up the end of the leash—another cloth belt tied to the collar—and held it loose between us. The collar we could pretend was an adornment, one no less weird than the soul breaker resting against my chest. The leash added a whole new disturbing level to the getup. It made it seem like Jamie was my property, a thought that made me squirm.

"Ready?"

Jamie looked away. I took two steps before he fell in at my side, tail down, shoulders stiff. My fingers on the leash felt dirty. Maybe I should have canceled. This wasn't fair to Jamie.

He could have come in human form, I reminded myself. I shifted Val to the opposite hip and pretended everything was fine.

Alex stood inside the windowed foyer of the meal-in-a-bowl chain restaurant, a coat draped over his arm, and when he spotted me, he stepped outside. The last time I'd seen him, he'd been dressed in slacks and a button-up, and he'd looked divine. Today he wore work apparel: navy blue scrubs adorned with his veterinary clinic's logo on the breast pocket and a white flannel shirt layered beneath the short-sleeve top. Nary a single dog or cat hair marred the entire ensemble, which meant he must have changed before walking to the restaurant. The loose garments drew attention to his shoulders and his biceps, and I suspected they did great things for his butt. Sunlight shimmered in his bright blue eyes, and his welcoming smile elicited a flutter in my stomach that banished my lingering drowsiness.

My mood lifting, I brushed my hair back from my face and returned Alex's smile.

"I hope you don't mind eating outside," I said when we stopped in front of him. I regretted starting with that immediately. I sounded absurd. The temperature hovered near freezing, the chill made apparent by each fresh gust across the nearby pond. No one in their right mind wanted to eat outside.

Persevering, I picked my words carefully so I wouldn't offend Jamie or come across as completely batty. "I'm temporarily in charge of this guy"—I flipped my hand to indicate the pooka—"while my friend sorts out his life." If Alex assumed my friend and Jamie were not the same person, who was I to correct him? "It's sort of a last-minute arrangement, but this place has heat lamps on the patio, right?"

"It does. So, who's this handsome fellow?" Alex bent and roughed up Jamie's ears.

Jamie jerked his head free, gave me a baleful look, then plowed his nose into Alex's crotch. Alex backed up with a wince, pushing Jamie's muzzle aside.

"Um, this is Jamie. Thank you for being okay with this."

"If you thought a dog—even a horse-size dog—was going to scare me off, you picked the wrong guy."

We shared another smile, mine full of gratitude for his understanding, his still tight in the corners from Jamie's full-frontal assault.

A disgruntled server turned on the heat lamps for us, dropped menus on the table, and hustled back into the warm interior of the restaurant. I settled into the seat farthest from the heater, being best dressed for the weather, and Alex pulled on his coat and joined me. It took a moment to adjust Val across my lap and situate myself in the chair so the knife hilt didn't dig into my spine. I only clanged the soul breaker against the metal table twice.

"The winter air really agrees with you," Alex said, openly studying me. "You've got a rosy-cheeked glow about you."

I smiled and ducked my head, shy in the face of his blatant admiration. "I could say the same about—"

Jamie jumped into the third chair, knocking into the table and sending it screeching across the concrete patio.

"Whoa!" Alex said, catching the table.

I shot a hand out to steady Jamie as he circled atop the wobbling mesh chair, all four feet squeezed on top of each other. No matter how he twisted, he couldn't fit his butt and his paws onto the small seat.

"Jamie, you can't sit up there. You don't fit," I said, rolling my lips in to hide my smile.

He jumped down, shoulders hunched in a pout.

"Should you tie his leash to your chair?" Alex asked, not bothering to hide his laughter.

"No, he should be fine. He can lie here next to me." I directed the last at Jamie.

The pooka flopped on my foot. I discreetly planted my other foot on the end of the leash just in case. Blinking to Primordium, I checked Jamie. *Lux lucis* coated his back where we touched, and I breathed a silent sigh. He was behaving.

When I glanced up, I shamelessly evaluated Alex's soul. For a norm, he had a beautiful, clean energy with splotches of gray and no *atrum*. Talk about *hot*.

"I'm really glad you called me," Alex said, toying with the edge of his menu. "I think there's a rule somewhere that you're supposed to wait a number of days after the first date before getting in touch, but I've never understood why."

I called it *not looking desperate*, which I'd completely botched.

"Why wait?" I asked, trying for nonchalant. "I had a great time on Friday."

"Tell me, are you always this honest, or only when it flatters my ego?"

"Definitely only when it's flattering," I teased back, but my stomach constricted. If he had any idea how much I lied to him, and how much more I omitted, he'd run from the restaurant and never look back.

The server returned to take our order, jetting out of the restaurant and hunching beneath the heaters. Alex ordered an Italian-themed noodle bowl. I selected a salad for its *lux lucis*, my soul's energy still sluggish after its excessive use last night, and I tacked on a curry dish to reward my taste buds. For Jamie, I ordered a meat-filled mac-and-cheese bowl and a spaghetti bowl, both in to-go containers.

"Are you sure you want to feed him that? I mean, won't his owner be upset?"

Alex's tone held an unfamiliar note and disapproval pinched his face. Right. I'd just ordered people food for a dog in front of a vet. That probably put me square in the *horrible human* category in Alex's eyes, but if I canceled the order, Jamie would make a scene.

"That's how he, uh, how his owner says he eats," I hedged.

"Well, if he gets sick, you know where to bring him."

Jamie blew through his lips, making them flap, and rolled his eyes. I pretended my seat needed adjusting. This was fast becoming a train wreck.

"Any big plans for the holidays?" I asked.

"The usual glamorous event: I'm throwing an office party that's really a fund-raiser in disguise. Very low key. The Placer SPCA brings by some kittens and puppies, and I do my best to get everyone tipsy and in a donating mood."

Jamie stood, ears perked, staring toward the pond. A bevy of imps rushed around the corner, a vervet perched like a grotesque jockey atop the largest. Shaped like an emaciated monkey, with piranha teeth, a scorpion tail, and scaly flesh, the vervet possessed enough intelligence to look beyond the pooka and take in the scene. Its ink-black eyes latched on to my pristine soul and a wicked grin split its face nearly in half. When the imps crashed into Jamie, the vervet sprang over the pooka, all four clawed feet and scorpion tail extended, and pounced on my chest. Razor teeth chomped on my soul.

I clutched the armrests and congratulated myself. Two weeks ago, I would have made a spectacle of myself jumping out of the vervet's path. A week ago, I wouldn't have been able to control my flinch. It took all my concentration and my expression froze on my face, but I managed to sit rock steady under the assault. Shoving *lux lucis* into the vervet, I watched it explode in a spray of *atrum* glitter; then I dropped my hand beside Jamie and built the *lux lucis* in my fist until it glowed like a small sun. The imps frolicking on the pooka bailed, diving mouth-first onto my body and dying just as fast.

". . . always dresses like Rudolph, which inevitably scares some of the dogs and makes the others want to attack her," Alex was saying. "Anyway, I'd invite you, but I don't think we're at the 'help me pimp my business' stage yet."

I blinked at him, trying to remember what he was talking about. Something about a party, right? When in doubt, flirt.

"I forget, does that stage come before or after meeting the parents?"

"I'm pretty sure it's interchangeable."

The last imp died in a puff of glitter. Jamie spun to face me, barking pointed words I didn't need to understand to interpret.

"Argue all you want," I told him. "We agreed that was the rule."

Jamie glowered. I glared. Then I realized I'd talked to him like he was human while Alex looked on in bewilderment.

"Ah, I'm trying a new method with him," I explained to Alex. "We're still working out the kinks. Like how when you're with me, Jamie, you have to behave."

Jamie's furry eyebrow knobs rose, and he glanced toward the pond. Alarm bells went off in my head. *With me* had been a poor choice of words. I lunged for the leash two seconds before Jamie took off. He hit the end of the slack with the strength of a small pony, and the rope belt bit into my palm. My chair slid with a painful shriek across the stones, caught an edge, and tipped. I scrambled to my feet as the choke of the collar brought Jamie up short.

"Wow! Good reflexes," Alex said with genuine awe. He stood and collected my chair, carrying it back to the table.

I remained rooted in place. The pooka's soul swelled from his body, all *atrum* and potent fury, eating its way up the leash toward me.

"You agreed to this," I whispered, my heart beating loud in my eardrums. The *atrum* crept closer, so dense I could hardly see Jamie's body through it. I relaxed the tension on the leash, fighting to keep my breathing even and not let my fear show. If Jamie decided to go super-nova right now, I wouldn't be able to stop him, and I wouldn't be able to protect Alex.

Jamie pivoted to face me. From this angle, he needed to take only a few steps back to slide out of the collar.

"The moment lunch is over, the collar comes off," I said, speaking too softly for Alex to hear. "All you have to do is sit beside me and eat. That's it. Then we go and we never, ever do this again."

Layers of *atrum* swirled inside his soul, black on denser black, all traces of *lux lucis* missing. Then his soul imploded, shrinking back into the confines of his body, and he stomped back to the table. I trailed after him on wobbly knees, fingers shaking with relief to see equal pulses of *lux lucis* inside his agitated soul.

When I sat, Jamie tried to squeeze into the small space between me and Alex.

"You won't fit there, buddy. Try the other side." Alex gently redirected Jamie with a push to his neck. His hands came away black with *atrum*.

"Jamie!"

Jamie gave me a flat look and circled my chair to flop down beside me. My eyes bulged, so many unutterable reprimands clogging my throat that I couldn't breathe. He had intentionally tainted my date! He'd known I'd see it. He'd known I'd do something about it. But he'd done it anyway.

Any sympathy I'd harbored for Jamie burned away beneath my fury.

I reached for Alex's hands, laying mine on top of his. His heat seared my icy fingers, and he turned his hands to cup mine. It should have been a nice moment, but the *atrum* ruined everything.

"I'm so sorry about this. I thought Jamie would be better behaved. He used to be such a good dog." I kept my tone light when I wanted to growl, but the twitch of Jamie's tail said my words had hit home. Rolling *lux lucis* in my palms, I fed it into Alex, wiping away the pooka's taint.

Alex's eyes widened the moment my *lux lucis* swept through his soul, his pupils dilating, his gaze dropping to my lips. Shock made my hands stiffen in his, and I withdrew from his touch. I hadn't expected him to feel what I was doing. I definitely hadn't intended it to elicit arousal.

"Don't worry about it. He's not that bad," Alex said.

A chill hit my toes and faded. I recognized the sensation, and it had nothing to do with the cold weather and the limited reach of the heat vents and everything to do with my sensitivity to *atrum*.

I peered through the mesh tabletop. Jamie leaked *atrum* in a small, growing puddle, all of it oozing toward Alex. My molars fused together in frustration. Yesterday at lunch with Niko, Jamie hadn't tried anything like this. If he had, it would have been a simple matter to clean it up, and not just because Niko would have helped. But with Alex, he pulled this petty stunt, knowing I'd have to pretend like nothing was happening or ruin my date and possibly my entire budding relationship.

Smiling tight at Alex, I focused on rolling *lux lucis* through my foot. When I had a good spin, I released it from my toes. The energy splashed against the tip of my boot and infused the leather. The more I pushed, the brighter the boot glowed, a tide of white inching up the calf-high shaft.

Peachy. I'd forgotten one of the basic laws of Primordium: Previously living material held *lux lucis*. The boots weren't porous like my wool gloves. All my efforts to shoot *lux lucis* from my feet to counter Jamie's *atrum* would be moot until I'd suffused the boot completely.

Scooting my chair back, I leaned down and planted a palm on the ground. *Lux lucis* rolled through my hand and speared off my fingertips, flashing across the *atrum* growing between Jamie and Alex, negating it.

"Stop it, Jamie," I hissed.

The pooka watched the servers bustle inside the restaurant and pretended to be deaf.

"Everything okay?" Alex asked.

I straightened and rubbed my palm on my pants. "I think he's all settled now."

More *atrum* leaked from Jamie, flowing across the patio toward Alex. If he'd wanted, the pooka could have flooded the whole restaurant in darkness with a single tsunami from his soul. This creep of *atrum* was pure taunt, reminding me he could wreak havoc at a moment's notice, with the added passive-aggressive, petty benefit of sucking the fun out of this date.

My hands balled into fists on my lap. Twenty minutes. He couldn't give me a twenty-minute breather to savor some normal time with Alex. Of course not. That'd be too considerate.

I'd cowardly hoped to avoid the confrontation brewing between me and Jamie until the sjel tyver were history and preferably after Pamela had left our region. But after this stunt, I was through putting off our fight. The moment the pooka and I were alone, we were having it out.

I propelled a gallon of *lux lucis* into my boot, loading the leather with energy until it shimmered brighter than the rest of my soul. Finally *lux lucis* leaked out onto the patio through the sole, and I shifted in my seat, stretching my leg to rest it in the puddle of *atrum*. My energy ate sluggishly through Jamie's, leaving a bright white splotch on the paving stones.

My fingers shook when I shoved my hair behind an ear. Between the *lux lucis* expended in the boot and killing the imps and vervet, I really needed to recharge, but the nearby emaciated bushes wouldn't suffice. One touch, and they'd die back to their roots, and wouldn't that freak out Alex?

"Madison?"

I blinked at Alex, realizing I'd missed his question the first time.

"Sorry. What was that?" How flattering was I? I couldn't even pay attention.

"I asked what your Christmas plans are."

Besides paddling the bottom of one irksome pooka? "The usual: Go over to my parents'. They live in Lincoln, so it's a quick drive."

"No big trips?"

"I wish. I'm too tied down this year, financially and with obligations." I glared at Obligation Number One beneath the table and shifted my foot to counter another creep of *atrum*.

The server burst from the restaurant with our food, tossed everything onto the table, and rushed back inside with a halfhearted, "Need anything else?"

I opened the takeout containers and dropped them next to me, forcing Jamie to move farther away from Alex to eat. Then I dove into my salad, willing the meager *lux lucis* in the lettuce to refuel all my expended energy. I had to salvage this date. No way would I allow one disobedient pooka to ruin everything with Alex.

I turned on my smile and, ignoring the dizziness framing my vision, asked, "What about you? After the pimping party, are you going anywhere?"

"To San Diego to spend time with my mom and sister. My nephew still believes in Santa, so that makes Christmas a lot more fun. Way better than hanging out at my dad's drinking beer like we do every other weekend."

"A sunny Christmas sounds heavenly right about now." I polished off the salad and stabbed the vegetables in the curry dish, chewing like a gerbil and trying my best not to look like a speed-eating contestant.

My phone warbled "Hail to the Chief" from my purse. I froze for half a second, then dove both hands into my bag. If Brad needed me, I'd have the perfect excuse to get Jamie away from Alex and get myself to a hearty source of *lux lucis*.

"I'm so sorry. I need to take this. It's my boss." I scooted my seat back, prepared to stand and walk a polite distance away. One look at Jamie stopped me. I couldn't leave the pooka unattended next to Alex. I'd have to be rude and stay. Meeting Alex's eyes, I said, "I'm sorry," one more time before accepting the call.

"We've got a frost moth issue at Maidu Park," Brad said. "Where are you?"

"Near Sierra College and Douglas." No need to inform him about my date.

"Good. Swing by the park before you come in."

"Right now?"

"Do you have something more important to do?"

I met Alex's eyes as Jamie licked up the last of his mac and cheese. My heavy sigh gusted across the receiver.

"No. I'll be there."

I hung up.

"Is everything okay? You look pale," Alex said.

Lux lucis loss will do that to an enforcer.

"Everything is fine. Well, not really. I'm annoyed and wish I could stay, but I've got to get back to work."

"Is there a sudden rush on bumper stickers?" Alex asked, going for teasing and falling flat.

"Some clients arrived early, but that won't stop them from being irritated if they have to wait." The lied flowed from my mouth so smoothly I almost believed it.

I stood, clutching the table when my vision darkened to a pinpoint before clearing. A few doses of *lux lucis* and I'd be as good as new. The trick would be making it to the nearest tree without face-planting.

Alex stood. "Do you need a to-go . . . ?" His question trailed off as he took in my empty dishes. His singular bowl was still half full. How embarrassing.

Jamie chased down one final meatball, then rose to all four feet and headed for the patio exit. I tightened my hand on the leash, giving it a soft tug to stop him. The black-and-white energy of his soul rioted within the confines of his body, but *only* within the confines of his body.

"It was really good to see you," I said to Alex. "I'm so sorry I have to rush off like this."

"I'll give you a call. Maybe we can set up something this weekend. That way your boss won't interrupt."

"I'd like that." *I'd like to live in a world where my boss couldn't interrupt a date.* I shoved the thought aside, not enjoying its flavor of self-pity.

Alex took my hand and pulled me to him. His fingers were furnace warm as they wrapped my cold digits in a gentle embrace.

"I'd be kicking myself all week if I didn't—" He leaned in, head tilted, and brushed a kiss across my lips.

My irritation took a giant step back, making way for a rush of happy hormones. The heat of his lips zinged southward, and I melted against him, opening my mouth and deepening the kiss.

Energy spilled across my tongue.

I gasped and stepped back. I'd just fed off Alex. First I'd zapped him with *lux lucis*, now this?

Alex wobbled and caught himself on the table, his eyes unfocused. When he zeroed in on me again, heat darkened his eyes, dilating his pupils. If I had to guess, I'd say he'd misinterpreted the dizzy drain of his energy as the light-headedness of arousal.

"Are you sure you have to go?" he asked.

"Yeah." It came out appropriately breathless, if not for the reason Alex thought. Oh God, *I'd just fed off Alex!*

I disentangled my fingers from his and walked away, trying to mimic a normal stride, my body tingling under his gaze. Jamie paced at my side, a good two feet between us. The moment I strode around the corner, I detoured to a small tree and siphoned a wallop of *lux lucis* from it—not as much as I needed to recharge, but less than would cause permanent damage to the sapling. More than enough to clear my thoughts. I'd consider the ramifications of feeding off Alex later. Right now, I had more pressing matters.

"You and I need to talk," I said to Jamie.

I reached for the collar and slid it off his neck. Icy *atrum* slicked my soul, coating my fingers. My thoughts scattered.

Jamie had always made sure I could safely touch him. Always.

I stared at the black energy smearing my fingertips, struggling to wrap my head around his betrayal. The pooka turned away and padded to the car.

15

LONG LIVE THE QUEEN

J amie morphed into a pasty human the moment he crawled into the backseat. I jerked my gaze away from a full white moon and wrenched my door open. By the time I had my seat belt buckled, Jamie had stuffed his legs into his pants and latched himself in on the right side of the car, as far away from me as he could get. I watched in the rearview mirror as he rubbed his throat with cold-pinkened fingers. A faint dark smudge of a budding bruise cut across his throat.

I winced in sympathy but reminded myself it'd been his fault, his decision to run, his call to keep going while dragging me across the patio.

The ignition caught, and I revved backward out of the parking spot, taking the turn onto Sierra College Boulevard fast enough to screech the tires. Anger built inside me, screwing a lump in my chest tighter and tighter. I plowed around the corner onto Eureka Road, the steering wheel creaking in my grip. The light turned red and I slammed on the brakes. The seat belt slapped my chest, and my anger erupted.

"What the hell was that back there?" I shouted.

Jamie yanked on his sweater and glared out the side window like a petulant teenager.

"What's going on with you?" The light turned green and I peeled across the line, most of my attention on Jamie in the rearview. "You smeared me with *atrum*! Alex too! And that stunt with your soul at the table? What were you thinking? We had a deal. You said you'd *never* use *atrum* on me."

Jamie whipped around to glare at me in the mirror. "You said *atrum* and *lux lucis* were equal. You said neither belonged on nonliving things. What happened to *that*?"

"How does that even compare? I'm a living thing. I'm a pure *lux lucis* living being, and you still mucked me."

His cheeks turned bright red, and he glared at me, nostrils flared. "I'm half *muck*. I couldn't help myself."

"That's a lie and we both know it."

"Then I finally did something right."

"What's that mean?" I drummed my fingers on the steering wheel, waiting in a left-hand turn lane before darting through an opening in front of oncoming traffic and barreling down a side street.

"Everyone says you're supposed to teach me to behave," he said. "I'm just following your example."

What did *that* mean? How had we gotten so far off point? "Fine. You want to take your grump out on me, that's one thing. But you changed Alex. He's a norm—"

"He likes you," Jamie spat.

"What does that have to do with anything?" Was he jealous?

"You kill everything that likes me. Why shouldn't I do the same?"

My jaw dropped. Jamie's scowl should have cracked the mirror.

"Because Alex never did anything to you!" I yelled when I found my words again. "Everything that likes *you* tries to eat my soul and kill me."

Jamie shrugged. His dismissive attitude spiked my fury to new heights, choking off any reasoning argument I might have formed.

I screeched into the Maidu Park lot, bouncing over the speed bumps. We barreled past the paved parking spaces and jounced along the gravel road that wrapped four empty baseball diamonds. I selected an unmarked spot close to the back half of the park and hit the brakes. We slid to a stop. I unsnapped my seat belt and twisted to face Jamie.

"Wait here. Don't feed anything, don't use *atrum*, don't change shapes. Got it?" There. I'd covered all the bases and I hadn't shouted, despite my blood boiling hot enough to melt the car around us.

"You're not my Brad." Jamie launched out the far door, pulling his shirt over his head.

"What?" I shoved my door open and jumped out, tangling Val in the seat belt.

Jamie glared at me across the top of the car. "We're bonded, not coworkers. You're not the boss of me. I don't have to do anything you say." He yanked his pants down. Still bent over, his body blurred and reconfigured into a Great Dane.

I gave myself whiplash looking for witnesses. Midday on a Monday, with the temperature resting near freezing, few people had bothered to venture out to the park. None were close enough to have noticed Jamie's freakish transmogrification.

Jamie stalked to the back of the car, golden eyes burning. His lip peeled back and he growled, soft and low. The hairs on the back of my neck stood on end.

"Jamie." I loaded the word with warning, but we both knew it meant nothing. I'd lost control of the situation—of Jamie—long before today.

He spun and galloped into the preserved open space beside the park.

"Jamie!"

I sprinted two steps and slammed against Val's strap. The thin leather cut into my neck and knocked the wind from me. Spinning, I yanked Val free of the seat belt. The buckle ricocheted around the door panel and cracked against the passenger door, leaving a dent and a deep scratch in the green paint. By the time I turned back toward Jamie, he'd disappeared.

I cursed and kicked a tire for good measure, the reciprocal sharp pain in my big toe only elevating my anger. I'd never catch up to the pooka now. Holding still, I strained to hear sounds of his progress. A lone car cruised by on the road outside the park. Birds chirped. A remote-controlled plane climbed toward the clouds with a whine more piercing than a child's shriek. Otherwise, a peaceful quiet wrapped the park, undisturbed by the crashing sounds a monstrous dog should have made tearing through the bushes and crunching through dried leaves. Even Primordium failed me.

I paced the length of my car and back, thoughts spinning.

Wait until Pamela heard about this. She'd probably go straight to Brad and demand he fire me. Or better yet, she'd call up the Triumvirate and have me jailed. At the very least, she would strip me of my title as enforcer and give my region to someone else.

Oh, hell, my region. The amount of evil one angry pooka could dole out was mind-boggling. He could defile everything and everyone I protected if he chose. The thought should have terrified me, but the bond distorted my emotions, funneling them into a different worry: What if Jamie got hurt? He didn't understand the world, not completely, and his time with me had been so sheltered he might not recognize danger until it was too late.

"Who am I kidding. If anyone gets hurt, it'll be *because* of Jamie." He hadn't shown an ounce of empathy for anything other than *atrum* creatures.

And Mr. Bond. And Dame Zilla, my traitorous conscience chimed in.

"Great. Two cats in the entire region are safe. I can go home and call it a job well done."

I braced my hands on the hood of my car and took deep breaths. Arguing with myself—*out loud*—in the parking lot didn't solve anything. I needed to get a grip. Jamie wasn't gone for good. He'd come back to me after he blew off some steam. In the meantime, I had work to do.

I swung open the passenger door and retrieved my palmquell, lighter, and pet wood from my purse, then dropped the emptied bag on the floorboard and tossed Jamie's clothes on top of it.

Replaying our conversation in the car, I stomped down the paved pedestrian path away from the baseball diamonds. Where the front half of the park had been groomed and gridded into sports fields, the back half had been left wild. My route took me along an elevated trail that followed the natural twists and turns of a creek, and I looked down on the surrounding marshes and thick oaks. Up until last week, this open space had been a haven for native flora and fauna. Then a salamander had been set loose among it, burning more than half the landscape before I could kill it.

I searched for signs of Jamie as I walked, peering into the dense brambles and trees, but he'd simply vanished.

If pookas could become invisible, someone would have mentioned it, I assured myself. I swallowed the urge to yell for him. Pamela had been right: I should have been a lot stricter with him. I wanted a do-over. If the inspector had shown up even two days earlier, she would have seen a happy, well-behaved pooka, and she could have stopped me from making the mistake of allowing him to use *atrum*.

A frigid breeze swept across the path, leeching the last of the heat from my jeans. My hair blew into my eyes, and I shoved it behind my ears, tugging my coat's collar up to cover my neck. I'd forgotten my beanie and scarf in the car, but I didn't want to waste time going back for them. Neutralizing the frost moths, then finding Jamie, took precedence.

The cold deepened with each step, and after I slipped on a patch of invisible ice, I stepped off the pavement to the dirt beside it and shoved my hands deep in my pockets. Maybe the cold would chase Jamie back to the car for me.

I rounded a bend in the trail, and the *lux lucis*–filled landscape bled to gray. Twisted charcoal trunks melded with the mud-churned hillside, the underbrush little more than charred tufts. Spindly burnt twigs, the leftover scraps of once-dense bushes, speared the slopes, but nothing had survived in the hollow where the salamander had tread. My steps slowed. Frost moths coasted through the gully on the ash-scented breeze, so numerous their electric-blue bodies created the illusion of a fluttering river of ice suspended in the air. A handful drifted over the far bank, flapping their way toward homes in search of people to feed on.

Brad had been putting it mildly when he'd called this an "issue."

Before diving in, I scanned the devastated grounds for Jamie, spotting nothing resembling the pooka in any form. *Just as well.* In his current mood, Jamie would probably let the moths feed off him just to watch me stumble as if punch-drunk.

But at least I'd have known where he was.

Sighing, I backtracked to the nearest trail leading into the hollow, mincing down the slope. Halfway to the bottom, my right foot slipped out from under me and I crashed to my butt and slid the rest of the way. Scrambling to my feet, I brushed mud from my pants, but not before the icy moisture sank through my jeans to chill my long johns and underwear. Just perfect.

I trounced to the edge of the frost moth swarm, sinking to my ankles in mud limned with ice. The suction wreaked havoc with my balance, and I stumbled against an ashy stump and righted in time to net seven moths in one sweep. After chasing away the rest of the flock with the lighter, I shoved the flame through the captured moths, pulsing *lux lucis* into their mouths for the final kill as they shrank. Then I staggered forward a few steps and repeated the process. Those moths died and the next batch took their place, but not before they sipped from my soul, adding their trademark emotional accelerant to my burning rage.

My thoughts spiraled around my utter impotence. I hadn't been able to stop Jamie from bolting, and it had nothing to do with my inexperience as an enforcer. *No one* could have stopped him, but I would still be blamed for my loss of control. Brad would lecture and yell. Pamela would claim me incompetent. As long as Jamie was acting out, I'd be viewed as a failure. What complete and utter ridiculousness!

My jaw ached, and I yawned to stretch the cramping muscles. Where was Niko when I needed him? One look at him, and all this frost moth–fed fury would transform into lust.

Oh, real classy, Dice. You just finished your date with Alex, but bring on the man meat so you can forget about your failings. I'm sure Niko would appreciate being given such an important assignment.

All my anger imploded, consuming me in my own self-hatred.

You kill everything that likes me. Why shouldn't I do the same? Jamie's words rang through my head.

Five more frost moths died as I wrapped my thoughts around that memory and flipped my ire back toward Jamie. How dare he threaten—

A blur of white blasted through the frost moths and rocketed up the slope to the tall oak standing alone at the top. A prajurit! Not just one, either. A handful of them darted among the low-hanging branches of the oak. I abandoned the frost moths and scrambled up the slope.

Brad hadn't known how long it would take for the local wiped-out population to be replaced by newcomers, but seeing some this deep inside our region had to be a sign of good fortune. Finally. I could use some positive news.

As I jogged closer, the speed of their movements and their jagged flight patterns didn't look quite right. The flash of a sword spurred me into a run. I broke off the trail and dashed through thigh-high weeds, heedless of the icy moisture soaking my pants. Drawing my pet wood, I extended it with a flick, then fumbled for my palmquell in my left hand as I ducked under the low outer branches of the oak's massive canopy. My boots slipped on the acorn-strewn ground and I stumbled to a halt.

A cage of white branches arched overhead, dipping to the ground in several places and turning the world around me into a prism of white lines. I lifted my palmquell and pet wood, searching the *lux lucis*–laced environment for black-bodied enemies, finding none.

The prajurit weren't fighting evil; they were fighting each other.

Two six-inch-tall duelers strafed past my head, swirling my hair against my cheek. They plunged almost to the ground before spearing upward to fight in the empty space in front of me. Both wore elaborately detailed jackets and pantaloons, with thick woolen wraps spun around their feet and ankles. Both fought with a sword in each hand, and both wore tiny woven crowns that glowed faintly. One was familiar.

"Lestari!" I cried, rushing forward. "What's happening? How can I—"

"This is a prajurit matter!" Lestari declared, speaking on top of the other queen's, "Keep out, human!" Neither woman's assault slowed, and neither looked my direction.

"Hang on. No one's the enemy here. We're all on the same side, just—"

Lestari barked a word I didn't understand, the other woman repeated it, and they flared apart. I had a moment to relax before they dove for me from separate directions, swords leading their charge.

I dropped to my knees with a yelp, thrusting my arms up to protect my head. Those swords might be the length of toothpicks, but they were scalpel sharp!

Satisfied I'd been cowed, the queens clashed back together in the air above my head. I remained kneeling, stunned by the assault. Now that I knew what to look for, I spied more prajurit fighting vicious skirmishes above and around the queens, zipping through the branches too fast to track. None of them came to the aid of their rulers; in fact, they seemed to go out of their way to give the women space.

The queens fought in a blur of wings and swords. Never more than an inch separated them as they spiraled through the air, their intensity and skill mesmerizing. My breath caught when the foreign queen slid through Lestari's defenses and sank her sword's tip into Lestari's thigh. Lestari dipped, falling away from the stab. The other queen rushed after her in a flurry of strikes, pushing Lestari backward until she hovered near a tangle of twigs at the end of a low branch.

I scrambled to my feet, a protest on my lips. Lestari faltered, swords wavering. I surged toward them, but the foreign queen struck too fast, one sword swinging high, the other low. Lestari blocked the upper strike as she exploded upward, spun on the fulcrum of their connected blades, and slashed her opponent's wing. The foreign queen fell, her piercing shriek spiking through my skull. I clapped my hands to my ears, stumbling forward with the intent of catching her before she hit the ground, knowing I'd be too slow.

Three warriors disengaged from the fight and dove over my shoulders, catching their queen between them. Her injured wing hung by a thread of muscle. Blood welled from the wound and fell in viscous *lux lucis*–charged drops to splatter the ground beneath her. A flurry of prajurit blasted past me to surround the wounded queen, and she wasn't the only one supported by comrades. Two swooped low, and my hand flew to my mouth when they lifted a dead warrior from the ground. Then, in a swarm, they buzzed through the oak's branches.

With a war cry loud enough to do the Vikings proud, Lestari's people chased the retreating prajurit, Lestari at the forefront. I remained frozen in shock until their tiny bright bodies were out of sight.

What had they been fighting over? What had been worth killing for?

A chill seeping up my forearms woke me from my trance. Lifting my arms, I examined my coat. Razor-smooth cuts split my sleeves, two per forearm. One had cut the sweater beneath. I stuck my fingers through the holes, dazed. The queens had been willing to hurt me to keep me from interfering, so willing that the apparent mortal enemies had teamed up in their effort.

Lestari and her warriors threaded back through the oak's canopy, flying in formation. The queen lit upon the branch nearest me and the warriors fanned out to nearby limbs, their bright bodies a subtle hue different than the white of the oak. I counted, surprised to find only six. They had looked a lot more numerous earlier. Oddly, all the warriors were male. Most were injured.

A small prajurit, shorter than Lestari by almost an inch, knelt in front of her and dug into a pouch at his waist. He retrieved a jar fit for a doll and a roll of cloth. After using his hand to slather the contents of the jar over Lestari's thigh wound, he pulled out a needle so tiny I could barely see it and stitched her flesh back together.

"I will forgive your interference this once," Lestari declared, hands on her hips. No part of her demeanor indicated she felt the medic's ministrations, though she did hold statue still. "But only this once, and only because you are Madison Fox."

My name sent a wave of reaction through the warriors, and even the medic paused to shoot me a glance. Having seven pairs of disproportionately large prajurit eyes focused on me made me shift in my boots.

"That's, um, very kind," I said.

The medic finished, applied more ointment, then wrapped Lestari's leg with the cloth. She winced and shooed him away, but he'd already launched toward the next injured prajurit.

"Lestari, what are you doing back here?" She had relocated to Grass Valley not three days ago after the death of her entire clan—to grieve and recover, I'd assumed. The last place I'd expected to find her was in the park, dueling it out with another queen.

Lestari zipped into the air, flying back and forth in a hypnotic figure eight. If her leg hurt her, she didn't give any indication of it.

"This is my territory. This is my home," she said.

"Of course it is, but didn't you—"

She spun, wings humming, expression intent. "You acknowledge my right to these lands?"

"Sure. But did you have to cut off her wing?"

"Only because she defended her neck too well."

I flinched, stopping short of taking a step back. Yes, the tiny woman frightened me. How could anyone so violent not accrue *atrum*? I spent my days killing evil creatures, but if I were to duke it out with another enforcer, I was pretty sure we'd both end up blackened with more than bruises.

If I continued to work with Summer, I might get a chance to test my theory.

A high-pitched, male-timbered voice above me said, "The Sunan would be wise to rest, since her own wing has only just mended."

Lestari crossed her arms and flew another figure eight before landing on a branch, her regal bearing daring anyone to suggest it wasn't her decision. Her landing lacked its usual grace, though, when she tilted off her injured leg and had to use her wings for balance.

"Foolish child," the male said, and I identified him as the medic.

Lestari shot him a look that should have knocked him off his perch, then sat and gingerly laid her bound leg out straight. Her fat, beelike abdomen protruded behind her, and the split lines of her body looked as if it should have been painful, but all the prajurit sat the same way.

"Daud, you're on watch," Lestari ordered. "Iskandar, patrol. I want reports every two hours."

Two warriors flew off, one with his ribcage bound in strips of gauze. Now that Lestari wasn't moving, I could see she had more than one bandage, including a gossamer stitch patching the thin membrane of her lower right wing. Tiny cuts and dirt smudged her face, and her clothing hung ragged at the seams. She might have made the forty-mile journey back to Roseville from Grass Valley in record time, but it hadn't been a peaceful trip.

"Do you expect another attack?" I asked.

"Always. Everyone wants my land. They are fools who see weakness instead of honed resolve."

The other prajurit were preying on Lestari, taking her territory after all her people had been killed? Talk about ruthless.

"What do you mean by 'everyone'?"

"Everyone. All the prajurit know of Isabel Dulat's heinous treachery."

The prajurit struck their wings together, generating a shrill, discordant chorus. I winced but didn't jump, expecting the reaction to the traitorous warden's name.

"All believe my territory is undefended," Lestari said.

"More than the queen you just—" I made a hacking motion with my hand.

"She was the tenth."

Holy cow. Ten battles in less than seventy-two hours? No wonder Lestari looked battered and beaten.

"Do territorial disputes always have to be settled by battles? We've had enough prajurit deaths. Couldn't you, I don't know, negotiate?"

"Do you mean peace talks?"

"Exactly!"

"Brad Pitt agrees?"

"Of course." I didn't even hesitate. Sjel tyver were invading and our region was vulnerable; we needed prajurit help now more than ever. Letting them kill each other wouldn't serve anyone any good.

The remaining warriors looked to Lestari with varying degrees of disbelief. Apparently not everyone shared my less-than-bloodthirsty sentiments.

"Good. The talks will be quick," Lestari said. "I will inform Brad of your promise to our claim here and to all land within one thousand wing beats of this tree."

"Was that your previous territory?" Her easy acquiescence made me suspicious. One thousand wing beats for such a tiny woman was what, a hundred feet? A thousand? How much territory did a prajurit clan need? What I knew about them wouldn't fill a page of Val—nor had the information he'd shared about our diminutive allies.

"Much more than my former territory is fallow due to the traitor. Much more."

The other prajurit smiled and nodded their heads. I squinted at Lestari, recognizing her smug expression; the last time I'd seen it, it had been on Brad's face when he talked about a permanent expansion of our region. I was beginning to think I'd missed something.

"Isn't your claim here plenty of territory?"

Lestari's hands flew to her swords. "You insult me!"

"I'm sorry. I—"

"Tell Brad we accept his offer to host the peace talks."

To host?

"Where is the pooka?" Lestari demanded. "I wish to thank him for his kindness and receive a prophecy."

"He's—" In the excitement, I'd forgotten about my falling out with Jamie, but the weight of it resettled on my shoulders, dragging them down. "He's around here somewhere."

A shrill, three-tone whistle sliced the upper range of my hearing. The prajurit sprang from their perches, swords leaping to their hands. Seconds later, the two scouts plunged through the branches, dropping on either side of their queen. After a rapid exchange, Lestari charged me, stopping so close to my nose that my eyes crossed to keep her in focus. I edged back a step. She buzzed closer.

"You brought a hostile pooka into *my* territory? Explain yourself."

"He's not hostile." At least not to prajurit. "Where did they—"

"Then why do my men tell me he runs with the black flies of *atrum* coating him? Where he goes, dark shadows follow. Where is his balance of sunlight?"

He had flies on him? What did his shadow have anything to do with anything? Or was she speaking in metaphors? I considered asking, but getting back to Jamie was more important than deciphering her questions.

"He's upset," I said. "Can you point me in—"

"Why is he upset? What did you do?"

Her tone snapped my spine rigid. "I didn't—"

This time, the bark of a dog cut me off. I whirled, scanning the vegetation beyond the oak's branches, searching for Jamie. Something black moved at the base of the ravine, deep in unburned undergrowth. Jamie. I couldn't let him out of my sight again.

"Excuse me, I must—"

"Eagle formation," Lestari snapped, cutting me off yet again. "Daud, take point. Iskandar, go afield. I want reports every two thousand beats." One warrior shot through the oak's twisted limbs, disappearing into the sky. The rest swooped into a loose arrow formation around Lestari, the tip of their V pointing straight up. A heavy drone filled the air as they hovered in place.

"The hounds approach," she informed me. "We must depart."

I jerked back toward Lestari, a cold ping of adrenaline tingling across my scalp. "The hounds?"

"Fix the pooka, Madison Fox," the tiny queen ordered, using the same imperious tone with me as she had with her warriors. "Fix him, or don't return to my territory again."

16

DON'T RUN; YOU'LL ONLY DIE TIRED

The prajurit shot straight up, weaving through the branches with dizzying speed. When they cleared the scraggly canopy, they zoomed north, away from the frost moths and the glimpse of moving *atrum* I'd spotted in the ravine.

"Wait!" I raced after them, slipping on loose acorns and catching my hair in sharp branches. By the time I reached the paved trail, the prajurit had flown out of sight.

I planted my hands on my hips and shouted after the haughty queen. "This is my territory, too!"

Announcing it to the empty air made me feel even more impotent than being ordered around by a pint-size woman.

"You know what I really need?" I asked the oak. "Another person telling me to get a grip on my pooka. I wasn't going to bother, but now that Brad, Pamela, Niko, *and* Lestari have ordered it, I guess I have to do it."

Channeling my irritation into my feet, I pounded back to the frost moth–filled ravine. I paused at the top of the slope, straining to catch sight of Jamie amid the dense white plants. The heavy crash of a clumsy creature running through the bushes drew my attention to the base of the slope.

Lestari had said *hounds*, right? One *atrum*-soaked pooka in dog form she might have mistaken for a hound, but she'd used the plural...

Twin corgis surged through the underbrush in near-perfect synchronization, fangs bared and snarling, their bodies so dark they should
have sucked in all the light of Primordium like canine-shaped black
holes. Not Jamie. Hounds. Dread chased ice through my veins,
freezing out all thoughts but one: *Hide*.

Despite the hounds' stubby bodies and the fact that neither stood
taller than my knees—and that I'd never live down the embarrassment
if anyone found out I'd cowered from *corgis*—I dove behind the
nearest thick oak at the top of the hill. I couldn't take on two hounds at
once with my bare hands. I shouldn't even attempt one without a net,
especially not hounds as healthy as this well-fed pair. The last time—
the *only* time—I'd taken on a hound, it'd been an emaciated weakling,
and even then it'd been a tough fight. Hounds were real dogs with real
teeth. If they took a bite out of my soul, they would also rip out a
chunk of flesh and tendon and bone. It wouldn't take much to provoke
an *atrum*-crazed hound's attack, either. The mere sight of me would be
enough to set them off.

I clutched the oak when the hounds bayed with excitement. The
nearest branch stretched well above my reach. I'd never be able to
climb the wide trunk, either.

Without meaning to, without wanting to, I drew my knife. Three
inches of blade wasn't much, but it was better than my bare hands.

I don't want to kill a dog. Please don't make me.

I peeked around the trunk. A pitch-black Great Dane flashed
between me and the hounds. I clamped my mouth shut on my knee-jerk
need to call out Jamie's name. The pooka galloped down the slope
toward the corgis, then past them, and the squat hounds charged
after him.

Had he intentionally saved me, or had that been a coincidence?

With shaking fingers, I sheathed the knife. Two hounds didn't
simply materialize out of thin air. Either his pookaness had attracted
them or he'd encountered two perfectly normal dogs and changed them
into hounds.

Like all animals, dogs were creatures of *lux lucis*. They didn't turn
evil on their own; for that, they needed human interference—or a
pooka's. It took time for a human to sully a dog's soul but scant
seconds for a pooka to turn a dog into a hound. All he had to do was
net a dog within his potent *atrum*, overwhelming and replacing the
dog's *lux lucis*, and the transformation would be complete.

As much as I hated the thought of Jamie stealing the free will of other creatures and altering their souls, not to mention him willfully spreading *atrum* in my region, I hoped he had turned these dogs. It beat the alternative, that the corgis had been tortured or had such an evil owner that they'd both been turned. Plus, if Jamie had changed the corgis in the last half hour, the *atrum* wouldn't have had time to sink into their consciences and change their basic natures, making them relatively easy to clean back into dogs.

Or so I hoped.

Keeping an ear trained on the receding sounds of the pooka and hounds, I forced my wobbly legs to move. I had a hound net in the trunk of my car. A car that I'd parked five miles away. Okay, a half mile away, but *come on*! Couldn't I catch a break? Why did everything involve running these days?

I dug deep into my reserves of energy and shoved into a sprint, my steps hobbled by the pain lingering in yesterday's overworked leg muscles. Freezing air sliced down my windpipe with each gasp, and when I reached my car, I had to pause my frantic search for my keys to focus on not throwing up. Popping the trunk, I overturned a cloth bag tucked in the corner. A single hound net fell out. If I'd had the lung power, I would have cursed. I'd been meaning to buy another net, but they were crazy expensive, and with a pooka in need of clothing and extraordinary amounts of food, I'd put it off. Plus, I'd had Jamie. He could easily protect me from a hound and he would never leave my side.

I was such an idiot.

I slung the net over my shoulder and slammed the trunk. The loud crash of the abused metal startled a flock of pigeons into flight but wasn't half as satisfying as I'd thought it would be. Stripping off my gloves, I untangled the net while I ran, rolling it into a manageable bundle of hemp rope and leather bindings. Then, keeping an eye out for wayward frost moths, I pounded down the slick slope back into the burn zone. This time, I managed to keep my feet. Bully for me.

Stalking along the muddy creek bank, I located the last place I'd seen the hounds, then followed their tracks. Where the squat hounds had run easily through fire-singed bushes and squeezed under the denser, sharp branches of living brambles, I had to fight my way, stopping frequently to untangle the net or Val's strap. After the third time yanking Val free of a limb at the cost of a shallow gash down the back of my hand, I unzipped my coat and stuffed him inside, strap and all.

"It's darkness or being scratched to bits," I said, knowing he hated being cut off from the world. Several gouges lined with grit and coated with ash marred his beautiful leather cover. "I should have done this sooner. I'm sorry, Val."

The cold leather spread a chill through my sweater to my stomach. Shivering, I zipped my coat. When I lifted my head, I looked straight into the eyes of a hound.

The corgi stood atop the bank on the far side of the creek, tail up, teeth bared. Its twin trotted up beside it, whining and licking its lips when it spotted me. With a harmonious bark, they charged.

I fumbled with the net. Too many plants obscured the area, clutching at the woven rope as I tried to spread it. The hounds bore down on me with growls that flipped a primal switch in my brain, igniting an age-old instinct to flee. Snatching the clumsy net to my chest, I darted toward the nearest slender oak and clambered up the trunk to the lowest branch six feet off the ground. The branch creaked and popped alarmingly but held.

The hounds cleared a fallen log in a tandem leap, bodies so close together they looked connected. Five more yards, and they'd be beneath me. I unfurled the net and powered *lux lucis* into it. The white energy caught in the fibers and spread, illuminating all scant four feet of the tight tapestry. The circular net was designed to capture a single, standard-size hound. I prayed it would work for two corgis that ran as if they were linked to a single brain.

Movement flashed in my periphery, and Jamie dashed by in his familiar role as Pied Piper–slash-pony for imps. A mound of dark bodies piled on his back and a trail of stragglers bounced in his wake.

"Seriously?!" I shouted. "Jamie, enough is enough. Come help me."

The pooka skidded to a halt, sending imps tumbling. Swirling black-and-white irises took in the stampeding hounds, then pinned me with a look of raw contempt. Spinning on a back foot, he galloped away before the hounds noticed him.

My breath caught in my throat, and the lump in my chest shattered, spearing straight through my heart.

The hounds reached the oak tree and leapt for me, their tiny legs inadequate for the task. I slumped over the net where it draped the limb in front of me. Breathing hurt. Jamie had abandoned me. He'd seen me in danger and he'd turned away.

One of the hounds scrambled up the slope of the trunk, its teeth snapping inches from my dangling foot before it fell back to the ground. I jerked my leg up, lost my balance, and tipped off the branch toward the open jaw of the second hound. My arms and legs spasmed around the limb, and I swung upside down. A hound's teeth snapped closed on my dangling hair, yanking out an eye-watering chunk. I cinched my limbs tighter around the branch, the soul breaker jabbing my chest through my coat. The pet wood in my front pocket felt like it'd drawn blood.

Heart beating in my throat, I righted myself. I'd deal with Jamie in a minute. First, I had to survive the hounds.

Gripping the branch with both thighs, I rolled the net into a tight spiral, positioning my hands to make it easy to throw. I'd only get one shot at this. If I failed and netted only one hound, or worse, missed them both completely, I'd be sitting in this tree until I could call Summer to rescue me. And I'd die before making that call.

Inching out along the branch, I lured the hounds away from the trunk. They spun in circles beneath me, springing on truncated hind legs to snap at the air below me. Carefully, I raised the net, swinging my arms to get a feel for the weight of it.

The limb cracked, dropping several inches before catching. I screamed. The hounds went wild, piling on top of each other to reach me. Before I lost my nerve—and the branch broke completely—I flared the net and flung it over them.

It landed askew, wrapping their heads, and the hounds tumbled together, loosing piercing, pained cries. In their flailing, one hooked a paw in the mesh, pinning it to the ground and freeing the other to back out and escape.

I leapt from the tree, landing flat on cold feet. Sharp pain exploded in both ankles, but I kept moving, motivated by visions of being mauled. Rushing behind the corgis, I grabbed the flopping edge of the net, kicking the nearest hound when it lunged for me. It fell on its side with a whimper.

"I'm sorry!"

I yanked the net snug across both hounds and pressed the ends into the muddy ground, then jumped back. The hounds growled and stilled, turning to press their noses to each other.

The net weighed no more than ten pounds and should have been easy for the corgis to escape from, but its powers were more psychological than physical, or maybe a combination of both. Every time the hounds moved, they flinched and whined as if the *lux lucis* zapped them. So long as the edges of the net remained in contact with the ground, the hounds wouldn't be able to escape.

Breathing deep, I ran my hands down my pants, wincing when splinters bit into my palms. My ankles ached from the bad landing, but since they flexed, I decided nothing was broken or sprained.

I should cleanse the hounds immediately. With them pinned, it would be a relatively easy task, but it'd take time. I wasn't going to give Jamie that much of a head start.

Any other day, netting two hounds at once would have induced a triumphant high, especially with the deluge of adrenaline bleeding from my tense muscles, but I kept replaying Jamie's contemptuous expression and abandonment. How had we gone from getting along so well to him hating me? Could we recover from this?

I shoved through the undergrowth after him, my steps as heavy as my heart. Jamie's trail proved easy to follow. If his hoof-size tracks in the mud had somehow been camouflaged, the slime trail of *atrum* would have been impossible to miss. I left the dark energy alone and concentrated on speed, fully aware that I'd catch Jamie only if he let me. What I'd do with him then, I wasn't sure, but I couldn't let his behavior stand. Playing with imps, protecting drones, besmirching Alex and then me with *atrum*, threatening Alex's life, forsaking me to hounds, actively spreading evil through my region—each time he acted out, he escalated. At this rate, it wouldn't be long before he embraced evil outright and wholeheartedly. When that happened, Niko would be called in, and with Pamela at his side, they'd kill Jamie.

I bent over and dry-heaved, hands braced to my knees.

As long as we're still bonded, there's still hope, I told myself. I didn't know if it was true, but it helped me push back into action. I didn't doubt we were still bonded, either. If my physical reaction to the thought of Jamie being harmed wasn't proof enough, my urge to wrap him in a hug and never let go—despite everything he'd done— confirmed the bond still manipulated my thoughts.

Jamie's trail angled up the hill to the road that circled the park. I clawed up the muddy bank and stood on the sidewalk, chest heaving. *Atrum* and muddy footprints led straight to the pavement, then vanished. I spun in a slow circle, scrutinizing the deserted sidewalk and neighborhood streets. No dogs barked. No imps rushed from the manicured lawns. No people stood on their front porches, convenient witnesses to point out the direction Jamie had gone.

He'd disappeared as surely as if he'd flown away.

I waited until I'd returned to the netted hounds before calling Brad. I'd put it off far too long already. In his capacity as warden, Brad had the ability to feel the movement of *lux lucis* and *atrum* in his region. He'd be able to help me track Jamie, but I'd have to first admit to losing control of the pooka.

"What's going on?" Brad demanded. "I'm getting some weird readings."

"I netted a pair of hounds. Corgis." Delaying wouldn't make this any easier, but I couldn't bring myself to lead with my failure.

"*Hounds?* Since when did hounds get into our region?"

His words confirmed my suspicion. "They were likely pooka made."

"Pooka made? What was he—" Brad cut himself off with a strangled sound, then much quieter asked, "Madison? You don't sound— Tell me what happened."

"Jamie and I had a fight. He ran off, apparently made the hounds, and mucked up the area with a lot of *atrum*." The words tumbled out fast, as if I could lessen their meaning by rushing through them.

"Where is the pooka now?"

"Gone." I braced for his explosion.

Silence reigned so pure I could hear a faint conversation between Rose and Pamela about their lunch plans in the background. I lifted the phone from my ear, preparing for the tsunami after the calm.

"Send me a picture of you next to the hounds. In Primordium."

His calm, matter-of-fact tone and the absence of any candy-laced profanity worried me far more than a full-blown berating.

"Me and the hounds? Like some disgusting hunting picture?"

"Something like that."

Frowning, I crouched beside the hounds, near their hind ends. Even with the net holding them, I didn't want to tempt fate by sitting with my back to their muzzles. Activating the Primordium picture app, I snapped a selfie of the three of us and sent it to Brad.

"You've got it."

Brad's silence sat heavy against my ear, and if I hadn't been straining so hard to hear something—anything—to clue me in to his thoughts, I would have missed his soft, relieved sigh. The picture combined with the sigh cleared up my confusion; Brad had feared the worst: that Jamie had tainted my soul. Asking me to send a picture with the hounds was his equivalent of getting my picture beside today's dated newspaper: He'd made sure I had sent a current image of my soul.

"I'm still me. I'm just—" I heard the bewilderment in my voice and closed my mouth. I didn't want to cry while on the phone with my boss. I didn't want to cry at all. I wanted to be mad. I wanted to get Jamie back and teach him how to be a good pooka and make every-thing normal between us again.

I covered the microphone with my finger and cleared my throat before saying, "If you felt the anomalies in the park, can you point me in Jamie's direction?" There. I had sounded professional and composed.

"Whatever the pooka was doing, he stopped before you called. I can't sense him now."

"You can't? But—"

"It's a good thing, Madison. It means he's not actively using *atrum*." Brad spoke with uncharacteristic calm.

My fingers clenched on the phone and I rubbed my temple with my opposite hand. Dried mud flaked off my fingertips, gritty against my sweat-damp forehead.

"How am I supposed to find Jamie?" I asked in a voice too small and distant to be mine.

"You need to take care of the hounds."

"But . . ."

"Cleanse the hounds. Finish the frost moths. The pooka might be back by then."

"Do you think so?"

"I think you'll feel better—we'll both feel better—if you eliminate the threats we can see."

It wasn't the assurance I wanted, but it had to do.

I hung up and stuffed the phone in my pocket. A pair of cyclists cruised by on the trail above me, out of sight but within hearing range. Birds chirped to each other, growing bolder now that I'd stopped crashing around their territory. Jamie didn't materialize.

Pivoting on the ball of my foot, I faced the hounds.

"You don't know it, but you want me to do this," I said, talking to work my nerve up. The hounds growled, low and menacing. "Trust me, you'll thank me when I'm done."

I planted a hand on each of their flanks and gushed *lux lucis* from my palms. Both hounds jumped, yipping when the net shifted against their fur. Yips became snarls and growls, drool dripping from exposed fangs, eyes wild with fear and evil intent. Observing them revived some of my anger. Nothing I did physically hurt the corgis, but all their *atrum*-skewed instincts demanded they attack and kill me, and holding still while I extinguished the dark energy coating their souls was akin to torture for them. Jamie would answer for this, and I'd make him see his behavior for the cruelty it was.

In theory, it might have been faster to transform the hounds one at a time, but it would have been disastrous. Trapped up against a normal dog, a hound would attack. It wouldn't remember that the dog next to it was its best friend and playmate. It would sense weakness and go for the jugular.

If the hounds had been imps or even vervet, they would have exploded into harmless glitter after the first three seconds of my assault. But they weren't insubstantial creatures, and my soul's energy fell into the hounds as if into a void. I stopped when dizziness tipped me onto my butt. After recharging from nearby trees, I returned to the hounds and repeated the process. Their *atrum* clung so thick and dense that I began to worry it'd never relent against my onslaught. Finally, the fur around my fingers turned gray, then white, and ever so slowly, shimmering *lux lucis* spread across the dogs' flanks. I pushed the evil energy away from my hands in twin tides so their muzzles and toes were the last to lose flecks of black. Easing back, I continued to ply the corgis with *lux lucis* until I met a slight resistance.

The dogs had long since quieted, and when I let go of them, they squirmed to peer over their shoulders at me, tongues nervously licking their noses. I ran my fingers through their thick fur, and two tails wagged tentatively.

"See. I told you I was on your side."

I checked their necks, dismayed to find them both without a collar.

It could have been Jamie's doing or they could have escaped a back-yard. I doubted they'd been abandoned. They were both too fat and, now that *atrum* no longer controlled their impulses, too friendly.

I started to lift the net, then thought better of it. If I let them loose, they might run off, and not necessarily straight home. I needed some way of leashing them. While I contemplated my next course of action, I stroked their foreheads. The one on the left lifted its head and laid it across the shoulders of the one on the right, and both dogs released contented sighs. Watching them, I realized I didn't need two leashes. As long as I kept one corgi with me, the other was sure to remain close. Unclipping the sheathed knife from my belt, I shoved it in my bulging jacket pocket, then unthreaded my belt. The corgi nearest me meekly allowed me to twine the leather around its neck, proving it had had plenty of socialization in its life. Sliding a hand under the net to get a better grasp on the makeshift leash, I freed the dogs.

They stood and wagged bushy tails, rushing to sniff my feet and knees and hands. After doling out more pets, I straightened and headed for the nearest tree, the net draped over my shoulder. The leashed corgi trotted at my side. The unleashed corgi followed close behind.

When I reached the first frost moth, I tethered the end of the makeshift leash under a rock. Navigating the uneven terrain was diffi-cult enough while holding a lighter and frost moths without adding corgis underfoot. Fortunately, the dogs' earlier activities seemed to have tired them, and they flopped down together to wait while I mean-dered back and forth through the burned landscape, killing the remaining moths. I took my time, scanning constantly for Jamie, but eventually I ran out of frost moths and my excuse to linger.

A fleeting hope that I'd find the pooka at the car added energy to my flagging steps, but I slowed again when the Civic swung into sight, alone in the vacant lot. I loaded the corgis into the backseat and stowed the net in the trunk, then idly practiced shooting trees and signs and fence posts with the palmquell, trying not to think too hard about how desperately I wanted Jamie to bound out of the nearest thicket.

When the tinny notes of "Hail to the Chief" rang from my jacket, I almost sprained my pinkie in my haste to retrieve the phone.

"Did you find him?" I blurted out.

"No. Where are you?"

My shoulders slumped and I dropped to sit against the Civic's bumper. "At the park."

"And the hounds?"

"Collarless corgis. They're in the car." I peeked through the windshield. The dogs had fallen asleep on top of each other.

"Take them to the shelter and come to the office."

"Now? What about Jamie?"

"We'll keep an eye out, but we can't wait much longer. The sjel tyv will return tonight and you need to be ready."

I blinked to normal sight and turned to face west. The sun sat an inch from the horizon, a dull glow behind thick clouds. I'd been at the park for hours. I didn't need Brad to spell it out for me: If Jamie hadn't returned already, he wasn't going to.

"Okay. I'm on my way." The words choked me.

I hung up and slumped over my knees. The clouds opened up, releasing a torrent of freezing rain. Tilting my head back, I let it wash over my face, then shoved to my feet. I gave the park one last look. Jamie was somewhere out there, getting rained on, with no shelter to rely on. He'd been the one to make the decision to tear off on his own, and he could have been up to untold evil, but as I got into the car and drove away, I couldn't shake the gut-wrenching sensation that I was giving up on him.

"I *will* find you, pooka of mine," I promised. I wouldn't abandon him, and I wouldn't let him abandon me.

Halfway to the shelter, driving fifty miles per hour down the four-lane road, my heart tried to burst through my sternum. It jackhammered against my ribs, frantic and sudden, stealing my breath and yanking my awareness inward. Terror flooded my system, chased by a cold sweat. I couldn't catch my breath. I couldn't even pinpoint the source of my blind panic. It simply *was*—omnipresent and overwhelming.

The honk of a car horn jerked my attention back to the road. Gripping the steering wheel with trembling fists, I struggled to makes sense of the lines, the lights, the traffic. My vision darkened, tunneling. I jerked the car to the shoulder and screeched to a stop amid a spate of blaring horns.

My hands trembled when I pressed my palms over my frenzied heart. My rib cage bounced in shallow breaths barren of oxygen. I forced myself to inhale and hold it, first for a single second, then for two seconds on the next breath, until I stopped hyperventilating. Something warm and wet splashed against my hands. I stared at the clear liquid on my shaking palm, then patted my face. Tears dripped off my chin.

I blinked to Primordium. Nothing evil disturbed the interior or exterior of the car. The corgis were still corgis. My soul remained unblemished. I craned over the dash to check the roof. Nothing.

Traffic blasted past close enough to touch, each car's passing rocking the Civic on its shocks. I snapped myself free of the belt and twisted backward, banging my head on the ceiling and my knee against the center console. The moment I squared off with the general direction of Roseville, my panic receded. Clutching the headrest, I squinted through the back window at a house with the misfortune of being located a driveway's length from this busy road. In my head, I saw much farther, all the way back to my region. All the way back to Jamie, because every fiber of my being screamed that he waited at the other end of this invisible line.

The moment I acknowledged it, the tether became a tangible sensation. It hooked to the base of my brain, sending pulses to my heart and head, and it stretched out toward Jamie, so tight it thrummed with tension.

I'd driven outside of the tether's range. I hadn't even considered the possibility. I needed to get back, get close to Jamie. I needed to—

The tether tugged against my brain shaft, moving parts of me never meant to be touched. I scrambled over the center console, flopped into the passenger seat, and flung the door open in time to vomit in the dirt. I remained braced in the open door, eyes locked on a piece of glass embedded in the soil, letting the fresh air and gentle rain wash over me until my stomach ceased sloshing.

Struggling, I righted myself in the passenger seat and located a water bottle. After swishing and spitting, I closed the door. The corgis whined, but I couldn't work up the energy to soothe them. Belatedly, I activated the flashers and listened to the rhythmic click timed with the lights.

Inhaling deeply, I rested a hand on my chest to confirm my slowing heartbeat. Jamie must have closed the distance between us.

Or the link had snapped.

Frantic, I probed my brain for the feel of the tether, encountering nothing. It had disappeared as if it had never existed.

With shaking fingers, I unhooked Val and opened him. Before I could say a word, text flowed across his page, the letters so slanted and jagged that I had trouble reading them.

This is beyond the bleed! We're not going to take this, not from that soggy, good-for-nothing, two-toned abomination!

I partially closed him, flipping him over so I could check his cover. Dirt and ash flaked off in my lap, and several long scratches cut into the leather, but all his injuries appeared shallow enough to be buffed out with a good polish.

Turning him back over, I asked, "Val, are you okay?"

Scourge of the armpit of five-day-dead roadkill! That's what that pooka is!

Ah. Straight to the point, then. "Did I— Do you know what just happened?"

Betrayal.

The word splintered my heart, inflating spikes of guilt through my lungs. "I didn't. I swear. I'm going back for him."

You should never have trusted that pooka. Never bonded him. You let him too close and he stabbed you in the back, Val continued without a pause.

Of course. Val saw everything in black and white, and despite his dual nature, Jamie fell squarely on the black side in Val's eyes. Unfortunately, it wasn't so cut and dry. Jamie's behavior today had been atrocious, but he hadn't acted in a vacuum. He hadn't deserved to be left behind, even if he'd abandoned me first. Damn it! Did this snarl of emotions mean the bond remained in place or merely that I had a conscience?

I told you he was trouble. I told you he'd tear you to confetti. He's a despicable, deplorable, loathsome, scum-breathing bête noire!

"Okay. I get it. You don't like Jamie. But what about me? What about—"

Pamela is going to be extremely disappointed. She told you what to do. She told you how to take charge. And you blew it. You were weak and useless.

With each word, my insides contracted, squeezing into a ball of misery. His text mirrored the dark voice of my conscience, and fresh tears lodged in my throat.

Now she'll think I'm a horrible handbook. Any respect Pamela had for me is shot. All because of that skin-shifting, evil-soaked bugbear.

Maybe if you talk to Pamela, you can convince her I was blameless. I couldn't—

I gently shut Val, slid him into his strap, and closed my eyes, reaching for Jamie and the tether. The roar of vehicles rushing past, the rock of the wind-blasted car, and the steady tick of the flashers all droned together, weaving a shroud of numbness that saturated my mind.

Maybe the bond is just dormant again, I reasoned. Since day one, it'd manipulated my emotions, but up until a few minutes ago, I'd never sensed the metaphysical link.

I tried to take solace in the thought, but it didn't stick.

I called Brad and explained my panic attack, listening to my own voice as if it were a stranger's.

"Did I break the bond?" I asked.

"How do you feel now?"

Sad. Lost. Confused. "Fine."

"Then the tether's intact."

The iron sitting on my lungs lifted and I took a deep breath. "Are you sure?"

"I'm sure. If it'd snapped, you'd be unconscious and I'd have felt the backlash of evil."

"You say the most comforting things."

"Can you still feel him?" Brad asked.

"No."

"That's too bad."

Which meant he still couldn't track Jamie, either.

"Should I come back?" I asked.

"Drop off the dogs, then get back as fast as you can."

I drove the rest of the way to the shelter without incident. I'd been there once before, also to drop off a hound-reverted-dog. His name had been Max, and he'd been half starved when we'd parted ways.

The staff remembered me, and the process of relinquishing the corgis into their care didn't take long. I explained where I'd found the dogs, and while they readied a kennel, I snapped pictures of the pair, then posted them to the Maidu neighborhood message board. The receptionist assured me she would disseminate pictures of the corgis on lost-and-found sites. In the meantime, they'd have a safe place to stay and food to eat.

I put off saying good-bye to the dogs as long as possible. Petting their heads, I smothered a fantasy of adopting them myself, or at least fostering them until their owners could be contacted. My life was already crowded with creatures who needed me to care for them, and adding two dogs—real dogs, not pookas who could take dog form—to my hectic life would be irresponsible and unfair to the corgis.

Before I left, the receptionist pulled me aside to a wall of pictures and tapped on the image of a midsize mutt with glossy black hair and a big doggy grin on his face. A smiling five-year-old girl draped across his back.

"That's Max now," she said.

"Really?" I stared at the photo, and a trace of optimism lightened my step back to the car.

I drove back to the office by way of Maidu Park, parking in the same spot I'd used earlier. When no pooka rushed to greet me, I cut the engine and climbed from the car. The rain had slackened and an arctic wind coming off the soccer fields promised the next heavy precipitation would fall in the form of snow. Darkness swallowed the paved trail and turned the ravine into a mesh of shadows. I blinked to Primordium and spun in a slow circle, looking for a Great Dane–shaped pooka, but my hopes didn't have far to fall when I didn't spot him.

17

WHIRLED PEAS

I clutched the steering wheel and hugged the slow lane like a first-time driver. Less than two miles separated the park and our new headquarters, and I spent every foot of it expecting another sensory-exploding panic attack. When I arrived without incident, it took another minute to relax my grip and slide out of the car.

A frosty breeze hit my derriere, stabbing straight through to the skin and reminding me of every wet patch remaining on my jeans. The Civic's dome light illuminated smears of mud ground into the driver's seat and floor mats. I checked the back. Despite the towel I'd lain down, the corgis had besmirched the tan seats and door panels with drying mud. To the uninformed eye, it looked like an enormous creature had gotten violently ill in the back of my car.

"When you're sliding into first, and you feel something squirt," I sang under my breath, and popped the trunk. Any other day, the destruction of the interior of my car would have inflamed a foul mood. Today, it barely registered as irritating. I grabbed a clean pair of jeans and long johns from a bag in the trunk, ignoring the identical change of clothes I'd brought for Jamie, and marched toward the office.

Due to extensive fire and water damage to our previous offices—and, apparently, a shoestring relocation budget—our new headquarters resided in a cramped shotgun retail space squeezed into the crotch of an L-shaped, run-down shopping center. The liquor store two doors down entertained brisk postwork business, and no one looked twice at our grungy, glass-front office lit up in all its lackluster glory. Some of that had to do with our receptionist Sharon, propped behind a podium in front of the door. Drab and stout, she served as the face of the office —one that said, *Go away and don't bother us again.* I'd originally assumed she functioned as little more than a gatekeeper to discourage the public from entering our undercover headquarters. More recently, I'd come to suspect she qualified as part of Brad's security. Deeper in the office, I spotted Rose at a plastic-topped folding table, neat rows of spray bottles lined up in front of her. Across from her sat Sam.

Could this day get any worse?

Sam and I had history, much of it unpleasant. I'd first encountered him when he'd broken into my car, but I'd recognized a soul worth saving. Teens were more malleable than adults, and he still had time to correct his moral path before it cemented into his personality. I'd tried to scare him straight, cleaning the smut from his soul and warning him against his bad life choices. Unfortunately, Sam had a bit of a kink for being bossed around by a woman, and he'd embraced the habit of stalking me.

It wasn't until Niko took notice that I learned I'd unwittingly addicted Sam to my *lux lucis* infusions. Until the Illuminea could wean him, Brad had stuffed Sam into the role of office intern of our fake bumper sticker company—the front of our CIA operation.

Sam was part of the reason my energy swap with Alex today had freaked me out. I wouldn't be able to live with myself if I addicted Alex to my *lux lucis*. Plus, I wanted his attraction to me to be genuine.

The door opened with a broken-bell *clank*. Normally I added extra cheer to my voice when I greeted Sharon, partially to amuse myself since she never responded in kind and partially because I'd made it my personal goal to win her over. Today I didn't care.

"If you see Jamie, scream," I said.

Sharon's dull brown eyes slid to me, then whipped back to the parking lot. Either that was her version of alarm or she hadn't liked my suggestion of a scream. Anything so animated fell outside her repertoire.

"My main Madison! Where've you been?" Sam swung into my face, and I squinted against the glare off his frizz of red hair.

While I was grateful my boss had fixed my mistake with Sam, having the teen in the office meant that not only did I run into him more often than before, but I also had to be nice. Worse, Sam had formed a friendship with Jamie, further increasing his presence in my life.

Or maybe not. Maybe I'd found the silver lining to Jamie running off. Except the trade-off wasn't worth it, and the thought did nothing to brighten my mood.

"Why so glum, Maddy?"

"Don't *ever* call me *Maddy*." I shoved past him.

"Sure, sure. No problem. Whoa, did I miss the mud fight?"

"Brad wants to see you," Rose said; then she pointed at Sam. "You. Sit. Use your brain. Do you think any woman that filthy is in the mood to chat?"

"Huh. Rose droppin' knowledge bombs. What else can you teach me about women?"

"So very, very much," she muttered.

Summer perched at the back table, arms stretched in front of her and her hands flat on the plastic top, her attention fixed on her arms and a scowl etched into her features. In Primordium, a fluid *lux lucis* net traveled up one arm, down the other, and back again. Either she wanted to show off or she was bored. Probably both. Being forced to wait on me likely hadn't improved her opinion of me or her mood.

Too bad.

I didn't slow until I reached the unisex bathroom at the back of the office, and I changed in record time. I splashed water on my face and used paper towels to wipe the worst of the mud from my coat, then stalked to Brad's office, pulling the door shut behind me. It was a token gesture, since the walls of the shoe-box space didn't meet the ceiling and some sounds would carry into the main office, but at least everyone no longer had a front-row seat to the impending show.

Brad sat back in his chair, one leg crossed over the other, his thick fingers threaded together and locked around his raised knee. No telltale redness marred his neck or face. If he felt the urge to berate me, he disguised it well. Not sure what to make of his silence, I stood with my arms at my sides and tried not to fidget. Brad ran his gaze over my body, the once-over devoid of sexual undertones and strictly an assessment of my soul.

"Come here." He stood and gestured for me to walk to the map tacked to the wall.

I sidled around the folding table and stood next to him. Brad's head barely cleared my shoulder, and the map had been hung to his height. I slouched to get a better look, the defeated posture feeling appropriate.

"You were here when the pooka ran off." He stabbed a pudgy finger at the map over a green rectangle representing Maidu Park. "Where were you when you had your panic attack?"

I traced the road lines and pointed to Hazel Boulevard near Oak Street. "Here-ish."

Grabbing a ruler from the desk, Brad laid it atop the map so it measured the distance between the park and my finger as the crow flies. "That's a little over three and a half miles away."

"That's the length of the tether?" Three and a half miles? What was the point of a tether at all? It wasn't as if I could influence Jamie from that far away even if we had been getting along.

Brad didn't answer me. "The shelter is here. That's another"—he shifted the ruler to take a new measurement—"three miles."

"So the tether stretched? It's almost seven miles long now?"

"Not likely. I don't think it's even three miles long. I've talked with other enforcers who were linked to pookas. Their tethers were never more than a mile, tops."

"But . . . it has to be, because this is where I had my panic attack." I jabbed the map for emphasis.

"How fast were you going?"

"When? During the panic attack?"

"And after."

"I don't know. Forty-five? Sixty?"

"So the only way the pooka could have kept up was if he could fly," Brad said, his tone leading. He'd already thought this through.

"But Jamie can't—"

"Jamie has a fourth form. One with wings."

"Hang on. He's never mentioned another form. If he can turn into a bird, why—"

"Not a bird. His fourth form probably doesn't have a *lux lucis* equivalent."

It took a moment for me to process his words. "Are you saying he has a purely evil form? But he's not pure *atrum*. He's still split." He had to be. I couldn't have already lost him.

"A dog is traditionally a *lux lucis* creature, but he had no trouble taking the form of a Great Dane. It's likely whatever shape he's in, it's *atrum* based, which would explain why he hid it from you before now."

I stared at the map and the distance I'd traveled, and I couldn't come up with another explanation that made sense. For Jamie to have stayed close, even within three miles of me, he would have had to be moving as fast as I'd been driving. Unless he'd hitchhiked with another driver both ways—highly unlikely—he had to have flown. On top of that, whatever his winged form, it flew faster than the average bird.

I stumbled to a folding chair and collapsed.

"Jamie can fly."

"Jamie can fly," Brad agreed.

"What sort of form am I looking for?"

Brad shrugged. "It's a guessing game. No one can predict any form a pooka will take. There's never been a pooka who could take the shape of a Great Dane before, or a mammoth."

"What does this mean for me? For us?"

Brad resumed his seat and rolled his chair up to the desk. "It means you're less likely to have another panic attack."

"But if Jamie can fly, how am I supposed to find him?" My question came out close to a wail, and I rocked back in my seat, gripping the plastic beneath my butt to ground myself.

"The bond works both ways. He will come back to you. As long as the link isn't severed, he'll always come back."

"When?"

"Hopefully soon." Brad ran a hand over his balding scalp, and for the first time I recognized his calm as a facade. "We're overdue for something to go right."

"Lestari is back," I blurted out. "I saw her today in the park. She's got a ragtag group of warriors with her. I actually came across them when they were mid-battle with another clan—the tenth battle she's fought since she returned, she said. Fortunately, she agreed to peace talks."

"Peace talks?" Brad sputtered. "She initiated *peace talks*?"

"Well, it was my idea—"

"Your idea! You involved yourself in a *prajurit land war*?!" His voice escalated to a roar that rattled the flimsy door. A familiar squiggly vein pulsed at his temple.

"Not personally," I reassured him. "I only said you'd approve."

He tensed, his face darkening from pink past magenta to purple. If his breathing hadn't been as audible as an enraged bull, I would have worried he was about to pass out. The table creaked, caught in the claws of his hands.

"We need the prajurit's help," I continued. "And Lestari looked in bad shape. I thought—"

"You thought you'd set *me* up to mediate a prajurit *land war*?" Spittle flew from his mouth.

"I don't think so?" In the face of his rage, my words came out a question.

"What exactly did you say?"

"That they should stop fighting, especially since the territory was already Lestari's."

Brad dropped his head into his hands with a choking sound.

"And I told Lestari you'd approve of peace talks. It was her idea for you to host them."

Brad collapsed forward and banged his forehead against his desk. I eased back in my chair, contemplating how quickly I could vacate the office. I'd seen Brad yell and rant and pace before, but I'd never rendered him speechless.

"The CIA's policy is to let prajurit police prajurit for a reason," he said in an eerily calm voice, addressing the floor. "Do you know why?"

"Because the prajurit are our allies?"

His head lifted, and he skewered me with a look that sealed my lips. Right. I should have realized the question had been rhetorical.

"Because peace talks can take *decades* to resolve," he said, his voice rising as he straightened. "The CIA steps in only in times of extreme need. No, don't." He lifted a hand to quiet my response. "I'm not using the phrase lightly. A sjel tyv does not qualify as an *extreme need*. It doesn't even come close."

"Oh."

Brad tipped his head to address the stained ceiling tiles. "Decades. I'll be retired and still mediating. I'll be dead and still mediating." He sighed and closed his eyes. When he opened them, he pinned me with a fiery glare. "What were you thinking?" he boomed.

"It might not take that long. Lestari already agreed to some territory in the park . . ." I trailed off, staring at Brad's hands. He'd raised them, possibly unconsciously, and squeezed them as if ringing moisture from the air between us. Or as if ringing my neck.

"What did you promise her?" he whispered.

"I'm not sure I really promised her any—" I took another look at Brad's expression, then babbled, "There's an oak in Maidu Park. She claimed everything within one thousand wing beats of it. I figured—"

"You figured you'd sabotage negotiations before they even began?" Brad leapt to his feet and planted his hands on the table, leaning toward me. The flimsy surface bowed and wobbled, spilling files to the floor. He didn't seem to notice. "Juicy frutti on my patootie! I'll look like I'm playing favorites! You've set negotiations back a year, and we haven't even begun."

I tried to squeeze out *I'm sorry*, but my throat had constricted too tight to make a sound.

Brad jabbed a finger in my face. "Out. *Out!* Now!"

I popped to my feet, knocking my chair over. I started to right it, thought better of it, and shoved the chair aside with my foot so I could open the door.

"Um, where am I supposed to go?" I asked.

"Fiddyment. Ask Summer. Now get out of my sight before I—"

I jumped through the doorway and pulled the door shut between us.

Summer and Sam stared with identical wide-eyed expressions.

"Ooooh, someone's in trouble," Sam taunted, but very quietly.

I bent to retrieve my filthy pants from where I'd dropped them outside Brad's office. "I'm ready whenever you are," I told Summer.

She snorted and stood.

I detoured to a stack of supply boxes and rummaged for duct tape. Sam helped me cut strips and use them to patch the sleeves of my ruined coat.

"Where's the pooka?" Summer asked.

"Around."

"What's a pooka?" Sam asked.

"A confidential account," I said, even though I knew better than to feed Sam's conspiracy theory that our office served as a front to a top-secret organization. It did, but no one would ever confirm as much to a norm, let alone to the troublesome teen.

Summer gave my soul an insultingly obvious examination. "You lost control."

"No." I hadn't lost control. Control was something I'd never had. I'd lost something more precious: Jamie's trust.

Rose paced outside the office, stomping as far as the thrift store beyond the Indian restaurant next door, then back. With her formfitting blazer flaring open to display her ample chest wrapped in an eye-popping teal top, she attracted a fair share of attention from the patrons of the liquor store.

The moment I stepped outside, she marched up to me. "Good going. I think you broke Brad."

"She's a walking disaster," Summer said.

"Stuff it." I'd had a crappy day, and I couldn't stomach dealing with Summer's attitude on top of it.

"Both of you, grow up, bottle that crap up, and ship out," Rose said in a shockingly harsh tone. "The illustrious inspector allotted me two hours to do a day's worth of work here after trotting me around as her personal lapdog lie detector. I don't need you two pissing in my emotional pool. Shoo."

I gaped at her. Minus any candy-tainted profanity, Rose sounded more like Brad than herself . . . which made sense. As an empath, she would have had the full sensory experience of Brad's explosive reaction to my unintentionally incendiary news.

"I'm sorry," Summer said.

"Very sorry," I said.

We jogged toward the parking lot, neither looking at the other. I glanced back to check on Rose. The empath stuck her head inside the office and bellowed in a tone that would have done Brad proud. "Sam, get out here, and come prepared with the best jokes you know."

By mutual consent, Summer and I took separate cars, and I did my best to avoid thinking about how empty my Civic felt without Jamie. Zipping out of the parking spot, I cut Summer off and led the way, winding through downtown and along a twisting network of parkways and boulevards rather than taking more direct, high-speed roads. If the convoluted route irritated Summer, that was pure bonus; keeping Jamie close was my top priority, and I wouldn't breathe easy until I'd made the entire drive without so much as a twinge of panic fluttering in my chest.

When we neared Fiddyment, where once-expansive farmland now crawled with homes connected by mazes of streets, I realized I didn't know the exact address of our destination. Pulling to the shoulder, I wriggled my fingers at Summer as she gunned past me to take the lead, deriving petty pleasure from her thunderous expression.

After zigzagging down several streets, Summer parked in the middle of a dense neighborhood, and I pulled in behind her. Turning off the car, I blinked to Primordium. A few drones dipped along the streets, pestering people returning home from work and aimlessly buzzing over fences and rooftops. If the tyv was in the area, none of the drones were in a hurry to get back to her.

"Are we in the right place?" I asked Summer when we climbed out of our cars.

"We might have been if you hadn't taken the scenic route. Who knows where the tyv is now." Summer peered behind me, into the Civic. "Seriously, where is the pooka?"

"Nearby."

"Don't play games with me—" Summer's phone rang and she jerked it from her pocket, answering with, "Pamela, I—"

The inspector must have cut her off. Summer's gaze shot to me and her free hand landed on the knife at her hip.

"She looks normal, for her," Summer said. "No, no sign of the pooka."

Damn it. Why had Brad told the inspector already?

I tilted my head back and scanned the dark skies, hoping I'd catch sight of Jamie. I might not recognize his current form, but I would recognize his soul anywhere.

Unless he's disguising it, cloaking himself with atrum, I reminded myself.

"Do you consider Madison a threat?" Summer asked, jerking my attention back to her. I thought I caught a glimmer of relief in her expression at Pamela's response, and her white-knuckle grip on her knife hilt loosened.

I rolled my eyes, turning my back on her so she couldn't see the trepidation behind my false bravado. Pulling out my phone to call Brad, I walked three houses up the street to the corner lot, stopping next to a giant inflated Santa. I didn't need an audience for this call.

My phone rang "Hail to the Chief" before I had a chance to dial. I hit the screen to activate the call.

"Tell me you've found the tyv," Brad said.

"That's my line."

"She's not there?"

I glanced up and down the empty crossroads. "We've seen some drones but no tyv."

"Hot tamales on a zagnut!"

I pulled the phone away from my ear to spare my eardrum. "I take it you don't know where she is either."

"Tyver don't disappear, not at night. They can disguise their daytime habitats, but they can't hide when they're feeding and laying eggs."

"Maybe she left our region?" I swiveled away from Summer's scrutiny. She'd pocketed her phone and stalked closer, making no pretense about listening in despite keeping a car length between us.

"She didn't fly out; she went *poof*," Brad spat. "One minute, I could feel her rotting nougat on my soul; the next she wasn't there."

"I take it that's not normal." I had an inkling where this conversation was headed, and I desperately didn't want to be right.

"Not even if I take into account Madison's law."

"Madison's law?" Did I want to know?

"It says every situation, no matter how straightforward, can be turned into a caramel cluster when you get involved."

Oookay. So he hadn't forgiven me yet for involving him in the peace talks. Pinching the bridge of my nose, I blurted out my question. "Jamie is helping the tyv, isn't he?"

Brad's heavy sigh gusted from the speaker. "Helping, hiding. Either way, I can't ignore the timing. Neither can Pamela."

"I had hoped you'd give me time to work things out with Jamie first before you notified her." I mentally congratulated myself for making it a statement, not an accusation.

"She's an inspector," Brad said. "She knew the moment Jamie disappeared."

Bile churned in my stomach and I started pacing, ignoring Summer's nosy presence. "What's she going to do to me? Fire me? Demote me?"

"Don't worry about the inspector, Madison. Focus on the pooka. You can fix this. I believe in you."

I couldn't tell if he was trying to convince me or himself, and it did nothing to reassure me.

"You haven't lost him yet," Brad said when I remained silent.

"He's helping out the most dangerous creature in the region! One that could kill me. What do you mean I haven't lost him?" My eyes stung, and I squeezed them shut and tilted my head back.

"You're still linked. You need to use your connection to draw him back and get him on track."

"How?"

"Any way you can. The sooner the better."

I rubbed my forehead. "Anything more specific?"

"Each pooka bond is different. See if the handbook has anything helpful. And stay put; Pamela is coming to you."

"Wonderful." I paced toward Summer, then away, listening to Brad breathe on the other end of the line. "How worried should I be right now? About the tyv?" I'd seen how fast she could lay eggs. If she remained hidden, she could cover the city with her spawn in a few industrious nights.

Brad hesitated.

"Don't hold back, boss. I need to know what we're up against."

"Right now, the situation is bad. Since we don't know where the tyv is, we don't know where the majority of the drones are. They're feeding unchecked, which means they're keeping the tyv strong. The stronger she is, the more eggs she lays. If we don't figure out where those eggs are, *bad* becomes *dire*. When those eggs hatch . . . catastrophic. A hundred thousand norms acting on their most base whims is not pretty. It's the kind of behavior that leads to riots and military action."

"Oh." I choked on the tiny sound, wishing I hadn't asked. Tugging off my beanie, I wiped nervous sweat from my brow.

"But that's worst-case scenario, Madison. Stay focused on finding Jamie and convincing him to listen to you again."

"Uh-huh." I gave myself a shake. "I'll do my best."

"I know."

"Okay. And, Brad? I'm sorry again about the prajurit."

He hung up on a sigh.

I tucked the phone into my pocket and checked our surroundings before meeting Summer's distrusting eyes.

"We need to stay put," I said.

"I know. Pamela is coming."

I blew out a heavy breath and resumed pacing, trying to shake the feeling of waiting for the executioner. Summer didn't help. Since her phone call, she looked as likely to shoot me as the occasional drones, and she maintained distance between us, as if afraid my failures would rub off on her.

Pulling Val from his strap, I dusted off his cover before lifting him to my lips and whispering, "All apologies must be heartfelt to be considered."

Apologies? The word splashed across Val's first page, the texture of the font conveying his incredulity. *You should apologize to me!*

"For what? You're the one who called me useless." *Weak and useless* had been his exact words.

You're making ME look bad in front of Pamela! The inspector's name received a caress of cursive and curlicue embellishments.

"Help me fix things, then. Tell me how to get Jamie back."

You should have been firmer with him. If you had, we wouldn't be in this predicament.

My fingers curled into his cover. "I don't need an *I told you so*."

When Pamela gets here, I want to talk with her.

"Can you help me?" I gave him a shake. I was practically begging; what more did he want from me?

I need to explain my side of the story. I can't let her think—

I snapped Val shut before he could finish his sentence. Call it childish or unfair, but it beat throwing him into the nearest pile of mud.

Locking him back into his strap, I resumed pacing.

A small sedan parked at the curb next to Summer. Two shining white women sat inside. The passenger's form-hugging glow marked her as an enforcer, and I recognized the driver as Pamela, but I gawked at her transformed soul. The last time I'd seen her, her soul had bulged around her like a deformed cloud, but now it had solidified into the sharp corners and lines of a warden's soul. Based on its shape, it looked as if her soul encompassed my region and Isabel's old region, plus the regions to the north and south, all of it compacted into a dense, powerful shimmer barely larger than the inspector.

Pamela swung open her door and marched to me. The other woman got out and greeted Summer.

"Hey, Grace," Summer said softly. Both enforcers remained near the car, but they didn't take their eyes off me and Pamela, no doubt eager for the show.

I recognized the enforcer's name, though I'd never met her. Grace had been an enforcer under Isabel and had since been cleared of all suspicion. I'd been relieved to hear the verdict of her trial since she watched over Lincoln, my parents' hometown. I would have loved to talk with Grace and beg for preferential treatment for my folks, but

Pamela filled my vision as she bore down on me like she planned to run me over.

"When did you last see the pooka?" she demanded, her British accent doing nothing to soften her tone.

"A few hours ago."

Pamela's lips pinched together; then she said, "Form a net. I need to test your purity."

I'd been expecting this, and I bubbled my soul over my heart on the first try. I'd had plenty of practice making nets since my first purity test, and my soul swelled a foot above my bulky clothing. Pamela thrust her hands into the bubble, her *lux lucis* hitting mine like a punch. I grunted but took pride in not flinching. With impersonal detachment, Pamela drove her energy into me, cycling through my soul, sampling and judging it. Gritting my teeth, I held my ground until Pamela stepped back and lowered her hands.

"You're clean."

"I know," I snapped, rubbing my arms to dispel the creeping, crawling sensation of my soul moving beneath my skin.

Pamela held up a thick plastic band with a small, hard box attached to it.

"This is a tracker," she said. "It will tell me where you are at all times."

"You're kidding, right?" I'd seen these types of anklets on TV shows. They were the type worn by criminals on house arrest. This had to be some sort of bad inspector joke.

"Take off a boot. I suggest your left."

"You're serious?" I squeaked.

"I can't be at your side all the time. The pooka has proven he can mask his movements. I won't let him hide yours, too. No matter what happens, I want to know where you are."

I crossed my arms. "I have a phone."

"And when the pooka returns, you'll use it to call me."

"And when you need to know where I am, you can call," I said, mimicking her falsely patient tone.

"Your pooka is volatile. No matter what happens to you, this"—she waved the tracker in my face—"will tell me where you are."

I narrowed my eyes, reasoning it out. She wanted a way to track me in case Jamie turned dark and took me with him. She believed I was that easily corrupted. *Weak and useless* seemed to be the going opinion of me.

Pamela snapped her fingers rapidly. "Every second you stand there, a tyv is defiling this region with more eggs. Pick an ankle. We're wasting time."

I bent and unzipped my left boot, slapped my sock-clad foot to the icy pavement, and rolled up my pants. Indignation boiled inside me thick enough to steam the air around me. Pamela squatted and attached the tracker over my sock. Heavy and cold, it squeezed around my leg like a shackle.

"Where you go, this goes, shower included. The only way to remove this is with a special key that I keep in my possession or by cutting it off. Don't cut it off. If you do, I will receive immediate notification and assume you've been compromised." She straightened to look me in the eye. "The moment the pooka is back in your control, call me. Until then, I'll be checking in on you regularly."

I bent to roll my pant leg down, my shoulders weighted with the avid stares of my fellow enforcers. Should we gather more CIA personnel to witness my humiliation? It could be a live-action cautionary lesson. *See, this is what happens when you fail to control your pooka. You get treated like a felon.*

I squeezed the sides of my boot around the tracker and yanked the zipper up. It stuck on the first try; on the second, the zipper flashed over the bulge of the anklet and bit into the flesh of my thumb pad. I flinched and shook the pain from my hand, then finished zipping the boot. I flexed my foot, and the unforgiving tracking box grated against my ankle bone.

Now the night was complete.

Pamela trotted down the street to her car and pulled a folded map from the door panel. Laying it across the hood, she tapped her finger against a section near the far left.

"We don't know where the tyv is, but we have a general area," she said. "Summer and Madison, you'll start here and work your way toward Festersen Park. Grace and I will start at the opposite end of this subdivision and work our way toward you. I've got a clan of prajurit sweeping the rooftops here and here." She tapped two locations on the map.

Summer and Grace circled the car to stand beside Pamela, but I remained next to the inflated Santa. I'd come out of my skin if I got close to any of the women. Pamela had broadcasted her distrust in me in the most public way possible, short of carting me off in handcuffs, and now she had the audacity to expect me to pretend nothing had happened and act like a team player. Summer and Grace were no better. They'd watched me be treated like a criminal, and their lack of protests said loud and clear they didn't trust me, either.

I wanted to scream. Not a single one of them could have controlled Jamie. He was too strong. He wasn't like us: He wasn't human and he wasn't pure *lux lucis*. He didn't fit into our rules, and he didn't have to follow them if he didn't want to. Not even perfect Inspector Pamela would have done any better in my shoes.

But I didn't say a word, because anything that came out of my mouth would sound like nothing more than delusions and excuses.

"If you find the tyv first, call. If you stop seeing drones, call." Pamela folded the map and opened the driver's door. She put one foot into the car, then paused. "Stay vigilant."

She spoke to all of us, but her eyes rested on Summer.

That's right, Summer. You'd better watch me for the inspector. I might spontaneously go rogue, and she's counting on you to take me down when I do.

Pamela and Grace left. I limped after Summer, my anger simmering so hot it blinded me.

18

IT'S OKAY IF YOU DISAGREE WITH ME; I CAN'T FORCE YOU TO BE RIGHT

Niko called before we'd cleaned the next block of its smattering of drones. I'd left his ringtone as Justin Timberlake's "SexyBack," and the first hard beat made me jump. The next made me want to smash the phone beneath my boot. I didn't need to be psychic to guess why the region's optivus aegis was phoning me.

"Brad told me you lost Jamie," Niko said when I answered.

"Did he? How nice of him to spread the word."

"Madison, this isn't good. For either of you."

"You think I don't know that? I've got a freaking tracking bracelet on my ankle courtesy of the inspector. I think things are beyond *not good*."

Niko remained silent for half a beat, then said, "Pamela gave you a tracker? That was smart."

I'd expected indignation from him. I'd expected surprise. I'd expected him to get off the phone, call the inspector, and berate her for being way out of line. I hadn't expected him to agree with her actions. I thought Niko had a higher opinion of me.

At least I knew now where we stood.

"I'm so glad you approve." My tone should have left frostbite on my tongue.

"She's making sure you're protected."

Keep telling yourself that. "Why did you call, Niko?"

"I wanted to make sure you understood the seriousness of your situation."

"I'm the woman wearing the anklet. I'm aware of the seriousness."

"Brad was obligated to tell me," Niko continued as if I hadn't spoken. "If I weren't already in the area, I'd be headed this way. A loose pooka is a dangerous pooka. You need to regain control. The longer he's on his own, the more likely he'll go dark and I'll be forced to take action."

My insides caved and the phone squeaked in my fist. *Take action.* What a lovely euphemism for *murder.* Jamie had been out of my sight for only a few hours, and already Niko threatened to kill him.

"Good-bye, Niko."

The cuff of pain circling my left ankle dulled, overpowered by the fiery cramp of my neck muscles. Even after hours of searching the skies for Jamie, the bitter mix of hope and desperation prevented me from looking down for more than ten seconds at a time.

The tyv remained elusive, which made every minute more frustrating than the last. For the tyv to be hidden from Brad's and Pamela's sensitive soul radar, she had to be cloaked by Jamie. Since the tether between us forced Jamie to stick close, we should have encountered the tyv eventually. For her to remain out of sight despite all four of us running a nonstop grid through the subdivision meant Jamie had to be herding her away from us, choosing again and again to protect the soul-devouring tyv rather than return to me. My emotions swung between heartsickness and fury, the erratic pendulum inspiring nauseous cramps in my gut.

Pamela dismissed me after midnight, well after the number of drone sightings had dwindled to fewer than two an hour. She and the other enforcers would remain behind in the hopes that with my departure, Jamie would be forced to uncloak the tyv. I couldn't tell if Summer resented me for getting to cut out early or if her contemptuous expression had frozen on her face. I was beyond caring.

They all walked me back to my car—not even a disgraced enforcer could be left unaccompanied while a tyv was on the loose—and I drove home on autopilot. I called Brad when I pulled into my parking space and cut the engine.

"Anything?" I asked.

"Nothing. It's too early for the tyv to have gone to ground. Jamie must have followed you with the tyv in tow."

I rested my forehead against the steering wheel. "Should I look for her? Is Pamela on her way?"

"No. We've decided to send everyone home, but you're on call. If the tyv turns up, I'll notify you. Until then, let the pooka wear himself out while you get some rest."

How? How could I possibly rest while Jamie was out there terrorizing my region, upset with me?

I clung to the weak hope that he would be waiting for me upstairs, but no pooka graced my welcome mat, and when I turned the key in the lock, I swung my door open into a dark apartment. A heavy thump followed by a series of increasingly loud meows announced Mr. Bond. I flicked on the light, and he and Dame Zilla blinked at me. I shut the door behind me and leaned against it, the heaviness of my heart sapping my will to move.

Her belly low to the ground, Dame Zilla crept up on the pile of muddy pants and towels I dumped at my feet. Mr. Bond ignored the laundry to twine through my legs, scolding me at top volume for letting his food bowl get empty. I took two steps into the apartment, unclipped the knife from my belt, and collapsed, flopping onto my back. My ankle throbbed at the change of pressure against the tracker, but the rest of my body welcomed being prone. Mr. Bond switched tactics, stomping across my stomach and settling on my chest. I wheezed in a breath and adjusted the soul breaker between us so it wasn't jabbing my breasts; then I rested a hand on my cat's soft back and closed my eyes. Mr. Bond started purring.

The serene moment lasted less than five seconds before Mr. Bond yowled and launched from my stomach. I gasped for air and sat up. Dame Zilla stalked from the towels to my feet. She sniffed the soles of my boots, then wrapped her tiny body around a boot and sank teeth and claws into the leather.

"Hey!" I shooed her away. She ran to the dirty towels, grabbed a hunk with her front legs, and disemboweled them with her back, her stubby tail slashing.

If Jamie had been there, he would have laughed and used my phone to take pictures.

Sighing, I removed my boots. The tracker hung loose enough around my ankle to fit my finger through the gap, and I savored a moment of holding the heavy band away from my bruised flesh. The left boot was ruined, the leather permanently stretched at the ankle in the square form of the tracker.

After allaying Mr. Bond's fear of starvation and plopping both wet and dry food down for him and Dame Zilla, I tossed everything I had on plus the second set of dirty pants and the muddy towels into the washing machine. Then I walked naked down the hall to the shower. No pooka meant no modesty necessary.

It didn't feel as freeing as I'd hoped.

I stood in the tub for several minutes after the water had warmed, holding the tracker under the gushing spout, hoping to drown it. An ugly bruise circled my ankle beneath it like a shadow. A dozen more purpling bruises marred my thighs and ankles, and my side had a fist-size black smudge below my ribs, though I didn't remember injuring myself there.

Good thing Alex and I aren't at the seeing-each-other-naked stage. Clumsiness could explain away only so much.

After showering, I took one look at my yellow polka dot and pink bunny pajamas—the ones Jamie had insisted on getting for himself, too —then dressed in sweats and a frayed UC Davis T-shirt. I switched the laundry to the dryer and forced myself to eat, alternating between staring at the door, willing Jamie to knock, and pretending the door and pooka didn't exist. Mr. Bond hid beneath the table, lying like a loaf across my slippered foot, while Dame Zilla tore around the front room, chasing a fake mouse covered in feathers.

Despite the late hour, I didn't want to turn out the lights and be forced to confront my emotions alone in the dark. Instead, I laid out an old towel on the table and placed Val on top. Using a damp cloth, I wiped mud and grit from his cover, then buffed his leather jacket with a water-resistant polish. I took my time caring for several deep scratches, but I didn't say anything while I worked. I tried not to even think. Every time I let my mind wander, it circled back to Jamie, the tyv, my deteriorating region, Jamie, the damn tracker on my leg. Jamie.

Finally, I opened Val. "What can you tell me about getting Jamie back?"

You didn't let me speak to Pamela! His words filled the page, every spiked letter loaded with indignation.

"I didn't think you'd want me to." I reassembled the polishing kit and folded the towel, wiping my fingers off on a clean corner. If I kept my motions calm, maybe I could fool my emotions to follow suit. My gaze slid to the door, and I jerked it back to the book.

I TOLD you I wanted to explain my side of the story.

"But then I'd have to explain mine. Like how you're supposed to help me, but all you do is complain. And how you put in the minimal effort possible and get in a huff when I ask for more. And how you let your prejudices obstruct your ability to do your job, and how if you'd explained how to handle Jamie earlier, I'd still have him under control. For the sake of complete honesty, I might have needed to include how you enjoy kicking your partner when she's down and playing the blame game."

Words started to form on his page, but I didn't read them and I didn't stop talking.

"But then I thought about how much you want Pamela to like you, whereas you only want me to be your caretaker, pamper you, carry you everywhere, and make sure you aren't bored. So I thought it best to hold off on chatting with the inspector—for the sake of your reputation, of course."

A flurry of words appeared and erased faster than I could follow, which I took to be Val's equivalent of sputtering.

"Well, you're all cleaned up and it's time for bed, so let's get you set up with your next audiobook. Good night, Val."

I closed him gently, though my fingers trembled with suppressed anger. Maybe I should give him to Pamela. Permanently. I could let the two of them bask in each other's stunning personalities.

The conversation had weakened the numb buffer between me and my emotions, and after I settled Val in the closet, the day's disappointments scrolled unbidden through my thoughts. Val's selfishness. Summer's holier-than-thou attitude. Ignorantly involving Brad in the prajurit peace talks. Jamie's behavior during my date with Alex. The tyv loose in my region. Jamie running away. The tracker on my ankle. Jamie's absence.

My whole body vibrated with the urge to pummel something, and I watched enviously when Mr. Bond threw himself against his scratching post, wrapping his pudgy body around a leg and pummeling it with his back claws. I needed a human version of a scratching post.

Flopping into my gray recliner, I stared at the door with eyes gritty from fatigue. My body was spent, but my mind refused to turn off. After an hour, when Jamie still hadn't appeared, I stuffed a spare key under the mat, left the front room light on, and went to bed.

A soft, snuffling sound woke me from a deep, dreamless sleep. I blinked at the dark wall, confused. The front room light. I'd left it on, but now the apartment sat in shadows.

Groggily, I rolled over. The tracker cut into my bruised ankle and I kicked out in annoyance, freezing a second later when I spotted Jamie. He stood in the center of the bedroom in his Great Dane shape, his body a dark outline in a dark room.

"Jamie." Relief, raw and unfiltered, filled my voice.

Jamie raised his head, and his golden eyes glowed in the faint light. He took a tentative step closer to the bed. I stretched my hand out to him and rested it on his forehead. Contentment flowed through me, unwinding tension embedded deeper than muscle.

I smiled. Jamie licked my hand, turned in a circle, and curled up as close to the bed as he could get. I wriggled to the edge of the mattress and dropped a hand over the side to rest on his back. We exhaled in unison, and I closed my eyes.

I had so many things to say to him, but the spell of the darkness, the bond singing harmoniously inside me, and his warm side beneath my hand stole the words from me.

The bed shook as Mr. Bond landed on it. He settled against my feet, his upper body propped across my soles. Dame Zilla curled into the crook of Jamie's leg, purring as loud as a mountain lion, lolling me back to sleep.

When I woke, Jamie was gone.

19

CAUGHT BETWEEN A STRONG MIND
AND A FRAGILE HEART

The snarled bond throbbing in the back of my head informed me of Jamie's absence before I opened my eyes. Squinting against the sunlight, I stared at his empty bed and tucked my dangling hand under the covers. For one sleepy moment, I wished he'd woken me and taken me with him. Then the weight of heartache, resentment, and anger settled once more on my chest, and I berated myself for doing nothing to stop him from leaving.

A heavy pounding rattled the front door. Throwing back the covers, I lurched out of bed, waking a chorus of protests from the muscles of my body. The tracker bounced against my bruised ankle, eliciting a throb of pain. Groaning, I hobbled across Jamie's bed, the fluffy blanket cold beneath my bare feet.

Sitting as tall as possible, with his ears stretched to elongated points, Mr. Bond stared at the front door from the safety of the kitchen, his blue eyes saucer round. Dame Zilla crouched behind him, poised to escape down the hall. When I stomped past, she hunkered lower, ears flicking in alarm. Given their nervousness, the knocking had been going on for some time.

I glanced from the crystal blue sky outside my third-story window to the clock on the microwave: 7:31. I'd had less than four hours of sleep.

A fist pounded on my door again, loud enough to wake neighbors. I

peered through the peephole. Pamela's white-blond head with its shock
of bright auburn over her temple filled the fish-eye viewer. When she
leaned back, her face telegraphed impatience.

I hesitated, then threw back the dead bolt and tugged the door open
as I blinked to Primordium. Pamela burst into my apartment, icy air
billowing over my bare toes in her wake. The inspector gleamed with a
radiant strength reminiscent of Niko, though the jagged edges of her
region-defined soul looked painful.

"Is the pooka here?" she demanded.

"No." The heater kicked on and I shut the door.

Pamela gave me a once-over, then swept the apartment with the
same critical stare. I glanced around, seeing the empty cat food bowls,
the cat toys, yesterday's mail strewn in front of the TV, a forest of
plants shoved around the edges of the living room, and not a single
drop of *atrum*.

Thank you, Jamie.

Dame Zilla decided she had been brave enough, and she slunk
down the hall and disappeared into the bedroom. Always an eager host,
Mr. Bond swung his tail up and sauntered up to Pamela to sniff her
pants. The inspector bent and sank her fingers into his thick coat,
sending a discreet trickle of *lux lucis* into Mr. Bond. He flopped onto
her foot, purring.

"What did you just do to my cat?"

"Wait here." Pamela straightened and marched down the hall.

I ran my hands over Mr. Bond. If I knew Pamela, that'd been some
sort of test, but Mr. Bond didn't look any worse for it. Giving him one
last pat, I hurried to catch up with Pamela. She might be a high-and-
mighty inspector, but this was my home, and I'd go where I chose in it.

Pamela stopped just inside the bedroom, and her eyes lingered on
the dog bed taking up most of the floor space. The folds of my cotton
sheets held lingering traces of *lux lucis*, but Jamie's bed looked charcoal gray in Primordium, free of a single speck of *lux lucis*—or *atrum*.
I let out a breath I hadn't known I'd been holding.

"Make a net over your heart," Pamela said, turning to face me.

My spine snapped straight and I crossed my arms over my chest.
"Right now?" Hadn't this wake-up been intrusive enough?

"The pooka was here. I felt him leave not twenty minutes ago. And
yet here you are in your pajamas, looking like you slept through it all."

I tugged self-consciously at my holey shirt, but my embarrassment died when I caught sight of the tracker protruding from the hem of my sweats.

"So, yes, right now," Pamela said, squaring off in front of me.

I wanted to protest again, but I *had* let Jamie waltz through here. In my drowsy state last night, I hadn't checked his soul before I touched him—or any time thereafter. Spreading my fingers, I examined the backs of my hand and my buttery soul. I looked clean, but what if Jamie had done something to me on a deeper level than I could see? Yesterday morning, I would have instantly denied the thought, but after he'd threatened Alex, left me to the hounds, and helped a tyv escape, I could no longer afford the luxury of trusting Jamie.

My hands curled into fists, and I dropped them to my sides. I gave my soul a push, centering the net above my heart. Pamela inserted her hands, cycling her *lux lucis* through mine, and my empty stomach roiled.

"You're clean."

I retreated to the front room, keeping my back to Pamela until my relief no longer showed on my face. Blinking to normal sight, I turned on a light and petted Mr. Bond.

"What happened with the pooka?" Pamela asked. She'd followed me, detouring to check the laundry room before planting herself between me and the front door. Did she think I'd make a run for it? Barefoot?

"Nothing happened. He came home after I was asleep."

"What time?"

"I don't know. After three?" I sidled around the dining room table and sat, stacking one cold foot atop the other. Putting the table between me and the inspector helped settle my ruffled soul. If I were feeling polite, I would have offered Pamela something to drink, but the purity test had excised my manners.

"What did you do?" Pamela asked.

"We slept." I wouldn't explain the contentment I had experienced when I'd laid my hand on Jamie; the moment had been too private—a shard of peace in an otherwise crappy week. I wouldn't tarnish it by giving it to Pamela to judge, especially since she'd misinterpret it as something nefarious.

"I thought Jamie and I would talk this morning," I added to fill the uncomfortable silence.

"Mmm." She uncrossed her arms and settled in the seat across from me, palms down on the table. Her eyes never left my face, but her expression softened. "I understand this all must be confusing, especially with the bond influencing you. A pooka bond is a double-edged sword. Through it, you can influence the pooka to choose *lux lucis*, but if the pooka goes dark, he can use it to influence you to choose *atrum*. You might not even recognize what's happening; the bond resonates his and your emotions between the two of you, which can muddy the distinction between your desires and the pooka's. More than one enforcer has been led astray by the bond's false feelings of harmony."

Harmony perfectly described what I'd felt last night, the pooka and I in sync for the first time in twenty-four hours. But it didn't mean Jamie had led me astray. It meant we'd taken a breather from our fight. Maybe if Pamela had ever been bonded with a pooka, she would have understood.

"You probably don't think I know what I'm talking about," Pamela said, eerily echoing my thoughts, "but I've seen the aftermath of several pookas who've gone dark and taken their enforcers with them. And Jamie has all the signs of turning evil. It's not pretty when they do."

"I know. He'd have to be . . . stopped." I couldn't make myself say *killed*.

"There's that, but there's also what he'd do to you."

The compassion in her tone made me shift uncomfortably in my seat. It'd been easy to brush off her warnings last night when we'd both been angry, but her concern proved harder to ignore.

"He has the ability to flood you with *atrum*, and if you are in any way complicit, it *will* change you. We would do everything in our power to save you, but not even extensive rehab always works. If it didn't, you would spend the rest of your life in prison where we could ensure you would never hurt anyone."

Prison? The anklet sat heavy against my leg—a foreshadowing or a warning?

I glanced away from Pamela's knowing green eyes. Had I let the bond sway my thoughts last night? Jamie and I should have talked, at least a little. I should have thought to make him promise to stay with me. Or better yet, I should have made him swear he'd not help the tyv again. Instead, I'd fallen asleep with my hand on his side. It'd felt so right, but . . .

My lips twisted. So much for preserving the memory of last night's peace.

Pamela stood. "Next time, call me the moment he's back. Don't wait."

When she left, I pressed my ear to the door, listening until she reached the ground floor before I reopened the door and checked under the mat. A shiny silver key lay centered beneath it.

Did that mean Jamie planned to return home later or had last night been good-bye?

Heat hit me like an open furnace when I stepped across the threshold of our grungy headquarters. Sweat broke out along my scalp, and I tugged my beanie from my head and stuffed it into my jacket pocket. The scarf followed. Sharon's flat brown eyes tracked me. I gave her a grimace, which was the closest I could muster to a real smile. If she noticed the difference, she didn't give any indication.

Stripping off layers, I threaded through the plastic tables. Only Will sat at his desk, and his attention was riveted on his computer, the soft click of keyboard keys barely audible over the rattling hum of the overbearing heater. I hadn't seen him or his sister Joy since we'd relocated offices, but their absences were commonplace. Though Will looked like an attractive human guy somewhere in his late twenties, his friendly face unlined by wrinkles, and his brown hair perpetually mussed, one look at his soul identified him as Illuminea. In Primordium, he radiated with a sun's healing light, so warm and inviting that I'd had to stop myself more than once from curling up against him to soak in his rays. From what I'd been told, Illuminea were beings of pure *lux lucis* who had chosen to take human form to better influence the world. I had a hard time wrapping my brain around it, but I didn't doubt it. Will exuded the calm, caring energy one might expect from the love child of a charismatic Buddha and an ancient redwood. In other words, he personified walking, talking *lux lucis*.

I tossed a "hi" in his direction and received a glancing smile in return, but nevertheless felt warmed and welcomed. Such was the power of an Illuminea—and the reason I avoided him: He didn't deserve to be subjected to my foul mood.

Brad looked up from his computer, his expression registering mild surprise when I stomped into his tiny office.

"No, I don't know where Jamie is," I said before he could ask.

Brad closed his mouth and swiveled away from his computer to face me. I plopped into the folding chair on my side of the desk, and it groaned as if criticizing my weight. In my head, I broke the chair in half and fed it to a cannibalistic cushioned chair that didn't have such a judgmental attitude.

"The inspector put a tracker on me," I spat.

"For your safety."

His soft words abraded already-raw nerves. My left leg jittered. I considered and dismissed getting into an argument about the tracker. The inspector outranked Brad; if she wanted the tracker on me, the tracker would stay.

"Jamie came by my apartment last night. He's gone again already." I threw the words at my boss like a challenge, the opening salvo to the argument I wanted to have. If he started yelling at me, I could yell back, and I badly wanted to yell at someone.

"You're looking for him?" Brad asked.

"As much good as it's going to do me." My leg bounced up and down, and I shoved to my feet, pacing two steps before running out of room. "Why is it so hot in here?"

"I had to leave the back door propped open for the prajurit. Peace talks begin in a few minutes."

I waited for him to get angry about the talks, but his uncharacteristic serenity remained unruffled. Irritated, I slammed the folding chair closed and shoved it against the wall to give myself more room to pace.

"Where's Niko?" If he was already tracking Jamie—if he had any way *of* tracking Jamie—I deserved to know.

"Right now, probably sleeping. He helped the enforcers in Auburn bring down two sjel tyver last night."

"Two?" People were *killing* the tyver in their regions while I couldn't even *find* the one in mine? Guilt piled on top of agitation. The urge to act, to fight or hunt or do something—*anything*—productive built inside me like a jack-in-the-box spring, ticking, ticking, ticking, set to explode without warning.

When I spun to face Brad, I caught a flicker of compassion in his eyes, and it tightened the coil of anger in my gut.

"I can't feel Jamie or the tether. I don't want to run around chasing my tail all day looking for him. He's faster than me. He doesn't have to let me catch him; he just has to stay close."

"True," Brad agreed.

I waited for his instructions. He was my boss. He loved to tell me what to do. When I was smart, I even listened.

"Well?" I demanded.

"Well what?"

"Tell me what to do!" The words roared from me. If we'd been in a cartoon, Brad would have been blown through the wall behind him, and his tuft of friar hair would have smoldered.

Instead, the biggest reaction I got was the appearance of the squiggly vein in Brad's temple, a precursor to anger but nothing close to the real thing. He smoothed a paper on his desk, not quite meeting my eyes, not quite looking away. I threw up my hands and resumed pacing.

"Sorry," I mumbled. "I don't know what's wrong with me." *Other than everything.*

"I can't tell you what to do. You're the one linked to Jamie. What do you think would bring him to you?"

"Here. I thought the familiarity of the office might make him show up, but that seems stupid now." Why would he want to surround himself with *lux lucis* people? Especially now. "I thought if he felt comfortable somewhere, he might stay long enough to talk, and we could . . . The parking garage!" I smacked myself on the forehead. I should have thought of his birthplace first.

"Did the handbook have any ideas what the pooka's fourth form might be?" Brad asked, interrupting my inner monologue of reproach.

"He's still mulling it over." That sounded better than admitting to our passive-aggressive fight.

I stalked out of Brad's office before he could ask a follow-up question.

"Hey, Madison. I heard about Jamie," Will said, cutting short my sprint for the front door.

"Is there anyone who hasn't?" I snapped. When I met Will's concerned expression, I heaved a sigh and apologized.

"How are you holding up?" Will asked.

I laughed. The sound edged close to tears, so I cut it off and shook my head. Giving voice to my internal turmoil wouldn't help. I didn't remember moving, but somehow I stood next to Will. Not too close, and with my hands to myself, keeping my metaphysical soul-bathing discreet. Go me.

"What are you working on?" I asked.

"My favorite thing: the office budget. Whoever invented Excel is my hero," Will said without a drop of sarcasm.

I peered over his shoulder at a chart filled with alarming red numbers and a lot of negative symbols. "That doesn't look good."

"We've had more expenses lately than normal," Will agreed.

I flinched at the offhand accusation, though I knew he hadn't meant it as one. Pretty much everything wrong that fell under the heading "lately" could be blamed on me.

"The destruction of our headquarters really set us back," Will continued. "Then the expansion of our region brought a lot of extra expenditures we hadn't budgeted for. But we've already got a solution. Joy and I have declined this month's salary, and I'm looking into other discretionary expenses we can defer. The region will prevail."

Other discretionary expenses? Alarm spiked through me. I hoped he didn't consider *my* salary elective.

"Um, how exactly does this office get funded?" I probably should have thought to ask the question earlier, but I'd been busy with a demon and a pooka and a region that went up in flames one week and froze solid the next. I decided to cut myself a little slack.

Will wriggled in his seat like a happy puppy. "It's all rather fascinating. I like to think of the CIA financial system as a series of nesting dolls, each one snuggled inside the next. It starts at the federal level . . . No, it's bigger than that, but I'm rusty on the global structure. At those heights, it changes from nesting dolls to something more like a series of fish that take turns swallowing each other. Or maybe it's more like an endlessly folding blanket; sometimes it starts from the right and covers the left and sometimes it folds diagonally . . ."

My eyes glazed over, but calculating how long it'd take me to recover from a month without pay snapped me back to the moment.

"I mean," I interrupted, "how do we make *more* money? What do we need to do for our region to change all those red numbers to black?"

Pink flushed Will's cheeks, but he made embarrassed look attractive. "I was rambling, wasn't I? I get so excited about the complexities of economics, I get carried away."

Especially with the metaphors. I kept the comment to myself and urged him to continue.

"To get out of the red, we need to get our region out of limbo. Best-case scenario, Pamela approves of us taking over the larger region. When she does, the expansion would come with an increased budget and all our financial problems would be solved."

"Just for fun, let's say Pamela denies us the expansion." I shifted my weight to my right foot, feeling the tracker loosen around my left ankle. I tried and failed to picture a future in which Pamela decided I was qualified to handle more territory. "Would we still . . . Would you go back to getting a paycheck?"

"Probably not for the next three or four months. Oh, don't look so worried. I pay next to nothing for my place and my friends are more than happy to keep me fed. And don't worry about yourself, either. Your salary is secure. However, Brad ran through his savings when he bought the handbook." Will gestured to Val resting against my hip. "So I suspect we'd get to call this place home for another few years."

We both surveyed the grungy office. I couldn't help but feel as if our new headquarters were a metaphor for the whole region—soiled and falling apart—and I was the root of the problem. Fresh guilt heaped on top of my internal avalanche of failure and frustration.

The front door whooshed open with a broken-bell *clank* and Sam sauntered in.

"Yo, yo, yo, Will-My-Man! And Mad-Dog Madison, in the flesh." He tossed a gesture in our direction, a cross between a wave and a finger point, and strutted past Sharon.

The receptionist's body remained glued in place, but her head swiveled to track the swaggering teen. The quality of her stillness altered, and beneath her drab polyester pantsuit, I suspected her muscles were primed to pounce. Oblivious, Sam tossed her a wink. He tugged a black beanie from his head, unleashing a riot of carrot-red hair that emphasized the flush on his pale cheeks.

"Oh, Sam, what did you do?" Will asked, his tone caught between horror and pity.

Sam scanned his own body, admiring his brand-new jeans and jacket. Slicking his hair back with one hand, he looked up through his lashes at me, his expression a masterful and practiced blend of inno-cence and sin. It might have worked better if he hadn't been ten years too young for me. Will received his own version of the look, a cocky-contrite grin topped by wide-eyed innocence.

"I'm just ridin' high on jolly Jesus cheer," Sam said. "It's the Christmas season." He stripped off his jacket to reveal a blue T-shirt so new it still had creases from being folded on a shelf.

I'd never seen Sam in anything remotely new. From what little I knew of his home life, he and his family lived in poverty, or at best, poverty adjacent. He could no more afford that new name-brand jacket than I could a Bentley.

I blinked to Primordium and sucked in a sharp breath.

Thick black *atrum* coated his hands, flaring up his arms to his shoulders in intertwining patterns reminiscent of Celtic knots. More spirals twined up his neck and around his mouth and jaw like the most grotesque facial hair design ever.

Only yesterday, the worst blemish on Sam's soul had been a smattering of soft gray. He would have had to work pretty hard to have acquired that much *atrum* in a day. Or had help.

"How's Jamie?" I asked through numb lips, following my hunch.

Beside me, Will stiffened.

"My boy is goals as fu—" Sam caught himself and gave me a cheeky grin. He dropped his beanie onto the desk in front of Will's and took an obnoxious amount of time arranging his jacket across the back of the chair, lingering to admire it when he finished.

"You two were together this morning?" I asked, drawing his attention away from the jacket I suspected he'd "purchased" with a five-finger discount and the help of a pooka.

"Sure, sure. We hung out. Had some fun."

"What kind of 'fun'?"

"The kind that makes me lit." Sam pointed to his ear-to-ear grin.

I fought to control my revulsion as *atrum* melted from his mouth down his chin. "Where is Jamie now?"

"Why you sussin'?"

"Just answer the question." In English, preferably. I understood about half of what came out of the teen's mouth.

Sam crossed his arms, his attempt to look tough ruined when he admired his own biceps encased in soft, never-washed cotton. "He said he had to fly."

I bet he did.

"I figured he'd be back with you. Aren't you two, like—" Sam wriggled his eyebrows, his smile shining again at full strength. "I get it. I totally ship you guys."

My life was complete. Sam approved of me and Jamie and whatever that caterpillar mating dance his eyebrows had implied about our relationship.

I crossed my arms, ignoring the gouge of the soul breaker into my ribs and forearms. Part of me wanted to shake Sam until some intelligence broke free inside his brain, but mostly I wanted to give the boy a hug and apologize. The point of Sam being in our headquarters, under the protection of the CIA, was to wean him off his addiction to my *lux lucis* infusions, not so he could become Jamie's pawn. Sam deserved better.

Brad marched from his office but stopped after two steps. He took in Sam, turned to glare at the propped-open back door, and then barked, "Will, clean him up and get him out of here. Pamela's on her way in."

A jolt of dread zinged down my spine, and I shuffled in place, checking the exits.

"Should I wait?" I asked.

"Only if you want to." Brad took one last look out the front windows to the parking lot, then retreated into his office.

I bolted for the front door and jogged to my car. Will would fix Sam's soul. He didn't need me to hang around to watch.

Peeling out of the parking spot before I'd finished buckling my seat belt, I gunned it for the mall. If I didn't find Jamie at the parking garage, I was screwed and so was my region.

20

INCONCEIVABLE!

Trolling for a parking spot at the crowded mall ate through my threadbare patience. I didn't have time to waste; Jamie needed to be brought back in line yesterday. As if helping out the tyv wasn't awful enough, Sam's condition this morning confirmed that Jamie spending time away from me only made him worse.

I wedged my Civic between two Priuses in a spot on the edge of the mall's grounds and marched past idling traffic, joining the flow of people streaming toward the massive shopping complex. A long outdoor courtyard jutted from the center of the mall, funneling patrons past loud-mouthed teens skating on the mini ice rink and toddlers shrieking on the all-weather jungle gym. While everyone else squeezed through the bank of glass doors into the welcoming jaws of Tiffany & Co., Burberry, and Louis Vuitton, I veered from the crush, stomping down an empty walkway between two expensive restaurants that wouldn't open until lunch.

The narrow brick walls muffled the irritating cacophony of the courtyard, and I breathed a sigh of relief, my breath frosting the air. Ice coated the right side of the cobblestone walkway, snaking frozen tendrils toward the opposite wall. I stuffed my hands deeper into my coat pockets and watched my step, not stopping until I reached the chain-link fence blocking the far end of the walkway.

Six stories of a half-built parking garage towered on the other side of the fence. The last time I'd seen the garage, the fence had been closer to the steel beams, the whole framework had been wrapped in enormous sheets of plastic, and a handful of CIA employees had stood witness to Jamie's birth and our bonding. Today, it bustled with machinery and construction workers in bright yellow vests and matching hard hats.

My hands fisted in my pockets as I took in the scene. A giant crater at the center of the garage floor had once marked Jamie's underground location, but it had been filled in and sealed with a thick concrete slab. Jamie had spent years—decades—under that very spot, incubating in the burgeoning *atrum* and *lux lucis* supplied by Roseville's expanding population, and in a few sweeps of a bulldozer, all signs of his birth had been erased as if it had never happened.

The nostalgic yearning to re-create a literal hole in the ground ate at my stomach with an almost physical pain.

Hello, bond.

A scuffle of a foot against the cobblestones behind me echoed against the walls, pulling me around. Jamie stopped halfway between me and the courtyard behind him. He'd arrived in human form, his glossy black hair falling across his forehead to shadow his golden eyes. A new coat—wool, black, double-breasted—hugged his body. He'd paired it with pale jeans and bright red sneakers. My pooka had style, all of it stolen.

The bond roared to life, pulling me two steps toward him before I regained control. I dug my fingernails into my palms, using the pain to override a wild surge of protectiveness, telling myself he was dangerous and in need of a reprimand, not a hug. It didn't work. Holding myself still and separate from Jamie hurt my heart—but not as much as the wariness in his expression.

"Hey," I said.

"Hey."

"I'd hoped I'd find you here." I hadn't expected him to appear human. The drive from the office to the mall exceeded our tether range, and to keep up, he would have had to fly. He'd never been able to retain his clothes through a change before, so how had he shown up dressed?

Jamie walked past me to the fence, hooking his fingers through the links and staring at the place of his origin. His expression remained closed, but the bond had given me a good idea how the sight would make him feel. I had to cross my arms to prevent myself from reaching out to touch him.

I'd been angry when I arrived, but the only emotion I felt now was the need to reassure Jamie that everything would be okay and I'd protect him.

You want to coddle him, Pamela's voice whispered in my head.

How much of my feelings were the bond and how much was me?

"I want you to come back with me," I said.

Jamie turned his head to look at me, his expression closed. I blinked to Primordium for insight into his emotions. The dual energies of his soul shifted and reshaped beneath his skin like a kaleidoscope, spinning fast and irregular.

"I'm afraid," I continued. "For you; for me. I want you to be safe, and I can't protect you when you're not with me."

"I'm doing fine on my own."

I shook my head. "I don't want 'fine' for you. I want so much more."

Jamie turned to face me fully, arms limp at his sides, eyes clouded.

"Come home with me. We can sort this out between us and fix the bad decisions you've made."

He stiffened. I'd said the wrong thing.

"You only think I've made bad decisions because I'm not doing exactly what you want."

"You're helping the tyv. The same tyv that would love to eat my soul and leave me comatose or dead." My earlier anger broke through the bond's suppressive strength, but I tried not to let it show. "Explain to me how that isn't a bad decision."

"I'm going where I'm wanted."

"What does that mean? I want you. It's you and me, tethered together, through good and bad, not you and a tyv. I'm here to guide you and help you be a good pooka. Doesn't my advice matter?"

Jamie sneered, and I flinched from the foreign expression on his face.

"*Your* advice? Don't you mean Pamela's?" Cynicism warped his voice into a stranger's.

"She knows what she's talking about. She's worked alongside a pooka before. She knows the right way to—"

"She doesn't know *me*." Jamie jabbed a finger into his chest. His soul frizzed from his body like static-charged cat hair.

I didn't back up, but I modified my tone, stripping away the anger so he could hear my sincerity. "Pamela knows what's right. I just want you to be a good pooka, and she can help."

"You don't want me. You want something that looks like me on the outside but not on the inside. You want a happy pretend-Jamie who will follow you around like a pet *Illuminea*." He spat out the word like an insult. "You don't even like me."

"That's a lie!"

"I know. I see." Jamie tapped his forehead. "You're fixed to one future now. I can give you a prophecy."

A jolt of fear rooted me in place. He'd said he couldn't see a prophecy for me before because we were too closely linked. How much separation had grown between us? Not enough to stop the bond from messing with me, but any weakening of my connection to Jamie scared me.

Jamie glanced down the alley to the construction site. When he looked back, the sorrow in his eyes unlocked my muscles, but he spoke before I could.

"The next time we meet, one of us will die. You will be the one to choose who lives."

Goose bumps raced down my body. I could see it in his eyes: He believed he spoke the truth.

"That can't be right." I reached for him when he turned away.

"Stay away from me," he snarled.

Atrum swelled in his palm, and he hurled the energy at me. Too dumbfounded to dodge, I took the brunt of it in the stomach. The chill of evil coating my soul stole my breath, and I stumbled backward, staring at my blackened chest in disbelief. Wild-eyed, I jerked around, seeing *atrum* splashed ten feet in every direction. Sputtering in shock and indignation, I spun back to Jamie, but he hadn't waited for me to recover. Shoulders hunched, he strode around the corner and didn't look back.

Jamie had attacked me.

My heart cracked inside my chest and I crumpled. The soul breaker swung forward, smacking against my forehead. The collision rang through my brain, the pain shattering my anguish-stricken shock. Swallowing a sob, I straightened and flared *lux lucis* through my chest, stomach, and thighs. The *atrum* burned away with startling ease, and my front flared beacon-bright before I regained control. Suspicious, I turned and ran a finger through the black smut on the wall, effortlessly tracing a clean line through the darkness.

Jamie hadn't been trying to hurt me; he'd used the *atrum* as a diversion so he could escape. The realization settled a soothing patch over my broken heart. His betrayal still hurt, and we were further from making amends than before, but he hadn't declared war on me. All hope wasn't yet lost.

I considered leaving the *atrum* and chasing after Jamie. He didn't have more than a minute head start on me, and if he remained human, I stood a chance of catching him.

The *atrum* made the decision for me when it bubbled from the wall, swelling into the shape of a chinchilla. The imp opened glossy black eyes, spotted me, and leapt from the vertical surface to sink its fangs into my shoulder. Light coat or not, the *atrum* couldn't be ignored. Left unchecked, it would fester into much stronger and worse evils.

My phone buzzed in my pocket, playing the opening chords to "Sweet Home Alabama." I dug it out with cold-numb fingers even as I killed the imp with a pulse of energy. After clearing my throat to make sure my voice sounded normal, I crouched at the rim of the *atrum* puddle and answered the phone.

"Hi, Mom."

"Hi, Madison. How are you? My mom senses are tingling."

If her "mom senses" weren't wrong as often as they were right, I might have been shocked by the timeliness of her call. "I'm good, Mom. Fine."

"You don't sound fine."

"I'm just tired." I planted a hand on the freezing cobblestones and rolled *lux lucis* from my fingertips, pleased when the rush of energy ate through twice as much *atrum* as it normally would. Jamie really hadn't tried very hard.

"You sure it's nothing?"

"I'm sure, Mom." *I'm losing control of one of the most dangerous creatures in my region and simultaneously destroying one of the most important relationships in my life, and I just found out I am either going to be dead soon or Jamie is. No crisis here.*

"In that case, your father and I are coming over."

"Now?" I jerked upright, lost my balance, and fell on my butt. Ice cracked beneath my backside, and I scrambled to the balls of my feet before moisture could soak into my jeans.

"No, we're in Reno, remember? The train doesn't leave for another hour. We're waiting it out at a diner with track-side seating." She paused and sniffed audibly. "Ugh. Everything I brought smells like cigarette smoke. It's in my hair."

"There won't be any smoking allowed on the train," Dad said, his voice faint.

"Right, dear," Mom agreed.

"Just think of how beautiful the return trip will be," he said. "The fresh snow will transform the tracks into glistening ribbons, like endless diamond necklaces strung across the wild mountainside."

I pulled the phone from my ear to stare at it, then pressed it to my face and whispered, "Is Dad okay?"

"He can smell the grease of the tracks," Mom said, her voice droll. "It's messing with his brain. His head will clear when the coffee gets here."

"Has he been like that the whole trip?"

"More or less."

My mom was a saint.

"So we'll see you this evening? We can't wait to meet our new granimal."

"Um . . ." With any luck, I'd be out killing drones and a tyv by the time they got home.

"Did you notice when we went through the mountain tunnels that the engine sounded like the prehistoric roar of a sabre-toothed tiger?" Dad asked. His voice got louder; he was either shouting or he had leaned toward the phone. "I'll make you a recording, Son."

"I think Dad needs a psychiatrist," I said.

"After this trip, we both might," Mom said. "See you tonight. I'll text when we disembark."

"Uh—" But she'd already hung up.

I was still banging the phone against my forehead when it started playing "Hail to the Chief." I shoved another handful of *lux lucis* through the *atrum* before answering.

"What happened?" Brad demanded. "I felt a flare."

"Jamie and I had a fight." I decided to keep the details vague. I recognized Jamie's use of *atrum* as a rebellious diversionary tactic, not an attack, but Brad might not see it that way, and I didn't want to give him any reason to call Niko. "Can you tell me where he went?"

"He's gone again? Sugar sticks on fried Snickers!"

I took that as a no.

"Madison, this can't go on. You need to get control of him or—"

"I know," I said, cutting him off so I wouldn't have to hear the rest of the sentence.

On the other end of the line, several high-pitched voices escalated in volume, the individual words all piled on top of each other and unintelligible.

"This is a peace talk," Brad bellowed, his voice partially muffled. "The first person to draw another's blood forfeits their rights—or their queen's rights—to any territory. Nonnegotiable!"

A flurry of voices swelled in response, then faded. Brad must have walked out of the room.

"How do you plan to find Jamie now?" he asked me.

The next time we meet, one of us will die. I rubbed a cramp in my stomach. "I don't think I can, not unless he wants me to."

"I think you're right. But we may not need him to come to you."

"What do you mean?"

"We just need to keep Jamie from helping the tyv tonight."

"How am I supposed to do that if I can't even get him to talk to me for five minutes?"

"We simply need him too tired to meddle," Brad said. "You need to keep moving. If he's too exhausted to fly, he won't be able to mask the tyv. I'll text you the address of your first destina—"

"Brad Pitt!"

Lestari's sharp, high voice blasted through the speaker, piercing my eardrum, and I jerked the phone from my ear.

"We have reached an agreement," she continued at a volume a carnival barker would envy. "The foul odors of this moldy building are offensive to us all. You will need to make other arrangements for the peace talks."

"I'm glad it took only an hour to come to a consensus about the smell of the room," Brad said, his voice laden with sarcasm. "It bodes well for the negotiations, which will happen here—"

Lestari attempted to interrupt, but he talked right over her.

"I will concede to bringing a rose to each queen to mask the unpleasant scent. However, *I* will choose the rose size, color, and variety. The roses will all be purchased by me from the same florist at the same location. All roses will have the same number of petals and length of stem, and all thorns will be removed."

I scoffed at his specificity, thinking Brad was taking the sarcasm too far until Lestari responded.

"So long as the rose color does not favor the clan colors of any queen."

"I will select bloodred roses, a color you all favor."

"Humph. Now about the platforms. They are made from inferior wood—"

"They are all the same material," Brad interrupted.

I swiped the last of the *atrum* from the wall and returned to the courtyard. Even knowing Jamie would be long gone by now, I paused to look for his unique soul among all the norms. When I didn't find him, I trudged to recharge among the cluster of trees near the parking lot. In my ear, Lestari and Brad continued to argue.

"Very well, I will bring a rug—"

"All platform adornment is forbidden."

"But—"

"To everyone," Brad said.

"The platforms are too small for those of us with a larger clan—"

"The number of warriors acceptable to accompany each queen is limited to four, per the 1929 peace talks of San Antonio and the 1877 peace talks of Montreal."

"Um, should I hang up?" I interjected.

"One moment, Madison. Sunan Lestari, I request a two-minute recess, as is allotted to all mediators once an hour."

"You have already been on recess for longer than two minutes."

"Yet you interrupted it, negating . . ." Brad trailed off with a sigh. "She's gone. Tomorrow I'm hiding the lemon drops. The queens don't need extra sugar."

I tried to summon sympathy for his plight, but my own worries edged out any other emotion.

"How accurate are pooka prophecies?"

"Why?" Brad asked after a brief charged silence, and I knew I had his full attention again. "Did he give you someone's?"

"I'm curious." *And the Understatement of the Year award goes to Madison Fox.*

I expected Brad to press for more information, but after a pause, he said, "One hundred percent accurate."

My heart plummeted.

"But only because he foretells all possible outcomes," he continued. "Most prophecies are so convoluted that people don't know they've reached the prophesied moment until they've already passed it."

How many possible interpretations of *One of us will die* could there be?

I walked to my car in a surreal haze. Maybe Jamie hadn't seen the future correctly. Maybe he'd misinterpreted it because we were too closely linked. Except we didn't feel close.

His soul had been so jumbled today, it'd been impossible to judge if his inner energies had tipped toward a greater mass of *atrum*. If it had . . . If the next time we met, he was more evil than good, irreparably evil, then he would have to die. . . .

Unless he embraced evil and killed me first.

A car horn bleated next to me, and I jumped, not realizing I'd stopped in the middle of the parking lot. I gave the driver a distracted wave and jogged out of the way.

Jamie had said I'd choose who died. That implied he wouldn't kill me, right?

Wait! Jamie's soul couldn't have turned darker yet. The only reason he could see those prophetic image bubbles he'd described was because of the balance of his soul. My relief flared, then collapsed in on itself: If Jamie's soul remained unchanged, then his prophecy was accurate, and one of us was destined to die. Soon.

I rubbed my temples with icy fingers, hoping to dispel the budding headache. Damn it, this was worse than the first time he'd run off. This time, he had embedded doubts in my thoughts, making me hesitant when I should have been acting. Maybe that'd been his goal all along. Maybe the prophecy was a lie, another way for him to buy time to escape. If so, it worked.

However, remembering the expression on his face when he'd delivered the prophecy made it impossible to dismiss it as a diversionary tactic. Jamie had believed one of us would die.

I braced a hand on the trunk of my car, taking deep breaths of frigid air.

Jamie said people's prophecies change. Nothing is fixed. Maybe by the end of the day, I'll do something to alter the future, and Jamie's prophecy will be erased.

Fortunately, Brad's plan didn't involve any interaction between the pooka and me today. Jamie's prophecy would never need to come into play.

The slender hope didn't make me feel any less nauseated. Nor did the bond, which vibrated beneath my skin, irrationally urging me to run to Jamie despite his prophecy—and without knowing which direction to go.

I shut myself into the chilled cocoon of my car and rested my head on the steering wheel. Closing my eyes, I counted my breaths. On the fifth, the person waiting for my spot honked their horn. On the eighth, a squeal of rubber on pavement announced they'd given up.

On the tenth breath, someone knocked on my window. I jumped, whacking my knee against the steering column. Pamela leaned close to the window, her shock of auburn hair peeking out of a stylish off-white beanie. The sight of the stern lines of her mouth and her hard eyes twisted my stomach into a knot of dread.

How had she found me?

Oh, right, the tracker.

I pushed open my door and stood, the press of the tracker against my bruised ankle throbbing with renewed pain at the reminder of its existence. Pamela scooted back to give me room. She held shiny silver cuffs in her left hand, looped over a thumb, and when she caught me staring, she tucked them into the back pocket of her pale jeans.

Had those been for me?

"Is something wrong?" I asked, my tone aggressive in anticipation of her answer. It wasn't a coincidence that she had shown up just after my confrontation with Jamie. If Brad had sensed the pooka's diversionary *atrum* assault, Pamela would have, too.

"You need a purity test."

I crossed my arms. "We did one less than an hour ago. Nothing's changed."

"Since then you've made contact with an out-of-control pooka. You also failed to call me when you had him in your sights, or afterward. Your behavior is suspect."

"There wasn't time! Not to call you and not for Jamie to taint me." The tracker squeezed my ankle when I curled my toes inside my tennis shoe, and I shook my foot in frustration. "Look at me. You can see I'm still pure *lux lucis*."

"You helped bring down a rogue warden. You of all people should know corruption can be hidden. Make a net."

I clenched my teeth and glared at the inspector. Arguing my innocence only made me look guiltier and prolonged the inevitable. I flared my soul above my heart, hating myself for capitulating and giving her power over me. Drawing in a deep breath, I braced a hand against the Civic to stop myself from backing up when Pamela reached for me.

There's nothing wrong with showing the inspector I'm clean. I'm not giving her any power she didn't already have as my boss. This isn't a violation any more than a lie detector test would be if I worked for the mundane CIA.

My reasoning helped soothe my irritation, enabling me to hold still as she sank her hands into my net. Foreign energy pulsed through me, burrowing into my body and *lux lucis*, hunting for the slightest fault or crack in my purity. My soul crawled, and maintaining the net took all of my concentration. When Pamela removed her hands, I took a large step back, knocking into the side mirror.

"See, I'm clean," I said before Pamela could speak. "I know I haven't exactly impressed you, but I'm not evil and I'm not going to allow myself to be changed."

"You're right, you haven't done anything to impress me."

I winced.

She strode to her car, double-parked behind mine, but turned back to face me before getting in. "This whole region is one false move from falling into complete chaos," she said, "and you're a weak link. You don't even recognize help when you see it."

Was she referring to herself? Did she think her repeated tests were helpful? They only emphasized her lack of conviction in my abilities and my character. Or did she believe her insults were beneficial? Was this her tough-love approach?

A blast of cold wind hit my face, making my eyes water, but I refused to blink and allow a tear to escape. I couldn't stomach the thought of the inspector thinking she'd made me cry.

21

THE BEATINGS WILL CONTINUE UNTIL MORALE IMPROVES

I flung myself into the driver's seat and cranked over the engine, slapping the dials to turn off the heater when it blasted cold air in my face.

If only Pamela's opinion didn't matter. If only Jamie would come back to me. If only Jamie hadn't revealed his horrid prophecy. If only I'd never taken this job.

"If only I'd never been born," I said out loud, using a wail not employed since my teenage years. The absurdity of my words broke the downward spiral of my thoughts. I backed out of my spot and did my best to leave my self-pity behind.

Twenty minutes later, I pulled into the parking lot at the Folsom Lake public beach. My route had included several miles-long stints at sixty miles per hour, and I hadn't felt the pull of the tether between me and Jamie once. I blinked to Primordium and scanned the skies, finding nothing but darkness and swarms of frost moths above me. Wherever the pooka was, he remained close, but he wasn't revealing himself.

Midday on this arctic Tuesday, the only company I had on the beach were a few bundled people and their Labradors. No slurry-souled Great Danes frolicked along the waterline or traipsed through the trees as I stomped up and down the rocky beach, killing frost moths that had congregated in the icy breezes off the lake.

Over an hour later, chilled to my bones, I folded my stiff body back into the Civic and blasted the heater on high. Driving across town to Roseville's jail should have taken less than half an hour, but due to holiday traffic, I sat in the car for a solid forty-five minutes, which gave my body time to thaw and my stomach time to wake up. Detouring to Whole Foods, I grabbed a premade sandwich and some overpriced snack bars. If Jamie had been with me, the bill would have been three times as high.

See, it's a good thing I'm alone today, I told myself.

Yeah, right.

As I predicted, all the evil Jamie and I had cleaned up four days ago had been replaced. The police station and jail collected too many people making bad decisions for it to stay clean long. Swaths of grimy *atrum* oozed down the main stairs and along the sidewalk in front of the station, even more in front of the jail. Plenty probably lurked inside, but since crawling along the floors of the station or jail lobby would likely get me arrested for suspicious behavior, I concentrated my efforts outside. When I could no longer feel my toes, I returned to my car. A ten-minute drive led to another lackluster neighborhood and a batch of vervet to be eliminated, then back to my car for a fifteen-minute drive to a park plagued by imps and frost moths.

Methodically, I checked off the locations Brad had texted me, zigzagging across Roseville to clean my region one city block at a time. For once, I was experiencing the life of a normal enforcer, performing spot-check cleanups rather than dashing from one overwhelming problem to the next. Maybe it would have been satisfying if it hadn't been an illusion, because this time my overwhelming problem chased me, maintaining his distance without testing the limits of our tether. An even larger, more disastrous problem—the elusive tyv and her drone cohorts—loomed closer with every passing minute as the sun sank toward the horizon. Meanwhile, our big plan consisted of me puttering around my region, putting miles on my car and torturing my body in the freezing temperatures all in the hopes that it would tire Jamie and maybe, possibly, hopefully—fingers crossed—help us with the tyv tonight. What a joke.

I should have fixed the rift between me and Jamie last night. Or at the mall. How many different ways could I bungle this?

Frustration swamped my melancholy, and the hairpin turn of my emotions fueled my irritation. I'd always thought of myself as easy-going and optimistic, but with the damn bond toying with my emotions, all I wanted to do was snap at the world and then curl up under the covers and cry. I didn't even trust my fatigue after I realized remaining in any location for longer than fifteen minutes made me feel more rested, even if I spent the whole time running around. That had to be the bond dictating what was best for Jamie. But what about his needs that weren't so easily translated through our metaphysical link? Was he getting enough to eat? He had the metabolism of a human-size hummingbird, which meant he required five times the amount of food I ate in a normal day. Where was he getting his nourishment today? What if he became too worn out to keep up with me the next time I drove off? What would happen to him? To me?

To combat my exhaustion, I stopped at a local convenience store for a soda and chocolate. The soda slid down my throat in an acidic rush, frothing back up in painful belches that burned the back of my nose. Stuffing the chocolate after it made me want to cry. My skin squeezed too tight on my body and my brain churned through anger and anxiety in nauseating loops, until I began to hope my gray matter would overheat and melt out my ears.

If that had been the extent of the day's tortures, it would have been agony enough to last a month, but Pamela piled on her own torments. Every hour, no matter where I was or what I was doing, the inspector tracked me down and shoved her hands into my soul. Each time, she arrived prepared to find me corrupt, cuff me, and take me away. I could read her intentions in her tense body language and increasingly closed expression—and in the insulting flicker of surprise each time she confirmed my purity. It took longer and longer for my soul to resettle after each test, and by three in the afternoon, the mere sight of Pamela spiked my blood pressure and set off anticipatory curdling sensations in my soul. It was almost enough to make me wish I'd been corrupted just so I could lash out and put a stop to the tests.

Almost.

The one bright spot in the day was a text from the receptionist at the dog shelter. The corgis' owners had seen my notification on their neighborhood message board and had rushed to retrieve them. The text included a picture of a happy couple, each with a corgi straining to lick their faces. It should have made me smile. It only made me miss Jamie and want to strangle him, which fit right in with the rest of my jumbled, contrary emotions.

I crawled home a little after four, with the sun less than an inch from the horizon. If our plan today had worked, I'd be rushing off in a half hour to hunt a powerful tyv and her bevy of drones. If it hadn't, tonight would be another fruitless endeavor full of hostility and suspicion. Either way, I planned on squeezing in a twenty-minute nap before whichever miserable ordeal fate assigned to me, and if Jamie also used the time to get some rest, so be it.

My parents stood on my doorstep, waiting for me. Both were bundled to their chins in thick coats, backs to me and the harsh wind rushing through the breezeway. Crap. I'd forgotten about Mom's earlier call. Tugging my phone from my pocket, I saw the tiny flashing light indicating a text I'd missed. I considered creeping back down the stairs and calling them from my car to cancel their visit. I could sneak up to my apartment after they left and get a few minutes' rest . . . but only as long as I was okay with accepting the Horrible Daughter of the Year award.

"Hey, Mom, Dad," I called, stomping up the last flight of stairs. "Have you been waiting long?"

They both swung toward me, smiling to see me, and guilt twisted tighter in my gut.

"We just got here," Dad said, setting down two bulging canvas bags to wrap me in a hug. I did my best not to sag against him. When I hugged Mom, I had to bend to wrap my arms around her shorter frame.

"That's quite a necklace," Mom said.

I lifted a hand to the soul breaker. It'd become as much a part of me as Val on my hip and the knife in the horizontal sheath across my lower back. Had either of them felt the knife during our hugs? What about the palmquell in my front pocket? I didn't have much practice keeping secrets from my parents, and I hated that interactions with them now felt like walking a tightrope of lies.

"I'm trying something new," I said. "What do you think?"

"It's . . . big," Mom said.

"Looks Turkish," Dad said. "Not sure that's the right outfit for it."

Fashion advice from a man wearing a jacket emblazoned with a giant Union Pacific logo across the back—I'd reached a new low. Biting my tongue, I fished my keys from my purse.

"How are you doing, sweetie?" Mom asked.

"Good."

"You look tired," Dad said.

"Gee, thanks, Dad."

"He's not being mean, Madison. You do look tired," Mom said.

"Yeah, well, it's been a long day." My tone said all too clearly that it would have been better if they hadn't come over. My face likely backed the statement up, because hurt flashed across Mom's expression. Guilt corkscrewed my irritation into a sharp knot.

Teeth clenched, I turned and fumbled to unlock the door with fingers stiff from cold.

"What's with the book?" Dad asked.

"It's the latest fashion. Very popular in New York."

"Really?" Dad asked. "Maybe I should get myself one of those straps. It looks handy."

"Oscar, she's teasing. That's her Christmas notebook."

Right. That's how I'd explained Val to Mom last time she'd seen him. I would have to come up with a new excuse once Christmas passed.

"So if I get my hands on it, I'll know what I'm getting for Christmas?" Dad asked.

My mom slapped his hand away from Val. The dead bolt finally twisted open, and I held the door open with the best smile I could muster. We hustled into the warm apartment and shed our shoes and coats in the tiny entryway, jostling each other. I draped everyone's coats across the short half wall between the dining room and front room, fighting down an irrational impulse to shove my parents aside to get some breathing room.

Mr. Bond sprang from the recliner and rushed to greet everyone, his dark tail raised high. After twining through my parents' legs and sniffing toes, he stuck his head in the nearest bag, then tried to dive in with his whole body, but the handle thwarted him.

"Where's the newest addition to the family?" Mom asked.

For a foggy moment, I thought she meant Jamie, and my stomach performed an acrobatic twist of apprehension, surprise, and dread.

"Uh . . ."

Dame Zilla crept out from behind the large *Howea* palm near the sliding glass door, her blue eyes wide and her tail low.

"Oh, look at her, Oscar! She's so tiny!"

I witnessed the precise moment Mom and Dad fell in love with Dame Zilla. Mom squatted, and that was all the kitten needed to know she was welcome. Her entire body language changed, and she trotted to my mom, head and tail high. Dad bent to scratch her head, and she revved her extraordinarily loud purr to full throttle. My parents melted.

I sidled around them, doing my best not to fixate on the recliner. Scooping up Mr. Bond, I carried him to the middle of the front room and away from whatever lay inside the bag. He mewled pathetically and raced for the bag the moment I let him go. I sank to the carpet, sitting cross-legged. The position ground the tracker against my bruised ankle, but it also hid it from sight. If explaining the knife would be difficult, the anklet would be impossible.

I tugged my sweater down to cover the knife, removed my phone from my back pocket, and settled Val on my lap. If I hoped to pull off normal with my parents, I needed to stay sharp. Stifling an unwelcome yawn, I ran a mental check of my life, trying to anticipate any questions my parents might have.

"You look ready to keel over," Dad said, taking a seat in the recliner.

"Keep the compliments coming." Good to know I looked as bad as I felt.

"Are you sure you're only tired?" Mom asked.

Someone pounded up the stairs outside the apartment, and I froze. If that was Pamela here to test my soul, I didn't think I could make myself answer the door—which would probably be as hard to explain to my parents as having a coworker show up just to touch my chest.

No, the chest touching would be the more difficult explanation.

And what if it was Jamie?

The footsteps fell silent, but I didn't breathe until the jangle of keys and slam of the door across the landing reverberated through my apartment.

"Madison?" Mom prompted.

"Uh." What was the question? Oh, right, they wanted a rationale for my haggard appearance. When in doubt, try honesty. "Work has been stressful. There's been a lot to, uh, learn lately, and I guess I'm just distracted."

Both cats were attempting to claw through the canvas bags now, and I latched on to the diversion.

"What's in the bags?"

"Gifts, of course." Mom shooed the cats out of the way, eliciting complaints from Mr. Bond. She pulled out a bag of treats and a catnip mouse for Mr. Bond "so he won't be jealous of his new sister getting too much attention"—she knew my fat cat well. She tossed the mouse, and Mr. Bond thundered across the front room and threw his body atop the tiny toy. While he was preoccupied, she hid the treats on the kitchen counter.

Dame Zilla got her own bag of kitten treats, her own mouse, and a cardboard scratching pad, which she promptly tore into, much to my parents' delight.

"You sounded so glum on the phone that we decided to bring a few things to cheer you up, too," Mom said. She turned so Dad couldn't see her face and gave me a funny look. "Your dad insisted on this magnificent souvenir."

She lifted a ceramic monstrosity free from the canvas bag. Longer than her hand and four inches tall, the bright yellow Union Pacific engine sat atop a pair of glossy black rails obscured by two white arcs of glittering snow parting in front of the engine like crests of water in front of a cruise ship. It was hideous, and my smile only grew wider when Dad chimed in.

"I got one for myself, too. You haven't lived until you've experienced the power of a locomotive surging through Mother Nature, the throb of the engine pulsing beneath your feet, the crisp mountain air filling your lungs. The exhilaration can't be matched."

"Mmm, yes, the surging and throbbing and pulsing *was* exhilarating," Mom said, her expression innocent except for the laughter dancing in her eyes.

"Imagine how much better it'd be from the engine, not stuck in the passenger car," Dad continued, missing Mom's teasing completely. "I need to figure out how to talk my way up there next time."

"I also snagged us each a copy of Ilona Andrews's newest book," Mom said, raising her voice to interrupt Dad's musings.

I snatched the book from her hands, wondering when I'd get the time to read it.

"And a Johnny Cash CD, because I couldn't help myself," Mom said. The album cover showed a young Cash, his hair styled into an impressive voluminous comb-back. In his twenties, decades after the style had passed, Dad had cultivated Cash's '50s look, which was when Mom fell in love with him. I wasn't sure if she'd fallen for Dad because he'd had a passing resemblance to Johnny, or if she'd come to love the singer because of Dad. These days, Dad's wiry gray hair tended to go any which direction in what we teasingly deemed his Albert Einstein style.

Mr. Bond tired of his mouse and investigated everyone's shoes, settling atop Dad's sneaker and sticking his head deep into its depths. Dame Zilla scaled the kitty tree, then bounced down and tore into the kitchen. Mr. Bond perked up and trotted after her, only to be ambushed when she burst around the corner, paws splayed, claws out. Mr. Bond administered three slaps to the top of her head, almost too fast to follow. She stumbled back, then jumped around him, swiped his tail, and kept running.

My parents laughed and I joined in, enjoying the chance to share the moment with someone. This sliver of normalcy felt like heaven. The jittery sense of doom that had ridden my shoulders all day faded with each passing moment in my parents' company, and the loosening of tension emphasized how tightly I'd been wound. The disjointed sensation of being a stranger in my own body disappeared, and I was just me, Madison, daughter of two wonderful people, mother of two adorable cats.

I walled off all thoughts of Jamie and sank into the happy moment.

"I don't remember you having so many plants," Mom said, twisting to take in the greenery lining the dining and living room.

I'd forgotten that she and Dad hadn't seen my place since I'd become an enforcer.

"I read an article about using plants to purify your home, but I think I might have gone overboard." The half-truth came easily and seemed to appease Mom's curiosity.

We listened to Dad wax about the pleasures of trains for another few minutes before Mom took pity on me and bundled him up. I saw them off with promises to send more pictures of Dame Zilla soon.

The quietness of the apartment enveloped me after the door closed behind them, and I flopped into the recliner, closed my eyes, and listened to the hum of the appliances and the muted sounds of my neighboring apartment dwellers.

My phone chimed. I cracked open one eye and used my toes to pull it to me. In a Herculean effort, I bent forward and retrieved it, opening the message app to Bridget's picture. Her text was short and to the point.

UP FOR COMPANY TONIGHT?

I glanced at the clock. It wasn't even five. Bridget would be at the office for another hour or longer, and we rarely hung out on week-nights because she liked to bring her work home. Mom must have sent up the "Madison needs cheering" flare, and Bridget had faithfully responded.

I would have scoffed at the transparency of the ploy if I hadn't so badly wanted to take Bridget up on her offer. Putting my shoes and coat back on and facing another night either aimlessly searching for the tyv or finding her and sprinting around fighting drones sounded as much fun as an ice bath. But the odds of reconnecting with Jamie would be better if I were actively out looking for him or at least keeping him moving around.

Resigned, I took a picture of my new tacky figurine and sent it with my response. No THANKS. MY NEW BEST BUD AND I NEED SOME ALONE TIME.

Bridget's text came back fast. WHOA! SAY THE WORD AND THAT CAN BE PART OF AN UNFORTUNATE ACCIDENT.

YOU'RE THE BEST. I hit SEND and flopped back in the chair. The knife pressed into my spine and my ankle throbbed. My eyelids sank until my lashes rested against my cheeks. Mr. Bond meowed from the vicinity of his food dish. I murmured a promise to feed him in a moment. Soft sounds of scratching emanated from the laundry closet: Dame Zilla in the litter box.

My eyes closed fully. A five-minute power nap was all I needed.

Mr. Bond yowled and head-butted my calf. Dame Zilla's enthusi-astic scratches switched from the litter to the dryer beside it, her tiny claws squeaking against the metal. I squeezed my eyes tighter and shoved my fingers into my ears. Someone pounded on my door hard enough to rattle it in its hinges.

I recognized the knock. The same sound had woken me this morning.

A lead ball sank into my stomach and anxiety fizzed through my extremities. The respite of the last twenty minutes evaporated before the echo of the inspector's final knock faded. My soul crawled in a purely psychosomatic anticipation of a purity test, and I chafed my forearms. My disappointing reality settled back on my shoulders: I wasn't "normal Madison," who could hole up in her apartment with her cats and her books and a soft blanket. I was a failed pooka bondee, the untrusted, unimpressive enforcer wearing a tracer anklet who needed to get off her butt and prepare to fight a soul-stealing creature.

Pamela pounded on the door again. I closed my eyes, searching for the serenity I'd almost attained, but it had fled. Wallowing in its loss wouldn't help me.

I heaved to my feet and peered through the peephole. Pamela shifted on the welcome mat to survey the sky above the stairs, no doubt looking for signs of Jamie. Or maybe she thought I hid the tyv on my roof. My nails dug into my palms. Resting my forehead on the cool metal door, I took a deep breath through my nose and let it slowly out of my mouth. Pamela was an ally, not an enemy, no matter what she thought of me. Grasping the doorknob, I jerked the dead bolt open and swung the door wide.

Pamela strode inside, assessing me, then my apartment with her cool gaze.

"You're due at the office."

"I know." I blinked to Primordium, preparing to make a net.

Pamela didn't slow, walking past me down the hallway to check the bedroom and bathroom, as if Jamie might be hiding in the closet or behind the shower curtain.

I closed the door and stayed on the welcome mat, arms crossed.

"Any pooka sightings?" she asked from my bedroom.

"Not since the last time you asked an hour ago." I didn't attempt to moderate the irritation in my tone.

Usually Mr. Bond was the first to greet a new guest, but Pamela's intense energy had sent him running for the dining room table, and he sat tall against a leg, eyes wide and ears tracking the inspector's decisive steps. Dame Zilla took her cue from Mr. Bond and hunkered between the recliner and the wall, slinking down the hall to the bedroom when Pamela came back to the front room.

"You need to draw the pooka back to you," she said.

"I know." *But how?* I didn't voice the question. If Pamela had the answer, she would have given it to me by now.

Without asking or giving me a warning, Pamela shoved her hands inside the *lux lucis* net I'd created over my heart, and my thoughts scattered. Her foreign energy pulsed through me, and I swayed in place, clinging to my soul when it attempted to scatter. When she withdrew her hands, my soul undulated and bile lapped up the back of my throat. I braced against the half wall and closed my eyes until my stomach settled. It wasn't my imagination; each test left me worse off than the last. How many more would I have to suffer through before the end of the night?

"Satisfied?" I asked, rolling my shoulders to alleviate tension cording my neck.

"For now. Let's hope your plan worked today and we find the tyv before it decimates your region. We've got a long night ahead of us."

On that cheery note, she let herself out. I threw the dead bolt and collapsed back into the recliner. Nausea churned in my stomach, and not all of it could be blamed on the purity test. I was sick at heart. Sick of trying so hard and failing. Sick of Pamela's tests and Pamela's mistrusting attitude. Sick of fretting over Jamie—where he was, how he was doing, and what trouble he was creating for me to clean up. But most of all, I was sick of worrying about the veracity of his prophecy and if I'd have to choose which of us lived.

The last thought doubled me over. I couldn't do this. Not tonight.

My cell phone was in my hand and I'd dialed Brad before I'd finished thinking it through.

"Why aren't you here?" my boss demanded.

"I'm not coming in. I'm not feeling well."

"Since when?"

Oh, how to answer? I had so many options. Since my parents' visit had reminded me that my body wasn't supposed to feel torn apart by tension. Since Pamela's umpteenth purity test had unmoored my soul from my body. Since the bond reinserted its pressure, wringing anger and worry together into a tight knot in the back of my head that wouldn't let me rest.

The next time we meet, one of use will die. You will be the one to choose who lives.

"Jamie hasn't corrupted me," I said, answering the true question my boss was asking. "Pamela can verify it; she was just here for yet another purity test."

"'Yet another'?"

"She's been testing me hourly."

Brad didn't respond, and the muted sounds of arguing prajurit filled the silence.

I was ruining his plan. If I stayed home, Jamie would get to rest, and all my efforts today would be for nothing. But if I stayed home, Jamie would be confined to the tether's range around my apartment.

That had to be worth something, and Brad and Pamela would have to figure out how to make it work for them.

"You need to come in, Madison."

"Not when you've got Summer there. She's all the enforcer you need." Bitterness curdled on my tongue. Pamela had made clear her high estimation of the other enforcer, just as she'd made clear—in actions and words—how little she respected me.

"Toffee on a turkey's tush! That's not how this works!" Brad shouted.

"It's how it works tonight," I said, and hung up.

I tossed the phone to the floor and bounced to my feet, agitation fueling my actions and burning through my earlier fatigue. Pacing the front room, I wondered if I'd gotten myself fired, then laughed, the bitter sound dying quickly. Brad couldn't fire me. Not so long as I was tied to a pooka, no matter how loosely. More likely, he would show up on my doorstep and drag me to work. Or Pamela would.

Screw that. I was taking tonight off. No one was telling me otherwise.

My inability to sit still, the nervous thrumming of my fingers against my thigh, my to-hell-with-the-world attitude told me I wasn't in my right mind, but only so much of my agitation could be blamed on the bond messing with me. The rest was work, plain and simple. Impossible demands, forced responsibility over outcomes I had no control over, repeated god-awful purity tests—what did Brad and Pamela expect I would do? Did they think all this pressure would mold me into the perfect, well-behaved little enforcer? Well, tough. Their plan backfired, and all I wanted to do was rebel.

I snatched up my phone and called Alex.

22

I'M A WOMAN. WHAT'S YOUR
SUPERPOWER?

"Hello, this is Alex."

His deep voice shot a thrill of energy to my already over-charged nerves.

"Hey. It's Madison, and I've got an unorthodox proposal for you."

"Oh?" His response came a half beat delayed. I'd caught him off guard. Or maybe I sounded as crazy as I felt.

"Want to go dancing?"

"Right now?"

"Tonight." When he didn't say anything, I prompted, "You do know how to dance, don't you?"

"I have rhythm," Alex responded with mock affront.

His words sparked a vivid image of his body pressed to mine. "Perfect," I said, and the word rolled off my tongue with an unexpected purr. I bit my lip, but since he couldn't see my blush, I pretended the sultry tone had been intentional.

Alex cleared his throat. "Are you sure there's somewhere open on a Tuesday?"

"I know of a place. What do you say? I've got a short skirt and a lot of energy to burn. And I won't bring a mannerless dog." *A short skirt?* My mouth was out of control, and I couldn't rein it in.

"Well, with a proposal like that, how could I say no? What time should I pick you up?"

"Seven." The club wouldn't get busy until nine, but I couldn't wait that long.

I hung up, shoved my feet into my shoes, and rushed from the apartment before I'd finished zipping my coat. After locking the door, I leaned over the railing to make sure no one was headed up to drag me to the office. The tracker squeezed my ankle, reminding me that no matter where I went, Brad or Pamela could find me.

I considered cutting the device off but dismissed the idea just as fast. If the tracker went dead, Pamela would assume the worst: that Jamie had gone dark and taken me with him. She would call in Niko to kill Jamie, and then she would come for me. Instead, I decided to make hunting me down as onerous as possible. If anyone had a problem with it, I could always claim I was doing my part to keep Jamie busy.

Invigorated by self-righteousness, I jogged to my car. My new rebellious attitude couldn't completely drown out a tiny voice of reason, which pointed out I was going to regret thumbing my nose at my boss and abandoning my responsibilities, but it only made me more determined to enjoy *now*.

With indulgence as my compass, I selected my favorite frozen yogurt shop for dinner, leaving with a tub of chocolate soft serve loaded with toppings. I ate it while I drove uptown to DSW, where I purchased some slouchy boots with impractical heels and peep toes that also did the trick of hiding the tracker. My last stop took me back to East Roseville and my favorite consignment store, Sei Bella, where I purchased the promised short skirt—a cherry-red number cinched at the waist but with oodles of extra fabric to flare when I twisted. When I returned home, I changed into the skirt, paired it with a slinky off-the-shoulder black top with tiny white polka dots, tucked Val into the closet with an audio book, dumped all my weapons into a drawer on my desk, and surveyed myself in the mirror.

Damn, I looked sexy. Not sweet, not pretty, but sexy. Not even the soul breaker, the one weapon I couldn't bring myself to leave the house without, marred the look.

If I spent more than a handful of minutes outside in this minuscule outfit, I'd freeze. Good thing I planned on being indoors. Checking the clock, I dabbed gloss onto my lips, swiped dark eyeshadow onto my eyelids, and added an extra layer of mascara. I left my hair down, but I brushed it until it glistened.

My bed got a quick cover straightening, and I stuffed Jamie's bed out of sight beneath it. Halfway back to the front room, I froze, realizing what I'd just subconsciously planned for. Then I lifted my skirt and checked my underwear. Bland tan cotton. This wouldn't do. I exchanged them for a seldom-worn pair of lacy black. Much better.

I ignored my dirty work coat with its duct-taped sleeves in favor of my fanciest jacket, a belted red pea coat several shades darker than my skirt, and as I sashayed to the door to answer Alex's knock, I admired the way a few inches of skirt kicked up below the heavier coat panels.

When I opened the door, Alex's eyes fixed on my bare legs, his eyebrows lifting. I smiled and stepped out, closing the door behind me. Freezing air hit my exposed legs, eliciting instant goose bumps that did nothing to quell the renewed energy humming through my body in response to Alex's appreciative look.

"Hey," he said, backing up to give me room to lock the door.

"Hi."

"Are you sure you're going to be warm enough?" In light gray slacks and a heavy coat, he looked winter-scrumptious and far more prepared for the night's temperatures.

"If I wore anything more, I'd be too hot."

"That would be a shame," Alex murmured, and his grin warmed me to my partially exposed toes.

After a discreet check over the railing confirmed we wouldn't run into Pamela on her way up, I trotted down the stairs to Alex's Volvo. He held the passenger door open for me, and I slid into the interior, appreciating the residual heat lingering on the leather seat beneath my bare thighs.

Alex removed his coat before sliding behind the wheel. Beneath it, he wore a fitted dark blue button-up, and he self-consciously patted invisible wrinkles from it when he caught me staring.

"I don't do a lot of dancing. Am I dressed appropriately?"

I laid a hand on his forearm to draw his attention from his chest, and he stilled.

"You look"—I let my eyes drift down his body—"really good."

"Really?" He leaned closer.

"Really."

Our lips met in a soft press, and I leaned into it, teasing my tongue across his bottom lip. He made a soft, surprised sound and deepened the kiss. The heat of his mouth and the velvet of his tongue against my lips speared pleasure southward in a dizzying rush. The center console gouged into my abdomen as I tilted into the kiss. He tasted of mint and Alex, and I couldn't get enough.

Alex shifted back in his seat, breaking the kiss and leaving me panting. Using his forefinger, he brushed my hair back from my face, the gesture a tender juxtaposition to his intense expression. His hand slid along the side of my neck, then retreated, and I shivered from the caress and again from its loss.

Releasing a deep breath, Alex started the car. Heat swirled from the vents and the chug of the engine filled the silence.

I leaned back in my seat and caught my lower lip in my teeth. I'd come on too strong, but my arousal, fed by the recklessness spurring my actions this evening, had surprised even me.

"So, where am I going?" Alex asked as he put the car in reverse. He had to clear his throat first and even so, his voice came out rough. Good to know I wasn't the only one affected by our kiss.

A charged silence and stolen glances filled the drive to the club, neither of us sure how to act after our intense greeting. Refusing to allow the awkwardness to cement around us, I popped from the car as soon as we were parked, grabbed Alex's hand when he came around the bumper, and bustled us into the warm interior of the club. I shed my coat at the door, handing it to the coat check boy.

"I'm definitely underdressed," Alex said, passing his coat to the waiting attendant without taking his eyes off me.

"I think you look delicious. Come on."

Peppy, bass-fueled music filled the dim interior. We'd arrived as a salsa class was winding down, and the patrons at the bar and tables tapped their feet and swayed along, watching the beginners stumble through the steps. I dragged Alex to the edge of the dance floor, and we did our best to mimic the steps of the students, laughing at our clumsiness.

With each carefree shuffle, my stress unraveled, and I savored Alex's warm hands in mine, my feet moving to a rhythm. I abandoned myself to the heavy beat, allowing it to align my brash energy into a single focus: this moment. Nothing else mattered, not the frustrations of my job, not my failings with Jamie, and not the future ramifications of blowing off the inspector. I gave the incessant, wild drive of the bond only one outlet—my body—and it lit through my nerve endings, turning every touch into a caress, every step into a seduction.

Alex proved to have a gratifying amount of hip movement for a white guy, and more important, a willingness to attempt the dance's sensuous steps. He spun me around with confidence, and while I may not have managed the correct foot placement, I gyrated my hips with gusto, each sensual twist grounding me in my body, reminding me it was much more than just a vessel for *lux lucis*.

The class ended and the music blasted louder as the dance floor opened to everyone. Most of the students stayed, breaking into partners, and everyone on the sidelines filled in the empty spaces on the floor. Alex steered us toward the center of the dancers, rolling up his sleeves to reveal sun-kissed muscular forearms. I fluffed my hair, smiling when Alex's eyes darted to the temporary gap between my shirt and skirt.

For another song, we mimicked the salsa dancers around us as best we could, but the limited hand-to-hand contact wasn't enough. I wanted more. Pulling Alex to a stop, I stepped into his personal space and settled his hands on my waist, then wrapped my arms loosely around his neck. Less than a hand's span separated us, and my sides tingled beneath the heat of his palms. Better.

Alex stared down at me, a question in his eyes. I smiled and rolled my hips, prancing through the same steps as before, and Alex followed. He slid his hands from my waist to my hips, subtly taking lead. *Much* better.

The contained strength of his hands encasing me, the feel of his muscles moving beneath his shirt, the brush of his leg against mine, my chest against his—each touch sparked a fresh zing of pleasure, soothing the agitation of today's purity tests. My frazzled soul settled into my body, calmed by unmoderated joy.

What we danced wasn't the salsa, but it fit the beat and we moved together in harmony. It didn't take long for the marginal gap between us to disappear, Alex's leg sliding between mine, our bodies rubbing deliciously against each other. I wished I'd gone braless. I wished I wasn't clothed at all and we were somewhere private.

Alex's left hand slid down the center of my back to splay across the top of my butt, his right hand gliding up my spine to hold me close. Guilt fired a warning shot through my pleasure, the sharp stab of the day's unpleasant realities attempting to usurp my joy. My pooka was out of control and up to untold evil. Brad was furious with me. Pamela likely plotted additional tortures to inflict on me. I should be—

I crushed all the *should* thoughts, locked them up with my guilt, and sank back into the dance with renewed vigor, writhing against Alex. Tomorrow would be soon enough to deal with the consequences of my actions. Tonight, I would enjoy myself.

Playing my fingers through the hair at the nape of Alex's neck, I pressed my lips to his jaw, and his hands tightened around me. A gentle tug on the back of his neck brought his lips to mine, and the molten heat of his kiss blazed straight to my core.

The next kiss set me on fire.

A tiny voice cautioned me to slow down, but Alex's tongue swept across mine, and I wriggled closer, squeezing his thigh between mine. I clutched his biceps for balance, enjoying the way they flexed beneath my hands, the round muscles filling my grip. Beneath his conservative clothing lay a well-toned body, and I was eager for the full reveal.

Without breaking the kiss, Alex's hands slid back to my waist, holding me in place as he eased back. I curled my fingers into his shoulders, straining to close the gap between us. His second step separated us completely.

"Come on." Alex grabbed my hand and pulled me off the dance floor. He angled for a table at the edge of the club, pulling me close once we were free of the crowd.

"I think we were getting in peoples' way," he said.

He had the sexiest lips, the kind I wanted to sink my teeth into.

"Can I get you something to drink?" he asked, pulling a chair out for me.

I ignored the chair and his offer, leaning up against the wall next to the table and beckoning him closer. He smiled but shook his head.

"Madison . . ."

I dropped my gaze down to his pants—mmm, yes—then peeked at him through lowered lashes. Normally I would have asked for a glass of wine, then attempted to talk to Alex above the pounding music. I would have taken it slow. But the purity tests and the bond had sheared the brakes off my usual restraint, exposing a wild energy I had no desire to curtail. I felt free and uninhibited and deliciously sexy. I didn't want to lose this feeling. Not quite yet.

Taking Alex's hand from the back of the chair, I drew him to me. My first kiss was soft, teasing. So was the next. On the third, I nipped his bottom lip, eliciting a satisfying groan. Alex caged me against the wall, leaving just enough space between us for his hands to glide down my slinky top, teasing over my nipples. I gasped, but he'd already moved to my stomach, his light touches inducing a shiver through my abdomen.

I slid a hand down the front of his shirt, past his belt, to glide down the hard length of him pressed against the front of his slacks. He growled, the primal sound completely at odds with his buttoned-down presentation, and it sent a thrill through me. My free hand fumbled for his belt.

Alex jerked to shackle my wrists, and he pinned them to the wall at my sides. His body crowded mine, and I strained against his strength, enjoying being caught.

"Madison." My name, uttered in a tone that bridged prayer and reproach, brought my eyes open. In the dim light, Alex's blue eyes glimmered a few shades lighter than black. Passion suffused his features, but when he leaned closer to me again, it was to rest his forehead on mine, not to kiss me.

I stared at him from too close, air gusting from me in choppy pants. My body hummed, supercharged and ready. He wanted me; I wanted him. What was the holdup?

The tempo of the music changed, vibrating against my spine through the wall. I blinked. The sound overwhelmed the pounding of my heart, the individual notes coming back into focus. From the corner of my eye, I caught flashes of hands and legs and feet—dancers. People. A lot of them. I'd completely forgotten we were in a dance club, and the dose of reality splashed cold water on my libido.

"Whoa. That got a little out of hand," I said, making no move to free myself.

Alex chuckled, the sound rueful. "Not that I'm complaining, but I'm not usually into exhibitionism." He lifted his head, and cool air rushed between us.

"Me neither." Making the most of my stolen evening of freedom was one thing; having sex up against the wall of a dance club was entirely too far. "I think I need a moment to, ah, cool down. I'll be right back."

I squeezed Alex's hand and smiled to show him I wasn't upset. He tugged the hem of my top down to cover my exposed stomach and pointed the way to the restrooms.

With each step away from him, my hormones settled and reality crept back in. My gaze snagged on the bartender's, and her wink ignited a slow blush from my clavicle to my hairline. How much had she seen? How much had any of the dozens of people in the club seen?

I wished I could chalk up my actions to raw chemistry, but I knew the answer was more closely linked to my problems than my attraction to Alex. I'd been so intent on distracting myself that I hadn't noticed when I'd crossed the line from rebellious to reckless. Thankfully Alex had maintained a clear enough head to stop us.

Oh God, what must he think of me now?

I started to turn to check his expression when Pamela emerged from the shadows, her short frame and shock of red hair unmistakable even in the dim light. Without saying a word, she grabbed my forearm and propelled me down the black-walled hallway to the bathroom.

The inspector gave me a shove, sending me stumbling through the bathroom doorway. She followed on my heels, and I retreated deeper into the tiny room. Both stalls were empty, but a middle-aged woman stood at the sink, washing her hands. At my clumsy entrance, she looked up, her gaze sliding between me and Pamela, lips thinning in disapproval.

"Out," Pamela barked.

The woman arched an eyebrow and snorted. She leaned into the mirror and touched up her lipstick, then made a point of thoroughly drying her hands before sauntering out. I used the time to straighten my clothing and run my fingers through my mussed hair.

A cold wash of panic had flooded my limbs the moment I'd recognized Pamela, followed closely by a wave of guilt. I'd blown off work to go *dancing*. I'd known Pamela could track me—a part of me had expected it. I simply hadn't cared.

I tried to summon that indifference now, but shame overwhelmed it. My behavior had been childish and petty, only I'd been too ground down by the jittery energy of the bond and the disjointed effects of repeated purity tests to see it earlier.

My responsibilities crashed back to my shoulders, twice as heavy for having been cast aside for a few hours. I had a duty to my region, and whether they knew it or not, a lot of people counted on me to show up to fight evil, even on days or nights when I'd rather be doing anything else. More important, I had Jamie counting on me to save him from himself. He might not see it that way, but he needed rescuing before his damn prophecy came true.

I took a deep breath, formulating my apology. I'd need time to extract myself from this date. I wouldn't walk out on Alex, not without a believable explanation. He didn't deserve that, and I didn't want to ruin the good thing we had going. But afterward, I would strap on my weapons and get back to work.

"Inspector, I'm—"

"No. You don't get to talk. Make a net."

My teeth clicked shut. Releasing a slow breath, I tried again. "Look, I didn't mean—"

A knife appeared in Pamela's fist, and she brandished it at me. I scrambled backward, slamming against the counter.

"Make a net. *Now*." Her tone, her body language, and her expression all said the same thing: She was prepared to use the knife. She had been acting as if she thought I'd attack her all day, though earlier she had only been prepared to restrain me with handcuffs. Apparently she'd upgraded my threat level.

Raising pacifying hands, I swelled a net over my heart.

"I'm clean. I swear."

"We'll see."

My jaw locked, I concentrated on taking deep breaths, doing my best to suppress my rising anger. I'd given Pamela reason to be suspicious of me. I hadn't exactly been acting like myself. Nevertheless, fury simmered through my contrition.

Resting the knife against my chest, the blade aimed at my throat, Pamela shoved her hands into my net. A corresponding convulsion jangled through my soul. One surge of Pamela's *lux lucis* through me undid an hour of Alex's restorative touches.

"You're clean." She slid her knife back into the sheath at her hip.

My soul writhed with the heebie-jeebie aftereffect of the test, sifting my anger to the surface and burying my half-formulated apology. I didn't bother to chafe my skin, knowing from experience that it wouldn't chase away the crawling sensation.

"I don't know how you expect us to trust you after this," Pamela said. "You're acting like you're under the pooka's influence—erratic and irrational. Or maybe you're simply lazy and selfish."

I jerked as the barb struck home. Calling in sick tonight had been pure selfishness, never mind that I'd been working myself ragged up until I made the call.

"You're a disgrace to illuminant enforcers," Pamela continued in the same flat, disappointed tone that worked like acid on my emotions. "You're doing your pooka no favors. All this unsupervised time will lead to nothing good. Now say good-bye to your date. You're coming with me." She gripped the handle and turned to open the door. "It's too bad you didn't stop to think about how your actions would reflect on your warden, especially at this juncture in his career."

I would have borne her censure for my bad decisions, and I could have swallowed being treated like a child, but her off-the-cuff comment about making Brad look bad was the final straw. I slammed a hand onto the door above her and leaned on it. The door slapped shut, jerking Pamela off center. I loomed over the shorter woman.

"No."

Pamela let go of the handle and backed up a step. She had years of training and experience fighting far more dangerous threats than me. Her subtle retreat wasn't a sign of intimidation; it'd freed up room for her to reach for the knife at her waist.

"No?" she asked.

"You don't get to pretend like anything I've done is the reason you're not giving Brad more territory—and I know that's what you were insinuating," I added when she tried to get a word in. "You were never planning on expanding our region. You've been trying to strong-arm Doris into that warden position since before you met me. So, no, don't try to pin that guilt on me."

"You definitely haven't done anything to change my mind."

I scoffed. "Have you found the tyv?"

"Your pooka is still hiding it."

"Fine. Call me if she shows up. Otherwise, I think you can handle doing nothing tonight without this lazy, selfish, untrustworthy disgrace of an enforcer." I yanked open the door, forcing Pamela to dance back or be struck. My heart pounded against my rib cage, my own brashness frightening me, but it took all my willpower to remain civil and I had nothing left for such trivial concerns as whether or not I had just set a torch to my career. "Don't bother coming by my house tonight. That was the last purity test you'll subject me to."

I stormed out of the bathroom, heels pounding loud enough to pierce the blare of salsa music. I didn't look back until I'd reached the end of the hallway. Pamela remained in the bathroom doorway, arms crossed, expression pinched.

Let her stew. I was done with her insults and her guilt trip.

Alex stood by the same table, expecting me to return refreshed and flirty. I plastered on a smile and put sway into my hips, but anticipation of Pamela grabbing my arm and dragging me outside made my movements stilted. When I reached the table unmolested, I scanned the club. The inspector skulked near the bar, not sitting but not approaching me, either.

"Let's dance!" My forced enthusiasm sounded more sincere shouted over the music, and Alex's wary expression turned my smile genuine. "Just dancing. I swear I won't jump you."

"Not that I'm opposed to being jumped," Alex said, reaching for my hand.

"But you prefer to be jumped in private," I said, finishing the thought for him. I added a wink. "Good to know."

Alex laughed and trailed me to the dance floor.

We danced. Not the salsa, but some bastard version of it, holding hands and going with the beat. I tried to regain my earlier enthusiasm, but Pamela's glare ate through my joy. Even after she left a few songs later, my carefree attitude remained elusive, my libido dampened. Alex's touch had lost its restorative properties, and my *lux lucis* fluctuated beneath my skin in crawling echoes of the purity test.

Pamela had sucked all the rebellious delight out of the evening, leaving me with a mass of worries. How badly had I screwed up? What repercussions would I face tomorrow? If I lost control of Jamie, the odds of being fired skyrocketed. The last several days had been terrible, but that didn't mean I didn't want my job.

Thinking of Jamie in terms of my employment set a knot in my stomach. He was more than a means to a job for me. He was my pooka and I loved him.

I glanced around the club, unconsciously looking for him. Where was the pooka right now? Was he safe? Was he warm? Was he helping the tyv destroy my region?

"Are you okay?" Alex asked, leaning close so I could hear him over the music.

I started to nod, but when I realized how hard I had to work to force a smile, I changed my mind.

"I think I'm more tired than I realized. Mind if we leave?"

We collected our coats and exited into the freezing night. The Volvo's icy leather seats against my bare thighs sent shivers rattling through me, and Alex cranked up the heat. According to the clock on the dashboard, we'd been out barely three hours. I was such a lame date.

Alex drove back to my place in silence. I peeked at him from the corner of my eye, trying to read his mind. He didn't look irritated by my mercurial moods, but he could have been hiding it. When he pulled into an uncovered parking space in front of my apartment building, he put the car in park and let it idle. The heater churned out a steady wave of warmth, and my shivers finally subsided.

"I'm sorry," I said.

"For what?"

"For tonight. I—" How to explain without sounding crazy? "It's just I've been under a lot of stress lately, and I thought dancing would take my mind off everything. And it did," I hastened to add. "For a while. But I just—"

Alex captured my fluttering hand, and I stilled.

"Hey, I had fun." He held my gaze, letting me see his earnestness.

The corner of my lips kicked up. "So did I."

Alex shifted his grip, his warm fingers stroking my palm before he brought it to his lips for a soft kiss. My jumbled thoughts unraveled and quieted.

"Then I think we had a successful date," Alex pronounced.

I leaned across the console and he met me halfway for a chaste kiss. A hum of pleasure sparked along my nerve endings, but after several minutes of awkward contortions around the clunky console, we pulled apart.

Staring into his lust-darkened eyes, I considered inviting Alex up to my apartment. I wanted him almost as much as I yearned to recapture the devil-may-care attitude I'd enjoyed before Pamela's interruption.

I let out my breath in a long exhale, leaving the invitation unspoken. My first time with Alex should be more meaningful than an excuse not to think about my problems.

"This stress. Do you want to talk about it?" Alex asked.

I shook my head, picturing the disaster of trying to explain soul-sucking evil creatures to Alex, let alone a half-evil shape-changing pooka I'd lost control of.

For a second I thought he might have been disappointed by my response. Or maybe relieved. The dim light made it hard to read his fleeting expression.

"I'm glad you called me tonight," Alex said.

"Me too."

I kissed him again, a quick good-bye kiss, and slid out of the car. A gust of cold air twined icy fingers around my bare legs, and I shuddered. Stuffing my hands into my coat pockets, I scurried up the walkway to the stairs, pausing long enough to toss Alex a wave as he backed out of the parking space.

Stomping up the stairs alone, I shook my head at myself. I was an idiot. I should have invited Alex up. We could have talked and made out. Sex didn't have to be on the agenda.

But sex would have been nice.

I scanned the sky and parking lot in Primordium, then blinked to normal sight when I saw no trace of Jamie. Where *was* he? The bond tangled with my emotions, stretching and sharpening them. Sleeping tonight would be difficult. Maybe I shouldn't bother to try. I could change and hunt tyver and make everyone happy. It'd be better than tossing and turning all night.

The fact that my thighs burned with fatigue and my knees wobbled rubbery and weak when I made it to the third-floor landing made me rethink my plans. Maybe if I took a sleep aid and achieved real rest, everything would look better in the morning. Maybe sleep would help heal my sore body and aching heart.

I shoved the key into the lock with unnecessary force, irritated that my decision to take care of myself had been accompanied by a dose of bond-enhanced guilt. The door required an extra push and opened with the soft sound of cloth rubbing on metal. My hand reached for the light switch on auto-pilot even as I realized the apartment was already lit. A white tube lined the inner doorway from floor to lintel, a new addition since I'd left. Had Jamie . . . ?

The pooka wasn't waiting inside.

Niko was.

23

I MAY NOT ALWAYS BE GOOD BUT MY INTENTIONS ARE

Niko sat in my recliner, Mr. Bond sprawled across his jean-clad lap, Dame Zilla snuggled on his broad shoulder, her face buried against Niko's dark neck.

My brain stuttered to process the scene. Niko looked at home in my apartment. With my cats. Mr. Dark and Deadly himself, relaxing in my recliner like he belonged. Like he was a natural part of my life. In all my fantasies about Niko, I'd never once imagined anything quite so domestic.

A wallop of thwarted libido tinged with tenderness blindsided me, giving rise to an impossible daydream of coming home to Niko at the end of a long day and snuggling with him in that chair, the bedroom just a few steps away.

Niko lifted an eyebrow at me.

I closed my mouth with a click. *Please tell me all that hadn't shown on my face.*

I stepped into my apart—

Invisible bands constricted around my feet and hands, tightening into knots and locking me in place. Panic iced my spine. I struggled, but it didn't make a difference; my limbs didn't so much as twitch. Frantic, I blinked to Primordium, searching for an escape.

Niko's soul shimmered with its trademark glossy strength, not a drop of *atrum* in sight. Both cats were pristine, as was my apartment. I couldn't turn my head, but straining my eyes left and right enabled me to make out gossamer strands of what looked like *lux lucis* spiraling from my hands to the white tube bordering the door frame. Despite their fragile appearance and glowing good energy, the cobweb-like substance held me as immobile as if I'd been bound by steel cables.

I jerked my gaze back to Niko. He remained seated, his bland expression confirming he'd known exactly what would happen the moment I walked through the door. He'd set me up! He'd broken into my house, befriended my cats, and *installed a trap*!

I fought the bonds holding me, succeeding in doing nothing but raising my blood pressure. Sweat blossomed along my hairline. My outraged exclamation rattled in my throat like a poor Ms. Piggy impression, my jaw locked closed, my lips immobile. Niko's eyes crinkled as if he found me amusing, and I willed the chair beneath him to catch on fire.

What if my neighbors stepped outside right now? I'd look like an idiot, frozen in my doorway like a cardboard cutout, held by ropes they couldn't see.

Mr. Bond had perked up at my entrance, and when I made no move to greet him, he jumped from Niko's lap and approached, meowing and waving his tail. I lost sight of him before he reached me, unable to tilt my head to track his movements. With my hand stuck holding the door open, Mr. Bond had unfettered access to the great outdoors. I started struggling in earnest. Mr. Bond was an inside cat. He had gotten out the front door twice in his life, and both times he'd panicked, huddling against the wall and yowling until I snatched him up. Both times he'd been outside less than twenty seconds. If it took me longer to rescue him, would he bolt?

Niko shifted, drawing my attention back to him. He tapped Dame Zilla's side, and her head jerked up. She chirped, looking around with a dazed expression the way she did when woken from a deep sleep. How long had Niko been here? Scooping the kitten up with one large hand, Niko stood and gently set her on the recliner's cushion. She immediately jumped down and ran toward me and the open door. I jerked to stop her, straining without moving.

"Good evening," Niko said.

"How dare you! Get me out of this!" I shouted, but with my lips sealed and jaw locked, it sounded like a badly hummed song. I released another Ms. Piggy scream of frustration.

"Close your eyes." Niko lifted a bottle. It resembled a dense cito spray, the contents sparkling with *lux lucis*. He depressed the nozzle and a fine powder swirled through the air, stinging my eyes. I clamped them shut, but tears leaked from between my lashes.

The web loosened in stages from my head down, and I fell off balance into my apartment. Niko steadied me, but I shook free and whirled to scoop a curious cat under each arm and deposit them both back in my living room. Niko shut the door as I straightened.

A roll of white cotton hugged the door frame, tacked in place by industrial-strength staples. The cobweb restraints had disappeared as if they'd never existed, and a fine white powder coated the welcome mat. I dusted off my hands and swiped tears from beneath my eyes, my fingers coming away smudged with mascara. More powder drifted from my hair. I looked like a bag of flour had exploded on me.

I glared at the mess on my carpet, then up at Niko, my hands balling into fists. I took a half step toward him, arm muscles bunched. A solid punch to his jaw would wipe that serene expression off his face.

Too much. My reaction registered as too extreme, but surprise fueled the volatile manipulations of the bond, firing my anger higher. I forced myself to the center of the front room and channeled my rage into volume.

"What the hell was that? And how did you get in here?"

"I used a key." He gestured behind him to the door and said, "That's for your protection."

I dug my nails into my palms, his calm and level tone rendering me speechless. Mr. Bond chose that moment to head-butt my shin. He rubbed his body against me and wrapped his tail up my bare leg; then deciding I'd been properly greeted, he trotted to his food bowl. Hunkering down, he crunched through dry kibble with relish. I eyed the full bowl of food.

Niko had fed Mr. Bond.

Swallowing my rant, I ground out a single word: "Explain."

"It's a nonlethal trap. It'll catch a pooka as easily as it caught you."

"Great plan. Nothing restores trust like a good trap." I shook powder from my hair and coat, holding my breath until it settled.

"It will give you time to talk to Jamie before he runs off. Again."

Because he knew better than me how to handle a pooka. Riiight. "If

Jamie had triggered your trap right now instead of me, what would you have done?"

"I'd have called you." His eyes tightened, the first sign of his calm demeanor cracking, and scorn laced his tone when he continued. "I'm pretty sure you would have cut short your date for Jamie."

"Well, your trap didn't work, so good night." *Take your imminent lecture with you.*

"I've got an assignment upstate and won't be around for a few days," Niko said as if I hadn't spoken. "Before I leave, I want to make sure you're prepared."

"So you decided to break in and make yourself at home." If I'd brought Alex upstairs, how would I have explained Niko waiting for me in my apartment? Or better yet, how would I have explained the trap?

Niko's lips settled in a flat line and he crossed his arms. "I had been told you were sick. When you didn't answer the door, I was concerned. It never occurred to me you'd be out."

"And naturally you decided to try your hand at trapping Jamie. Without running it past me."

"Where is your head at?" Niko thundered, the fury and volume startling me. "You've got an *out-of-control* pooka doing who knows what in your region, and you decide to go on a *date*? I thought you recognized the seriousness of the situation, but I guess I was wrong."

"You think I don't know how serious this is?" I matched Niko's tone, indignation turning my body rigid.

"Clearly not, if you're prioritizing your sex life—"

"How *dare* you!"

"Look at yourself. Look at your actions!" He lowered his voice, but his tone grew harsher. "I'd expect this from a teenager, but not from you. Not with how much you claim to love the pooka."

Bite me. "Because all I've done is ignore the problem. I haven't hunted the tyv all night and Jamie all day. I haven't run myself ragged—"

"This is what you consider ragged?" Niko asked, gesturing to my slinky top and short skirt with the blade of his hand.

"Get off your high horse. I needed a break. Do you know what it's like to have this damn bond in your thoughts?" I jabbed two fingers against the back of my head where the bond snarled at me to attack Niko because he wanted to trap Jamie, where worry had morphed into something viscous that made each swallow feel like it'd choke me. "It distorts everything, and the longer Jamie is gone, the more it yanks me around."

Tears, unexpected and unwelcome, welled in my eyes. I spun away before Niko could see them and stormed down the hall, uncaring that I tracked dirty footprints and powder through the house. I tossed my coat on the bed. A new, thick white drape smothered the window, Velcro holding it tight to the wall. Another trap? I throttled my tears and marched back to the front room.

"What have you done to my window?" Unfamiliar white in the corner of my eye caught my attention. A tube of cotton clung to the frame around the sliding glass door. I pointed at it. "And that? What have you done to my place?"

Niko hadn't moved, but his body language had changed. He didn't look angry so much as cautious. Good, because I was in the mood to break something, and right now he was at the top of the list.

"The bedroom curtain is a ward, the strongest I could find on short notice. That"—he pointed to the sliding glass door—"is another trap. If Jamie breaks the bond, you're going to need protection. Your weak energy wards aren't going to cut it."

"You think Jamie would come for me? That he'd attack me if he went evil?" I'd intended the questions to sound righteously indignant; instead, I sounded uncertain, the memory of Jamie's expression when he had thrown the ball of *atrum* at me countering my loyalty to the pooka.

"Believe it or not, I don't want to see you hurt."

Too late. This whole week had been one painful experience after the next. I might not have the wounds to show for it, but if I had to take much more of being torn in two by Jamie's rebellion and my responsibility to bring him in line, I'd shatter.

"Which is why you need to pull yourself together and treat this seriously," Niko said. "If you don't get control of Jamie before I return, I'm going to have to do it for you."

His threat stole my breath. He wasn't saying he'd bring Jamie back to me or even take over the bond. He was saying he'd kill Jamie.

"Over my dead body."

My words landed in the silence and stuck. Niko closed the distance between us, gripping my jaw and staring into my eyes. I jerked free with a harsh laugh.

"You think I'm already tainted." I'd seen the doubt in his eyes. A hollowness yawned inside me, and I struggled for balance, readjusting to the loss of Niko's trust. Bitterness lapped into the emptiness, and my face twisted into something ugly. "I thought you knew me better."

"So did I."

"Don't. Just don't. I've had enough guilt trips for the day. If you require proof, here it is." I shoved a bubble into my soul above my heart, and the net swelled to engulf Niko's hand, still raised between us. Repeated practice today had improved my technique; even Jamie might have been impressed with the basketball-size net.

Niko glared into my eyes and pulsed his *lux lucis* into mine. I braced myself, prepared for the discordant impact of his energy and the intrusive sandpaper slide of his soul through mine. Instead, our energy met in a soothing, intimate caress. Every cell of *lux lucis* in my body snapped to attention and magnetized on Niko, thrumming with awareness. Between one breath and the next, my entire body woke up and turned on, surpassing even the meteoric speed of my arousal with Alex.

I stumbled back and my net collapsed with the sharp pain of a rubber band snapped against my skin. Niko flinched. Heat rushed to my cheeks and my dark shirt couldn't disguise the press of my hard nipples. I compressed my lips and held my breath, refusing to let my chest move, refusing to give in to the impulse to bite my lip.

Niko took a deep breath and turned his back to me, bracing his hand against the door. After a long, quiet fifteen seconds—I counted—he opened the door, and I thought he'd leave without saying anything.

"This activates the web," Niko said, squatting and indicating a toggle switch at the base of the cotton frame. "Flip it this way to deactivate it before you walk out or in. Flip it back to prime it. I've installed an app on your phone. It will tell you if the trap is tripped."

So much for him calling me if he'd caught Jamie tonight; my phone had been here all along.

"Those will free Jamie." Niko straightened and pointed to two spray bottles of powder on the half wall beside the door; then he turned enough to look at me. "Take one when you leave, otherwise you won't be able to free him. Don't get caught in your own trap or you'll be stuck until one of us happens along. It would be difficult to explain to norms."

"What makes you think I'm going to use it?"

"Because you want the pooka to live." He stepped across the

threshold and turned back to face me. "Try to stay alive." Pulling the door almost closed, he flicked a dark finger across the toggle, activating the trap, then shut the door.

Hail pounded my skull as I sprinted from my car to the office the next morning, adding insult to headache. Sleep had been slow to come last night, and I'd woken more times than I had counted, phone in hand, bringing up the trap app before my bleary vision came into focus. More than once I got up and opened the door to check the empty landing for signs of Jamie.

I missed the pooka with a fierceness that made my chest ache. I resented him for abandoning me and leaving me to deal with the fallout. Every time I thought about him spreading *atrum* through my region and helping the tyv, my heart sprinted in my chest and my fists clenched with impotent anger. Over and over, these conflicting emotions cycled through me.

Sometimes they all bombarded me at once.

I yanked open the door to my headquarters, wincing at the obnoxious *clank* of the broken bell. Heat gusted over me, carrying the combined scent of stale fast food and roses. Ah, Ode de Dumpster, the smell of my illustrious headquarters.

Sharon sat behind her podium at the helm of the empty desks. From outside, she had appeared to have the office to herself, but the squabble of high-pitched voices that assaulted my eardrums as I crossed the threshold proved she wasn't alone. The peace talks were still in full swing.

Sharon's flat brown eyes bore into me with a suspicious heat she had previously only directed at Jamie. My spine snapped rigid and I glared back.

"Lay off me. I'm clean," I growled.

The receptionist pivoted in her chair as I passed, her actions unequivocally aggressive. Holding her stare, I swung wide and didn't turn my back on her until I had a table between us. When I glanced over my shoulder at her, she'd resumed her usual position, but she continued to monitor me in a small mirror propped on the podium.

My steps slowed as I neared Brad's office. This conversation was going to suck.

Just get it over with.

Taking a deep breath, I forced myself to step up to Brad's open doorway.

My boss stood in the limited free space behind his desk, hands placidly clasped in front of his stomach, face bland as he listened to a prajurit in front of him. She rested on a small wooden platform screwed into the wall about four feet above the floor. Four warriors flanked her, crowding the narrow ledge. None of them had swords in the sheaths at their waists, and judging by the scowls on their faces, it was fortunate everyone was unarmed. A dozen more platforms ringed Brad's office, each with a red rose resting at the center. The sweet-rich odor of the cut flowers wafted from the office and coiled in the back of my throat, a heavy but welcome relief from the musty old-food scents emanating from the break room.

When Brad noticed me, his expression danced from surprise to relief to annoyance with comical speed, finally settling into an unreadable mask.

"Excuse me. I need to confer with my enforcer," he announced, cutting off the tiny queen.

Her protests were overridden by a chorus of prajurit speaking at once.

"Madison Fox?"

"Is that her?"

"Madison Fox, you promised me—"

"You said you favored working with the *Ek Emas* clan—"

The drone of their wings grew until it sounded as if a small engine were running in Brad's office, and the scent of roses intensified.

Brad whirled to face the prajurit. "Anyone who leaves their designated platform will incur a five-wing-beat decrease in their territory."

As one, dozens of prajurit feet hit the wooden platforms and silence replaced the hum of their wings. Grumbling under his breath, Brad exited his office and pulled the door shut behind him. Since the walls of his office stopped short of the ceiling, the attempt to barricade the prajurit inside and give us privacy was more symbolic than anything else, but it did help cut down the noise when the prajurit resumed their shrill arguments.

"I wasn't expecting you so soon," Brad said, speaking at a normal volume.

I checked his forehead. No vein pulsed at his temple. His face remained pink but not flushed. I waited.

"Are you feeling better?" he asked politely. Indifferently. Like he was talking to a stranger.

"Not in the least."

"I'm sorry to hear that."

I ground my teeth. Why wouldn't he yell at me and get it over with?

"Did you send Niko to check on me last night?" I asked.

"Niko doesn't take orders from me."

I'd been prepared to defend myself and I'd rehearsed my explanation. If he got angry, I could get angry right back. I didn't know what to do with this quiet disappointment. I shuffled my feet, fidgeting with my jacket zipper tab, each tick of silence between us feeding my guilt.

"Jamie gave me a prophecy yesterday," I blurted out.

Brad's eyes widened. "He what?"

"He said he couldn't before because we were too closely linked, but then yesterday, when we . . . spoke at his birthing grounds . . ."

"Did he specifically say it was a prophecy?"

I nodded.

"What did he say?"

I hesitated, but I needed to tell Brad—because I needed his guidance and because I needed to no longer be alone with the knowledge. Still, I couldn't shake the feeling that by speaking the words aloud, I gave them more power.

"He said, 'The next time we meet, one of us will die. You will be the one to choose who lives.'"

Brad sank into the nearest chair, his meaty hand covering his mouth. I thrummed my nails against my thigh, tension tightening my shoulders.

"It doesn't mean what it sounds like it means, right? Because I don't want Jamie to die and I don't want to die, either."

Brad rubbed his hand up over his forehead, his eyes refocusing on me. "The wording of prophecies can be tricky. They don't always mean what you think they mean." He didn't sound convinced. "You've had no contact with him since?"

"What do you think?"

Brad didn't respond to my sarcasm. I paced away from him and back.

"You need to prepare yourself," he said softly.

"Prepare . . . ?"

"It's going to happen soon."

"But Jamie can see a year into the future—"

"Your bond won't last a year in its current fragile state. If it breaks, we'll know exactly where he's at, and we'll have to . . ."

I glanced away from my boss's pitying look. How was I supposed to prepare myself for that? Draft up my will or sharpen my knife?

A cold sweat broke over my head, sluicing down my body, and I wobbled to a chair and collapsed. The stifling heat of the office compressed my lungs. I yanked off my coat and scarf, tossing them atop the desk. Massaging my forehead, I concentrated on taking slow, deep breaths until the urge to vomit subsided.

Pamela strode into our headquarters, her keen eyes bouncing between me and Brad. My stomach flipped. Last night's shouting match in the club's restroom replayed in my head, and I didn't come out looking rosy. Then again, neither did the inspector. An echo of my former indignation sputtered to life, enough to enable me to straighten my spine and meet Pamela's gaze.

Rose trailed after her. Dark circles underscored the empath's eyes, and her steps lagged despite it not yet even being ten.

"Prophecies are private," Brad whispered. "There's no rule that says you are required to share a prophecy. With anyone."

I jerked to look at his face, but he'd already turned away to greet the inspector. Was he cautioning me not to share the prophecy with Pamela? Or had he merely been telling me my rights?

Pamela stopped on the other side of the table, scrutinizing my face. I wondered if I looked as sick as I felt.

"I'm glad to see you're here, Madison. It saves me a trip. Any sign of the pooka?"

I shook my head.

Her lips tightened, but she didn't state any unnecessary cautions. Pulling out her phone, she sent a quick text message. I folded my hands in my lap and Brad waited patiently at Pamela's side. Rose marched to her desk, grabbed a water bottle, and downed two aspirins. The inspector's phone chimed, and we all watched her read the text.

"Good. Doris says she'll be here in twenty minutes," Pamela announced, putting her phone away. "She's your backup today, Madison. Where you go, she goes. We don't know what state the pooka is in, and I'm not letting you out alone."

"But—"

"As long as you're with Doris," she continued, overriding my hesitant protest, "I won't need to do any purity tests on you."

"Some company would be great," I said.

Pamela smiled a genuine smile that contained no malice and didn't disguise the worry in her eyes. "I thought you'd agree. However, the moment the sun sets, I want you here at my side. No excuses."

I nodded, not quite believing she was letting me off so lightly. If not for the impending doom of Jamie's prophecy, I might have felt genuine relief.

Pamela turned to Brad. "We're going to need every prajurit available once we figure out where the tyv has been laying her spawn. How are the peace talks coming along?"

"About how you'd expect," Brad said. "Every queen feels she deserves as much land as Madison promised Lestari. None will concede they're not yet ready to rule, not even those who can't muster four warriors to attend them during the negotiations. Plus none of the strong queens want to allow a weaker queen into their clan for fear of future mutiny."

While he talked, he ambled toward the back of the office, taking Pamela with him and leaving me in relative peace.

Rose shoved her chair across the aisle to sit next to me. I glanced up, making a feeble attempt to rein in my rioting emotions. The empath didn't need to be subjected to the mess tangled between my head and heart. Judging by her sympathetic expression, my attempt to exude calm fell flat.

"I thought you were avoiding the office during the peace talks," I said.

"Pamela asked me to come in this morning."

We both glanced toward Brad and Pamela, who had their heads bent together, deep in a strategy discussion that I didn't strain to hear; they'd tell me what I needed to know when it pertained to me. The prajurit had fallen blissfully quiet, and the throbbing in my head receded, the sharp pain becoming a dull ache behind my eyeballs.

Rose broke the seal of a second water bottle and passed it to me. When I took a breath to thank her, a cloying lavender and vanilla scent lodged in my throat. I swished a mouthful of water, but even after I swallowed, the heavy odors coated my tongue.

"New perfume?" I asked, striving for a polite tone that didn't sound like I was choking.

"Last-ditch coping strategy."

Ah. Vanilla and lavender were calming scents. Rose must be desperate if she was relying on aromatherapy to distance herself from other's emotions.

"Is it working?"

"It's better than popping aspirin every twenty minutes and dying from liver failure before Christmas." Rose flapped the top of her apricot blouse and grimaced.

I took another drink and scanned the parking lot for Doris. If I sat in this pathetic office much longer, I'd become mired in its depressing atmosphere.

"I'm just going to say it: You look like hell," Rose said.

I huffed a laugh, glancing toward the ceiling and blinking back the tears stinging my eyes. "You would too if you'd bonded a pooka turning evil."

Rose's commiserative hum opened a floodgate, and my problems tumbled out.

"I've tried everything with Jamie. I followed Pamela's instructions to the letter. She said be firm. She said not to let him use *atrum*. But when I laid down the rules, he didn't listen. It's not like I could force him, either. He's got all the power and the worst I can do is get mad and yell. It's like trying to discipline a child without being able to follow through on the threat to spank them. I have no leverage, no ability to enforce any rule. Then he ran off, and when I tried to talk to him, he threw . . . he threw it all back in my face. Maybe I need to be stricter with him. When I get my hands on him, I'll lock him down and not let him up until he sees things my way." Somehow.

"What about affection?" Rose asked softly.

I blinked, straightening in my chair. "You're not suggesting . . . ?" Rose knew my relationship with Jamie was platonic. The thought of trying to win him back by sexual means made my insides want to curl in on themselves.

"No! No, nothing like that." Rose swiped her hands down her thighs and shuddered. "I mean, you've tried being strict with him. You've tried yelling. You've scolded. Maybe that's not what he's going to respond to. Maybe he just needs someone to talk to, some attention that isn't demanding or controlling."

"But Pamela knows about pookas, and she said—"

"Who cares what she said?"

"I do!"

Rose cocked an eyebrow at me. "That's not what I heard."

"Fine. I *should* care. She could teach me a lot. She has experience and—"

"And no idea what it's like to be bonded to a pooka."

I flopped back in my chair. Rose wasn't saying anything I hadn't thought.

She leaned forward. "Have you considered Jamie might be acting out because he doesn't feel welcome or . . ." She hesitated. "Or loved?"

I opened my mouth, but the truth of her words stole my breath. I'd been so determined to stick to the inspector's rules to prove I was a good enforcer that I hadn't allowed myself to dwell on how cruelly I had been treating Jamie. I was his anchor, the one person around whom his world revolved. He didn't have a support network of friends to turn to for advice or comfort; he had me. And I'd stopped treating him as if his opinions and emotions mattered. I'd changed up the rules, gone back on my word, and turned every moment together into a test. In doing so, I'd been telling him he wasn't good enough, that he needed to change to be worthy of my affection. In words and deeds, I'd told him that despite his half *lux lucis* soul, I didn't trust him. I'd acted as if I expected him to become evil—as if he already was evil.

No wonder he'd rebelled and run away.

It'd been exactly what I'd done, too. Pamela's repetitive purity tests had hammered home her lack of trust in me and her belief that I would turn evil at any moment. Just like Jamie had with me, I'd struggled to prove Pamela wrong, and when I'd failed at an impossible task, I'd rebelled and run off.

"Oh, Rose, what have I done?" I swiped a tear from my cheek with the back of my hand, not quite meeting my friend's eyes.

"You've been human. You made a mistake." She lifted a hand to forestall my self-recriminations. "It's no longer about what you've done; it's about what you're going to do."

I nodded. It sounded so easy and logical coming from her, but— "I don't even know where to start."

"Try doing what you normally do."

"Make a mess of everything?" My joke fell flat, and I swiped another tear from my cheek.

"Follow your heart and your instincts. It's worked for you in the past. Now pull yourself together. Pamela's going to come back over here and want me to report on your emotional state, and it'll go better if you're not crying."

"You're going to tell on me?" This had been another test?

"Don't give me that. I care about your emotional well-being, and so does Pamela. She's worried about you. We all are. If Jamie turns dark and gets to you . . . You're a very strong enforcer, Madison. You could do a lot of damage, and we couldn't predict the harm the *atrum* would do to your psyche." Rose glanced toward Pamela and Brad, then leaned closer and whispered, "You scare her, or your potential to make everything go sideways scares her. Which is why she's doing everything she can, including using me, to keep control over this situation."

"She does like to be in control," I agreed, bitterness twisting my mouth.

Rose shrugged. "Who doesn't?"

When she leaned back in her chair, Brad and Pamela broke off their conversation and walked back to our table.

"How is Madison?" Pamela asked.

I fisted my hands under the table and glared at the inspector. She could have pulled Rose aside or waited until I left. Instead, she spoke as if I weren't there, making a point of letting me know she didn't trust me. Brad gave me a small nod that I didn't know how to interpret, but he didn't intervene.

"She's about how you'd expect: Frazzled, irritated"—Rose delivered the understatement with a small smile—"mourning her broken relationship with Jamie and eager to fix things."

Pamela studied me, searching my eyes as if she were trying to peer inside my head. "Do you sense any darkness in her?"

"Traces of self-loathing and heaps of guilt, but nothing worse."

My cheeks flushed with embarrassment, both that Rose could feel my shame and that she'd given voice to it.

Pamela nodded, apparently satisfied. "Good. Go with Doris today, Madison. Your strategy yesterday was sound: Tire the pooka so he won't be a problem for us tonight. Coordinate with Brad, and be back here in time for hunting the tyv at sundown—if we can find her."

"Are you here to capture Jamie if he shows up?" I asked Doris after our first stop as we walked back to the car. We'd burned through a moderate swarm of frost moths congregating behind a 7-Eleven, and I had just enough moth-enhanced anger to consider tackling the older woman and wrestling my keys from her if she gave me the wrong answer.

Doris snorted. "I'm here to make sure you don't die. I'm your bodyguard."

If she'd said that to anyone else, they would have collapsed with laughter. Doris's short, wiry frame, permed gray hair, and wrinkled face were the antithesis of a stereotypical bodyguard. But I could see the tensile strength of her soul, and I accepted her words at face value.

She halted and spread her arms wide, tilting her head back to belt out the chorus line from the song Whitney Houston made famous. "And I-I-I-I-I will always love you!"

I scanned the horizon, ever hopeful that I'd spot Jamie—and dreading seeing him, too. *The next time we meet, one of us will die.*

"Not even a clap? No smile?" Doris poked my ribs. "Child, you're in a bad way."

Don't I know it.

Lunch came and went without spotting Jamie. Determined to make Doris's presence superfluous, I attacked each new cluster of evil with single-minded fervor. When I was slicing through herds of imps or burning through flocks of frost moths, my thoughts quieted. For those limited seconds or minutes, I floated in a cocoon of purpose, free from worries and regrets, and I became ruthless in achieving those moments of peace.

As had become my habit, I kept the palmquell in my left hand and used every opportunity to practice my marksmanship. Most of the time, I hit what I aimed at, even vervet swinging from eaves and trees above us. Doris offered a few pointers and the occasional praise, but for the most part she left me alone with my thoughts and stayed out of my way.

Though we never encountered anything stronger than a small wraith, the nonstop activity sapped my strength. I slouched into our shabby headquarters shortly before five that night, pausing on the threshold for one last inspection of the parking lot and sky. During our day zipping back and forth across my region, I hadn't once felt the stretch or pull of the bond. Not once. Either Jamie had kept close, or our tenuous connection had thinned too much to matter.

"I've worked with enforcers who had decades more experience but who weren't half as dedicated as Madison," Doris said, drawing my attention. The retired enforcer stood in the middle of the office, reporting to Pamela. "She's understandably preoccupied, but otherwise a model enforcer."

I tried to keep the surprise from my face, never having expected to hear such high praise from Doris.

"Good to hear, especially after her actions last night," Pamela said.

Doris gave me a pat on the shoulder as she left. "Good luck tonight."

I waited near the door, searching the sky and stretching knots from my calves. Dancing in three-inch heels last night, then being on my feet all day today had done my legs no favors. Sharon's flat gaze bore into me, mistrust written across her stoic features.

"Have you eaten?" Pamela asked.

I shook my head, not wanting to explain my loss of appetite. "Any sign of the tyv?"

"It's too early to tell. You should rest while you can. I plan on keeping us moving all night."

Oh joy. The throbbing ache in the soles of my feet encouraged me toward the nearest chair, but relaxing under Pamela's suspicious supervision was out of the question. Besides, despite my attempts to lose myself in my work today, I'd had a lot of time to think—not just about my relationship with Jamie, but also about my actions in general. I owed more than the pooka an apology.

"I think I'll get a snack." I tossed my jacket and beanie on a table and ambled to the break room for privacy. Pamela trailed after me, forcing me to open and choke down an entire yogurt to maintain my ruse. The inspector fussed at the coffee maker, taking her time doctoring her cup of coffee, then sipping it while staring out the door, as if by not looking at me she could fool me into thinking she wasn't monitoring me. Did she expect me to make a break for the back exit and run out? Then what? I still wore the tracker. She could pinpoint my location no matter where I went.

I headed for the bathroom. The inspector followed, stopping to lean against the wall when she noted my destination. I gave her a flat look through the gap of the closing door and made sure to snap the lock with extra force. A box of a room, the bathroom fit right in with the rest of the office: drab, uninspired, and tired. The overhead light flickered on and a fan roared to life.

Cocking a hip against the sink, I slid Val from his strap and opened him.

It had been twenty-four hours since I'd last cracked his spine. Leaving him closed had been a passive, quiet cruelty, one that turned his cover into his own prison of solitary confinement. I expected his first page to be filled with a justified rant or maybe some much-deserved insults in all caps. Instead, a blank page stared back at me.

"I'm sorry, Val." I kept my voice low, below the drone of the fan. If Pamela were so crass as to press her ear to the door, I didn't want her listening in on my side of this conversation. "I've been self-centered. It was wrong of me to treat you so poorly and ignore you."

I didn't like it. The words printed small and prim across the center of the page.

"I know. I shouldn't have let my anger get the better of me." I hesitated. As much as I wanted to blame all my thoughtless behavior on losing Jamie and the bond's emotional manipulation, I needed to accept responsibility for my actions with Val. Clearing my throat, I continued. "I was . . . I *am* jealous of how highly you speak of Pamela. It made me act petty. But it's okay for you to like other people more than me."

I waited, but Val didn't jump in with a polite protest and a proclamation of his love for me above all others. His silence stung my ego.

"What I'm trying to say is I shouldn't have prevented you from talking to other people, even if you wanted to say bad things about me. Maybe especially if you had an opinion I didn't agree with."

Pamela's not the same as I remember. Val took his time forming the sentence, as if picking each word carefully. *I do not like the way she treats you.*

That made two of us, but I found myself shaking my head. I didn't approve of Pamela's methods, but none of her actions had been malicious or ill intended, and it felt cheap to bond with Val by tarnishing his hero. "She's just doing her job and making sure my region is protected."

So are you. You're a good enforcer, Dice.

Pathetically grateful for his meager praise, I hoped it meant he'd forgiven me. "Thank you, Val. I may not know any other handbooks, but I'm glad I got paired with you."

So you're not going to sell me?

"What?" My exclamation echoed in the tiny room. More hushed, I asked, "What are you talking about?"

The region is bankrupt and you don't think I'm useful, but I am worth a lot.

Oh Val. "I would never sell you. Not to save the region, not even when you're being a pain in the ass. You're my friend, and you're stuck with me."

You're not always sand in my binding, either.

A backhanded compliment and a bit of flair in his font: Val was cheering up.

"Are we okay?"

Yes. Thank you for talking to me. He barely let the words land before he wrote over them. *I want you to know that if I had any knowledge about how to bring the pooka back, I would tell you.*

"I know. Do you want to talk with Pamela now?"

Val hesitated. *Maybe later.*

I'd expected more enthusiasm, but he might have restrained himself to spare my feelings.

Essentially, nothing about my situation had changed, but as I exited the bathroom, my steps were lighter. One relationship repaired, one to go. If only mending things with Jamie would be so easy.

Pamela wasn't standing guard outside the bathroom door, as I'd anticipated. She'd moved to pace in a tight circle in front of Brad's office.

"Do you feel that?" Brad asked her.

She nodded. "I'll need a contingent of prajurit—"

"I'm on it." Brad pivoted and stepped into his office. "I need six volunteers to—"

The chorus of prajurit voices drowned out his next words.

Summer had arrived, and when she glanced in my direction, her look should have incinerated me. I thought her opinion of me had been bad before I'd stranded her alone with Pamela to aimlessly hunt the tyv last night, but apparently there had been deeper depths to plumb.

"Nice of you to join us," she said, ice in her voice.

I met her disdainful gaze with a sense of remorse. I kept screwing up with her, undermining any possibility of us forming a friendship.

"I'm sorry about last night. I—"

Summer turned her back to me and walked away.

Just like that, my regret dried up. Jaw locked, I grabbed my coat and stuffed my arms into the sleeves. When no one moved toward the exit, I laid Val open on the table so he could participate. He greeted Summer and Pamela, the words appearing in large font easily visible from several feet away.

"Ah, hello," Summer said, eyes flicking up to meet mine, then back to Val.

"What's going on?" I asked.

"I'm sensing drones. Close. Within the pooka's tether range," Pamela said, her tone grim. "The fact that he's not hiding them . . . This could be the pooka's turning point, Madison. If he's become stronger in *atrum* than *lux lucis*, it would hamper his ability to provide a neutral camouflage."

My heartbeat pounded against my eardrums, and my voice warbled when I spoke. "Or he could have decided to stop helping them."

"He's had no reason to change his mind," Brad said, stepping out of his office. An entourage of prajurit fanned out around him. "Just . . . just be prepared."

The room swam, and I braced a hand on the table. They had to be wrong.

24

ARE YOUR REFLEXES GOOD? I WANT TO TRY SOMETHING

T he drones didn't politely wait in one location for us to show up and kill them, nor could Pamela get a consistent lock on them. I didn't know whether to be relieved or frustrated. If the balance of Jamie's soul was tilting toward evil, making it harder for him to disguise the drones, at least the transition wasn't fast or seamless. However, the longer it took us to locate the drones, the more time they and the tyv had to spew evil across my region and eat the souls of my norms. I couldn't win, and the tangle of my conflicting hopes twisted my stomach into knots.

"It's only a matter of time," Pamela said, craning to examine the roofs we passed. She sat in the passenger seat of my car, and with Summer following, bringing the prajurit in her vehicle, we snaked through crowded subdivisions for an hour, making frequent U-turns and backtracking according to the pulses of evil sporadically registering on the inspector's soul. "I'm picking them up more frequen— Turn around, they're headed that way."

I flipped on a blinker and looped through a sleepy intersection, passing Summer. I didn't dare chance looking for drones myself. Doing so would require switching to Primordium, where road lines, sidewalks, and the traffic lights all blended into the same gray tone. Instead, I concentrated on being an exemplary chauffeur and keeping my mouth shut. The less the inspector and I said to each other, the better.

"There! Got you, sucker," Pamela exclaimed, pointing due east.

Unable to fly over the line of houses in front of us, I sped back to the main road and raced around the long block. We made a right onto East Roseville Parkway and took the first left, entering an apartment complex. *My* apartment complex. We came in through the west entrance, over three city blocks from my actual building, but I still wanted to laugh, or perhaps cry. Jamie couldn't have made this situation worse if he had tried.

"Clearly the pooka doesn't respect you, and he definitely doesn't care for your safety if he's bringing the tyv to your backyard," Pamela said.

"Or it means he's not in charge of where she goes," I countered.

I wished I believed myself, but I'd yet to meet an evil creature Jamie couldn't overpower with his innate strength, including the tyv. If he had a way of communicating with her, not simply disguising her whereabouts, then it wasn't hard to picture him in charge. Guiding the tyv to my doorstep fell in line with his escalating rebellion.

Following Pamela's directions through the convoluted jigsaw puzzle of three-story buildings squeezed around old oak trees, tennis courts, and pools, I selected an empty parking spot far from my apartment. When I shoved from the car, icy air scraped down my esophagus, carrying a bitter mix of wood smoke, exhaust, and swamp. I exhaled, my breath a white fog in the yellow lamplight. Cars occupied almost every parking space, and lights illuminated the interior of dozens of apartments, but no one lingered in the cold with us.

High above, well out of the range of my palmquell, drones crisscrossed the sky, their mixed-energy bodies transforming the black expanse into a seething patchwork. Their numbers had doubled, tripled, as if all the drones Summer and I had killed had been resurrected over the last two nights, back to feed once more on my region. I shuddered and tightened my grip on the palmquell, its familiar shape in the palm of my hand steadying my nerves.

Summer parked and opened her door, pressing back against her seat when a flurry of prajurit blasted through the opening. Of the six queens Brad had selected, only two had more than three warriors in her clan. I recognized Lestari and her warriors, who hovered nearest me. The rest fanned out, all keeping an equal distance between themselves and the other clans. Drafts of arctic air from their wing beats stirred strands of hair against my face, tickling my numbing cheeks.

Pamela divided the prajurit into two groups, three queens per group, designating the queens with the most warriors to be each team's leader. Then she selected a warrior from each group, assigning the two men the task of scouting and serving as messengers. I braced for a slurry of arguments, but the prajurit remained silent, their differences set aside for the battle.

"No clan has jurisdiction here, and no deeds performed today imply future territorial rights," Pamela announced. "Clan *Hujan Gembira* has spent the last two days stockpiling supplies and will arrive shortly. I want a poison bead dropped down every chimney in this complex and in every chimney within a thousand-wing-beat radius. No exceptions."

Dismissed, the queens of each group clustered together, lifting higher while they discussed strategy. The warriors fanned out, ever watchful. One scout zoomed over the closest building and out of sight, and the prajurit who remained as our go-between messenger settled onto the warm hood of the Civic.

Pamela's misshapen soul pulsed over her left thigh, and she stiffened. "Damn, the tyv is strong." Her hand drifted to the soul breaker at her neck as she swiveled to stare unerringly south. Not taking her eyes off the horizon, she said, "Madison, you're at my side at all times. If I can't reach out and touch you, you're too far away. Keep up."

She broke into a jog, angling across the parking lot and up a muddy slope to a walkway. The prajurit warrior buzzed from the Civic's hood after her, and I chased them, dividing my attention between the ground and sky. Summer caught up to us, and our pounding footsteps echoed against the nearby buildings.

Dashing past manicured landscaping, we burst into a spacious quad. Muddy slopes and waterlogged lawns surrounded the central fenced-in pool, and towering apartment units boxed us in on three sides. I skidded to a stop. We'd found the tyv.

Inflated half again as large as the last time I'd seen her, the tyv loomed atop the building to our left. Her massive wings spanned the width of an apartment, and her grotesquely bloated body wouldn't have fit through the sliding glass door. Shuffling on six sturdy legs, she dragged her abdomen soundlessly across the roof tiles, aligning her rear with the nearest chimney and depositing an egg into its depths. Drones buzzed around her, flitting across the roof and crawling along her body, but when she lifted her ponderous bulk into the sky, few assisted her.

She had not only grown larger, but she had also grown stronger. A lot stronger.

Oh, Jamie, what have you done?

The tyv lit upon the next rooftop and crawled from chimney to chimney, pausing to stab her spearlike mouth into unlucky drones and drain them of their partially digested *lux lucis*, leaving the victims little more than emaciated black shadows.

"We're too close," Pamela whispered, and I startled, released from the horror that had frozen me in place. "Let's circle the pool. We need to put distance between us and— Bloody hell. What are they doing now?"

A cluster of drones over twenty strong peeled from the roiling mass and formed a tight circle above us, needle proboscises angled down, dark multifaceted eyes glossy with hunger. *Lux lucis* churned strong in each of them, making them easy to track against the dark sky.

"That's not normal drone behavior," Summer said.

"No, it's not." Pamela spared a glance for the prajurit warrior hovering near my shoulder. "Go. Get to safety."

He raised a sword, tapped his fist to his chest, and rocketed toward the nearest tree, his white body blending into the *lux lucis*–saturated branches.

"We should get to cover, too," I suggested.

"Stay together. Summer, watch our backs." Pamela pivoted to put her back to Summer's, her rough grip on my forearm spinning me around with her. It didn't matter which way I faced; drones filled the sky in every direction. At some invisible signal, they fell upon us.

"I hope your aim has gotten better, Madison," Pamela said. "Stand your ground."

The drones swarmed in a complex, multidirectional attack. I fired a blur of *lux lucis*, pulling energy from my soul in a steady drain and feeding it through the palmquell. Drones exploded, filling the air with a cloud of *atrum* particles, but the three of us couldn't hold off the nonstop attacks for long. I heard Summer's muffled cry first, spinning too late to kill the drone that had struck her. She bolted.

Sharp pain lanced through my shoulder and neck, staggering me. When I regained my balance, I sprinted for the nearest oak. I needed to get to cover. My sneakers slipped in mud and I went down on one knee, springing back to my feet and not stopping until my back pressed to rough bark. Gulping in air, I checked the canopy. White limbs arched above me, dwindling into slender branches and spindly twigs. Beyond them, drones swirled and spun, but none swooped low enough to attack.

Closing my eyes, I sucked in deep breaths, keeping one hand planted on the tree to absorb its *lux lucis*. I'd made it to cover. I'd—

The fog of false urgency cleared from my thoughts. *Crap.* I'd run.

I shoved from the tree but stopped after two steps, taking stock of the situation. Summer crouched in the stairwell of the same building the tyv crawled atop, hidden from the monstrous creature's sight while she fired through the open backs of the concrete steps at the drones assaulting Pamela.

The inspector hadn't budged, and her soul visibly dimmed as she unloaded a continuous blur of bullets into the ceaseless drones. For every evil insect she killed, two more jabbed her soul, their bites draining her even faster.

My sprint to cover had been the smart tactic. Even Summer had sought out a more defensive position, so why didn't Pamela? At the very least, why didn't she employ evasive maneuvers?

Stand your ground. It had been the last thing she had said, and it must have been her intent when she had been struck by the first drone. Every drone afterward only reinforced her determination to remain rooted in place. Pamela could no more move than I could have stopped myself from running for the tree.

The inspector possessed one of the strongest souls I'd ever seen, but even she couldn't withstand this assault forever, and she certainly couldn't take out all the drones by herself.

"Stay there," I yelled to Summer. "I'll get her."

I yanked my pet wood from my pocket and flicked my wrist to extend it, pumping *lux lucis* down the wand's length. With my palmquell in my opposite hand, I charged.

Get Pamela to cover. Get Pamela to cover, I chanted, keeping my gaze locked on the inspector. I fired into the sky but didn't pay attention to where my bullets landed. I couldn't allow myself to be distracted in case a drone struck. If a random impulse stranded me out in the open, the drones would drain my *lux lucis* even faster than they devoured Pamela's. Slashing blindly overhead with the pet wood, I barreled into the inspector.

"We need to move," I barked.

Her eyes latched on to me with feverish intensity. I grabbed a fistful of her jacket, but the pet wood made me clumsy, and she shrugged out of my grip. Spinning, she seized my right wrist. Fine. That worked, too.

"Let's go." I tugged, ready to pull her with me.

Pamela dropped her palmquell.

"What are you—"

She slapped a handcuff over my right forearm and cinched it tight, then snapped the other cuff to her left wrist, locking us together. I stared at the shackle in shock.

Pain jabbed through my back as a drone pierced my soul and swallowed a mouthful before buzzing skyward. I threw my palmquell aside and slapped Pamela with the full weight of my body behind the swing. Her head snapped back, and the crack of sound ricocheted through the buildings before the pain registered in my palm. I grinned. That had been damn satisfying.

Pamela dipped into her stance and cocked her fist. I danced backward, stumbling when my trapped wrist canted my balance. My foot slipped off the edge of the sidewalk into the mud and kept sliding. Crashing to my butt, I slid under Pamela swing by pure accident. Our connected wrists jerked her off balance and she slammed down on me with the force of a small vehicle, punching the air from my lungs.

Uncomprehendingly, I gaped at the sky, my entire field of vision boiling with drones. My pulse pounded, a deep accompaniment to the ringing in my ears; then my lungs remembered how to function, and I sucked in oxygen with a cavernous moan that set me coughing.

Fiery pain radiated from my right shoulder down to my wrist, where my hand kinked awkwardly against my side. A sharp ache, slowly numbing, informed me I'd have a new Bowie sheath–shaped bruise across my lower back. I'd landed in mud, not on the concrete sidewalk, which had probably saved me from a broken tailbone and concussion, but with the icy muck oozing into the gap between my coat and pants, I found it hard to be grateful.

Pamela floundered, her knee grinding into my thigh, her free hand pinning my hair to the ground. I groaned, and she froze, looking around with sudden awareness. Most of the drones had retreated into the airspace outside the range of our palmquells, but a handful broke away, dropping down to make the most of our helplessness. My left hand fisted on nothing, and panic carved through my midsection. I'd thrown the palmquell . . . there.

I wrenched my hair from beneath Pamela's hand, the sharp pain eliciting unbidden tears. Residual *lux lucis* gave the weapon a soft glow against the gray mud where it lay, useless, out of reach. I'd lost hold of the pet wood, too. Grunting, I braced my hand on Pamela's knee where it jabbed into my thigh, and shoved. The inspector toppled onto her butt, snapping the cuff against my wrist and twisting my arm painfully.

I'd done nothing but prove—repeatedly—my devotion to my job, my region, and *lux lucis*. Even at my most rebellious, the worst I'd done was take a night off and get embarrassingly intimate with Alex in a dance club. Yet the handcuff shackling me to Pamela's side reaffirmed how little she trusted me and how little faith she had in my ability to maintain my true *lux lucis* nature. Fury and humiliation pulsed through my limbs, leaving me shaky, my control thread-thin.

When the drones struck, this wouldn't be pretty.

The glint of white bullets winked through the air, and the lead drone exploded into *atrum* dust. The two behind it kept coming. Pamela flared a beam of *lux lucis* from her palm, a shining sword made of the pure energy of her soul, and cut the next drone in half. The third veered wide, wings blurring to gain altitude.

Summer sprinted to us, tossed Pamela her discarded palmquell, and swung around to fire at approaching drones. She looked like a Native American Wonder Woman, her stance wide and confident, her expression fierce as she protected us. Whatever organization the drones had possessed disintegrated, and they disbanded, scattering beyond the range of Summer's *lux lucis*.

I sat up, ignoring the throbbing of my back, and massaged my numb thigh, using my right hand to purposely jerk Pamela off balance. If she thought she could lock herself to me *and* call the shots, she was in for a nasty surprise.

Rolling to a crouch, I prepared to drag the inspector to my palmquell. She shocked me when she pocketed her weapon and retrieved a tiny key. Without saying a word or meeting my eyes, Pamela undid the cuff from my wrist, then from her own.

I snatched the metal bands from her loose grip and chucked them over the fence. They hit the pool water with a soft *plop* and sank out of sight in the deep end. Jaw fused, I glowered at Pamela, daring her to say something. She looked away first, but only to shoot a drone barreling down on me. Anger simmering hot enough to counter the frigid creep of wet mud down my backside, I hobbled to collect my palmquell, then my pet wood.

Not waiting for Pamela's instructions, I stomped across frozen, dead leaves to the nearest oak. Summer and Pamela followed, each of us giving the other space as we recharged from the massive tree's freely given *lux lucis*. Pamela took the largest draw, but the old tree's bright white trunk didn't so much as flicker at the energy loss. I rubbed my back against the trunk, scraping mud from my jacket, then bent and swiped the back of my legs against the rough bark. The abrasive surface proved better at removing wet mud than my gloves, but it did nothing to counter the chill.

The tyv had disappeared during the attack, and with buildings blocking our view and so many drones choking the sky, we couldn't tell which direction she'd gone. Fortunately, we had an airborne spy.

"She's beyond that building, moving east," our prajurit scout said, pointing across the pool. "Clan *Hujan Gembira* requests additional supplies."

"I'll see they get them." Pamela fired off a short text to Brad even as she continued to speak. "Stay hidden. The drones are behaving peculiarly."

The prajurit saluted and launched from the branch in the opposite direction as the tyv.

"Stick together," Pamela said.

I glared at her back and took the opposite path around the pool.

We jogged up a gently sloping road lined with covered parking, our eyes on the rooftops, slowing only when forced to defend ourselves from wayward drones. Even then, I maintained a steady walk and still hit my targets, each kill a vindication countering Pamela's low opinion of me.

As we drew alongside the building where the tyv roosted, a battery of drones dropped in a tight formation, attacking from directly above. Clustered together, they should have been easy targets, but the moment we started shooting, they scattered, only to regroup to my left, closer than before. A bristle of soul-devouring, control-stealing proboscises jabbed toward me. I fired again, my white bullets accompanied by Pamela's and Summer's. Between us, we killed seven drones, but the rest flared wide, twisting as fast as a school of piranhas to charge from a new direction. Their attacks were growing in sophistication, and it was only a matter of time before they overwhelmed us again.

Acorns popped underfoot as we dashed to an oak and spun, putting our backs to the trunk. The drones might have been invisible to normal people, but they had enough substance to prevent them from passing through solid matter. With the network of limbs curtailing a bold attack from above, they were forced into head-on rushes beneath the branches, and they died en masse before reaching us.

"I've never heard of drones coordinating like this," Summer said during a lull.

"They're not acting alone," Pamela said. "The pooka must be behind this."

I didn't want to admit it, even to myself, but I'd been thinking the same thing. Jamie had helped the tyv and drones the last two nights, disguising their activities from us. It stood to reason he could communicate with them. Maybe he could teach the drones or at least give them orders they'd respond to.

Or maybe he led them.

I stared up at the sky full of flying creatures with dawning horror. Jamie couldn't be a drone, could he? Human, dog, mammoth—all his other forms were solid, tangible, and visible to normal people. I'd been envisioning his fourth form as something like an evil prajurit, small enough to be overlooked by norms yet with physical form. But an insubstantial drone . . . ?

It fit. It explained how he'd been able to trail me across the city without attracting attention. It could explain why I hadn't spotted him tonight despite knowing he was close. Where better for a dual-energy pooka to hide than among *lux lucis*–carrying drones? Was it really such a stretch of the imagination to accept he could have a nonmaterial form? He changed shapes. His very existence defied the laws of physics, so why couldn't his body refute basic cellular density, too?

I cursed my own stupidity and started looking for a drone calling the shots.

If he's here and we encounter each other— I cut off the thought. I couldn't allow myself to dwell on Jamie's prophecy.

Aside from variations in size and negligible differences in the amount of *lux lucis* lighting up their abdomens, all the drones looked alike. My best chance of pinpointing Jamie was through the process of elimination. I dismissed the drones arriving from far afield and those departing, just as I dismissed the grunts assisting the tyv's flights. To command his troops, Jamie would need to remain close to the attacking drones, and he wouldn't want to be distracted by carting around the tyv every time she flew to a new chimney. He also wouldn't behave like a normal drone. They flew in an aimless, agitated cloud, but he would move with purpose. Which narrowed my focus to the drones swirling at the bottom of the flock, especially those that dipped low enough to feed on us.

I rubbed the crick in my neck, smearing mud on my scarf. The perpetual motion of the drones made it impossible to keep track of which I'd eliminated from my pool of suspects, and after ten minutes of making myself dizzy spinning in circles beneath the oak's branches, I decided I needed to change strategies.

The tyv launched for the next roof, her bulk dwarfing her small contingent of support drones. To follow her, we had to brave a parking lot and tennis court, both lacking convenient cover. If Jamie was going to organize another coordinated strike, it would be then.

I jogged out from under the tree with Pamela and Summer. I needed to force Jamie to reveal himself, and I couldn't do that by acting predictably. So instead of raising my palmquell and sighting on the nearest drones, I tucked the weapon and my hand into my pocket. Unable to leave myself completely defenseless, I grasped the middle of the pet wood and raised it above my head, holding it horizontal. A gentle push channeled *lux lucis* down all three feet of the slender rod. The wand wouldn't deter a drone attack, but at least they'd have a hard time jabbing me without receiving a deadly wallop of *lux lucis*. As ready as I'd ever get, I planted my feet and tipped my face to the sky.

"What are you doing?" Summer asked, stopping in front of me.

"Give me a minute. I need to concentrate."

"Figure out how to concentrate and walk at the same time," Pamela snapped.

I let her words wash over me and focused on spotting the drone that didn't belong. The last thing I needed was another impulsive fight with the inspector spawned by the confluence of a stray thought and a drone bite.

The riotous mass of insect bodies split, the underbelly of the swarm branching into tight lines that descended like enormous spider legs uncurling from the pulsing body. My heart pattering in my chest, I spun in a slow circle, scanning the oncoming drones, looking for any anomalies among them. My fist tightened around the palmquell, but I didn't draw it. If struck, I wouldn't have the wherewithal to divide my attention between killing drones and looking for Jamie. I sucked in a harsh breath, vulnerability running weightless fingers through my midsection.

"Bloody hell. Is it the bond?" Pamela asked. "Madison, talk to me."

Jamie. Jamie. I mentally chanted his name, aligning all my thoughts to fire on that single desire: *Find Jamie.*

The lead drones zoomed into range. I scanned their foreign faces, seeing no trace of intelligence in their mesh eyes, feeling no hint of recognition. The drone on my right adjusted its flight to aim its arm-length proboscis at my chest. I locked my knees and elbow, holding my idiotic stance like a parody of the Statue of Liberty, unable to tear my gaze from the sharp tip of the drone's mouth. *It will only hurt, not kill me.* My internal chant faltered, degrading to meaningless syllables, and I bounced to my toes, preparing to run—

Bursts of white light streaked over my head, and the drone exploded. The one behind it veered wide, missing me by several feet. Summer and Pamela closed around me, firing into the descending hordes. Letting out a shaky breath, I stood like an antenna between them and wrestled with my instincts. Fighting or fleeing made sense. Standing still took extreme concentration.

Find Jamie.

Drones bore down on us, unflinching and unfazed by the *lux lucis* bullets tearing into them. Their mindless flight paths eliminated them from the possibility of being Jamie in disguise. Tearing my gaze away, I spun to track two drones that dodged bullets, darted overhead, and swung back for a second pass.

Which one of you is not like the others? I sang in my head, the old *Sesame Street* song at odds with the silent battle raging around us.

Pain jabbed through my torso, quick as a whip crack. The sting hadn't faded before a second lash cut across my shoulders. *Find Jamie.* I darted my gaze from one drone to the next, categorizing patterns among the chaotic sky. There, the fastest dodgers. They tended to zigzag as they retreated, not looping back until they were beyond range of our bullets. There, the opportunists. They drafted off two or more larger drones, only exposing themselves once they were near enough to feed.

Pain stabbed through my neck and into my lung, stiffening my spine. I sucked in oxygen, barely getting a breath before the next strike took me through the heart and another spiked across my fore-head. Panting, I squinted to see around the heavy black-and-white abdomens filling my vision, shuddering as another whip crack vibrated through my soul. As fast as they'd surrounded me, the drones zipped heavenward, disappearing back into the seething cloud.

Not Jamie. He would have remained near the bottom to monitor the attack.

Which one of you is not like the others?

There! One drone hovered in place, only for a moment, but the anomalous behavior might as well have shouted, *I'm different!* Fixated, I sprinted after it.

I saw the chain-link fence a second before I crashed into it. My forehead smacked against the metal, setting off a gong inside my head. I stumbled backward, vision dancing. The chiming rattle of the fence muffled the sound of ripped cloth, and cold air seeped into my jeans above my knee. The pet wood tangled with the metal mesh and I twisted it free. Through it all, I didn't—couldn't—take my eyes off the drone I suspected to be Jamie.

It darted back in the opposite direction, and I whirled to follow. A sheet of fluid *atrum* and *lux lucis* blanketed my vision, resolving into a cluster of drones. They converged on me, feeding in agonizing jabs as I staggered after the Jamie drone.

Bright white bullets cut across my vision.

"Come on, Madison. Fight back. At least *use* your wand." Exertion turned Pamela's soft British accent harsh. Footsteps pounded closer, and the volley of bullets doubled. The drones around me exploded into thick *atrum* glitter. Holding my breath, I ran through it, afraid of losing sight of maybe-Jamie.

The drone pivoted on a wingtip to face me. Staring across the thirty feet of pavement separating us, I hunted for a sign of the pooka hiding in the skin of this drone. The battle receded, unimportant, and not even Pamela speaking so close to my ear that her breath disturbed strands of my hair broke my concentration.

I need proof. My left hand jerked from my pocket and extended, palmquell in my fist, bullets flying before I'd finished the thought.

The drone rocketed toward me, taking five hits to its bulky abdomen. It didn't dodge or weave. I'd misjudged. Jamie would be smart enough to avoid being hit. I unloaded another volley into the rushing drone. All seven shots hit, and it kept coming.

My eyes widened. The sixth shot should have killed it. No drone could survive twelve powerful slugs of *lux lucis*.

"Jamie." His name slid from me on an exhale of relief and disbelief. I'd found him.

I'd shot him.

Had the bullets hurt him?

Jamie bore down on me, the bright dot of my reflection swelling in the hundred facets of his enormous insect eyes. I threw my arms wide, not sure if I was trying to stop him or hug him, and he hesitated.

Time stood still while I soaked in the sight of him.

Now that I knew what to look for, I could discern subtle differences between my pooka and normal drones. His mixed-soul abdomen gleamed with the density of his powerful energy, his ebony *atrum* glossy instead of matte, his *lux lucis* pure and undiluted. Proportionally, he resembled his Great Dane form, his segmented body as thick as a dog's and his legs just as long, though toothpick thin. The gossamer blur of his wings was both wider and thicker than his drone counterparts, as if he needed more aerial power to compensate for his greater metaphysical bulk. Of all his drone features, his proboscis seemed the most true to form. Longer than my arm and dreadfully sharp, it poised in line with my heart as Jamie assessed me.

I searched his foreign features, looking for some hint of his feelings.

White bullets streaked through the air, pummeling his side. Jamie darted over me, dragging the tip of his proboscis through my shoulder. I braced for a slash of pain, shocked when the contact elicited a wrenching brokenhearted ache instead.

"Jamie!" The shout burst from me, echoing back from the tall buildings.

"Summer," Pamela warned.

"I'm on him."

Summer thundered past me, her hair streaming out behind her, her soul blazing as bright as a mythical avenging angel's. I sprinted after her, following Jamie. My heart dropped when he disappeared behind a building. I couldn't lose him. Not now.

Pamela's booted steps echoed mine, the older woman easily keeping pace as I tore around the side of the building and crunched through a tangle of low shrubs. I hurdled a hedge and swerved through parked cars, bursting into an opening in front of a semicircle of buildings. Summer halted, her palmquell chasing a single drone across the sky. Slug after slug of *lux lucis* hammered Jamie. I barreled into her, knocking her sideways.

"Hey!" She straightened, bringing the palmquell back up.

I spun a kick to the back of her knee—a move I hadn't known I possessed—and followed it up with a stiff shove to her shoulders. Summer toppled. Fury contorted her features. She rolled to her feet faster than I expected, but then Pamela stood between us.

"Stay back. She might not be in control." The inspector crowded Summer, walking her away from me.

"I lost him," Summer said.

"He'll be back. He can't resist Madison. She's the one you need to watch. We need to save her from being turned."

I shook my head. We needed to save Jamie. I hunted the skies for him, finding the pooka immediately. He hadn't gone far, circling at the bottom of the evil throng.

"Jamie." He didn't respond to my call. Could he hear me? Did drones have ears? I had no option other than to act as if he could. "I'm sorry. I had to be sure it was you. I won't shoot you again. I promise. I just want to talk."

I pressed the tip of the pet wood against my thigh and collapsed the wand, shoving it and the palmquell into my pockets. Jamie ignored me, swirling through the drones. I lost sight of him a few times, but it didn't take long to pick him out again.

"Fight the bond, Madison. Whatever it's telling you, you need to stay strong," Pamela urged. "He's not the pooka you bonded. Look how dark he is. He's turning evil—"

"He's not evil; he's angry." *Lux lucis* still sang bright in Jamie's soul. I wouldn't give up on him until the last drop faded.

"He's helping the tyv. He's evil and needs to be stopped. Push through the bond—"

I tuned Pamela out. Pacing away from her, I waited until Jamie dipped below the second story of the nearest building before trying to speak to him again.

"I miss you, Jamie. I want you to come home. I want us to work together. I won't make you do what you don't want to."

Pamela scoffed. "That's a foolhardy promise you can't keep."

"Please," I said, raising my voice to drown her out. "I know I was cruel . . ." Every memory of Jamie's hurt and bewildered expressions, every haunted and confused look he'd given me over the last several days hammered through my mind, a montage of guilt and regret that ate acid through my heart. "Can you forgive me?"

The pooka flew higher without responding, corralled a ball of drones, and rode them down to earth.

"Get to the tree," Pamela ordered.

"But Madison—"

"She's under the pooka's thrall. We have to let this play out."

The inspector was wrong. The bond had no hand in manipulating this emotional scene. My heartfelt plea was as authentically me as it was desperate.

The knot of drones split in two, the larger group going for Pamela and Summer, who had retreated to stand with their backs against a building, spindly trees spread in front of them. The rest of the drones—at least fifteen and led by Jamie—dive-bombed me.

"I'm not going to fight you anymore, Jamie." I locked my knees and didn't take my eyes off the pooka, refusing to acknowledge the drones behind him.

"Look at her. She's leaving herself defenseless—"

"Stick to the cover," Pamela said.

Lux lucis blasted the drones behind Jamie, exploding three into black glitter, but the remaining dozen didn't slow. My lungs constricted, bound by fear and a soul-deep sorrow when Jamie didn't slow, either. His sharp snout jabbed through my chest and I crumpled beneath a wave of heartsickness. The drones struck a second later, and I bit down on a scream, collapsing to my hands and knees as pain crackled through me.

When I looked up through eyes blurry with unshed tears, Jamie burst through a cloud of black glitter, a handful of drones on his tail. Summer had planted herself in front of me, and she fired bullets so fast her soul's glow visibly softened. Determination defined every line of her body. I gathered myself to tackle her but hesitated when Jamie zipped past her. She had plenty of opportunities to hit the pooka, but all her shots landed on the drones behind him.

I pushed to my feet, locating Pamela pressed to the closest building, holding off a line of drones. Summer should have been with her; instead, she had thrown herself in danger to defend me. I couldn't fathom her motives, and I wasn't going to waste time trying to decipher them now. I had a pooka to save.

"Jamie," I called, and hope surged through me when he flew back to me, circling just out of reach. I spun with him, dizzy and tripping over my own feet. "I shouldn't have changed the rules on you." I could feel Pamela's eyes on me, judging my words and actions, but I didn't care. The tenuous, lingering hope I'd maintained of impressing her had died the moment she snapped that handcuff around my wrist. I was through trying to appease her. "I should have trusted you, Jamie. I *do* trust you. I love you."

The pooka shot straight up, returning with a pocket of drones, but they all attacked Summer, driving her toward Pamela and away from me. Jamie split from them, skimming the ground, tracing a wide arc around me. I reached for him, yearning to close the emptiness between us.

"Come back to me. You're my pooka. I'm your person. I won't let anyone change that. You belong with me and I belong with you."

Jamie darted toward me, then away, agitation plain despite his strange form.

"She's moving! She's coming this way!"

"Get your soul breaker ready."

The panic in the inspector's voice sent a tingle of alarm through me, but I was more afraid that if I looked away from Jamie or said the wrong thing now, I would lose him. Forever.

"Forget the prophecy, Jamie. I don't believe it. You're safe with me. I won't let anyone hurt you. No one has to die today."

Jamie flung himself sideways a split second before a wall of *atrum* and *lux lucis* crashed to the ground, cutting us off from the rest of the world. My heart skittered up my throat, choking me. I'd forgotten . . . I'd been so intent on Jamie—

The wall twisted, bringing into view a giant triangular head coated with a sea of malevolent ebony eyes. My thoughts scattered beneath the weight of the tyv's ravenous regard.

25

NEVERTHELESS, SHE PERSISTED

T ime turned to molasses, clutching at my legs and arms. The tyv looked as if she had stepped from a Japanese horror movie titled *Attack of the Mutant Mosquito*. She dwarfed the nearby SUVs, her bulky abdomen swollen to elephantine proportions, her antennae clearing the second-floor balconies. Barbed hairs stabbed from her segmented legs and clawed feet, and fine black spikes bristled across wings longer than helicopter blades. My heart thundered in my chest as I cataloged all the ways she could kill me, fixating last on her proboscis. Protruding like a lance from between the hundreds of eyes coating her face, it ended in an obscenely sharp, angled tip that exposed the hollow interior. The sight of the tyv's long tongue flicking out the opening to taste the air like a snake broke my trance.

I backpedaled, my steps slow and cumbersome. The tyv had walled Jamie and me off from Summer and Pamela, pinning us between a building and her body.

I locked eyes with the pooka, seeing past his foreign face to the fear radiating from him. His legs stretched toward me, as if he could pull me to him, and his body blurred into a streak of black and white, closing the distance between us with inhuman speed.

Time snapped, releasing me.

I ran.

My fingers scrabbled for my soul breaker, yanking it free—

Agony speared my torso and exploded outward. I crumpled, the world titling as I crashed to the frozen pavement. Pain tore through my body, each pulse impossibly sharper than the last, my soul ripping apart skin and muscle and bone as the tyv sucked it through my impaled torso. The bitter scent of copper assaulted my nostrils. My fingers spasmed, blindly searching for the soul breaker, but I couldn't feel anything except terrible, breathless agony. The tyv shoved closer, her black pebbled eyes swelling to consume the light. I convulsed, thrashing, and my final breath gusted from my tortured lungs.

I rested against the chest of a prehistoric mammoth, cradled against his thick fur. Warm. Safe. A shiver wracked my body, and I snuggled closer. I didn't want to think about the cold. If I did, I'd remember . . .

No. Here, now, *this* was all that mattered. The mammoth and me. I'd been here before, when Jamie had first bonded with me.

Jamie.

My eyes snapped open. A white haze misted my vision, fogging my view of the tyv hovering above me, her wicked snout poised to plunge back into my body. I sucked in a shuddering breath, lifting a feeble hand to ward off the unstoppable blow.

A tiny drone rocketed into sight, driving his body into the tyv's head and knocking aside her proboscis.

"Jamie," I screamed. It came out a thready whisper.

He zipped in a tight circle around me, and my *lux lucis* twirled beneath my skin, tracking him as if he'd become a magnet to my soul's compass. Fighting dizziness, I closed my eyes, springing them back open because the darkness only made it worse. Jamie flew another lap around me, exposing the mist for what it was: a *lux lucis* net swelling from the pooka to cocoon me. Jamie zipped behind me, then shot over-head. Inside my chest, my soul rolled, then caught up against an internal hook and stuttered. The vibration rattled my organs, and I hunched to the side and threw up.

The net imploded, collapsing into my body and capsizing my equi-librium. I vomited again, shivering and sweating. When my vision cleared, I checked my hands. They glimmered with *lux lucis*, touting a strength completely at odds with the tyv's attack. She had peeled my soul from my body; I'd felt every tortured millimeter she'd stolen. I should have been dead.

The tyv reared on her hind legs, wings spread, antennae twirling in agitation. She filled the sky, eclipsing the three-story buildings around her. A lone, minuscule drone flitted around her eyes, distracting her. She swiped at him with mandibles and antennae, her wrath temporarily diverted, but Jamie couldn't hold her off much longer.

I staggered to my feet, gasping when icy-cold pain pierced my thigh, then warmed. I glanced down and blanched. I had found my soul breaker. The sharp hooks had sliced through my pants and embedded in my left thigh. Blood seeped from the twin wounds, soaking my jeans.

Gingerly, I grasped the weapon's handle. My fingers didn't want to work, clumsy from cold and trauma, and my fumbling jostled the razor tips in my flesh. Grimacing, I yanked the soul breaker free. Pain flared anew and fresh blood gushed down my thigh, but my leg held my weight.

Jamie dipped close to the tyv's massive eyes, jabbing with his sharp mouth. She flailed, raking her front legs through the air. I wouldn't get a better opportunity. Fist locked around the soul breaker's curved handle, I charged the tyv and punched the weapon into her side with all my strength.

At the last second, she swept her abdomen away from me, turning a piercing blow into a grazing cut. I floundered for my footing, shuffling backward. Ignoring me, the tyv sprang toward Jamie, her clawed foot skewering his abdomen, the tip protruding out his back. Jamie spasmed. A scream welled in my throat, choked off by fear.

The tyv landed over fifty feet away, half atop a row of parked cars. With a vengeful stomp, she pinned Jamie to the pavement. He struggled, his wings trapped beneath him, his slender legs scraping ineffectually against the tyv's thick, barbed appendage. If he could have overpowered her with either *atrum* or *lux lucis*, he would have, and his unprecedented helplessness terrified me.

I lurched into a limping sprint, my heavy steps too slow. The tyv pivoted and plunged her proboscis into Jamie. His legs stiffened and his whole body convulsed.

"No!" The denial roared from me.

The sky dropped.

Hundreds of drones converged on me, choking the air with their thorny legs and distended abdomens and piercing mouths. Pain crackled through me, sharp but meaningless. Only Jamie mattered.

I had lost track of all my weapons except the soul breaker, which wouldn't work on drones, but it didn't matter. *I* was a weapon. I grabbed *lux lucis* and shaped it into a sword. The blade extended three feet from my hand. A remote part of me marveled at the weapon. I hadn't known swords of pure energy were possible until an hour ago; I hadn't known how to make one until it crystallized in my hand.

I pushed the wonder aside, formed a second sword on my other hand that protruded past the soul breaker clenched in my fist, and kept running. My grasp on my *lux lucis* slid, as if I were holding oiled glass. I had the uncanny feeling that if I lost my grip, the blades would detach and my soul would simply drift away.

If I had possessed any terror to spare, the foreboding sensation would have made me hesitate, but my desperation to save Jamie over-whelmed everything.

I lurched blindly through the drone-choked air, orienting on glimpses of Jamie's limp form and the tyv greedily consuming his precious, powerful life force. My *lux lucis* blades scissored the air in front of me, extensions of my pumping arms, slicing through drones and exploding them into harmless glitter. I cleared a path, but each kill whittled away precious energy. Halfway to the tyv, the blades stuttered, shrank, and I tripped, my coordination faltering. I curbed my energy expenditure, extinguishing one sword, shrinking the other to knife length. If I reached the tyv but had no *lux lucis* left, Jamie and I would both die.

The tyv's thorax lay across the hood of a Lexus three cars away. I couldn't watch Jamie's feeble struggles. Instead, I locked my gaze on the increasingly bright energy—Jamie's energy—swirling within the most vulnerable part of the tyv's body.

Rigid fingers clamped around my forearm, spinning me from my target.

"Stand down, Enforcer," Pamela ordered.

"Let me go! She's torturing him!"

I swung a punch at the inspector, but she caught my fist and forced my hand to my side. She evaded my kick just as easily. I'd taken Summer down so effortlessly earlier, but my fatigued limbs betrayed me now.

"You don't have the strength. The tyv will kill you." Summer clamped down on my right wrist, holding the soul breaker in front of me, where it couldn't hurt anyone. As much as I struggled, I couldn't budge either woman.

"She's killing him!"

"Stop fighting us. We're here to help," Summer said.

Abruptly, the drone mob ascended, and only then did I realize the two women had been holding them at bay with *lux lucis* nets used like shields to surround us. A clot of drones broke from the main mass, sweeping under the tyv and lifting her. For a second, Jamie dangled from her clawed foot, then dropped back to the ground, limp.

"Now!"

Pamela and Summer released me, sprinting for the tyv. They struck blows across her underbelly before being swarmed by unencumbered drones. The tyv beat her massive wings, gaining altitude. If she had been wounded, it didn't show. She and her minions cleared the nearest rooftop and disappeared.

I lurched to the pooka. "Jamie. Jamie!" My voice broke, and I collapsed to my knees beside his broken body. An oily mix of *atrum* and *lux lucis* seeped from his abdomen, spreading in an uneven pool across the pavement.

"You said I'd get to choose," I sobbed. "I didn't choose you. You were supposed to live."

His legs twitched and he turned his head toward me. My heart lurched and I reached for him, hesitating over his unfamiliar body. I couldn't stroke his head without touching his eyes. He had no hands to hold.

I pressed down on his abdomen, desperate to staunch the seep of his soul. Jamie's insubstantial body shifted beneath my palms like the surface of a waterbed. *Atrum* ate into my fingers, sharp and stinging. I flinched but maintained pressure, only yanking my hands back when a violent shudder cascaded through Jamie's body. Damn it, I was making things worse.

"What can I do? How can I help?"

Jamie thrashed, long legs clawing at nothing. I grabbed for him, and painful black bands seared my arms where he clutched me in return. Together, we righted him. He released me and stood on shaky legs, thrummed his wings, and wobbled into the air.

"Stand clear," Pamela ordered.

I jumped, having forgotten the rest of the world existed. The inspector stood behind me, palmquell raised and aimed at Jamie. Summer sheathed her soul breaker and walked to stand with Pamela.

"Lower your weapon." I glared at her, expending precious *lux lucis* to erase the coils of *atrum* from my arms before she saw them. "He's hurt. He needs help."

When she didn't alter her stance, I struggled to my feet. Swaying, I planted myself between Pamela and Jamie.

"I won't let you shoot him."

"He's wounded and that makes him twice as dangerous—to himself and others," Pamela said. "We need to contain him."

She took a step to the side. I tracked Jamie's labored flight and shifted to keep my body between his and the inspector's. He'd taken a lot of abuse tonight; a few *lux lucis* bullets might be too much for his system.

When Summer stepped forward, I tensed, but she only set a hand on Pamela's forearm. The inspector shot her a sharp look.

"He's not threatening anyone," Summer said, surprising me again. "After all that's happened, he's still bonded with Madison."

Pamela's lips tightened, but she dropped her arm.

I spun back to Jamie, keeping Pamela in my peripheral vision. Black and white energy dripped from the pooka, dotting the pavement beneath his erratic flight. As surely as if he were losing blood, he wouldn't survive if he continued to hemorrhage his soul's energy. He needed to be bandaged, but nothing would stick to his drone body. I couldn't even touch him. I hated this helpless feeling.

The next time we meet, one of us will die. I wouldn't let his prophecy be true.

"Let me help, Jamie. What can I do?"

Jamie wriggled his proboscis, his tongue flicking out the sharp tip. Then he turned and flew away, his fatigued wings barely lifting him above the bushes next to the road.

"Jamie, please!"

I slogged after him, my inability to skim obstacles forcing me to take a longer route. When he disappeared around a building, I followed the trail of his bleeding soul, pushing extra speed from my fatigued limbs.

I lost my footing on the sloped ground, fetching up against a tree at the edge of a marsh bank. Jamie's trail led straight to the cattail-choked water and vanished. My heart sank. I couldn't track him across the soggy ponds. Scanning the far side of the marshes, I searched for any telltale movement of a drone.

"Jamie!" The swamp swallowed my shout.

Damn it, Jamie, why did you fly off?

Behind me, the lock on a sliding glass door clicked and the door rumbled open.

"Everything okay down there?" a masculine voice asked.

"We're fine," Summer said, laying an arm around my shoulders and surreptitiously supporting me. "Just a bad breakup. I'll get her home."

She discreetly tucked my palmquell and pet wood into my pocket, and I allowed her to turn me away from the marsh and guide me back to the parking lot. I needed to get to the other side of the marsh, which meant I needed my car. Orienting on the surrounding buildings, I determined the quickest route back to where we had parked and started walking. Summer dropped her arm but stayed close, as if she assumed I'd fall over and she'd have to catch me. Pamela trailed us, eyes on the empty sky, worry pinching her eyebrows.

Other than our footsteps scuffing the pavement and the distant sound of a car's motor, the complex slept silently around us. It seemed impossible that the residents ensconced behind those walls could have been oblivious to the swarms of drones, let alone the whale-size tyv. I tried to muster concern for the tyv's current whereabouts, but I couldn't think past my worry for Jamie.

"Here." Pamela thrust a small, familiar vial into my hand. Liquid *lux lucis*.

I unscrewed the cap and sipped, grateful for the rush of warmth that slid down my throat, hit my stomach, and burst outward to my extremities, refilling my depleted reserves. This wasn't the first time my soul had needed a pick-me-up after a battle, and experience had taught me that the surge of strength was nothing more than a temporary stopgap until I got proper food and rest. It was also going to inflict one hell of a hangover when its effects wore off, but tomorrow's pain didn't matter. I'd risk far worse for Jamie, and I'd take any enhancement I could get right now.

I tipped the vial to my lips for a second draw, but Pamela plucked it from my fingers before anything hit my tongue.

"That's enough," she said.

I spotted a shortcut along a pathway between two buildings and cut in front of Pamela to take it. Urgency flooded me, but my coordination lagged, forcing me to walk; anything faster and I'd end up flat on my face.

"The pooka was commanding the drones. Do you know what that means?"

I pretended I couldn't hear Pamela.

"It means his fourth form isn't a drone at all. It's a tyv. Given enough time and *atrum*, he will metamorphose into the smartest, most deadly sjel tyv this country has ever seen."

The plodding pace I set couldn't have been the cause of the breathy quaver in her voice. She was scared.

Tough.

"Do you really think that's going to happen?" Summer asked.

"I don't plan on finding out. He needs to be stopped. Now."

Wrong answer. Clenching my fists, I vowed not to let Pamela near Jamie. Which meant before I rescued him, I needed to get away from the inspector without raising her suspicions.

"But he saved Madison. You saw his *lux lucis* net—and what he did to her soul."

"This time. He saved her *this time*. We need to capture him while he's weak and we stand a chance of holding him."

Her use of *we* grated. I wanted to stop listening, but I couldn't tune them out. It made me sick that I'd put my trust in Pamela, believing her superior rank and experience gave her a better understanding of how to coach Jamie. I should have trusted myself. If I had, maybe Jamie would have trusted me to help him rather than fleeing. Maybe he wouldn't be dying in the first place.

"Can you tell where he went?" Summer asked.

My steps faltered and my heart kicked against my rib cage as I waited for Pamela's answer.

The inspector hesitated. "No. But we can follow the trail."

"Not through the swamp. Even if we drive up and down the banks, we could search all night and not find him," Summer argued.

Morosely, I agreed with her, but that wouldn't stop me from trying.

"What about the tyv? Can you sense her?"

Pamela huffed out a breath. "Of course, but the pooka is our first priority. She's gained too much strength from him, and even with the little we weakened her tonight, she's more than a match for the three of us. We need to cut off her access to the pooka. Our smartest move is to confine him before he regains his strength."

It was all I could do to keep my expression passive and not snarl at her.

"I'm going home," I announced when we reached our cars.

Pamela assessed my face, then my soul, and I tried to let her see my exhaustion without revealing the growing jitter inside me, urging me after Jamie.

"If I see Jamie again, I'll do everything I can to hold him." Truth. I wanted him back more than ever, but it didn't mean I'd be using Pamela's suggested method of force. "Right now, I can barely stand. I'm not up for any more confrontations."

"You're abandoning the hunt for your pooka?" Pamela asked.

Her words sliced razor blades through my heart. *Never!* I wanted to shout. *I'll never abandon him!* Instead, I ground my teeth and forced out words she'd accept. "Summer was right. He's got too much of a head start. Unless he wants to be found, we could search all night and not encounter him." I didn't have to fake my despair.

"Fine. I'll let Brad know. Make sure you eat before you fall asleep."

"Do you need an ME for that wound?" Summer asked, pointing to my leg where I'd skewered myself with the soul breaker.

"It's not as bad as it looks." In Primordium, the gray of my pants and my blood blended together. The lack of any traces of *lux lucis* in the stain meant the wound had stopped bleeding. I didn't have time to waste on a medical enforcer. My leg functioned, and thanks to the frigid temperatures, the exposed wound and flesh around it had lost all sensation. Even if the cuts had been more serious, finding and healing Jamie took precedence.

I sank into the Civic and tugged my seat belt in place. I didn't turn on the heater; warmth would bring pain, and I was barely functioning as it was. I shoved into gear as Summer shut her door beside me, and I backed out before she'd turned on her car. Still viewing the world in Primordium, I drove down the middle of the winding streets. The marshes flowed on either side of the complex, and Jamie could circle back virtually anywhere. If he did, I didn't want to miss him.

Summer followed, Pamela in the passenger seat. I hadn't really expected Pamela to take me at my word and trust I'd sit idly at home,

but it grated that she made Summer tail me back to my apartment. She
had the damn tracker—

The tracker. The moment I left the complex in search of Jamie,
Pamela would know. I'd have to chance that she was too busy looking
for my pooka to remember to spy on me. Nevertheless, I pulled into
my assigned parking spot and turned off my car. To maintain the farce,
I climbed out of the Civic and tossed the two women a lethargic wave
when Summer slowed to take in my performance. When she didn't
immediately drive away, I ground my teeth and trudged toward my
apartment. In case Pamela was watching, I didn't turn when her engine
revved and she drove off.

I made it as far as the sidewalk lamppost before I abandoned my
act. Bracing a hand against the metal pole, I counted backward from
one hundred, giving Summer time to clear the complex before I
returned to my car. I wracked my brain for where Jamie might have
gone to recover but came up blank. He didn't have anyone. He should
have had me, but I'd ruined—

A single drone careened across the sky, skimmed the barren canopy
of the enormous oaks, and crashed onto the third-floor landing.

My feet started running before my brain caught up.

26

I WANT TO BE THE PERSON MY DOG THINKS I AM

Hang on, Jamie. I'm coming.

When my foot hit the first stair, I remembered the trap across the door. Dread flipped my stomach, and I took the steps two at a time, rattling the concrete-and-metal frame.

Jamie, pale, naked, and human, curled against my door, his soul sluggish inside his body. A puddle of *atrum* and *lux lucis* leaked onto the welcome mat beneath him.

"Jamie!"

The pooka lifted his head and my heart skipped a beat when I saw the slow spin of his dull black-and-white irises. *He hasn't come home to die. I won't let him.* Stripping off my coat, I barreled up the last three steps and wrapped his folded frame, far less concerned with modesty than his warmth. He didn't quite track my motions, as if I were moving too fast for his eyes to keep up with.

"Let's get you inside." I crouched close to him, unlocked the door, and deactivated the trap. I thought I felt the weight of his disappointed gaze, but when I checked his face, his eyes were closed. He might not have even noticed the trap, but that didn't lessen my guilt.

"Come on. A few more steps, and you're home. Safe." I tucked an arm around his rib cage and helped him stagger across the threshold. Heat blasted me, stifling but welcome. We made it a step beyond the postage-stamp laminate foyer before he collapsed, curling on his side into a fetal position. I went down on my knees with him, shutting the door with my foot and shooing the cats away when they trotted over to investigate.

Jamie's soul fluctuated and sputtered, bits flaking from him to drift to the carpet like metaphysical snow and soot, but I was more concerned that despite no visible wound to blame, he continued to bleed *atrum* laced with *lux lucis*. I switched to normal sight, leaving his side long enough to flip on the light. A vicious purple bruise marred the pale skin of his stomach, and blackened patches crisscrossed his knees. Dirt streaked his body, but a careful examination revealed no blood. I sat back on my heels with conflicted disappointment. A physical wound I could treat, but this . . . ?

"How can I help? Should I call the ME?" Was he breathing? "Jamie? Jamie!" I shook him, frantic. He dragged in a ragged breath but didn't open his eyes.

"Hol—" His voice cracked. When was the last time he'd had water? "Hold me."

A shiver rattled his body, and he moaned. Cursing my helplessness, I snatched a blanket off the recliner and wrapped Jamie, then hugged him tight. Dark circles underscored his eyes, his cheeks gaunt above chapped lips. With every passing second, he grew more fragile, his soul bleeding out on the carpet.

"Don't give up, Jamie. Your prophecy was wrong. I won't let you die." I squeezed him, but not too tight, afraid of hurting him. "There must be something more I can do."

"Use your soul," Jamie rasped.

"How?"

"Net me."

He wasn't a pure *lux lucis* creature—wouldn't being held in a *lux lucis* net hurt him? I crossed my fingers and flared my soul from my chest, thankful for hours of practice capturing frost moths. Pushing the net into a bubble large enough to encompass a human tested my control, the task made more difficult by the sounds of Jamie's labored breathing. Once I had him enveloped, I expected the pooka's *atrum* to cancel out my *lux lucis*, depleting my hollow strength. Instead, all his sloughing energy washed up against my net and held, trapped.

This is what he had meant when he had said *Hold me*.

Jamie released a soft sigh and relaxed.

"This is enough? This will help you heal?"

"Yes."

Silent, grateful tears rolled down my cheeks. I sat cramped around my pooka until my legs fell asleep. Afraid of resting my weight on Jamie, I stretched out in front of him. Val's spine jabbed my ribs. I slipped him free of his strap and slid him under the recliner, where the cats couldn't pester him.

Unimpeded, I curled my body around Jamie, facing him so I could monitor his breathing, flexing and adjusting my net until it fit snug against him. All of his soul pulsed within the confines of mine, leaking good *and* evil energy, yet it made my heart sing with how right it felt. How different from Pamela's purity tests! I settled an arm over Jamie's blanketed back, hugging him close.

Dame Zilla crept up to sniff Jamie's hair, her muzzle pushing through my *lux lucis*. Neither my net nor the pooka's leaking soul seemed to concern her, and after satisfying herself with Jamie's scent, the kitten pranced behind him to my hand, bracing her front paws on his back so she could rub on my fingers. I started to shoo her away, but the faint smile curving Jamie's lips stopped me. After a few minutes, Dame Zilla lost interest in my uncooperative petting and curled up on the cushion of the recliner. Mr. Bond flopped across my feet, uncaring that he ground my ankle bone against the tracker. His purr rumbled to fill the quiet apartment.

I lay there, unmoving, at first listening to the heater kick on and off, then to the sleepy sounds of neighbors waking and heading for work. My soul ached like a muscle held tense for too long, but it was a good pain. Jamie slept or lost consciousness, lying so still it would have alarmed me if not for the assurance of his breath across my face and the rise and fall of his chest beneath my arm. Gradually, his soul ceased to flake, the fluctuations settling beneath the press of my net. I checked his stomach wound frequently, cautiously hopeful when it looked as if the seepage slowed, but I wasn't convinced it wasn't wishful thinking until it stopped leaking altogether. Eventually the mixed energies pooling beneath Jamie shrank, absorbing back into his body.

"Did you mean it?"

Jamie's timid, rasping voice startled me. Vulnerability pinched his mouth, and a bleak hope swirled in his eyes when he opened them.

"Every word of it," I said. "I love you, and I'm so, so sorry."

"You didn't say that just to get me here?" Jamie peered over my shoulder at the active trap on the sliding glass door, then at the inactive trap around the front door. Niko had turned my apartment into a glorified cage, and fear had prevented me from doing anything about it. I wished I could go back in time and tear down the traps before Jamie saw them.

"Everything I said was in the hopes you'd come back here, but only because this is where you belong—with me. You're free to go." I choked on the words. "But I hope you won't."

Jamie closed his eyes. "I love you, too."

His soft smile cut through the knots of guilt corseting me. My chest expanded, and I took my first full breath in days. Swiping tears from my eyes, I said, "You really scared me with your prophecy. I can't tell you how glad I am that you were wrong."

Jamie's eyes opened. "My prophecies are never wrong."

My stomach gave an anxious lurch, and I pushed up to an elbow. "We met again, and we're both alive. That means—"

"You died," he said.

"No, I didn't."

"The tyv separated your soul from your body. Your heart stopped beating."

"How do you know?"

"Drones and tyver can hear heartbeats."

Okay. Val had failed to include that tidbit of information in his tyv description. But more important: "If I died, then how . . . ?"

"I stole your soul back from the tyv and I held it to your body, sort of like what you just did for me." Jamie's smile contained timid pride. "Except I had to bond with you again to get it to stick."

"You took my soul back," I said with all the intelligence of a recording. "How?"

"We're connected: I have a bond with your soul. Retrieving it was like gathering scattered pieces of my own. Only it was yours." Jamie shrugged.

I opened and closed my mouth. I understood our connection had been forged on a deep level, soul to soul. What I didn't understand was his ability to collect disconnected pieces of his soul, or mine, for that matter. When I expended my soul's energy, I could no more draw it back than I could reattach cut hair or pat skin cells back in place after being scratched. Once let go—or stolen—my *lux lucis* became inert and unmalleable.

I shook my head. I'd ponder the mechanics of it later.

"You bonded with me again?"

"It seemed the best way to save you."

"Did it change anything between us?"

Jamie lost his pleased smile. "The bond might be stronger than before."

"Good."

His eyelids, which had fluttered down to conceal his eyes, sprang wide, and he grinned at my emphatic acceptance of him.

"I think you can let go of me now," he said after the moment passed.

I collapsed my net. My soul swirled within the confines of my body, tingly and languid after its rigorous stretch. I'd lost some of my glow, too.

"Are you hungry?"

"I want to sleep."

If Jamie was turning down food, he must have been exhausted. I assisted him down the hall. Despite my repeated offers to use my bed, he opted to lie on his giant dog bed. I pulled an extra blanket over him and, unable to let him out of my sight just yet, sat by his head and stroked his hair. Mr. Bond sprawled across the remaining space on the round mattress, kneading the soft blanket, his eyes closed in bliss and his purr a lullaby.

Just when I thought Jamie had fallen asleep, he spoke.

"I stole a car with Sam."

Well, that explained the state of Sam's soul the last time I'd seen him.

"I don't think I should do it again. It really changed him."

I couldn't keep my surprise from my face, but Jamie's eyes were closed and he missed it. "I would prefer if you didn't, too, but I doubt you're responsible for the new *atrum* on Sam's soul. Something tells me you didn't have to push him too hard to convince him to take the car." I'd caught Sam breaking into cars—mine and other people's—more than once.

"It was his idea. He's a much better driver than me."

My heart fluttered at the frightening image of Jamie behind the wheel. It also clarified how he'd been able to meet me, human and fully clothed, at the mall.

Forcing my fingers to keep a steady rhythm through his hair, I said, "We'll see about getting you driving lessons, if you're interested."

He didn't respond, and when I lifted my hand to check, his face had gone slack with sleep.

I tiptoed back to the front room, drawn to the sliding glass door. The sun had risen, but the pale, butter-white rays looked as cold as the frost thick on the ground. Clouds built on the horizon, promising another storm.

Lack of sleep, *dying*, the relief of Jamie returning home, the tightening of our renewed bond—all of it messed with my head and prevented me from succumbing to my body's exhaustion. I retreated to the shower. The hot, soapy water burned the cuts on my thigh, but once the blood washed away, I was reassured I wouldn't need stitches.

Jamie didn't stir when I gathered my flannel sleepwear and dressed in the hallway. I found Mr. Bond circling the recliner, stretching his paws as far under it as they'd go. I shooed away the overweight Siamese and retrieved Val, then distracted Mr. Bond with fresh food.

Have you given any thought to declawing that beast? Val asked when I opened him up.

"I think he loves you."

Love should neither hurt nor leave one disfigured.

"Wise words, Val."

I grabbed a cleaning rag from the cupboard and sat on the floor, wrapped in a blanket. Holding Val over a large potted plant, I swiped the bulk of the dirt from his cover, then opened him again.

"Sorry about tonight's rough treatment."

It's all part of the job. Val's text somehow conveyed his pride, the stems of the letters tall and straight.

"You heard everything Jamie said, right? About the second bond?"

Yes.

"What do you think?"

It's unprecedented. Then again, so is being brought back to life by a pooka.

"Do I look different to you?" I didn't know if I was asking because of the second bond or because of my second chance at life.

No. Do you feel different?

"I don't know. Maybe. When I held Jamie in my soul, it felt . . . euphoric. That's the polar opposite of how it felt with Pamela. Even Niko didn't feel that . . . that joyous."

That's the bond at work. Part of its role is to keep you and Jamie in sync. What better way to do that than to make it feel good. Plus, Pamela and Niko are human. Jamie is a pooka, and pookas bend all the rules.

"So everything is normal?"

With you, I don't think that quaint word will ever apply.

After making sure he didn't need anything, I tucked Val safely into the closet. He opted not to listen to any books, claiming he needed quiet time to think, but I suspected he didn't want to chance waking Jamie, and his pride wouldn't allow him to acknowledge any softening of his feelings toward the pooka.

My stomach grumbled, so I ate—and ate and ate. In addition to my extreme expenditure of *lux lucis*, I hadn't consumed much the previous day, and the combination gave me the appetite of a sumo wrestler. I gorged on half a gallon of yogurt, a pear, a cold bean burrito, and an entire bag of salad, stopping only when I felt too stuffed to move.

After standing in the bedroom doorway, watching Jamie sleep until it began to feel creepy, I settled in the front room recliner and wrapped myself in a blanket. Dame Zilla rushed to my lap and curled her almost weightless form into a tight ball across my thighs. Mr. Bond gave her a sour look and flopped across my dirty shoes.

The tracker jabbed my ankle, and I used the toes of my opposite foot to slide it into a more comfortable position. What I really wanted was to cut the cursed contraption off.

My hand paused above Dame Zilla's back, arrested by the thought. Jamie was back with me, under my guidance. All of Pamela's dire predictions of me being turned evil had been disproved. The situation no longer warranted the tracker. I *could* cut it off!

If only I believed Pamela would see it my way.

I almost rose to get the scissors anyway, but logic stopped me. The moment I severed the tracker's band, Pamela would show up. In fact, the tracker was probably the only reason the inspector hadn't already barged in. I'd done exactly as I'd promised, coming home and staying put. I could tolerate the dull pain and annoyance for a while longer if it meant delaying Pamela's intrusion in my restored relationship with Jamie.

Leaning back, I closed my eyes. Drones rushed me, a flurry of dark bodies through which I could see the tyv holding Jamie pinned to the ground, devouring his life.

My eyes snapped open. The wards remained strong and bright around the sliding glass door. No mixed-energy mutant mosquitoes flew against the Primordium-dark sky. Dame Zilla shifted, stretching out and resting her chin on her extended legs. I ran my fingers through her downy fur and took intentional, deep breaths to slow my pulse.

It's over. Jamie's safe. I'm safe.

My phone rang and I lurched to answer it before it woke Jamie, speaking a soft "hello" into the receiver.

"Madison?"

"Alex?" I scrambled to remember a reason for him to be calling. Had I stood him up for a date I didn't remember? Did we have lunch planned for today? No, that had already happened. My thoughts jumbled together, canceling each other out and leaving my mind blank.

"I didn't wake you, did I?"

"No. I've been up awhile. It's a workday." I felt smart for adding the last fact. I couldn't remember what day of the week it was, but knowing it wasn't the weekend felt like a victory.

"Oh, good. I had a few minutes between surgeries, and I was thinking about you."

"I'm flattered?"

He chuckled. "The two are completely unrelated. Actually, I'm calling about this weekend. The forecast says this storm will clear before Saturday morning. I thought I could show you one of my favorite hiking trails. If you're still dog-sitting that Great Dane, I bet he'd enjoy it a lot more than the restaurant patio. And I'll bring my dog, too. It can be a play date for them."

The poignancy of having a second chance with Jamie, one that would include nonwork outings, brought tears to my eyes. My pooka was back with me, and safe. It was also sweet for Alex to design a date around the dog he thought I was watching. I opened my mouth to thank him, but no sound made it past my emotion-choked throat.

"Oooor"—Alex drew out the word when I didn't respond—"it's an awful idea, since it's supposed to be freezing and the trail will be muddy and—"

"No. It's not that." My voice caught, and I cleared my throat. "It sounds great, but I can't. I need to take care of a friend this weekend." I didn't know when Jamie would be up for leaving the house, and I wasn't in any rush to share my time with the pooka. Choosing my words carefully, I parsed out what I could share with Alex without scaring him off. "My friend has been sick for a while now, and it got really bad last night, but I think the worst is past."

I noticed how careful I had been not to use a gender-specific pronoun. I was doing my best to be honest with Alex, as much as I could be, but if I told him my friend was a man, he might get the wrong idea. Or maybe I was overthinking it. "Actually, I owe you an apology. I've been a complete basket case about this for several days. The dancing—that was an attempt to blow off steam. I shouldn't have used you like that."

"Trust me, I didn't feel used." He paused, and I heard people talking in the background and a dog bark. "Is there anything I can do to help?"

Restrained curiosity colored his voice, but he didn't pry for information. More points to him. I assured him I just needed time and hung up after promising to call him in a few days to set a date for our hike.

I hoped I was doing the right thing with Alex. I really liked him, which made lying to him difficult. Keeping all the important parts of my life a secret from him would only get harder the closer we got. It wouldn't just be my weird hours I'd have to find excuses for. How would I explain the new bruises and cuts I acquired with alarming frequency? What would he say about all the weapons I carried? Most of them looked harmless, but the knife couldn't be easily dismissed. And what about Jamie? I wouldn't be able to introduce him as a pooka or explain our bond. We'd need a cover story . . .

I shook my head. Now, while sleep deprived and crashing after an extreme adrenaline overload, was not the time to attempt to answer tough questions.

I contemplated the phone in my hand, then dialed the office. An enforcer kept her warden in the loop, especially when she had good news for the first time in days. Besides, if I didn't call Brad, he'd call me, probably right when I got to sleep.

"Jamie is with me," I said when he picked up.

He didn't respond for a second, and the indistinct arguments of prajurit queens filled the phone line. "I'm coming to you."

"No. Please. We're both fine. Jamie is asleep and I'm exhausted."

"Pamela told me you almost died. Hang tight. I'll be there—"

"I *did* die. Jamie brought me back to life. He rescued my soul."

"He what?!" The background chorus of prajurit silenced at his outburst.

As succinctly as possible, I filled my boss in on the night's events, including how I'd helped heal Jamie in my apartment.

"I think we mended the rift between us, but if you come rushing over here, Pamela will, too. At least give us a few hours of uninterrupted sleep first."

He paused. "Send me a picture of you both."

"Okay." I understood his need for proof that neither of us were dark.

I scooted out from beneath Dame Zilla, walked to the bathroom mirror, and snapped a shot of myself, using the app that took pictures in Primordium. Then I took a picture of Jamie curled up on his dog bed, his soul a gentle swirl of balanced energy. I sent both pictures to Brad.

"I'll give you until three p.m.," he said, relief softening his voice.

"Thank you."

A knock on the door tugged me from sleep sometime later, but Dame Zilla's sharp claws scratching my inner thigh as she launched from my lap finished waking me. Clouds blanketed the sky, casting the afternoon in deep shadows. The recliner creaked as I sat up, and I listened for sounds from the bedroom, wondering if the knock had woken Jamie, too. Beneath the hum of the refrigerator, the apartment sat silent.

Too silent.

27

TIME TO GET CHOCOLATE WASTED

I rushed down the hallway, heart in my throat, and swung into the bedroom, grabbing the door frame to stop myself before I tripped over Jamie's bed.

The pooka lay sprawled on his back, mouth open, sound asleep, oblivious to my panic. I blew out a deep breath and hugged myself. Jamie was safe. He hadn't gone anywhere while I'd slept.

I would have stood there until my heart settled, but another knock echoed through the apartment. Dreading a confrontation with Pamela, I scurried back down the hall. *Maybe if I pretend to not be home . . .* Except so long as I wore the tracker, the inspector knew exactly where I was.

I put my hand on the dead bolt and checked the peephole. Bright red curls filled the magnified circle. Relief rushed through me, and I opened the door, a finger to my lips.

"Hi!" I greeted Bridget in an enthusiastic hush. "Jamie is asleep."

"Okay." Bridget stepped over the threshold with exaggerated care, pausing just inside the door to take in my apartment. Her eyes widened as they swept across the jungle of plants and the puffy white buffers casing both doors.

"You're going to have to tell me who your decorator is," she said.

"Shouldn't you be at work?" I took her coat. Beneath it, Bridget wore an obvious office ensemble: a gray pencil skirt and a peacock-blue silk top.

"I'm at the dentist." She slipped out of her spike heels and handed me a Tupperware. "I brought cookies."

I peered through the clear plastic. Peanut butter and chocolate sandwich cookies. She'd brought the heavy artillery.

"I hoped I'd catch you at home since you've been working nights lately. I'm glad you're taking time to rest."

I squinted at her over the container of cookies. "How bad did my parents tell you I looked?"

"The words *gaunt* and *haggard* might have been used. I can't say they were wrong."

"Stop. You're going to make me blush."

Mr. Bond, who had been cowering in the kitchen, frightened by my dashes up and down the hall, trotted out to greet Bridget with friendly chirps. He twined through her legs and accepted a few pats before settling in for some serious shoe sniffing. Emboldened, Dame Zilla crept out from behind the recliner, her tail springing up when Bridget crouched and held out her hand.

"You must be Dame Zilla," Bridget said in the same voice she used on babies. "You're adorable, yes you are. Are you keeping Mr. Bond on his toes? He needs someone to chase him around and eat his food."

I set the Tupperware on the dining room table and helped myself to a cookie.

"So, how's the region?"

I grimaced, picturing the enormous tyv loose somewhere, ready to rise and wreak havoc again tonight. "It's definitely been better. Last night was a doozy."

I decided not to tell her about dying. It sounded too dramatic, especially since I felt fine. Tired and sore, but basically fine. Bridget wouldn't be here if she weren't concerned for me; I didn't need to add to her worries. However, since she wasn't blind, humility seemed the best approach.

"I managed to cut myself on my own weapon."

"Badly?"

"I didn't need stitches. It's this sucker that hurts more." I turned around and lifted my shirt to reveal my lower back. Landing on my knife's sheath had given me a radiant purple and black bruise the width of my back.

Bridget winced in sympathy. "Aspirin?"

"Yes, please."

She retrieved two capsules from the bottle in my cupboard and brought it to me with a glass of water. "Did I wake you?"

"Yeah, but I needed to get up soon anyway." I swallowed the aspirin, hoping it'd counter the headache building behind my eyes. Ah, the joys of liquid *lux lucis*.

Bridget nibbled on a cookie while she roamed the front room. She gave the puffy traps on the door a poke. "Do I need to be worried?"

"Not as long as you don't hang around outside, especially at night."

"I meant about you."

"Other than the fact that I'm destroying my wardrobe faster than I can replenish it? No."

Bridget studied my face and let the comment stand. "I've been researching pookas."

"Oh?" I had Val. It'd never occurred to me to look anywhere else. "What'd you learn?"

"That they're shape changers."

I tried not to let my surprise show. "You got that from . . . ?"

"The Internet. There were other myths, like how they drink blood—"

I shook my head.

"And spoil fruit and crops."

"That's a weird one."

"But all sites agree on shape-shifting."

A soft rustling emanated from the bedroom. Bridget appeared not to notice, just as she probably didn't realize her tone had taken on the inquisitive cadence she used in a courtroom.

"Does Jamie have any other forms?" A slight squeak in her voice betrayed her, as if she couldn't believe she'd spoken such an incredulous question.

"Funny you should ask." I could hear Jamie coming down the hallway now, his stride audibly human. *Please be clothed. Please be clothed.*

The pooka stopped at the edge of the front room, clearly unsure of his welcome. I let out a relieved breath: He wore a long-sleeve thermal shirt and flannel pajama bottoms. Better yet, a healthy pink flushed his cheeks, and the skeletal shadows that had haunted his features last night had been softened by rest and a restored soul. The last of my internal tension unwound, and I gave Jamie a welcoming smile. With his ebony hair haphazardly sleep tousled and his bare toes scrunched into the carpet, he looked young and insecure, and I wanted to smother him with reassurances.

"Jamie, you remember Bridget, right? Bridget, this is Jamie in his human form."

Bridget had gone perfectly still, mouth agape in shock. Jamie's eyes bounced from her to me.

"Bridget's the only norm I trust not to reveal your secret," I added. "With her, like me, you can be yourself."

Jamie's tiny smile stretched to a full grin, and I couldn't help but beam back at him. Bridget narrowed suspicious eyes at me, but I raised my hands in silent testament to the truth of my words.

"Hi, Bridget," Jamie said. "I liked your backyard. Your lawn smelled so much better than the ones around here. Maybe Madison and I can visit again soon."

I laughed, partially at Bridget's dumbfounded expression, but mostly because hearing Jamie talk about the two of us as a unit again filled my heart with joy.

Jamie spotted the container of cookies and made a beeline for it. His eyes lit up when he opened the lid and breathed in the sugary aroma. He stuffed a cookie into his mouth and shot me a wide-eyed look. Another cookie followed before he'd swallowed. Bridget watched him as raptly as if he were putting on a performance.

"What are these?" Jamie asked around a mouthful of crumbs. "Why haven't we had them before?"

"They are cookies. We didn't have them because you have to make them by hand, not purchase them in a store."

A third cookie disappeared into Jamie's mouth. "Are they hard to make?"

"I don't know. Bridget?"

Bridget jumped as if she'd been goosed, a bright flush staining her freckled cheeks as she turned to me. Using a hand to direct her words toward me, she hissed, "The way I greeted him last time! Why didn't you stop me?"

"I liked it," Jamie said.

Bridget gathered herself and addressed Jamie directly. "You're really the . . . the dog? But that's . . . that's . . ."

"Impossible?" I suggested. "Welcome to my world."

When Jamie and I pulled into the parking lot of our dilapidated headquarters less than an hour later, my sugar buzz battled with nervous anticipation, and I drummed my fingers anxiously on the steering wheel. Seeing Pamela screwed the knots in my stomach tighter. She barred the front door with her body, seeming oblivious to the tiny snowflakes layering her hair and crossed arms. On the other side of the office's glass front, Sharon glared from behind her podium.

I parked but didn't remove my hand from the key in the ignition. The urge to fire the car back up and tear out of the lot nearly overrode my sense of duty. With a heavy sigh, I pocketed my keys and shoved from the Civic. Frozen snowflakes tapped my face, the sharp, cold points reminiscent of imps' claws. I double-checked our surroundings. The only *atrum* in sight existed in Jamie's soul.

Echoing my sigh, the pooka climbed out of the car, shutting the door softly behind him. His wilted posture and downcast eyes drew me around the car to his side.

"I don't care what she says. It's you and me doing this together," I said.

Jamie nodded, not meeting my eyes.

I'd put off leaving the apartment as long as possible. The thought of confronting the tyv again made me queasy. So had the thought of facing Pamela. I dreaded the strain she and others would put on my untarnished new bond with Jamie. More important, I worried about my pooka's health. He'd been so close to death just a few hours ago, and his soul still had a fragile quality to it. Running around at night in the freezing cold couldn't be good for his health.

I guessed the same could be said about me, but sitting out tonight hadn't been an option.

The fluid energy of Jamie's soul fluctuated with agitation, and tension stiffened his stride as we marched across the parking lot. I tried not to read too much into my own flush of nausea-laced anger at the sight of the inspector, chalking up my reaction to a conditioned response from all of Pamela's purity tests.

Jamie's hand fumbled for mine, and I wrapped my chilled fingers around his warm palm. The nausea receded. I took a deep breath and relaxed my shoulders. In my periphery, Jamie did the same.

Pamela drew up straight, tucking one hand into her coat pocket and dropping the other out of sight at her side. Most likely, she had a weapon in each hand, something designed to take me down or capture Jamie. Maybe both. Whatever plans she had for him, she'd have to go through me first. I slowed and shifted to keep myself between Jamie and the inspector, giving my hand a shake to free it in case this came down to a fight. Jamie clung tighter.

The door burst open behind Pamela, and Brad stepped halfway out.

"Madison, Jamie, get inside."

"Not before I test Madison's purity," Pamela said.

"Inside." Brad's tone brooked no argument.

"Come on, Jamie." I had to jostle him to break his staring match with Pamela.

The inspector stepped off the sidewalk to give us plenty of room to pass. I nudged Jamie through the door, following close on his heels, our hands clenched tight enough to cut off circulation. I didn't turn my back on Pamela until Brad stepped between us.

Heat rolled over me, and I broke out in an instant sweat. I'd dressed for the elements, complete with long johns beneath my duct-tape-patched jeans, whereas the office had been set to tropical temperatures for the prajurit. The tiny, winged people swooped close to the ceiling, milling in discreet groups. Several dipped down to greet me and Jamie. I made sure to be polite, but I didn't let Jamie stop walking until we stood in the small open space at the rear of the office. The back door remained ajar for the prajurit, and I positioned us near it. If Pamela tried to cage Jamie or harm him in any way, we were out of here.

Was I being irrational? I didn't think so, but if I was, I didn't care.

Unzipping my coat, I tugged my scarf loose with one hand, then stuffed my beanie in an overcrowded pocket.

"How are you feeling?" Brad asked, stopping to lean his butt against the closest desk, his pose more forced than casual.

"Fine."

"We need to determine if you're being unduly influenced," Pamela said, squaring off in front of me. Her gaze flicked to my hand locked with Jamie's, then back to my face. "The purity test is as much for your good as it is for the pooka's."

I could either argue and make a fuss or I could submit and we could all move on.

"Fine. But I'm through with the ankle tracker." I tugged Jamie to the nearest desk and grabbed a pair of scissors. Bracing against the pooka for balance, I lifted my foot, pulled up my snow pants and jeans, and severed the strap of the hateful contraption.

Brad's indrawn breath hissed softly, and I glanced in his direction. His round face remained stoic, but a flush crawled from his collar to his crown as he took in the ugly bruise circling my ankle.

An alarm squawked in Pamela's pocket. She pulled out her phone and swiped the screen, cutting the sound off midnote. I resisted the impulse to pulverize the tracker beneath my heel, tossing it atop the desk instead. When I pulled my pant leg back down, I felt thirty pounds lighter.

The front door bleated its broken-bell *clank*, announcing Summer. The enforcer murmured a greeting to Sharon, then strode in our direction, stopping next to Brad. She didn't greet anyone, in deference to the obvious tension, but when she spotted my hand joined with Jamie's, a small smile curved her lips. More surprising, it didn't disappear when she met my gaze. Something last night had changed her opinion of me, and of Jamie, too.

"You cannot be touching for the test," Pamela said.

I squeezed Jamie's hand, then relaxed my fingers. "It's okay."

He let go but didn't step away from me. Nodding to herself, Pamela pocketed a strange little prism and gestured for me to make a net.

Gritting my teeth, I suffered through the longest purity test to date. Despite holding a net a fraction of the size I had created to heal Jamie, I strained to maintain it while Pamela's hand rested inside my soul. The vertiginous pulses of her energy through mine tightened cramps in my stomach, making me regret indulging in a fourth cookie.

"Clean," Pamela finally announced.

The prajurit broke into conversation, speaking a foreign language and conferring in small circles. I reached for Jamie, finding his hand extended to me. The instant we connected, my disjointed *lux lucis* settled.

"I think Madison and Jamie should sit tonight out," Brad said, directing his words toward Pamela. "They need time to recover."

"No," Jamie said. "I have to kill the tyv. Tonight."

I blinked at the ferocity of his tone. "*You* do? *You* want to take part in bringing the tyv down."

"She's my responsibility." Anger tightened his face, but his soul swirled with no more agitation than when Pamela had inflicted her purity test on me. "She killed you, even after I told her you were off-limits. Tonight, she dies."

I gave his hand a shake to loosen his grip. "I'm not dead. I'm right here."

Pamela snorted. "Maybe she was confused, since you were leading drone attack after drone attack against Madison."

"I could handle the drones." I glared at the inspector. If she wanted a fight, I'd give her one.

"I knew you could," Jamie said. Worry furrowed his brow and he looked at his feet when he added, "I wanted to see what you'd do after you recognized me. I wanted . . ."

"Proof that I still loved you. I know. I understand." It was exactly this vulnerability that had enabled the tyv to prey on him. She had used his confusion and yearning for a place of belonging to her advantage. Or maybe sjel tyver didn't have such complex thoughts and she'd only capitalized on the opportunity Jamie had presented. Either way, the blame for last night's events—for all the screwups with the tyv—fell on my shoulders.

"What are we up against?" I asked.

"Summer and I whittled down the tyv's drone support after you went home, but not enough to starve her anytime soon. We'd be better off tonight if we hadn't wasted so much time searching for the pooka. You should have reported in immediately, Madison."

I gave the inspector a flat look. "I was busy."

Summer cleared her throat. "*Can* the tyv be killed?" she asked.

"Everything can be killed." Pamela crossed her arms, her expression grim.

"The tyv is stronger than you think," Jamie said. "She's been using my energy. Before she attacked Madison, I gave her power—enough to evolve her eggs."

His words went through Brad and Pamela like an electric shock, rippling outward through the prajurit. For a second, the only sounds in the office were the hum of prajurit wings and the clacking of the break room refrigerator.

"What does that mean?" Summer asked before I could.

Jamie tugged me to face him, his expression pleading. "I wanted to balance out the region. I thought if there was more *atrum*, I wouldn't look so bad to you."

Oh, Jamie. "You look perfect to me." I owed him a hundred more apologies. A thousand.

"How much time do we have?" Pamela asked.

"Hours." Jamie squared his shoulders and turned back to the group. "She's almost done laying eggs. She'll wait as long as she can, but the weather's going to warm up fast over the next few days, and she'll have to take her offspring north."

"How would she know it's going to get warmer?" Summer asked.

"Nature sings about her rhythms and changes, and weather is just another language to sjel tyver."

Who knew my pooka was a poet?

"Are you certain they'll hatch tonight?" Brad asked.

Jamie nodded.

"Someone explain what's going on," I demanded.

"Thanks to the pooka, all the eggs he kept hidden from us won't hatch as drones," Pamela said. "They'll hatch as sjel tyver. Their accelerated evolution will make them ravenous. If dozens of tyver sweep through Roseville at once . . ."

My imagination filled in the rest of the horrifying scenario. Sjel tyver stole memories from norms. A horde of tyver unleashed en masse on the citizens of my region would result in an epidemic of amnesia, followed by a rash of fear, and humans were prone to unfathomable acts of stupidity when scared. Homicidal mobs, riots, war. Roseville wouldn't be the only area affected, either. As the tyver fled north to their colder breeding grounds, they'd wreak havoc on every town and city in between. And if a clutch of newborn tyver saw one of us? I didn't want to contemplate the odds of surviving against multiple sjel tyver intent on stealing my soul. One tyv had been more than I could handle.

"The prajurit have poisoned thousands of chimneys," Brad said. "How many eggs could they have missed?"

Jamie hesitated, then whispered, "Hundreds."

My warden blanched. His gaze darted to Pamela, and I saw the moment he acknowledged the death of his dreams of expanding our region. The inspector would never grant Brad more responsibility after this catastrophic bungle. His shoulders slumped and he rubbed his forehead with one meaty palm. He allowed himself two deep breaths and one resigned glance around the shabby headquarters before drawing himself up straight.

"Every egg we kill is one that can't hatch," he said. "I'll get a map and we'll grid out where—"

"The tyv is more important than the eggs," Jamie interrupted. "I must kill her."

"Last night already proved you're no match for her," Pamela said.

"Last night, I was weak—"

"And she's gotten stronger." Pamela glared down Jamie. "She's only going to get more agile once she's done laying eggs. Brad has the right strategy: The clock is ticking and we need to destroy as many unborn tyver as possible. I'll call in extra enforcers to defend areas where the eggs are most likely to hatch. Any tyv that makes it out of a chimney alive, I want an enforcer there to kill it."

"You don't understand." Jamie dropped my hand so he could emphasize his point. "The sjel tyv guides the eggs' rapid metamorphoses. Their minds are all linked to her. If she dies before they hatch, they die. Or they devolve to drones."

"Is that true?" Summer asked, looking to our superiors for confirmation.

"I've never heard that's how it works." Pamela glanced to the prajurit, who all shook their heads, then to Brad.

"Jamie is the one who can transform into a tyv," he said. "If anyone would know, it's him."

"We're going to trust the word of a pooka?" Pamela seemed to be talking to Brad, but she maintained eye contact with Jamie. "Not twenty-four hours ago he was working with the enemy and nearly got his enforcer killed."

"*Did* get his enforcer killed," Jamie said softly.

Summer's eyebrows danced to her hairline.

"Still here." I waved my hand, and the movement broke Pamela's fixed stare. "Ready to kill a tyv."

The inspector eyed us all, even the prajurit. Finally, she nodded. "We'll need Niko."

"I already texted him. He's a few minutes out," Brad said.

"If I'm in the field, I won't have time to coordinate the additional reinforcements we'll need."

"I'm on it." Brad finished punching the surface of his cell phone and raised it to his ear. After a second, he barked, "Rose. Call Joy and Will. I need everyone at the office ASAP."

He hung up and turned to the prajurit. "My esteemed queens, the time for talk is over. My region and your future territories are under attack of an extreme and undeniable nature. I claim Power of War. Do you accept?"

Wings hummed and tiny hands dropped to sword hilts as the queens assessed each other. Tense seconds dragged by; then the first queen dipped into a bow.

"I accept," she said.

One by one, the others agreed, each regal and measured in her response and in no way hurried. Brad bounced on his toes with impatience, barely letting the last queen speak before he barreled on.

"I'm honored to have you all as allies." He called forward four queens, Lestari among them, and designated them as clan leaders. The rest of the females and their warriors he divided between the newly elevated clans. When they protested, he overrode them. "I expect full cooperation and peace within your ranks until the security of my region and your territories is fully reinstated. At that point, you are free to work out conflicts among yourselves. The peace talks are officially dissolved."

Judging by the prajurit's open scowls and hands clenched around sword hilts, the peace Brad had instituted wouldn't last long. But at least they'd agree to put off killing each other until after we destroyed the tyv and her offspring. Now all we had to do was survive a battle against the strongest evil creature any of us had ever encountered. One who'd already killed me once.

Piece of cake. Right?

Right?

"Jamie and clan queens, with me," Brad ordered. "We have seventeen minutes until sundown, which means we have half that time to disseminate territories, grid out infected neighborhoods, and build a battle plan." He hustled into his office to stand before the wall map of our region. Four queens broke away from their clans and zipped over the top of the office wall. Jamie shuffled after Brad, his shoulders hunched. Since the office couldn't accommodate another person, I shifted to stand where Jamie could see me through the open doorway and I, him; if we couldn't maintain physical contact, visual contact was the next best thing.

"How did you find him last night?" Pamela asked. She'd followed me, keeping Jamie in her line of sight, too.

"I didn't need to. He came home to me."

Her eyebrows flickered in surprise. "Good. We can work with that. He's more connected to you than I thought. You'll have a much easier time keeping him under control now." Pamela lowered her voice. "The key is to not give an inch. He's angry with the sjel tyv right now, but it'll be up to you to make him see that all *atrum* creatures are just as bad. You have the advantage right now. Don't lose it."

I pinched my lips and nodded, as if I put any merit in her advice or had any intention of following it.

Inside his office, Brad drew careful lines across his laminated map, divvying up our region for the prajurit while Jamie drew Xs in clusters over residential districts to denote egg locations. The pooka's marks darkened a daunting portion of the map.

The front door clanked opened and Niko entered, immediately stripping off his puffy black coat and beanie. Normally the sight of him gave my heart an extra patter, but our last encounter had left me sour. I turned away and crossed my arms while Pamela brought him up to speed. Outside, snow settled on the bushes and limned the cracks in the pavement, but it wouldn't present a problem driving. The string of freezing days and anomalous snowfall had chased most Roseville residence indoors, too, which would make our jobs easier *and* deprive the drones of fresh food. For a fleeting moment, I wished I were one of the norms, curled up inside under a blanket, but then I remembered the tyv holding Jamie down, and I tuned back in to the conversation.

"She went to ground along the southern border of the region. I lost track . . ." Pamela paused, her attention turning inward.

I examined the contorted lines of her soul. Despite last night's perpetual use of *lux lucis*, she hadn't lost a shred of definition. If Brad were to attempt to do the same, his soul would blur back into his body's shape. It took a special person or a special kind of control for the inspector to be able to maintain the structure of her soul while actively using its energy.

Whatever she felt stir in the map of her soul wasn't apparent to me, but when she refocused on us, Pamela announced, "The tyv's awake."

Anticipation, sharp and nauseating, squirmed through my stomach. I gave my body a quick weapons-check pat-down.

Niko touched my arm, drawing my attention to his face. Worry kinked his eyebrows as he scrutinized me. "Are you up for this?"

Way to make me look weak in front of the inspector, Niko. Glowering, I leaned into his personal space. "Are you going to try to stop me?"

Surprise flickered across his face; then he broke into a grin. I bared my teeth at him, keeping my growl checked.

"There's the Madison I know. Good to have you back." He had the audacity to clap me on the back. Worse, his mild approval settled in a warm glow in my gut. Pathetic.

Brad barreled out of his office. "The wardens to the north of us have been warned, and they'll spread the word. I've got six enforcers coming in from Sacramento and Elk Grove, and Rose will be here any minute to cart the prajurit to the farthest locations. The rest have left. Where's Jamie?"

Brad's shoebox office was empty. I spun to check the larger room, catching Sharon's eye in the mirror on her podium. The stoic receptionist twitched her head, her eyes flicking to look over my right shoulder—her version of screaming and pointing. I whirled and raced for the back door. A wooden wedge held it ajar for the prajurit, and the blazing interior lights transformed the twilit landscape beyond it into an impenetrable shadow.

Jamie better not have . . .

I burst through the door and stumbled as my feet caught in a soft bundle. Jamie's clothes. Dread constricted my lungs.

Blinking to Primordium, I scanned the sky. An empty black void stared back at me.

She's my responsibility.

"Damn it, Jamie!" He'd gone after the tyv. Alone.

28

WITHOUT ME, IT'S JUST AWESO

Niko jostled me aside and sprinted to the far side of the back lot. I already knew he wouldn't find my pooka, but a kernel of hope rooted me in place.

How could I have been so oblivious? Jamie must have walked right by me. I should have recognized his guilt and kept a closer eye on him. He'd barely healed from his last encounter with the tyv. He wasn't up for another one-on-one battle with her. She would kill him.

When Niko shook his head and trotted back to the office, I took one last look at the sky, then scooped up Jamie's clothes and hugged them to my chest.

Hang on, Jamie. I'm coming.

I barreled back inside, swerving to avoid a collision with Pamela. "Let's go. You can ride with me."

Pamela seized my arm and pulled me up short. "I thought you had control of him."

"*That's* what you're focusing on?" I jerked free. "Jamie needs our help. We don't have time to waste on this bullshit."

Ignoring me, Pamela turned to Brad. "This changes everything. We can't trust anything the pooka said. For all we know, he just set us up for a trap."

"He wouldn't!"

Pamela shook her head. "No one blames you, Madison. You were tricked like the rest of us. He made you think he's not evil—"

"He didn't make me *think* he's not evil. I know it."

"That's the bond brainwashing—"

"No! I know Jamie isn't evil because I've held his soul in mine." My hands shook, and I tightened my grip on Jamie's clothes. "He didn't trick any of us. What you saw was exactly what he is—what I've felt: a blend of good and evil. Right now, that part-evil pooka is out there, alone, trying to save us all. He's doing what any of us would do: He's trying to atone for a mistake, and it's going to get him killed."

Pamela gave me a sympathetic look. If she tried to pat my shoulder, she'd lose a hand.

"Then the best thing you can do is stay here and use the tether to hold him," she said. "You can keep him away from the tyv where he can't make things worse. That's your top priority."

I hesitated, tempted, though not for the reason Pamela assumed. But then I shook my head. Her plan might keep Jamie safe, even if that wasn't her intent, but it would also deny my pooka his free will. As much as it terrified me to think of him fighting the tyv, I couldn't deny him his choice. Doing so would tear a rift between us that no amount of apologizing could mend.

"I trust Jamie." My voice quivered with earnestness. "And last I saw, we could use all the help we can get taking down the tyv. We have the same goal, Pamela. Please, don't try to stop me."

I spun on my heel and ran for the front door. Summer fell into step beside me, and I shot her a grateful look that she pretended not to see.

"Brad? She netted his entire soul?" Pamela asked softly enough that I don't think I was supposed to hear.

"The whole thing. She said she had to for him to heal."

"I told you she'd surprise you," Niko said.

"Turn left here." Pamela pointed, and I obediently cut through the intersection and powered down a sleepy neighborhood street.

I'd been so intent on chasing Jamie that I'd reached my car before I realized I didn't have a means of tracking him. The bond had sat silent at the base of my skull, telling me Jamie hadn't gone more than a half mile from me, but not pinpointing which direction. I'd pulled out my cell, intending to call Brad, but then Pamela had marched out of our headquarters and assumed command again as if my outburst had never happened. Per her orders, Niko and a prajurit clan rode with Summer while Pamela piloted our miniature convoy from my passenger seat. I knew better than to assume the inspector's motives and mine aligned, but so long as she helped me find Jamie, I was more than happy to be her chauffeur.

Feathery snowflakes brushed the windshield, too light to stick and promising a freezing night ahead of us. Festive Christmas lights outlined rooftops, blinking a rainbow of colors across snow-blanketed lawns adorned with plastic blow-up Santas and snowmen. Our traditionally balmy city had transformed into a winter wonderland.

I blinked to Primordium, the monotone reality ominous and depressing in contrast to the holiday decorations. Drones buzzed across the dark sky, slipping silently over dull gray rooftops. We'd been following a zigzagging course along the border of my region for the last fifteen minutes, and judging by the increased number of drones, we were getting close. The steering wheel squeaked in my white-knuckle grip, and I fought the urge to speed through the narrow streets. Somewhere nearby, Jamie faced off against a giant tyv, believing he had to sacrifice himself to atone for his bad decisions.

Come on, Pamela. Find the damn tyv already.

I flashed back to normal sight in time to avoid a pothole. When I glanced skyward again, a flurry of white flakes cut dizzyingly through the illumination of my headlights.

"Right," Pamela instructed as we neared the next intersection.

I flipped on my blinker and turned right, ignoring the stop sign. Without slowing, Summer cruised through the empty intersection behind me.

"There." Pamela's fingernail clacked against the windshield. She pointed toward a low ranch-style house adjacent to a nondescript office building. A four-foot-tall chain-link fence wrapped the building and parking lot, and a faded sign proclaimed it to be part of the Roseville High Joint Unified School District.

I slowed and chanced Primordium. Drones cluttered the sky, and a blur of black and white swirled behind a tangle of white birch branches.

"Park here," Pamela said.

My brain finally put the enormous shape together, and I screeched to the curb. We'd found the tyv.

I burst from the car as Summer parked behind us and cut the engine. When I checked the fence again, the tyv had disappeared.

"Stay close," Pamela said, readying her weapons. "No one goes up against a tyv alone."

If I hadn't learned that lesson the hard way last night, I might not have waited for the others.

Summer and Niko climbed from her car, and a flurry of prajurit zipped out behind them, each carrying tiny satchels filled with poisonous pods to kill incubating tyver in the surrounding chimneys. Niko placed the resupply sack of seeds onto the roof of the car, speaking quietly with the scout prajurit. I leaned over the fence, straining to catch a glimpse of the tyv behind the office building, every second of delay corroding my caution.

When Niko and Summer finally joined us on the sidewalk, I didn't give Pamela a chance to speak.

"The tyv is on the other side of this building. We all know what to do. Let's get going."

"Not so fast, Madison," Pamela said. "If the pooka is helping the tyv—"

"He's not." I glared at the inspector, and she returned the look, undaunted.

"If he is, then we take him down first."

I balled my fists and shoved them in my pockets. "Fine. For the sake of expediency, if Jamie is helping the tyv, we focus on him. Since he's not, we go after the tyv. Jamie's not strong enough to take her down himself, but that's not going to stop him from trying. I—*we*—need to back him up."

"We stick together and move as a unit," Pamela said. "No one attacks the tyv alone. Keep that thought in the forefront of your mind. The last thing we need is someone playing hero and getting themselves killed. Again." She gave me a pointed look.

"Got it." Summer patted her soul breaker for a third time, her expression tight.

I rocked in place, eyes glued to the sky where I'd last spotted the tyv. Plenty of drones swooped through the air, but the tyv's massive body remained out of sight. The memory of her pinning Jamie to the ground, sucking down his life, spiked through my brain. If she had him pinned again . . .

"Let's go." The fence's icy links pinched my fingers through my gloves as I scrambled over it. Val's strap caught on the top, slamming me against the freezing metal weave when I landed on the other side. I lost precious seconds untangling him, but my imagination raced onward, supplying horrific visions of Jamie tortured and dying.

"Madison, hold up." Niko gripped the top of the fence and vaulted over, landing beside me. Pamela and Summer clambered after him, rattling the fence against the posts in a piercing chime. I bounced on my toes, and when Summer's feet touched down, I spun and dashed across the snow-slick pavement. Heavy footsteps fell in line behind me.

I tore across the empty parking lot and down the side of the office building, straining to see beyond the legion of cypress trees behind it. It wasn't until I careened through a narrow gap in the fence and broke through the tree line that I recognized the location. Four wide-open baseball fields sprawled in front of me, glossed with snow. To my right, behind another barrier of trees, sat a football stadium. My fight against the tyv had come full circle; we were back at Oakmont High.

Tonight, the stands were empty, the school grounds devoid of victims. The tyv would never have come here on her own. She must have been chased or lured here by Jamie. My clever, clever pooka.

I slid through icy mud on a well-worn trail beaten into the grass, my gaze locked on the chaotic jumble of drones looping around the massive tyv. Shockingly, drones clashed with drones, tearing each other apart with sharp mouths and barbed legs. Even more astounding, tight clusters of drones attacked the tyv, jabbing their proboscises into her massive thorax. In retaliation, she pulled the smaller creatures from the air and eviscerated them. *Atrum* glitter hazed the atmosphere around the tyv, distorting the epic battle.

The tyv jumped, buzzing to land halfway across the field. My feeble hope that the battle had weakened her died at the sight of her unaided flight. Most of the drones were slow to follow her, locked in their own skirmishes, but one broke from the masses.

Jamie.

If I'd had leftover lung power, I would have called out to him. Instead, I conserved oxygen and redoubled my speed.

"Bloody hell. Slow down, Madison!"

Jamie's drone form had altered. He was larger, his thorax thicker, his abdomen sleeker. Pamela had been right; his fourth form wasn't that of a drone but of a tyv. Where before he'd been the size of a Great Dane, now he dwarfed the nearest drones. Only next to the tyv did he look small, like an SUV next to a locomotive. He wasn't hiding his true nature, either, and his limbs, wings, and face swirled with the monochromatic oil of his soul, the twin energies flexing and shifting within the confines of his body in a most un-tyv-like way.

He'd barely cleared the riotous cloud of drones when they converged on him again, attacking with the same ferocity they'd exhibited with the tyv. My stomach lurched, and a harsh wheeze-whimper escaped my throat. Fifty yards away, I couldn't do anything to help him.

Jamie ducked and evaded, landing a solid strike to the tyv before peeling away to confront the drones around him. A fresh contingent of evil mutant mosquitoes swept from the seething sky, dividing to attack the tyv and Jamie's assailants, and the air thickened with *atrum* dust once more.

Jamie wasn't fighting the tyv alone; he used drones against her the same way he'd used them against me. Unfortunately, for every individual Jamie commanded, the tyv controlled five more. Even as I sprinted across the uneven sod, her drones tore through those around Jamie, forcing him to retreat. By the time he'd gathered another squadron, the tyv had jumped again, this time toward the football stadium.

I altered course to follow, ignoring the white bullets whizzing over my shoulder just as I ignored the trio of drones that split from the battle and buzzed me. I had no fear of being struck. My thoughts had aligned on a single, clear point: *Save Jamie*. Nothing would alter that.

The sharp tips of drone proboscises sliced through my shoulders, and I stumbled but kept running, eyes locked on my pooka. He dove for the tyv's thorax, but she pivoted, and before Jamie could reverse course, her sharp claw hooked his abdomen and yanked him toward the ground. He lashed out, slicing the leg holding him and escaping, but as he flew away, a trail of *lux lucis* and *atrum* dripped from his wound. A flurry of drones enveloped him, and he powered through them, then spiraled away from his attackers.

Hang on, Ja—

Agony wrenched my legs out from under me, and I fell face-first into the snow, my momentum rolling me onto my back. I clamped a hand over my burning side and blinked through blurry vision at a hefty drone hunched over me. Dimly, I followed the line of its proboscis to where it disappeared into my hip.

My soul wrenched sideways, tearing fractures through my body. Fresh tears clouded my vision, and my brain labored for an explanation. It came on another burst of pain.

It's not a drone; it's a tyv.

Not *the* tyv, but another one, smaller but no less deadly.

With numb fingers, I clutched the curve of the soul breaker, tugging it from its sheath. In slow motion, my hand swept toward the tyv's head. The barbed tips of the soul breaker met a rubbery resistance, and for an agonizing second, I thought I wouldn't be strong enough to penetrate the tyv's metaphysical exoskeleton. Then the soul breaker punctured the tyv through its multifaceted eyes and didn't stop until they pierced its thorax. I shoved *lux lucis* through the weapon, and the miniature sjel tyv exploded in a mushroom cloud of *atrum*.

I scanned my surroundings with dull eyes, echoes of pain quaking through me. The riot of evil insects blurred into an incoherent mass above me, newly hatched tyver indistinguishable from their smaller drone counterparts. When none changed course to attack me, I tried to stand.

My legs didn't respond, so I rolled onto my stomach. The palmquell in my pocket stabbed my ribs, Val jabbed my hip, and wet snow stuck to my cheek, numbing my face. Still clutching my soul breaker, I stretched out my arms and swept aside the snow, absorbing *lux lucis* from the frozen grass beneath it. Energy curled through me, faint and welcome. When I'd depleted the meager supply of *lux lucis* within reach, I army-crawled past the dead patch and collapsed on my stomach again. Grass held little energy, but stranded in the middle of the field, I didn't have another option. Twice more, I dragged myself to a new location and consumed the grass's *lux lucis* before I contemplated attempting to walk to the nearest tree. I pictured the series of dead-grass angels I left behind and worried what the groundskeeper would make of them. The absurd anxiety in the midst of so much danger lodged an inappropriate giggle in my throat.

"Are you injured?" Niko demanded.

I rolled my head back. He stood beside me, his attention focused on a clump of incoming drones. One after the next, he shot them from the sky, exploding their bodies well before they drew close. I twisted to peer behind me. His footsteps marred the snow next to my mutant angels. He'd been standing over me during my stuttering recovery, and I hadn't noticed. It also explained why no drones had attacked me in my weakened state.

"I'm fine," I answered after too long of a pause. *Fine* covered a range of physical states, I'd learned, everything from *I'm not dead yet* to *I'm refreshed and ready to fight*. Right then, I decided *I can move* met the qualifications of the word.

It took two tries to get to my feet, but once my legs were beneath me, my balance returned. Clutching the soul breaker, I took stock of the battle. Not much had changed, at least not in the sky. Drones drove Pamela and Summer away from us, and a tyv hiding in their midst struck Pamela before either woman saw it. Summer killed it an instant later, and the drones scattered. Before the women could collect themselves, another cluster of drones broke from the aerial battle to attack them, half splitting to angle for Niko and me.

"We need to regroup with the others," Niko said, tracking the drones. When they drew within range, he fired. Every single shot hit its intended target.

"They're wasting time on drones. They don't matter. We need to take out the tyv and save—" *Jamie*. The tyv had injured him. I spun in a circle, eyes on the sky, staggering when the sudden rotation stole my balance.

Jamie plummeted from a seething ball of drones, spiraling out of control toward the ground. My heart leapt to my throat, my feet moving before I consciously gave them the signal to run.

"Niko!"

"Wait!" He cursed, but the pounding of his footsteps assured me I wasn't alone.

A string of drones broke from the mass to chase Jamie, closing the gap. He caught himself inches above the ground, spinning with uncanny skill to dart in a new direction. Less than half the drones made the turn with him, the others scattering before regrouping. The pooka didn't slow or hesitate, striking straight for the tyv. I pushed energy into my sluggish legs, feeling as if I were running in sand. The tyv crouched less than ten yards from me. If I could squeeze more speed out, I could time my attack with Jamie's—

"On your right!"

Niko's shout brought my head around. A giant drone barreled down on me, proboscis extended. Despite a dozen *lux lucis* bullets puncturing its thorax, it didn't explode or slow. *Tyv!* I stumbled when I tried to dodge, and the tyv skewered me.

Pain spiked through me, stealing the last of my coordination. I fell swinging, slicing my soul breaker through the tyv's abdomen. It shuddered but clung to me, pivoting its body to shift its abdomen out of reach. My soul ratcheted around the twisting tip of its proboscis, searing molten fire through my limbs. Thrashing, I jabbed the tyv again and again until finally the soul breaker hit its thorax and *lux lucis* gushed through my palm into the tyv. *Atrum* glitter mushroomed above me.

I collapsed onto my back. The dusty remains of the tyv faded to gray, settling on my heaving chest. I flopped an arm over my nose and mouth to avoid sucking the particles into my lungs.

"Incoming," Niko bellowed.

A pair of tyver dropped between me and Niko, both focused on his bright soul. Niko wielded a slender soul breaker as if it were an extension of his hand, punching and thrusting, forcing the tyver back. Despite his efforts, they herded him away from me.

Shoving to my feet took Herculean effort. On limp legs, my arms dangling as heavy as sacks of wet sand, I stumbled after Niko and the tyver attacking him. When I realized I would be useless in my current state, I altered course, lumbering to the nearest hedge and draping my body across it. *Lux lucis* leapt from the sharp branches and icy leaves, flooding my body. Acutely aware of Niko's peril, I sank into the energy, willing it to hurry. Through the network of branches, the thicker trunk stalks and roots, all the way down to the tiny hair-thin feelers deep in the soil—every scrap of *lux lucis* in the plant surged to me, and I drained it dry before pushing upright.

Niko's skirmish had carried him halfway across the field. Only one small tyv remained in front of him, and even as I straightened, he thrust his soul breaker into it, exploding the evil creature. Without waiting for the dust to settle, Niko jogged toward me. Far behind him, almost back at the fence line, Summer and Pamela fought an endless assault of drones and tyver.

I turned away, locking my sights on the gargantuan tyv. Pamela and Summer had each other; Jamie had no one.

If Jamie had weakened the tyv, it hadn't been by much. At the rate she consumed drones, she might have actually been getting stronger. Jamie, on the other hand, visibly leaked *lux lucis* and *atrum* as he dove for the tyv again. If he maintained his solo assault, it would be suicide.

"Ready?" I asked Niko, who had caught up and was recharging on a nearby sapling.

"Any chance you're headed toward Pamela?"

"Nope."

I stumbled into a run. Niko sprinted in my periphery. The width of the track and the empty grass behind the goalpost separated me from the tyv, but drones and small newborn tyver cluttered the airspace. Palmquell in one hand, soul breaker in the other, I ducked and wove through the throng, burning through energy I couldn't spare in an attempt to avoid being struck. I couldn't distinguish between drones and tyver, not without slowing, so I shot anything in front of me and dodged the rest. Niko kept pace beside me, and I had a sense of him shooting drones that attacked from above and behind us, but I didn't bother checking. I trusted the optivus aegis to cover my back and to warn me if anything got through his guard.

I pelted across the soggy track, searching the sky for Jamie, and almost flubbed the transition to the grassy football field. Catching my footing, I spotted my pooka zigzagging through a cloud of drones to punch his proboscis into the tyv's thorax. A fine spray of *atrum* gushed from the wound, dying back to a trickle. Countless additional glossy rivulets of *atrum* already seeped from puncture wounds in the tyv's side, but they might as well have been paper cuts for all the effect they had on her.

Jamie retreated, but the tyv chased him skyward, catching him on a barbed claw. He flailed and fought, but she clung to him. Together, they floated through the air away from me, carried by the tyv's momentum, and when she landed, she drove her foot into the ground, pinning Jamie. The pooka spasmed in her grip. Ducking her head, the tyv stabbed her thick proboscis into Jamie's thorax. His body shuddered and convulsed.

Last night's nightmare replayed in front of me: Jamie helpless and dying; the tyv devouring the pooka's powerful energy, gaining strength even as she killed Jamie; and me, too far away to do any good.

A sob escaped me. Niko no longer ran at my side. All the smaller tyver I'd avoided had converged on his brighter, stronger *lux lucis*, driving him toward the stands. He yelled at me. My harsh breaths drowned out his words, but I could guess he ordered me to wait. Even at full strength, I wouldn't have had enough energy to bring down a tyv the size of a semi-truck by myself. But Jamie didn't have time for me to wait for Niko to catch up. He needed rescuing *now*.

Without Jamie to direct attacks against the tyv, the drones and smaller tyver avoided the air space close to her, leaving me a clear path. I sprinted up behind her, terror giving me an extra burst of speed. The urge to bury my soul breaker into the pulsing blend of *lux lucis* and *atrum* of her thick abdomen warred within me. Stabbing the distended segment wouldn't kill her, but it might distract her from Jamie. Or it might chase her away, Jamie still impaled on her claw, and destroy any chance I had of rescuing him.

Thorax. It has to be the thorax.

My lungs burned, each gasped breath searing my esophagus. I ducked unnecessarily when I passed under the sharp, ten-foot arch of her back leg. Her abdomen curved upward to a tiny insect waist where it connected with the round thorax, and through the gap beneath her body, I spotted Jamie. Pinned on the tyv's far side, his feeble struggles went unnoticed by the gorging monstrosity.

I pushed everything I had into the next three strides and impaled the tyv on my soul breaker. The weapon's barbed tips punctured tiny holes in her thorax. I pulsed *lux lucis* through the soul breaker, then withdrew. *Atrum* gushed from the wounds in twin fountains, and I side-stepped to avoid the poisonous spray. My soul didn't contain enough *lux lucis* to overpower her vats of *atrum*, so I used Jamie's method: I kept stabbing. Eventually, she would bleed out.

"Let him go, damn it! *Die!*" I yelled, the words unintelligible between my ragged breaths and sobs. Working my way up her thorax, I stabbed again and again, opening dozens of cuts in her side, my stumbling steps propelling me ahead of the spurts of *atrum*.

The tyv shifted, and I lurched to follow her, seeing too late that she'd ripped her horrid proboscis from Jamie and turned her attention to the puny enforcer harassing her. In one seamless strike, she impaled me.

Agony tore my world to shreds and rebuilt it in torturous waves of misery. My soul imploded toward the tip of her sharp mouth, rending bones, shredding nerves and muscles. I clung to my soul. Pain intensified, melting my organs.

With an anguished cry, I flung my *lux lucis* away from the tyv. The torment retreated a fraction and my vision cleared.

A white haze filmed the air, casting the monstrous tyv's eyes in a soft, dreamy glow. Hundreds of my reflections stared back at me, a diminutive woman kneeling in the snow, mouth agape, eyes saucer-wide with shock. My chin dipped to my chest as I followed the line of the thick proboscis to where it punctured my gut. Pain ratcheted and eased, and a bulge of *lux lucis* slid up the tyv's tubular mouth. *My lux lucis.* I blinked away the fuzzy black spots in my vision and braced a weak hand on the tyv's wicked proboscis. I met resistance; then my hand sank into the creature's raw *atrum*. I jerked back, and my hand reappeared, blackened with evil soot.

The tyv ripped another mouthful of my soul free, pain bowing my spine, and I searched for Jamie, needing to see him one last time.

Pinned by her claw, he convulsed, jackknifing up around her leg over and over again. No, not convulsing; fighting. When the tyv had latched on to me, she'd shifted her bulk toward Jamie, and each time he jerked upward, his proboscis struck her thorax. Each time he fell back, *atrum* spurted from a new wound into a widening puddle. Impaled, his soul so faint I could almost see through him, Jamie still hadn't given up.

I wouldn't either, not until he was free, but . . .

Shouldn't I be dead already? It hadn't taken the tyv this long to detach my soul last night. Befuddled, I fought through the pain to focus. The white glow . . . my *lux lucis.*

I'd netted the tyv! A fatalistic thrill pinged through me.

I hadn't caught the whole tyv—she was too large for my paltry soul to encompass—but I'd netted her head. The maneuver had been muscle memory more than conscious thought, an attempt to escape the focused pain of her proboscis. By some miracle, it'd worked, too. Thinning my soul had slowed the tyv's ability to consume it.

And I could move.

I jabbed the soul breaker into the tyv, my hand a lead ball on a limp wrist. The weapon prodded the tyv with the force of wet paper. I fumbled to channel *lux lucis* through the tiny hooks, but stopped when my net threatened to collapse.

As defenses went, it was pathetic.

I mustered another weak stab. The soul breaker's hooks slid across the tyv's proboscis, scratching long welts into her intangible flesh. She jerked, tearing the sharp tip of her mouth from my gut. I screamed. Collapsing sideways, I caught myself with my right hand still fisted around the soul breaker, my tendons crunching under the awkward impact. Through the shimmer of my soul, the tyv's large, foreign eyes contemplated me. When she flicked her tongue out, tasting my net, flames sizzled across my nerve endings. When she swallowed, agony toppled me onto all fours. Without touching me, she consumed my soul.

I clung stubbornly to the net. Even with pain muddling my thoughts, I remembered the net was the only thing keeping me alive. Keeping me *and* Jamie alive. I'd given up on my own survival—the moment I'd flung my soul around the tyv, I'd forfeited my life—but the net forced her to slow down, and the longer she focused on me, the more time Jamie had to escape.

"Save yourself." My words squeezed through my constricted throat, barely audible. Jamie's insect head tilted in my direction, a multitude of spinning irises meeting my gaze. Then, his movements clumsy and exaggerated, he stabbed the tyv's thorax. I waited for him to withdraw, to let the newest wound bleed like he had the rest. His proboscis bulged and contracted, and a dark lump of *atrum* disappeared down his throat. The faint ribbons of *lux lucis* twining through Jamie's soul faded, darkening. Another swallow ate through the glow of *lux lucis* in his abdomen.

I shook my head, my sluggish thoughts having no problem grasping the danger of Jamie feeding on the tyv. If he consumed too much *atrum*, he'd be irrevocably altered. He wouldn't be my pooka. He'd be alive, but he'd be something darker, evil.

That isn't what I meant! I wanted to shout.

The tyv jerked her head toward Jamie, coming up short against the edge of my soul's net. I pitched sideways, wrenched off balance by the displaced energy of my soul. Fire sparked through my synapses. She yanked her head again, angling her sharp proboscis for Jamie. Again, she slammed into the intangible internal wall of my net. A backlash of pain cracked my skull. My soul lurched and my stomach heaved.

The tyv spread her wings and bunched her legs, alarm stiffening her enormous body. When she tried to lift her head, my soul held it pinned. When she twisted to stab Jamie, my soul brought her up short. Moaning, I clung to the net even as it tore my body apart. Throughout her struggles, Jamie didn't relent. Mouthful after mouthful of evil energy siphoned down his throat into his abdomen, blackening him even as he visibly strengthened.

Had his return to me been a lie? Had he told me what I wanted to hear? Had I lost him and not even realized it?

No. My heart denied the thought. Holding Jamie's soul in mine had been peaceful, comforting—even euphoric. I hadn't made that up, and Jamie couldn't have faked it. If he had turned evil, I would have felt it. Plus, he'd had plenty of opportunities to steal the tyv's dark energy before tonight. He wasn't acting on some nefarious plot. He was martyring himself to save me.

Oh, you stupid, wonderful pooka.

The tyv finally thought to lift her leg, hauling Jamie to her mouth. I staggered to my feet and stumbled in the opposite direction, dragging her head with me. Running against the pressure on my soul felt like peeling my tendons from my legs. My knees buckled. I crawled, flaying the flesh from my own bones. The tyv jabbed her proboscis into my back, ripping a hunk of my soul from my body. I crumpled to the snow. My vision narrowed, darkening to a pinprick. I fought to stay focused on Jamie. He ripped free of the tyv and blasted into the sky, and my heart flew with him, plummeting back to despair when Jamie spun to sink his claws and proboscis deep into the top of the tyv's thorax. *Atrum* swelled to fill his emaciated form.

I couldn't allow him to make this sacrifice. If he turned dark, Pamela or Niko would kill him before the night was over. I couldn't let all his wonderful potential be corrupted in the name of saving me. I'd made this choice. I'd decided to fight evil. Jamie had merely made the mistake of tethering his life to mine, and I refused to be his downfall.

The tyv floundered and fell, the impact of her huge body soundless on the grassy field. I gathered the last of my strength. I'd get one shot at this.

Retracting the net, I channeled all my *lux lucis* into the soul breaker and rammed it into the tyv's thorax.

29

WHAT DOESN'T KILL YOU WILL
PROBABLY TRY AGAIN

The soul breaker sliced into the tyv's thorax, and my *lux lucis* sank into her weakened body. She struck back, ramming her deadly proboscis into my side.

Pain shredded my thoughts, all but one: *Save Jamie.*

The tyv latched on to the spindly remains of my soul, trying to swallow it whole. With every ounce of my diminished strength, I shoved my energy in the opposite direction, pushing it through the soul breaker.

It hurt. *Oh God, it hurt!*

I screamed until I ran out of breath and pain closed my throat. Full-body tremors toppled me to my knees, my teeth chattering uncontrollably. Inch by inch, my soul ripped in two.

Jamie. Must save Jamie.

I peeled another layer of my *lux lucis* from my bones and thrust it down the soul breaker's short arms. My fragile energy slid into the void of *atrum* comprising the tyv's massive thorax, disappearing without a ripple. High above us, drones mobbed in a widening chaotic blur of legs and wings and segmented bodies, forming a deadly, living cyclone of evil.

The tyv swallowed, tearing another scream from me. I jabbed the soul breaker deeper into her thorax, shoving through the dense *atrum* of her body until her evil sludge coated me from my knuckles to my elbow. With the last of my strength, I ripped *lux lucis* from my marrow and thrust it through the soul breaker.

The pressure inside me snapped. My tattered *lux lucis* surged through the soul breaker and tore into the tyv. Her thorax collapsed. A tsunami of *atrum* engulfed me, thick and malevolent, replacing the all-encompassing agony of the tyv's proboscis with a biting, burrowing, smothering pain. Gravity spun, and I smashed against the frozen field. My teeth clenched, I fought against the invasion of *atrum*, but my *lux lucis* sputtered and gave out. A cold trickle of tears leaked down my temples into my hair.

The darkness thinned, imperceptibly at first, then faster as the tyv's imploding energy rebounded and exploded skyward in a tight column. Soundlessly, it lifted, leaving me panting and limp with pain. Higher and higher the *atrum* surged before billowing into a dense mushroom cloud, and still the energy climbed. The tornado of drones fractured, individuals scattering across the sky in pandemonium. I blinked heavy eyelids, tracking the expansion of the toxic cloud's onyx rim as it overtook fleeing drones. It stretched wider than a trampoline, than a hot air balloon, than the football field—and it continued to spread.

I flopped onto my back and dragged the soul breaker onto my stomach. I tried to smile, but I couldn't tell if my lips moved. Inside my head, I performed a victory dance. I'd killed the tyv. She wouldn't harm Jamie ever again.

A blissful numbness stole through my limbs—snow or *atrum* induced, I couldn't tell and I didn't look. It didn't matter. I wouldn't survive the inevitable fallout of the tyv's atomic cloud. I had expended everything I had for Jamie.

Where are you, my pooka?

Drones buzzed in disarray, but a few were already straightening from their directionless flights, homing in on something behind me. *Niko,* I decided. They must have caught sight of his soul, or Summer's or Pamela's. Without the tyv to control them, the drones were reverting to their base instincts, hunting the nearest food source: my coworkers. Perversely, a cheerful spark came and went with the thought—the others were strong; the drones didn't stand a chance.

Jamie, where are you? A tyv broke from the drones and plummeted toward me, proboscis extended—death on the wings of a mutant mosquito. My heart pattered in my chest, the beat erratic. I struggled to rise, succeeding in little more than a shuddering wriggle. The tyv bore down on me, filling my vision. When it landed, it caged me inside its six legs, its long body covering but not touching me. I strained to see around it, hunting for my pooka, needing to see him one last time. My right hand feebly twitched the soul breaker toward the tyv's thorax before falling back to my chest.

The tyv tipped its head, angling its proboscis down the length of my body so it could lean its multifaceted eyes close to mine, filling my vision.

A kaleidoscope of *lux lucis* and *atrum* swirled in the tyv's eyes.

"Jamie?" My voice cracked.

Atrum bathed him from proboscis to abdomen, the only *lux lucis* visible on him spinning faintly in his irises. Fresh tears blurred my vision. He'd consumed too much *atrum*, and it had changed him. I'd done everything I could to save him, but it'd been too little.

"I don't care . . ." I swallowed and rasped in another ragged breath. "I don't care how dark you are, I still love you."

Jamie reared onto his hind legs, spreading his front four legs and wings wide, towering over my prone body. I tensed in anticipation of his final strike.

This isn't his fault. He was trying to save me.

I couldn't move. The only defense I could muster was a child's: I squeezed my eyes shut. My breath wheezed and rattled, my heart skipping in my chest. When nothing happened, I opened my eyes. Jamie still stood over me, his insect body horrifically tall from this perspective. Behind him, the sky shimmered, the *atrum* fallout brightening. Faint swirls of *lux lucis* particulates twined through the black mass, collecting into tiny clumps as they fell—metaphysical snowflakes among poisonous ashes. Faster, the *lux lucis* coalesced, tightening into a singular mass separate from the exploded remains of the tyv. It fell over us, tenting us from the descending *atrum* for a breathless moment; then it transformed into a singular, blinding-white stream that shot into Jamie.

I gaped in wonder.

Lux lucis rolled through his ebony body, transforming him back into the pooka I knew, the twin energies corkscrewing in the confines of his body. Impossibly, he'd collected the parts of his soul the tyv had devoured. The darkness wouldn't consume him; he wasn't lost.

The tenuous tension holding my consciousness to my body

released. Jamie was safe. I closed my eyes and opened myself to the peace of death.

It came on a rush of warmth that soothed my body's lingering pain. "We need to move."

Jamie's voice burst loud across my eardrums, jolting my eyes open. I blinked into his human face, his eyes whirling pinwheels of *lux lucis* and *atrum*. A white haze stretched between us, siphoning from his naked chest directly into my heart.

What are you doing? My throat refused to work and the question didn't make it outside my skull.

"I can't retrieve your soul. It's too damaged." Jamie glanced up. The tyv's massive thundercloud of *atrum* had broken, unleashing its evil energy on the field below—with Jamie and me centered at the heart of the fallout. The first flecks landed on me, stinging. Odorless, tasteless, and chilling to the soul, the black dust thickened the air, settling on my frozen legs and arms, polluting my esophagus and lungs with each breath. The stream of *lux lucis* Jamie fed me weakened, *atrum* eating through his clean energy before it could settle in my body. Black splotches took root and spread across my torso. Panic floated at the edges of my thoughts, held at bay by a surreal, dreamlike fog.

Is this death? Am I dying?

"Sit up. Come on, you have to help me." Jamie squirmed a weak arm beneath my shoulders, but I couldn't locate my neck muscles, and my head flopped back.

You can't die today. Not after Jamie worked so hard to save you, my subconscious chided. *You're in shock. Snap out of it.*

"Can you stand?" Niko's urgent baritone rumbled in my ears.

No.

"I can't lift her."

Don't cry, Jamie.

"Here." Niko slid an arm under my knees, another along my back, and I soared through the air, settling against his warm torso. *Lux lucis* realigned in my chest like a compass needle, pointing to Jamie. "Can you run?"

I can fly.

The horizon bounced—the stands, the black cloud, Jamie's worried eyes. The pooka clutched my hand in his, our fingers both so cold I couldn't feel his grip.

The moment we passed beyond the *atrum* cloud, energy gushed into my chest, rushing down my body, stripping away the *atrum* and my buffer of shock. Gasping, I squeezed Jamie's hand, twisting in Niko's arms to see the pooka better.

"Careful," I croaked. "Don't give me too much."

Jamie sobbed and nodded. Niko didn't stop until an entire baseball field separated us from the rain of *atrum*. The moment he set me on my feet, I reached for Jamie, and we clung to each other, wobbling on weak legs.

"I thought you died—again," Jamie said.

"Me too."

"You saved me."

I hugged Jamie's shivering, naked form to me. "*You* saved *me*."

"You both saved each other," Niko said. "Neither of you should be alive."

I leaned back to smile at Jamie. His jaw chattered, but he grinned through it.

"No more." I tapped his chest where *lux lucis* continued to feed from him to me. "You need to conserve your energy."

"You sure?"

I closed my eyes and assessed my body. My knees trembled and my eyelids didn't want to open back up, but it was exhaustion, nothing more. "Yes. Thank you."

Jamie tapered the line of *lux lucis* connecting us to a thread before cutting it off. My knees buckled, and I would have fallen if Niko hadn't caught me with an arm around my waist.

"I'm going to change. It's too cold to be human."

In a seamless morph of flesh to fur, Jamie bent and assumed his Great Dane form. His soul bubbled and settled inside his new shape, his *atrum* glossy black, his *lux lucis* pale and drained. Even weakened, the good energy didn't succumb to the stronger evil energy. In fact, it almost looked as if more white sloshed inside him than black.

Jamie circled once and flopped against my feet in the snow-churned grass. Niko helped me sit next to him, and I draped an arm over the pooka's back. He sighed and closed his eyes. Niko unzipped his coat and laid it over Jamie, earning another happy sigh from the pooka.

Sheets of *atrum* rained onto the stadium, track, and football field, the downfall so thick it obscured everything beyond the outer edge. The sharp wind didn't affect the evil cloud; it remained anchored above the tyv's final location, as if not even death could negate the formidable creature's power. Her dispersed *atrum* didn't lose its potency, either, settling into a dense, dangerous black layer across the school grounds. A smattering of drones flitted through the tyv's remains before scattering toward the horizon, their flight paths uncoordinated and random. Only a handful of newborn tyv stuck around, diving after Summer and Pamela to die against their soul breakers.

The icy chill of the snow seeped anew through my wet pants and long johns, and my chest rattled with a weak shiver. Jamie and I needed to get warm and dry before we caught colds, but for the moment, resting beside my pooka seemed more important, my hand on his side, taking comfort in the rise and fall of his breaths and the steady thump of his heartbeat.

"After all that, you're smiling?" Niko asked, incredulous.

I shrugged. "I'm alive."

Niko shook his head and took a step away from me, then paused, his shoulders stiff. Abruptly, he spun back, knelt, and gripped my upper arms. Holding me firm, he leaned close enough for his breath to fan across my face, his expression serious.

I expected a lecture. Instead, he kissed me.

I gasped at the shocking heat of his lips against mine, so hot they almost burned. Niko slid his tongue between my open lips, and with it a tendril of his *lux lucis*. A riot of electric sparks shimmied beneath my skin, igniting a path of molten fire from my mouth downward, thawing my frozen body. I moaned against Niko's lips and his hands tightened with bruising strength around my arms. His tongue teased over mine again, then again, jolting pleasure through my sensitized nerves. Far too soon, he broke the kiss, nipping my bottom lip in parting. I opened my eyes, blinking at the passion reflected in his.

"Whoa." The word slipped from me on an exhale.

The corners of Niko's eyes crinkled with his barely-there smile, and he released me. I sagged, catching myself against Jamie.

"I'm glad you're alive, too," Niko said.

He jogged away to assist Pamela and Summer before I caught my breath. Just as well. I probably would have said something stupid.

Jamie lifted his head from his paw, his whirling eyes meeting mine with a question.

"I'm just as confused as you," I said.

Whether because of the pathetic state of our souls or fear of the pooka, the drones didn't bother us. For once, I got to be a bystander, too tired to do more than pet Jamie's side while the others dashed back and forth across the baseball fields, killing tyver.

"It appears you two need more help than they do," a male voice said from right beside me.

Jamie and I jumped, and I fumbled for my soul breaker before I recognized Gavin Holt, the local medical enforcer. His footsteps in the snow proved he hadn't materialized out of thin air, but I hadn't heard or seen him approach. I must have been more out of it than I realized if he'd been able to sneak up on me in the middle of an empty baseball field.

Dropping to his knees beside us, Gavin wrapped Jamie and me in thick wool blankets, then checked my pupils and pulse, poking and prodding with the detachment only a physician can exhibit. Barely older than me, with thick brown hair, kind eyes, a lean body, and a blazing soul, Gavin looked every part an enforcer, medical or not. He'd come prepared with his black doctor's bag and a thick wooden staff, and experience had taught me he was as deadly with the staff as he was skilled as a medic.

"How did you know we needed you?" I asked.

"I've been on call since the tyver showed up. Brad sent me the moment he felt everything go—how did he phrase it?—'graham crackers in gum balls'? Is it true the tyv was as large as a tank?"

"More like a double-decker bus." I ran my hand down Jamie's side, reassuring myself once more that he was safe.

"No wonder it took four of you to kill it."

I shook my head. "Just Jamie."

"Really?" Gavin asked, impressed.

Jamie poked me with an icy nose and woofed.

"Okay, I helped. Ow!" I batted Gavin's hand away from my thigh where I'd cut myself on my soul breaker the night before. I didn't need to look to know the wounds had reopened.

"You're injured," he said, gesturing to the bloodstain on my pants. "Let me see."

"No. It happened yesterday and I'm fine. I'm not pulling my pants down in the snow so you can say the same thing."

We had a similar argument when Gavin prodded my tender ribs.

"It doesn't hurt unless you jab it with your pointy finger," I groused. "Leave it alone and it'll be fine."

"You do realize I'm the doctor here, right?" Gavin asked, but he shifted his attention to a cut on my forehead. I grumbled and hissed as he swabbed disinfectant over the wound and bandaged it, and again when he tended road rash on my palms. I didn't remember getting either of the injuries, and I resented having fresh pain inflicted now after everything I'd suffered tonight. Yet somehow I found myself promising to drop by his office tomorrow for a full examination and whatever torture that entailed.

When Gavin finally helped me to my feet, a litany of pains clamored for attention. I yearned for my soft bed. Failing that, I wished Niko would offer to carry me to my car. Since he and Pamela had turned their attention to cleaning the taint of *atrum* from the stands and football field, I gave up on my selfish fantasy. As I hobbled across the infinite snow-covered baseball fields supported by Gavin, with Jamie stumbling against my hip, Niko and Pamela used powerful sweeps of *lux lucis* to eat through the settled *atrum*, recharging frequently on nearby shrubbery and trees. Oakmont High's landscaping would need a complete overhaul in the spring, but a few dead fields, shrubs, and trees were worth the sacrifice to prevent the massive blanket of evil energy from tainting students when they returned to school.

Summer plodded across the field, angling to meet us at the chain-link fence, weariness sloping her shoulders. Despite the clear skies, she clutched her soul breaker in a white-knuckled fist. *Shell-shocked,* I decided, recognizing her dazed look by the feel of it on my own face. Her soul guttered more faintly than mine, and when Gavin offered her liquid *lux lucis*, she took a sip. I waved aside the flask when she offered it to me.

"Are you sure you don't want some?" Gavin asked.

I shook my head. A tiny shred of the *lux lucis* inside me was mine; the rest was pure pooka energy, and I wasn't sure how liquid *lux lucis* would interact with it.

"Then I insist you eat," he said.

"You have food?"

"What kind of ME would I be if I didn't?"

Even Jamie, trudging nose down at my side, managed to perk up enough to wag his tail.

The short chain-link fence separating us from our cars might as well have been the Great Wall for how insurmountable it appeared in my weary state, and I almost wept with relief when Gavin climbed the fence and returned with bolt cutters. Snapping the chain holding the gate closed, he rolled aside the barrier, and we limped out to the sidewalk.

While Gavin examined Summer, I took Jamie to my Civic, popped the trunk, and laid out my spare clothes. I had his doggy vest, but after he'd spent the last half hour lying in the snow, it wouldn't be enough to warm him back up. Fortunately, his human form was similarly proportioned to mine, right down to our identical height, and my pants, shirt, and sweater fit him. After he changed and dressed, we huddled in the same blanket on the back bumper of Gavin's van, shivering together.

Summer slumped beside me while Gavin rummaged inside the vehicle. With enough clearance inside to stand, an array of cubbies and bins filled with supplies, and rear side-by-side double doors, the van served as a fancy incognito ambulance. My gaze glanced off the stretcher attached to one wall, and I wiggled my toes, grateful beyond words to be walking away from another battle. When Gavin handed us each our own thermos of hot chicken noodle soup, I decided the van was magical.

Summer finally sheathed her soul breaker, though she kept one hand on it while she sipped the steaming soup. Neither of us relaxed until Pamela and Niko strode through the gap in the trees. The memory of Niko's kiss tingled across my lips. Even exhausted, he walked with a predatory grace, vigilantly scanning the surroundings for the next attack. Pamela had her own version of that cultivated wariness honed from years as an elite enforcer. For some reason, I didn't find it sexy on her.

Niko glanced at me and our gazes collided. A shiver that had nothing to do with the snow slid through my body, petering out almost before it'd begun. Later. I'd figure out what his kiss had meant later. In Primordium, I couldn't read the subtle change in Niko's expression, but the loosening of tension from his shoulders and hands told me he'd been worried.

Silently, I handed him back his coat. He shrugged it on, then climbed into the van with Pamela to confer with Gavin. From the snippets I caught, Jamie and I were the subject of their whispered conversation, but I couldn't muster the energy to eavesdrop. With exaggerated care, I drained the last drops of soup from my thermos, then leaned back to savor the warmth spreading from my stomach through my body.

"You know you're insane, right?" Summer asked. She stared at the sky, eyes unfocused.

"I am?"

"Oh yeah." She bumped my shoulder with hers. "All the best enforcers are."

I smiled at my toes.

Summer took a drink from her thermos, then twisted to look me in the eye. "I misjudged you. I'm sorry."

"I'm sorry I kept giving you reasons to misjudge me."

She huffed a short laugh, shook her head, and went back to drinking her soup. I contemplated my toes some more, enjoying the companionable silence.

Maybe all hope of a friendship between us wasn't lost, after all.

Brad's tiny Fiat rocked up against the curb behind the van, and Pamela, Niko, and Gavin climbed out to greet him. My boss ignored them, rushing straight to me. He stopped close enough for his long coat to brush against my bent knees as he scanned my body, then Jamie's, checking our souls. Softly, he grasped my chin and leaned forward until he filled my vision and my eyes crossed trying to keep him in focus.

For a panicked second, I thought he was going to kiss me, but he only stared, his eyes bulging with an emotion I couldn't read.

"Mr. Pitt? Brad?" I squeaked when he didn't say anything.

He squinted, then nodded and stepped back. "How is she?" he asked, directing his question to Gavin.

"Roughed up but remarkably resilient."

I would have said *battered but alive*, but Gavin's assessment sounded nicer.

"She and Jamie took out the tyv by themselves," Summer said. "They make a good team."

I shot her a surprised look. She returned it with a fatigued smile.

"What's happening with the rest of the region?" Pamela asked.

Brad rubbed his hands together, a satisfied grin replacing his concern. "We're in the clear. Jamie was right: No more tyver have hatched since the main tyv died."

A collective sigh of relief resounded from our small circle.

"So it's over?" I asked.

"Just about. The assisting enforcers are reporting a significant drop in the number of drones hatching since you killed the tyv. It's going to take longer to destroy all the eggs, but the prajurit queens assure me that by the end of the week, our region will be free from threat of spawning drones."

"If I never see another tyv as long as I live, I will be a happy woman," Summer said. "Can I go home?"

"Yes. Thank you again for your assistance. I'll speak with your warden regarding bonus compensation," Brad said.

Summer nodded wearily, handed her blanket to Gavin, and departed.

"You should head home, too, Madison," Brad said. "I'll check in with you tomorrow. Jamie, I appreciate what you did here tonight. I consider you an invaluable asset to our region and to Madison. When you get a chance, I hope you'll share any information you have about sjel tyver that can help us in the future. But after you both get some rest."

An unspoken accusation radiated from Pamela's disapproving body language when Brad didn't mention that tonight's catastrophe could have been avoided if Jamie hadn't gone rogue to being with. If Brad had, I would have insisted on taking the blame. If I hadn't alienated Jamie, making him feel like an unloved disappointment, he wouldn't have acted out. The monstrous tyv and all the evil she'd wrought on our region lay squarely on my shoulders.

Jamie and I shoved to our feet, and I unwrapped the blanket from around us, shivering as the freezing air sapped away the nominal heat we'd generated. I handed the blanket to Gavin, whirling back toward Jamie when he made a soft, pained sound. Electric-white energy caged my pooka, the sizzling bars of *lux lucis* extending from a multifaceted crystal prism in Pamela's hand. Jamie's arm brushed the prison and a spark of *lux lucis* surged into him. He jumped as if shocked. A whimper squeezed out of his throat as a jagged patch of *lux lucis* jolted up his arm, vibrating through the rest of his soul's dual energies. He closed his eyes and swallowed hard.

I reached for Jamie, pulling up short before I touched the cage, not sure how it'd affect the pooka if I disturbed the wicked white lines.

"What are you doing?" I demanded of Pamela.

"You're in no shape to take charge of the pooka right now," she said. "You're too weak, and even if you weren't, your motives are questionable. You stand here before us because you are infused with the pooka's own soul. We cannot predict how this will affect you, let alone how much control you'll be able to exert over the pooka."

Maybe it was due to my brush with death; maybe it was because I'd battled a house-size tyv and facing down the inspector no longer scared me; maybe it was because weariness saturated every cell in my body—or maybe it was because Jamie's soul swirled inside me, helping me see from a different perspective—but in that moment, I saw the truth behind Pamela's actions: She was scared, impaired by her limited knowledge, and trying to do what she thought was best. In all her years working for the CIA, she'd met only one other pooka, and she'd made the mistake of assuming they were all the same. She believed the methods used with that pooka could be applied to all pookas. I'd fallen prey to the same faulty logic, and it had torn Jamie and me apart. Fortunately, I'd learned my lesson: Jamie was one of a kind, and he deserved to be treated as such.

Then I got another look at Jamie trembling inside the inspector's trap, and my anger roared to the surface. However, losing control wouldn't sway the inspector. Gritting my teeth, I modulated my voice when I said, "Pamela, you can't hold him, and you can't control him."

"Don't fight me on this, Madison. It's for your own good. For everyone's good."

Everyone's but Jamie's. "You don't understand. You can't dictate his actions, and neither can I because I don't have any control over Jamie. I never did."

Pamela tensed, her hand tightening on the prism. "I know, but I'm glad you're admitting it. It'll make this easier. You're a good enforcer, but you're not up to handling a pooka this powerful."

"You still don't get it." My fingers itched to snatch the prism from her, but I hesitated, wary of the unfamiliar weapon's powers. Frustration laced my voice as I continued. "Jamie is a pooka. He chose me, not the other way around. He instigated the bond—twice actually—"

"Three times now," Jamie whispered.

Brad's eyebrows danced up his forehead. "Three times?"

"Is that healthy?" Niko asked.

Gavin shrugged. "I don't think there's a precedent to cross-check against."

Pamela didn't react, but the cage tightened around Jamie, brushing his shoulders. He flinched, then flinched again when the slight movement pressed his knees against bars of *lux lucis*, zapping jagged lines through his soul. A tiny squeak escaped his throat, and I thrust my hand through the prism's energy to steady him. *Lux lucis* crackled against my flesh, biting into my skin as if it had an electric current. Hissing, I jerked my hand back and shook it. The white energy shouldn't have affected me. It definitely shouldn't have hurt.

"I have no control over Jamie because we're partners," I said, resuming my argument but gathering myself to act. The moment the inspector let her guard down, I would rip the prism from her grasp and free Jamie myself. "I'd no more try to control him than I would attempt to control you or Niko."

"Are you saying the pooka outranks you?"

My nails bit into my palms. "I'm saying he's a friend and an ally. Hasn't he earned the same respect and consideration as the CIA's other allies? Would you cage a prajurit?"

"A prajurit doesn't have a soul composed half of *atrum*. He's evil—"

"Enough! You're letting your eyes and your prejudice blind you. So Jamie has *atrum* in his soul. He also holds more *lux lucis* within him than you do. You're punishing him based on what he *could* do, not what he *has* done. Look at his actions. He's been nothing but genuine." The inspector tried to interrupt, but I overrode her. "When he felt hurt, he lashed out. When he felt loved, he protected and defended. He doesn't need to be controlled. He needs to be loved." I sucked in a harsh breath and let it out, lowering my voice and sinking sincerity into my words. "Jamie chose me. He and I will determine how he lives, not you."

I swept my gaze over the others, looking for objections. Niko's impassive expression told me nothing and Gavin watched me warily, but Brad gave me an infinitesimal nod of support.

The inspector studied me as if seeing me for the first time.

"You can't take him from me," I said.

"I don't have to stay in here?" Jamie asked.

"Of course not," I said.

Before I could demand Pamela release Jamie, the pooka flexed his soul. Jagged blades of inky *atrum* sliced through the powerful *lux lucis* bars. The light of the cage intensified, but Jamie's *atrum* countered it, burrowing into the cracks he'd created. His dark energy spiraled up the rigid white lines of power, peeling back the *lux lucis*. A backlash of mixed energy whipped toward the prism, and Pamela chucked it into the street. *Atrum* and *lux lucis* imploded inside the weapon, and when the crystal clattered to the pavement, the glossy prism transformed into a cracked gray rod. The inspector backpedaled, eyes wide with shock, hands fumbling for the knife at her waist. Jamie retracted his soul and reached for my hand with a blazing-white palm. I squeezed his cold fingers in mine. None of the others had moved.

Schooling my expression, I pretended I'd known all along that Jamie—even at half strength and bone tired—could break her cage.

"I appreciate your concern, Pamela," I said, "but I can take it from here. Good night."

30

SOME CAUSE HAPPINESS WHEREVER THEY GO, OTHERS WHENEVER THEY GO

Pamela allowed us to walk away that night, but she showed up on our doorstep the next morning, and she didn't leave our sides for the rest of the week. I shouldn't have been surprised. If Jamie's heroic battle against the tyv and nearly dying to save me and my region hadn't proven to the inspector that he had a good heart, then destroying her torturous cage and thumbing our noses at her authority certainly wouldn't have convinced her, either.

As much as I didn't want to care about her opinion, I couldn't afford not to. Pamela outranked me and my boss, and if she decided to, she could still strip me of my title as an enforcer, or transfer me away from my region, or . . . There were too many ways she could make my life miserable, and so I ungraciously allowed her to shadow our every move. While Pamela studied us, judged us, and waited for Jamie to swamp me with evil, I did my best to treat her the same way I wanted her to treat Jamie: with respect and as an ally.

Telling myself I was being the bigger person helped. Venting my frustration on straggler drones helped more.

I reinstated the old rules with Jamie: He promised not to alter anyone's soul—human or otherwise—and we both agreed neither metaphysical energies belonged on inanimate objects. Jamie tested me repeatedly, going out of his way to exterminate all traces of *lux lucis* from inanimate objects wherever we were, including at home. I didn't object, and my lack of reaction gave him the reassurance he needed that I would stick to my word this time. I never asked him to use *lux lucis*, letting him choose when he wanted to help me clean up *atrum*, and though he didn't assist with the extermination of any imps or vervet, he didn't try to stop or dissuade me.

After three days of fervent use of his *atrum* to wipe out all inanimate traces of *lux lucis*, Jamie left the rest alone. I didn't comment on that, either.

Surprisingly, Pamela didn't interfere. Some of my words must have penetrated past her preconceived beliefs about pookas, because she didn't attempt to tell either of us how to behave—and judging by her scowls and occasional white-knuckle grip on the hilt of her knife, not speaking up cost her. I wished I could have gotten a picture of her horrified expression the first time she witnessed Jamie's unrestrained play with imps. Pamela had seen him interact with the chinchilla-like evil fluff balls that first night at the high school, but I'd killed the imps quickly, afraid of her potential retaliation against Jamie. Now I took my time, in no hurry to suppress Jamie's fun. Even after the extreme control Pamela had seen Jamie exert over the dual energies of his soul, I think she still expected his frolicking to transition into an *atrum*-spewing rampage. Instead, he laughed and cavorted with the enemy until the last imp willingly leapt to my glowing fist and died. His great evil act afterward? Convincing me to stop at In-N-Out for milkshakes we didn't need in the cold weather.

As the days passed and Jamie and I worked in peaceful accord, performing normal cleanup around the region, Pamela's suspicious body language gradually softened, even if she never fully relaxed. To be fair, I never could shake my stiffness in her presence. I respected her *lux lucis* skills and strength, and I respected her position, but too much had transpired for me to like her. Trusting Pamela remained elusive, too, though I told myself she'd made her decisions with the best intentions. She had attempted to take Jamie away from me; no matter how hard I tried, no matter how professional I wanted to be, I couldn't look past that.

Fortunately, Pamela's other duties prevented her from following us around forever. When we were finally granted our first unchaperoned, work-free day, I already knew exactly what we were going to do. In keeping with my unspoken vow to introduce Jamie to more fun, I'd decided to go all out for Christmas this year, starting with a tree squeezed in among the jungle of plants in our front room.

"So, there's a man in a red suit who is flown around by slave reindeer at night every winter solstice, and he drops presents down chimneys?" Jamie asked after my broad-strokes explanation of the holiday during the drive to the tree lot.

"That's the myth of Santa." More or less.

"Is he related to tyver?"

"Uh. Maybe," I hedged. We hadn't discussed how he felt about tyver since one had nearly killed him, and I didn't want to needlessly disparage one of his forms. "Santa's presents aren't eggs. They're things people want, like toys and games, and he delivers them all on the night before Christmas."

"To everyone? In one night?"

"Yep."

Jamie narrowed his eyes at me. "Is Santa a real creature?"

"Well, I've never seen Santa."

Jamie frowned. I should have known he was too smart to be fooled, even if he technically was young enough to believe.

"But I'll let you in on a secret: Adults have been pretending Santa exists for centuries. It's a global conspiracy, and we all sneak around getting presents for our loved ones; then we wrap them up and put them under the tree to be opened on Christmas morning. That way, everyone gets to play Santa."

Jamie's eyes lit up. "Even me?"

"Even you."

I let Jamie select the Christmas tree—which involved a meticulous inspection of every single pine in the lot before he picked a small Douglas fir. To assuage Val's jealousy, the handbook got to pick the tree topper. I received a lot of strange looks, walking around Target holding an open book up to the shelves of glitter-encrusted stars and gauzy angels. Val chose a gaudy light-up winged chipmunk holding a hymnal book that bore a striking resemblance to a certain sentient handbook. I also gave them both free rein in selecting ornaments, and Jamie and I staggered from the store, our arms loaded with bags and our hearts full of good cheer.

Bridget came over to help decorate the tree, and we cranked up the holiday tunes, propped Val out of reach of the cats on a high bookshelf where he could be part of the conversation—if disjointedly—and turned our plain tree into a glistening jewel. Bridget's initial acute embarrassment around Jamie transformed into avid fascination, and the pooka soaked up her attention. I marveled anew at my friend's adaptability, feeling blessed to have someone so understanding in my life.

"He's really sweet," Bridget whispered to me when Jamie was out of hearing range. "I can see why you're besotted with him."

"'Besotted'? Ew. That makes it sound flirty."

"You do realize he's absolutely gorgeous, right?"

"He's less than a month old, so put your eyes back in their sockets."

"Easy, mama bear. It was just an observation."

Bridget wasn't the only woman to notice Jamie. Everywhere we went, he turned heads. Objectively, I could acknowledge that he was strikingly handsome. He also exuded unchecked confidence and curiosity, a combination that worked like catnip on teenage girls and drew the eyes of older women. But to me he was just Jamie, my pooka. As of yet, he remained oblivious to the attention he garnered, and I hoped he retained his innocence for a long, long time. I wasn't prepared to have the interspecies sex talk with him.

Dame Zilla waited until the tree was fully decked before scrambling up the slender trunk. The Douglas fir's quivering limbs and the chime of disturbed ornaments sent the kitten into a frenzy, and she leapt to the carpet and tore through the house, every hair on her body standing on end. When Mr. Bond deigned to rise from his prized position on the recliner to sniff fallen ornaments, the kitten charged him, only to scare herself before getting within reach and tearing away again. Tail puffed, Mr. Bond slunk back to his chair, giving us baleful looks when we dared laugh.

Though I had plenty of opportunities to mention it to Bridget, I didn't bring up Niko's kiss. I'd given it *a lot* of thought. Every time I tried dismissing it as a spur-of-the-moment, we-both-survived-a-near-death-experience impulse, I would remember the almost-kiss on the wildfire-ravaged hillside. I had proof now that it had been more than frost moths prompting him that day. Mr. Dark and Deadly was genuinely attracted to me—a thought that sent nervous butterflies through my midsection and a giddy flush to my cheeks every time I contemplated it.

However, since I hadn't seen or heard from Niko since that night, I wasn't sure anything between us had changed—nor could I decide if I wanted it to. So I kept the kiss to myself. If I told Bridget, she would want it to dissect it from every angle, and then I'd be forced to define my feelings. Plus, the last thing I needed was to spend more time reliving the tantalizing memory of Niko's lips and *lux lucis*.

But, *damn*, the man knew how to kiss.

Instead, I told Bridget about my public sexual mauling of Alex—which she wholeheartedly approved of, even if she did make fun of me for it—and of our promised hiking date after the holidays.

"I get to go as a Great Dane, and Madison says Alex has a dog, so I get to meet another friend," Jamie chimed in.

"That should be . . . interesting?" Bridget shot me a bewildered look.

Nerve-racking and *potentially disastrous* were how I described it to myself, but I would make it work.

Fingers crossed.

After Bridget left that evening, Jamie, Val, and I settled around the dining table to decorate Christmas stockings. Jamie had finished a whimsical, paint-and-glitter portrait of Dame Zilla on the kitten's new stocking and I was in the midst of attempting to use a tube of glitter glue to re-create Val's finicky artistic design atop his stocking when a familiar pounding knock drowned out the music. Mood souring, I answered the door.

"Hi, Pamela."

"May I come in?"

Grudgingly, I opened the door wider than a crack and allowed the inspector into my home. A familiar nausea churned in my stomach as I ran through the possible reasons for her presence, and a subconscious impulse lifted my hand to cover my heart. During the last week working together, Pamela had never once asked to test my purity, and if she thought to do so now, I'd assist her right back over the threshold.

She stepped inside, eyes darting from the decorated tree to Jamie, surrounded by art supplies at the table, a glitter smear across his chin. Her eyes widened at the sight of his yellow polka dot and pink bunny pajamas, then bounced to me, taking in my identical outfit. Using a clean finger, Jamie slid Val, open, across the table so the inspector could more easily see the huge *Hi, Pamela!* splashed across his page.

"Is something wrong?" I asked.

Pamela started and focused on me. "I'm leaving town."

"Really?" My face stiffened as I attempted to mask my relief and happiness behind a professional facade. "That's, ah . . ." What was the polite response here? *Don't let the door hit you where the good Lord split you?* No, that couldn't be right.

"I'm not here for a hug," Pamela assured me. "I'm here in an official capacity. Unless you have a valid objection, I'm granting the expansion of your region."

My breath whooshed out in shock. "You are?"

"Brad has the skills. His deft negotiations of the prajurit peace talks and his coolheaded leadership during the tyver invasion proved he hasn't lost the edge that once made him one of California's top wardens. But I didn't think he had an enforcer to back him up."

"What changed your mind?"

"When I first read Brad's reports about you, I thought he had exaggerated them to make his region look better. When I met you, I was sure of it."

Ouch. But she wouldn't be Pamela if she wasn't brutally honest.

"You're inexperienced, and from an outsider's perspective, dangerously rash. But I mistook your compassionate nature"—Pamela's eyes flicked to Jamie, making her meaning unmistakable—"as a weakness. I see now the truth of Brad's assessment. You're fast becoming an enforcer to be reckoned with. But if you feel overburdened with your current responsibilities—"

"No. Definitely not. I want the larger region." Did she honestly think I would stand between my boss and his fondest wish? Besides, I had gotten used to the extra territory. To go back to our former region would feel cramped, especially with Jamie at my side. We needed more space to explore together.

"Very well. I'll let Brad know." Pamela reached for the doorknob, splitting her parting words between me and Jamie. "I'll be keeping an eye on your progress. Best of luck."

I didn't need luck; I had Jamie, and together, we could do anything.

AUTHOR'S NOTE

I originally intended Madison and Alex's first date to be part of *A Fistful of Frost*, but no amount of plot wrangling made it fit into the novel. I also was loathe to skip over the date and leave you with only a recap. So instead, I'm offering it to you here as a bonus. I hope you enjoy the story . . . even if it's not the perfect night Madison fantasized it would be.

A FISTFUL OF FLIRTATION

A MADISON FOX SHORT ADVENTURE

1

FLUENT IN BLARNEY

I paused at the threshold of the restaurant, astonished by the crush of people packed into the elegant foyer. A wave of cologne and perfume wafted over me, underscored by aromas of mouth-watering dishes being served to people lucky enough to have nabbed a seat.

"Looks like we'll have to fight our way through," Alex said.

"I had no idea this place was so popular," I said, raising my voice to be heard over the clamor.

"I don't think it is."

I gestured to the milling crowd. "Do you want to tell them that?"

People near us glanced in our direction and attempted to squeeze to the side to make room. Somewhere beyond this well-dressed throng hid a computer screen with details of our reservation, but I couldn't even pinpoint the host station.

A trio of women wormed through the press of people on their way out, and I stepped aside so they could exit.

"Now's our chance." Alex grabbed my hand and angled his lean body into the gap.

I squeezed close behind him, enjoying the sensation of his long fingers wrapped around mine. I wasn't a teenager holding hands with a boy for the first time, but the giddy sensation fluttering in my stomach belied the fact.

Madison and Alex sitting in a tree . . . I squashed the child's limerick before it gained momentum, but I didn't try hard to abolish the image of Alex's lips on mine.

I had fantasized about this date ever since Mr. Bond's first visit as a kitten to Alex's veterinary clinic almost three years ago. I was sure every unattached woman who had been through those doors had given a relationship with the handsome Dr. Love at least a passing thought. I had been smitten since the first flash of his bright blue eyes and easy-going smile. It didn't hurt that Alex possessed a swimmer's body— long and muscled, with broad shoulders and sun-kissed skin. His competent and calm demeanor with my baby boy, aka Mr. Bond, had heaped an extra thousand points in Alex's favor.

I had assumed he had a girlfriend, and his unavailability had remained a matter of conjecture during the intervening years, because no amount of verbal gymnastics had enabled me to navigate from "Sorry my cat tried to claw your arm off when you checked his temperature" to "Are you seeing anyone?" Who could have guessed all it would take to get him to ask me out would be to show up at his office dressed like a video game character, sporting rescued kittens in my gun holsters?

We slid between a stoic couple and a cluster of businessmen in an assortment of navy and gray blazers and squished up to the host station. Alex released my hand, and I used the pocket of space around us to shrug out of my coat and drape it over my arm. A discreet check ensured my skirt hadn't gotten caught up in the coat and I wasn't flashing anyone. Score one for me.

The teenage hostess glanced up from a screen in front of her, a serene smile fixed in place. A sleek black dress hugged her slender frame, makeup painted her youthful features into a lifelike approximation of a porcelain doll's, and heels twice as tall as mine elevated her to shoulder height. At her age, I had been working at a bookstore where the number of customers rarely tipped into the double digits in an entire afternoon. I would have crumpled under the pressure of coordinating this busy restaurant's guests, let alone doing it in spike heels. Teens these days were made of sterner stuff.

"Love party for two," Alex said.

"Excuse me?"

Alex leaned closer, obviously thinking the hostess hadn't heard. He packed a lot of charm into his smile. "Love for two."

She blinked her eyelash extensions, a flush rising in her cheeks. He had short-circuited her.

"Love. It's his last name," I clarified to speed things up.

She blinked again, then started as if I had poked her. "Right. Mr. Love." She trailed a finger down the computer screen. "We've got your table right here. Please follow me."

She snatched up a pair of menus and darted from behind the counter so fast I feared for her ankles.

"Does that joke ever get old?" I asked soft enough for Alex's ears only.

"What joke?" His confusion cleared from his face a second later and chagrin replaced it. "Darn it, you try having this last name."

"I'm surprised you don't introduce yourself as *Love, Dr. Love.*"

A faint pink tinged his cheeks. Teasing Alex was fun.

"She's getting away," he said, indicating the hostess, who had failed to notice we weren't on her heels.

"Should I let her know the Love party is chasing her?"

Alex smiled as he shook his head, settling his hand on my lower back to guide me in front of him. The heat from his palm saturated the thin material of my dress and chased a shiver up my spine. Alex's eyes dilated fractionally. I forced myself to look where I was going before I ran into a server balancing a flotilla of food on an enormous tray.

A long mahogany bar sprawled down the right side of the restaurant, accompanied by an array of matching high tables and dozens of minimalistic stools. Packed elbow to elbow, people occupied every scrap of space in the bar and overflowed into the foyer. When we traversed the invisible line dividing the entrance from the dining area, the crush fell away, replaced by dark wood tables, cloth-backed booths, dim light, low floral arrangements, and soft violin music. Here was the atmosphere Alex and I had been expecting. I took a deep, unobstructed breath and lengthened my stride.

The hostess led us to a small table near the wall, and Alex waited for me to slip my coat over the back of the chair and sit before he took his seat. Thankfully, he didn't try to tuck my chair in under me. I had never mastered the art of timed sitting; plus I was perfectly capable of moving a chair on my own.

"What's with the crowd?" I asked the teen as she handed us our menus.

"Matchmaker Brewery is unveiling a limited release of their Flirtation IPA tonight. Last year they sold out in four hours."

I tried to appear suitably impressed, but since I had never heard of the brewery, I probably didn't succeed.

"If I'd known it would be this busy, I would have picked somewhere else," Alex said as the hostess scurried back to her post. "It's not too late if you'd like to leave. I know this great place in Loomis. They serve stellar chicken marsala."

The restless impatience of the patrons at the entrance couldn't penetrate the candlelit dining floor, and the noise level had dropped so the hum of conversation among the diners served as an auditory cocoon. I didn't want to change a thing. Besides, I couldn't jaunt off to Loomis on a whim, not without bringing Jamie.

"No, this is perfect. Maybe next time," I said. My stomach flipped when I realized I had proposed a second date.

"I'm holding you to that," Alex said, and we shared shy smiles.

I nestled my clutch between me and the seat back, making sure the side with my phone rested against me so I would feel it vibrate if Rose called. Rose had assumed responsibility for Jamie tonight, a boon for which I owed the empath an enormous favor of her choosing. Jamie might look like an ordinary teen boy, but he was neither ordinary nor a teen. He wasn't even human. Born less than a week earlier, he had risen from the soil beneath the mall's new parking garage as a fully formed mammoth. In actuality, he was a pooka, and aside from masquerading as a woolly prehistoric creature, he also could take the form of a Great Dane and a human man. His ability to shape-shift worried me less than the powerful energies of his soul—exactly half of it good *lux lucis* and half of it evil *atrum*. But he had promised, repeatedly, to remain human tonight and on his best behavior. With any luck, Rose would have no reason to call me.

"Good evening, my name is Sergi. I will be your server tonight."

I glanced up at the doughy face of a man in his early thirties. Pea-sized rubies glittered in his ears, matching the muted maroon of his uniform shirt, and a short black beard gave much-needed definition to his rounded jaw.

"Can I start you off with mixed drinks or one of our craft beers?" Sergi asked as he poured two glasses of water.

I glanced at the drink menu and ordered a sangria; Alex went with a glass of Flirtation.

"They haven't tapped the keg yet, so it's going to be a while," Sergi said.

"That's fine. I want to see what all the fuss is about."

Sergi took our appetizer order and strode away. I perused the selection of entrées, pretending I hadn't scouted my options online earlier, then set the menu aside and took a sip of water. While Alex flipped through his menu, I let my gaze skim over the other patrons and wracked my brain for a conversation topic.

"I have a confession," Alex said, setting down his menu.

"Oh?"

"I'm horrible at first dates."

"You are?"

"I never know what to say."

I laughed, my budding nerves evaporating. "Well, you haven't started any sentence with, 'I heard on NPR the other day . . .' I think you're doing just fine."

"What do you have against NPR?"

"Nothing, but I'd rather learn about you than a news story."

Alex's smile crinkled the corners of his eyes. "What do you want to know?"

"Hmm." I tapped my chin, affecting a serious mien. "Start with the basics. Where are you from?"

"I lived most of my life about ten minutes up the freeway in Newcastle, went to college at UC Davis, then moved to Roseville to start my clinic. It sounds like a boring life trajectory, but I love this area and I love what I do."

"Would a fellow Aggie judge you?" I had seen Alex's diploma in his office, so I had known he graduated from my alma mater. He had been a senior when I was a freshman. Like an idiot, I had been having flings with men my age at the time, not mining the upperclassmen for prime dating material.

"You went to Davis, too?" Alex asked, surprised.

"Yep. Your story is remarkably similar to mine, only I went from Berkeley to Davis, then came to Roseville for work."

"Right, your job at the bumper sticker company."

My smile tightened, and I took a sip of water to cover it. As far as Alex knew, my career had stalled in a sales position at Illumination Studios, a small-scale bumper sticker company. Explaining that Illumination Studios was actually an undercover branch of the CIA—the

Collaborative Illumination Alliance, not the Central Intelligence Agency—and defended the region from evil creatures that viewed human souls as prime sustenance wasn't exactly first-date material.

Hi. I use the energy of my soul to kill evil creatures you can't see. There's lots of hand waving, petrified wooden wand swishing, and knife stabbing involved, and this entire city's citizens depend on me to keep them safe. Oh, and did I mention I can examine your soul and judge exactly how good or evil you are?

Discussing anything about my real job would be relationship suicide, so I deflected like a champ.

"It's not a job my career counselor mentioned, but I find it fun and challenging. Plus occasionally I get to wear spectacular outfits." I waggled my eyebrows at Alex.

"It's a definite perk," Alex agreed, his eyes darkening.

I congratulated myself in steering him to the memory of me clad in costume, my chest inflated to five times its normal size by a padded bra, and my hips wrapped in a scrap of spandex tighter than my normal underwear. Hopefully the mental image would derail Alex from further questions about my job.

Sergi returned with my sangria as an enthusiastic cheer rocked the bar.

"Sounds like they've tapped the keg," Sergi said dryly.

I glanced past Alex toward the eager crowd, and a shot of adrenaline snapped my spine straight when I spied an unexpected and wholly unwelcome face.

Niko.

2

EVERYBODY CHILL, I FOUND THE BEER

N iko stood out from the crowd like a panther among peacocks. While everyone else chatted and laughed and jostled to get their drinks, he scanned the room with his dark eyes, his expression neutral, bordering on grim.

As the optivus aegis for Northern California, Niko served as a super-enforcer, defending the upper half of the state from evils too large for individual enforcers like me to handle solo. Lately, he had spent an excessive amount of time in my region, helping me ferret out first a demon, then a rogue warden. Since he didn't live in the area—that I knew of—he was the last person I expected to see tonight.

His presence could signify only one thing: trouble.

With a sinking stomach, I blinked from normal vision to Primordium. Color leeched from the restaurant, turning the surroundings into a monochrome world of white and gray, life and not life. On this metaphysical plane, the tan booths, black napkins, and metal utensils all were the same charcoal gray of inanimate objects. The flame of the votive candle in the center of the table vanished, as invisible in Primordium as the shadows and shimmers it cast on our glasses. A directionless, ambient light replaced the warm glow of the overhead lamps, casting no shadows yet providing definition to the objects around me. Only evil, or *atrum*, registered as true black.

Trying to be discreet, I scanned the restaurant, hunting for a source of evil that might have drawn Niko here. A handful of onyx chinchilla-like imps bounced among the legs of the people near the bar, but any gathering of more than twenty people tended to attract a few of the dark side's lowliest minions. If I got a chance, I would take them out, but they weren't reason enough to abandon Alex. They certainly weren't the reason Mr. Super Elite Enforcer himself graced us with his presence.

When no demons revealed themselves in the guests, no smears of inky *atrum* pointed to a hidden lair of a monster, and no servers emerged from the kitchen coated in vervet, I let out a slow breath and turned back to my date.

When my eyes lit upon Alex, I soaked up his soul's patchwork of white and soft grays. I had admired him in Primordium before, but reexamining his basic good nature took away my trepidation. Niko wasn't here because of my date. Maybe he wasn't here because of me at all. If I ducked just right, he wouldn't even see me.

One glance at my glowing white hand abolished that delusion. Niko couldn't help but spot me. Among a restaurant of people sporting a mishmash of white, gray, and black souls, their every immoral trans-gression staining them with corresponding darkness, my pristine soul stood out brighter than a spotlight. The only person brighter than me in this room would be Niko himself—

Or the woman standing next to him.

Tall, thin, in a sheath dress that made her legs look like they started in her armpits, she scanned the room at Niko's side, her soul aglow with vibrant strength. Curiosity squirmed through me. I had met a couple enforcers in the area, and she wasn't one of them. Was she Niko's girlfriend or an enforcer from another region? Both?

I squashed my inapt dismay before it could fully form into jeal-ousy. I was on a date with Alex, an absolutely wonderful man who I liked very much. I had no reason to wish Niko were single or regret it if he weren't. In fact, Niko being on a date would be the best possible reason for his appearance. Then I could be assured no horrid evil crea-ture was plotting to destroy my evening.

I finally worked up the courage to look at Niko, unsurprised to find him staring back. My heart plummeted to my stomach when he gestured me to his side.

Maybe he simply wants to check in to see if I'm here for work, I told myself. *For all he knows, this dress and these heels and this hot man and intimate setting are all part of an elaborate undercover sting.*

"It's going to take a minute for me to get your beer, sir," Sergi said to Alex. "I'll do my best to fight to the front of the line."

They were still discussing beer, which meant I had packed fifteen minutes' worth of roller-coaster emotions into a few seconds. Go me.

I did my best to maintain an easy smile while Sergi prattled on about the specials, all the while railing against the unfairness of my life. I had been working my butt off since I took over as enforcer for Roseville. I had taken out a demon, stopped a horde of salamanders, unraveled a turbonis, defended our headquarters from attack, bonded a pooka, and learned how to push, roll, and spin *lux lucis* to eradicate all manner of evil creatures. It'd been a long two weeks. I deserved an uninterrupted date.

Alex and I had already postponed our date twice, both times because of my job. Tonight was supposed to be my moment of normal, my peaceful night where I got to pretend to be Madison the saleswoman who lived alone with her cat, not Madison the enforcer who always had to put the well-being of the people in her region above her own happiness.

I grimaced. That was unfair. Niko wouldn't be here without good reason. I would just go see what he had to say, then get back to my date. No doubt it was nothing he and his shining companion couldn't handle.

"So, that's a no to the fish," Sergi said, taking in my expression.

"Oh, ah, yeah no, that's a no," I said with the eloquence of a third grader giving a speech in front of the class. Fumbling for my menu, I flipped to the salad section and ordered one with blood oranges and honey-roasted walnuts. I had been planning on getting a butternut squash ravioli, but I couldn't bring myself to order a *lux lucis*–depleted dish with Niko watching. I saved myself from being a dating cliché by adding a side of sweet potato fries.

After Sergi departed, I excused myself from the table under the pretense of washing my hands. As soon as I strode beyond Alex's line of sight, I angled across the restaurant for Niko and the shining woman beside him. They pushed through the crowd at the bar to meet me, steps unfaltering as they killed the smattering of imps that had flocked to their bright souls.

"Did Brad send you?" Niko asked.

"No. Did he send you?"

"No."

I circled Niko until he stood between me and Alex. With luck, even if Alex turned around, he wouldn't see me. I blinked to normal sight and double-checked my date's location. So far, so good.

"Niko is here because of me," the mystery woman at Niko's side said.

I stopped trying to spy on Alex and gave her my attention. At five-ten, not many women looked me in the eye, especially not when I was in heels, but for her I had to look up. Everything about the woman was long—her legs, her admirably defined arms, her wavy ebony hair that cascaded over her chest, her straight-cut bangs that brushed her enviously long eyelashes. With skin the color of roasted hazelnuts, full lips, and eyes straight from an Egyptian princess, she had won the gene lottery big-time.

Between her and Niko, who radiated his special blend of sex and danger in gray slacks and a black V-neck sweater a few shades darker than his skin, it was a wonder the whole restaurant hadn't combusted.

My shoulders relaxed. This had to be a date.

"Madison, this is Daphne. Daphne's a medical enforcer in Sacramento."

Not, *This is Daphne, my girlfriend.* Crap, were they on a date or not? Not that their dating status mattered. *My* dating status mattered.

"It's nice to meet you," I said. "I hate to be rude, but is there a threat I'm unaware of? If not . . ."

"If I'm right, yes," Daphne said, dashing my hopes. "The ME community has been investigating the source of scattered outbreaks, and we think we've pinpointed it to the Matchmaker Brewery."

Outbreaks? The word coming from the mouth of a medical enforcer conjured images of a deadly, *atrum*-borne plague sweeping the nation, the tide of evil snuffing out enforcers in an inexorable wave of death and destruction, and it all started in my region with patient zero contaminating the world under my watch.

"How bad is it?" I asked.

"Right now, manageable."

"Daphne was the first person to put it together," Niko said. "We've had seemingly random increases of evil across Northern California. It seemed to move like a disease, and the origin was always a restaurant."

"At first we thought it was tainted food," Daphne said, taking over the explanation. "But when I started examining common factors, it became clear our culprit was the beer. More specifically, whenever Matchmaker did a tap takeover or brought in a shipment of beer, outbreaks followed."

"If Brad didn't send you, why are you here?" Niko asked.

"I'm on a date." It came out whiny, but I couldn't help it. According to them, my perfect evening was about to be blown to pieces.

"Oh no! Talk about bad timing," Daphne said. "He's a norm?"

I nodded glumly and peeked over Niko's shoulder. Alex fiddled with his napkin-wrapped silverware. Any minute he would check for me. It didn't take long to wash one's hands. He had to be getting suspicious.

Following my line of sight, Daphne let out a low whistle. "Look at that soul. You found a good one."

"I know."

"We've got this covered," Niko said. "Go back to your date."

"Yes, we're all over this," Daphne assured. She gave Niko's bicep a familiar squeeze. "Between the two of us, we can handle it."

I clutched my stomach. A huge part of me yearned to accept their offer and walk away. But when I tried to picture myself sitting across from Alex, ignoring Niko and Daphne's battle against whatever weird evil Matchmaker was brewing, the image wouldn't form. This was my region, my responsibility.

That didn't stop me from wishing Alex and I had chosen a different location for our date or that I had taken Alex up on his earlier offer to switch restaurants. I could have been blissfully unaware of Niko and Daphne's activities. But I was here, and I would help.

"Thank you, but I knew what I was getting into when I took this job." Okay, that had been a flat-out lie, but it beat trying to explain my sense of duty. If I had to voice my noble sentiments, I might talk myself out of them.

I blinked to Primordium and scanned the restaurant.

"Do you know what we're . . ."

At the far end of the bar, a steady stream of beer gushed from a fresh tap, filling mug after mug with frothy, liquid *atrum.*

". . . looking for?" My mouth finished the sentence without input from my brain, horror numbing my lips.

This wasn't going to be the quick fix I had hoped for.

3

FINISH YOUR BEER; THERE ARE SOBER PEOPLE IN INDIA

"It's in the beer," Daphne and Niko said simultaneously.

"I thought it would be a person," Daphne said.

Niko was already moving. "I'll get the keg."

"We'll handle what's poured," Daphne said, stepping into the space Niko had vacated. Their actions looked coordinated; obviously this wasn't their first time working together.

Niko spun back, his hand brushing Daphne's forearm to get her attention. "Madison's new. She'll need—"

"A quick lesson," Daphne said. "Got it."

Cute. They even finished each other's sentences.

Niko muscled through the crowd toward the foyer, then cut through the main dining room and circled to the other end of the bar, where the bartender poured a never-ending stream of *atrum*-polluted brew.

"Come on. The less these people drink, the better." Daphne slipped into the throng, twining her thin body into the smallest openings between people and tossing apologetic smiles in her wake. She didn't have to shove too hard, either; most people took one look at her and made room for the goddess in their midst. I squished through in her wake.

"Since we can't stick our fingers in everyone's glasses, we're going to have to roll our *lux lucis*," Daphne said over her shoulder. "Precision is the key."

She sidled up to the bar between two men who were among the first to receive the tainted beer. They leaned aside to accommodate her, and she spread her smile between them. I monitored her hand. A flurry of white energy looped with increasing speed beneath her skin, then speared from her fingertips and flared across the bar top to the first mug. Half of the energy hit the side of the glass, flowed around the base's curved edge, and ricocheted over the lip of the bar, disappearing into the sink beyond. The other half hit the mug straight on, climbed the smooth glass, and spilled into the foamy head of beer. *Lux lucis* collided with swirling *atrum* and ate through it, cleansing the beer from the top down and leaving a pale shine of good energy behind.

The other man picked up his beer and drained it before Daphne's *lux lucis* reached it. I gawked in horror as twelve ounces of *atrum* slid down his throat. He looked to be in his thirties, and he had maintained a decent ratio of *lux lucis*, with only a handful of dark gray patches marring his soul. I waited for a black smear of *atrum* to blossom on his throat, but he set down the glass without an outward effect. I shuddered to think what the ingested *atrum* was doing to his innards.

"Can I buy you a drink?" he asked, fingers latching on to Daphne's wrist when she stepped back.

She smiled. "I can't drink because of the baby." She rubbed her flat belly.

The man released Daphne as if she had scorched his fingers, mumbling something inaudible before turning away.

"Works every time," Daphne whispered.

"I'm definitely stealing that line."

She laughed, but most of her attention remained riveted on the glass she had cleansed. "Look at how it's glowing. Infusing *lux lucis* in liquid is almost impossible unless there's a living agent involved. It's got to be coating the active cultures, which is what the *atrum* was feeding on, too. Damn it! I should have thought of this before. These microbreweries take pride in not pasteurizing their beers, and that's all well and good until evil spores take up residence."

Eating *lux lucis*-filled foods increased overall levels of good energy in people, so what would consuming high quantities of *atrum* spores do for the norms at the bar? When I asked Daphne, her frown deepened.

"Thanks to the delivery system, the *atrum* will hit their bloodstream almost instantaneously, and it'll start affecting their judgment just as fast. Like alcohol, the impact will vary based on each person's tolerance level and weight, only in this case, their gender and muscle mass will matter a great deal less than the overall state of their souls."

She shoved through another cluster of people, planted a hand on the bar, and shot *lux lucis* into three mugs at once, all without breaking her explanation.

"Hopefully the effect will be as temporary as the effect of the alcohol, especially if we keep everyone from drinking more than a few ounces. I've got the bar covered. You take the tables."

I pivoted, earning an elbow to my bicep from an exuberant woman behind me. A row of tables marched down the outer edge of the enclosed bar, the high-top surfaces square oases in the crush of people. A single server whisked through the beer enthusiasts, balancing a half-empty tray of mugs overflowing with tainted beer. Behind her, a dozen innocent hands clutched evil-blackened mugs.

I shoved into action with none of Daphne's grace, careening off the back of a heavyset man and fetching up against the nearest table hard enough to spill the drinks. Tossing out apologies, I planted my hands on the tabletop and flipped *lux lucis* from my fingertips. Not too long ago, looping *lux lucis* through my palms would have taken all my concentration. Fortunately, I had had plenty of practice, and three-inch-wide bands of white energy rolled across the table like the unfurling of the world's tiniest carpets. Both angled wide, glancing off the mugs' edges. The white energy arced tight to the glasses before careening out of sight off the table. Adjusting my angle, I fired again—and again, and *again*—before finally hitting a glass straight on. *Lux lucis* raced up the side of the mug, fell into the half-empty glass, and ate through the *atrum* in a bright flash. The beer continued to glow brighter than the hand of the woman who held it. With any luck, the extra *lux lucis* would counter the *atrum* she had already consumed.

Four of my next five attempts hit their targets, and I squeezed to the next table. Each passing minute ratcheted the tension in my shoulder blades tighter, and the bulk of my stress had nothing to do with the innocent norms I rushed to save. My absence from the table strained the boundaries of a normal restroom visit. I had passed the plausible hand-washing time frame minutes ago. I might get away with the excuse of a line having delayed me, but much longer, and I would run the risk of Alex thinking I was either sick or had fallen into the toilet. Or worse, had ditched him.

I scanned the restaurant. Alex had his head bent over his phone. Dread churned in my gut. Had he decided I was too much of a flake for him, first pushing the date twice, now disappearing before the appetizer arrived? Was he concocting an excuse to leave? It would be easy enough to pretend someone had called him with an emergency at the clinic. He would gracefully extricate himself from what was fast becoming a non-date, and my most promising romantic encounter in months would end with me cleaning up evil spores instead of the make-out session I had been fantasizing about for the last three years.

The noise level of the patrons at the bar jumped several decibels, raucous laughter competing with masculine bellows. I ceased even a modicum of politeness and boldly elbowed my way between drinkers. Speed mattered far more than people's opinions of me. My accuracy improved with each table, spurned by my urgency. I had to get back to Alex before our date imploded.

When the flurry of *atrum*-clouded drinks slowed, replaced by mugs of faintly glowing brew, I checked on Niko. Somehow, he had worked his way behind the bar to the Flirtation tap. Actually, his location wasn't much of a mystery, considering the female bartender working beside him, sneaking glances at him out of the corner of her eye. Whatever Niko's reason for asking to work the tap, she had no doubt leapt at the chance to invite him behind the bar.

A gauntlet of tainted drinks still stood between me and freedom, but despite my perceived sense of eternity since I had left Alex at our table, no more than ten minutes had passed. This could work.

I checked the dining room, and my gaze collided with Alex's. I froze. He had twisted in his seat to stare at me with a puzzled frown, his mouth tight. Our artisan cheese appetizer sat untouched in front of him.

Oh crap.

He mimed, *What are you doing?*

I mimed, *I'm so sorry. I'll be right there. Please don't leave. I'm so sorry.* I wasn't sure how much of that came across in my frantic pointing, but he must have gotten the gist because the corners of his mouth curved.

Screw being bold; I switched gears to outright rude and jabbed my fingers into the kidney of a man in front of me. He had made the unfortunate decision to chat up a woman seated at the bar, and his wide frame blocked my route to the next table. With a grunt of surprise, he staggered to the side. I slid into the empty space, pausing to grip the table and spear *lux lucis* toward half-finished beers sitting there.

"What the hell?" the kidney-abused man exclaimed.

I had already moved on to the next table—the last table! I bulldozed through a gaggle of businessmen, touching their hands to zing *lux lucis* into the glasses they held, then planted myself near the table, where a dozen more mugs rested on the surface: round two, as of yet untouched, each mug inky with *atrum*-poisoned cultures. I could feel Alex's stare boring into my forehead, but when I glanced up, he had turned back toward the table.

I flung *lux lucis* toward the cups, haste screwing with my aim. The meaty hand that slid down my waist and groped my butt cheek made me miss the table entirely.

I whirled to confront the pervert, but Daphne beat me to it. Materializing at my side, she grabbed the man's middle finger and jerked it backward toward his forearm in a strike too fast to follow.

"Did she give you permission to touch her?" Daphne asked.

"Hey, that hurts!" the pervert exclaimed, drawing the attention of his friends.

Daphne leaned forward, putting her weight on his strained digit. The man collapsed into his seat. None of his friends came to his rescue, but several laughed. Daphne smiled, nice and sweet, adding more pressure to his finger. Sweat popped out on the man's brow.

"I didn't mean anything," he protested.

I wrenched my eyes from the scene and pumped *lux lucis* into the drinks.

"Because that makes it all better," Daphne said, her voice dripping with disdain. Her free hand dipped into her bag; then she pressed her fingers to his wrist. "Next time you're thinking about violating a woman's body, ask yourself if you'd want a man to paw at you like an animal."

"But I'm not gay."

Daphne slid her gaze around the table, meeting the eyes of the pervert's friends. "See if you can explain to him what he did wrong before he gets himself truly hurt. Try using small words."

She released the man's finger and his hand slammed to the table. The rest of the men parted and Daphne and I escaped, stumbling free into the quieter foyer.

"It's official: You're my hero," I said.

"We make a good team. That would have been a lot worse without your help."

"Speaking of which . . ." I glanced over her shoulder. A row of booths blocked all but the top of Alex's head from sight. "Are we done?"

"Niko and I need to make a visit to Matchmaker in the morning to track down the source, but yes, we saved the day here."

"Great. I hate to cut and run, but—"

"Your date. Of course." Daphne glanced over her shoulder, then guided me closer to the exit and out of sight of the dining room. "Can I give you some friendly advice? Balancing this life with a norm is hard. The trick is to keep your lies simple and believable. Here." She pulled an expensive phone from her bag. "Take this to the hostess. Tell her you found it in the bathroom. Then tell your date the same thing. He'll understand why it took you so long to get back to him."

I stared at my salvation, feeling misty-eyed. "You're a genius."

"I've dated my share of norms. Now go. Hurry." She gave me a good-natured push toward the hostess.

I felt Alex's eyes on me when I paused to talk to the teen manning the counter, and when I scurried back to our table, he watched me the whole way. I wanted to check my dress for beer stains, but I forced my head up and settled for skimming my fingers through my mussed hair.

"I'm so sorry!" I exclaimed before I had finished sitting.

"Everything okay?"

"Yes. I found a brand-new iPhone on top of the hand dryer. I thought I knew which woman's it was, which is why I headed into that mess at the bar, but it turned out I was wrong, and by then I was stuck. It was like beer aficionado quicksand in there and—"

The words choked in my throat. A pint of black beer sat on the table in front of Alex, more than a third missing.

4

I FINALLY QUIT DRINKING FOR GOOD;
NOW I DRINK FOR EVIL

"Sounds like you did your good deed for the day," Alex said, the tension melting from his expression. Seeing my gaze fixated on his beer mug, he added, "It's not bad."

"That's what everyone was saying." The words came out breathy. "Mind if I have a sip?"

"No. Go ahead."

Alex shifted the glass away from himself toward me. I tried not to snatch it from him, but the beer sloshed in the glass when I grabbed it. Lifting it to my mouth, I gathered *lux lucis* in my lips and released it into the beer when it lapped against my lipstick. I had never attempted such an intimate transfer of energy, and I strained myself cross-eyed to check the beer. The glass tipped too far and liquid rushed into my mouth, hit the back of my throat, and the bubbles went straight up my nose.

Choking, I started coughing the moment I found air. I grabbed my napkin and covered my mouth, gasping between coughs. My vision blurred and I did my best not to blink and ruin my mascara. Alex took the beer back, though I made sure it shimmered with a healthy *lux lucis* glow before I relinquished it.

"I guess it's not all they promised," Alex teased.

"My lungs certainly aren't impressed."

Alex handed me my glass of water and I took a sip. The cool liquid soothed my burning esophagus. Taking a deep breath, I settled back in my seat and dabbed my eyes.

"Shall we?" Alex asked, gesturing to the cheese platter.

"Definitely. I'm starved." I checked my soul. I had expended a great deal of *lux lucis*. Normally I would have ducked outside to find a tree or sturdy bush from which to replenish my reserves, but leaving Alex again wasn't an option. Good thing I had ordered a salad. It would provide me with enough *lux lucis* to tide me over until we left.

I slathered a soft goat cheese on a hard round of bread and smiled at Alex before taking a bite. Mentally, I celebrated. It may not have been graceful or ideal, but I had saved the day *and* kept my secret identity intact.

Three cheers for Madison, the super enforcer. Hip, hip, hooray! Hip, hip—

"So, a two-cat home. Are you ready to be outnumbered?" Alex asked.

His question caught me off guard, because between Jamie; my Siamese, Mr. Bond; and Val, the sentient handbook, I was already outnumbered. I used to describe my one-bedroom apartment as cozy, but now *snug* seemed a more apt adjective. Nevertheless, I couldn't wait to pick up the tabby kitten from Alex's clinic after dinner. She had been one of three cats I had rescued while in costume, the most sickly of her litter. The other two had adopted out while she had been busy being nursed back to health.

Despite already having fallen in love with the kitten, I had ulterior motives for adopting her. Being an enforcer kept me busy—really, really busy. I had logged more hours at work in the past week than I had at home, and most of my home hours had been spent unconscious. Eventually, I would get this job figured out and find my rhythm, or so my boss promised, but until then, Mr. Bond suffered. I hoped the addition of a kitten would relieve his unaccustomed loneliness. Plus, Jamie had expressed an interest in a pet, and a kitten was a lot better than the fire-breathing salamander he had wanted to bring home.

"If I had the space, I'd have a dozen cats," I said. "What about you? Do you have a menagerie of your own?"

"One dog and three cats."

"That's it?"

"Most people think that's a lot," Alex said.

"Sure, for a normal person. But you're a vet. You must see dozens of animals in need of a good home each year. I think four pets shows admirable restraint."

"Well . . . I wouldn't mind another dog."

"Aha! The truth comes out." I polished off the last bite of some sort of delicious herb-infused cheese and remembered my manners in time to wipe my fingers on my napkin rather than lick them clean.

"I've got enough yard for another dog. But no more cats. Three are enough, and I vacuum up enough cat hair every week that there might already be a fourth I don't know about."

"To shed is to love," I said, and Alex laughed.

When he excused himself to wash his hands, I watched him walk away. His gray slacks did great things for his behind, and the blue shirt pulled nicely against his shoulders. I dropped my eyes back to the table when he reached the wall partitioning the restaurant from the bathroom and glanced my way.

Once he slipped out of sight, I gave myself a quick once-over, checking for food on my dress and using a small mirror in my clutch to examine my teeth. No embarrassing clumps of bread wedged between my molars, but my skirt did have a smattering of beer stains. At least they were all below waist level and therefore hidden by the table.

I forced myself to check my phone. I didn't want to see a message light blinking or a text telling me Rose needed my immediate assistance. Closing my eyes, I sent up a quick prayer to all gods everywhere, then flipped my phone over and stared at the screen. No light flashed, no messages crawled across the screen.

"Thank you, thank you, thank you," I whispered as I shoved my phone back in my purse and nestled it against my back. One job-related hiccup was enough for this date.

I gave the Matchmaker patrons the stink eye and spotted Niko and Daphne at the end of the bar. Food sat in front of them. They'd made a date of it. Good for them.

Dinner arrived as Alex resumed his seat, and I tackled the challenging task of consuming a salad gracefully. It forced me to eat slower than normal, which corresponded with my plan to savor this date. Alex must have been on the same wavelength, because he put a lot more attention on me than he did his fancy fish risotto. The conversation flowed naturally, the occasional silences easy instead of awkward. We talked about movies and books and places we'd traveled, cars we'd owned, and our favorite late-night haunts in Davis.

Then Alex stumped me with a deceptively simple question: "What do you like to do for fun?"

I lowered my fork to my plate, pondering the last time I had gone out. Aside from celebratory drinks with my best friend, Bridget, after I had been hired, being an enforcer had kept me too busy and too tired to do much outside of work. Before I had fallen into this crazy world of soul magic and fighting evil, I hadn't had the funds to do much of anything. I didn't have a go-to hobby that didn't sound lame. *I like to read* fell under the *what keeps me sane* category. Everyone liked hanging out with friends. Saying I enjoyed drinking with Bridget wouldn't make the greatest impression.

"I like to get out in nature," I said. Mainly to recharge my depleted *lux lucis*, but it was something I did for fun more and more lately—if you defined *for fun* as *to stay alive*.

Alex lit up. "Really? Me too. I love hiking. Have you ever been on Stevens Trail?"

I shook my head.

"What about Foresthill Divide Loop? It's a fast eleven miles with some spectacular views."

"I haven't caught that one," I murmured. Eleven miles? That sounded like torture.

Alex deflated a little. "The American River Trail?"

"I guess I'm a city nature person. Parks, the beautiful open spaces around Roseville . . ." I could at least point to those on a map.

"We'll have to change that," Alex decided. "Once you watch the sunrise over the American River canyon, you'll be hooked."

I decided it wasn't a good time to let him know I thought sunrises and sleep went hand in hand. Maybe he knew something I didn't. Or maybe with him, exercising before dawn would be worth it.

Sergi proved to be an astute server and chose that moment to approach our table and rattle off the dessert specials: a lemon tart, a crumble coffee cake with expresso bean and chocolate glaze, and a chocolate truffle cake with chocolate mousse and chocolate ganache.

"I might have been able to say no to two types of chocolate in a dessert, but not three," I said. I glanced at Alex. "Want to indulge with me?"

"Yes." Heat infused his bright blue eyes, sharpening their intensity.

I swallowed, then fought the urge to wet my lips when Alex's gaze dipped to them. My fingers curled around the cushion of my seat.

Pouncing on Alex before dessert arrived would be in bad form, but remaining seated took serious willpower. Darn it, why had I said yes to dessert?

I turned to cancel the order, but Sergi had cleared the dishes and departed while I had been lost in Alex's gaze.

A commotion at the bar drew my attention. People near the left side, closest to the bathroom, had started clapping. Farther to the left, beyond the partition to the restrooms, a middle-aged man emerged, dressed in a black shirt emblazoned with FLIRTATION in gold. He wore his dark hair short, yet possessed enough beard for two men, and the wiry black mass engulfed him from chin to chest. From his expression, the applause pleased and embarrassed him, and he took a mock bow, exposing the stylized MATCHMAKER logo on the back of his shirt.

Judging from the beer enthusiasts' response, I pinned him as the brewmaster. I blinked to Primordium. With the state of his beer, it seemed unlikely he hadn't picked up some residual taint.

Residual proved to be a massive understatement.

Dense *atrum* fuzz coated the man's soul like black mold on a decomposing corpse. It oozed over him, shifting with unseen currents, collecting in his hands and crawling from his mouth when he opened it to greet a woman near the end of the bar. A flurry of *atrum* spores skittered from the brewmaster's hand to the woman, crawling like a swarm of ants up her arm, coating her to the elbow before he released her. When she reached for her drink, some dove into the liquid, and the neutral beverage ran dark with *atrum*. Oblivious, she brought the glass to her lips, swallowing the evil energy even as more spores flocked from her hand to her face.

My stomach revolted. I swallowed convulsively, fighting bile, and fumbled blindly for a weapon. My clutch held my pet wood and a knife. The wand of petrified wood served as the perfect medium for funneling *lux lucis* into evil creatures without me needing to physically touch them, and I *definitely* did not want to touch the brewmaster. The knife channeled *lux lucis*, too, but it had the added benefit of cutting through physical objects.

The man turned, exposing his front to me, and my fingers spasmed on my purse. An enormous growth swelled from the brewmaster's stomach. Solid black, oblong, and covered with three-inch-long writhing feelers, the growth spawned spores that squirmed across his soul to swamp his momentarily clean hands. The *atrum* migration exposed lengthy leech-like tentacles stretching from the growth around the brewmaster to embed in his spine.

I tore my gaze from the horror show and scanned the bar for Niko and Daphne. From their position at the opposite end of the bar, they couldn't see the brewmaster, and they wouldn't be able to get to him quickly once they noticed him, either. Already a cluster of people had gathered around the brewmaster, and he spewed evil spores among them. Given a few more minutes, the whole bar would be crawling with *atrum* ooze.

The first infected woman turned, and I flinched. Writhing black fuzz coated her entire face, multiplying and skittering down her neck.

Alex turned back toward me, having twisted to see what all the fuss was about.

"Madison? Are you okay?"

I focused on his concerned expression, my mind blank. He glanced down at my hand clutching my purse.

"Um." Keep the lie simple. The advice only worked when my brain wasn't jammed in terror mode. The imprint of my phone through the soft leather of my bag finally kick-started a thought. "My phone. It's ringing. Well, vibrating."

"Oh?"

I fought my facial muscles back to something I hoped resembled embarrassment, not panic. Behind Alex, the brewmaster infected another couple. Damn it. If a single person left the restaurant with those spores on them, there was no telling how many people they'd infect. I talked faster.

"It's been doing it for a while, which means it's my best friend."

"Let me guess: your safety call?"

"You got me." It hadn't occurred to me to set up a fake emergency call with Bridget in case the date tanked, but it made a worthwhile excuse. Talking too fast, I said, "Good thing you turned out to be a lot of fun. Let me go take this so she'll stop calling me and we can enjoy that cake."

Spiderlike spores puffed from the brewmaster's mouth and fanned across a platter of drinks, burrowing into the liquid. The thought of cake combined with the visual made my stomach riot. I pressed a hand to it, holding it in place, willing everything to stay put.

"I'll be here," Alex said, his smile wide.

"Thanks for understanding," I said as I stood.

My eyes sought out Niko's, and he sprang from the barstool, reading the panic on my face for what it was. He and Daphne shoved through the crush of drinkers, their progress painfully slow.

I scurried across the restaurant on fear-numb legs. I *so* didn't want to tackle this monstrosity solo, but waiting wasn't an option.

5

NEVER GET HIGH ON YOUR OWN SUPPLY

My steps landed clumsy, the enforcer half of me hurrying as fast as manners allowed, the other half of me, the half concerned with self-preservation, trying to put on the brakes. I fisted my clutch in front of me like a shield, fingers locked on the zipper tab. I couldn't stab the brewmaster in public; I couldn't even pull out a knife without someone calling the police.

I shook my head at my thoughts. I wouldn't stab the brewmaster even if we were alone, not without first determining if he was truly evil or a victim, but every time I caught sight of the fuzzy creatures spurting from his mouth, the more I wished for a quick, easy solution. I forced myself to admit that even my nonlethal pet wood wasn't an option. Polite society frowned on poking people with sticks.

Whoever invented the rule had never seen anything quite so disgusting as the *atrum* fungus growing on the brewmaster. If I could show them, stick poking would become all the rage.

I shoved my hand through the wrist strap and let the clutch dangle from the bend of my elbow, flexing stiff fingers. The salad had done my soul wonders, restoring my *lux lucis* to respectable levels. If only it could have strengthened my courage, too.

Taking a deep breath, I rounded the wall of the bar and stepped up behind the brewmaster.

Plant a hand on him, douse him with lux lucis, *and get the hell out of here,* I told myself. My hand hovered inches from his back, refusing to make contact. Spores crawled down the man's shirt. From my new, far-too-close perspective, I could see their individual shapes, each one a miniature version of the massive growth attached to his stomach— tiny tentacles, feelers, and all.

A whip of black shot from the man's back and circled my wrist. I gaped at the noodle-thick band of *atrum* connecting the two of us. It wound cold and slimy against my soul, the sensation slowly fading to a numb nothingness.

I jerked my arm, and the tentacle burrowed deeper into me, stretching without breaking. The brewmaster turned as if I had tugged on his shirt. He smiled, black fuzz dripping from his mouth, and took my extended hand in his. *Atrum* invaded my soul.

"I hope you're enjoying tonight's Flirtation," the brewmaster said, sinking a wealth of innuendo into his statement.

Fungus rolled down the man's chin into his beard. Smaller spores floated on his exhalation to cling to my face and shoulders. I held my breath and tried to tug free. The brewmaster tightened his grip. A second, revolting tentacle burst from the growth on his stomach to twine up my forearm, and an army of spiderlike spores charged up the connection. The moment they touched my pristine soul, they began to divide and multiply.

The repugnant organisms were self-replicating. Could this nightmare get any worse?

"My name's Craig. Has anyone ever told you that you have the most striking eyes?" the brewmaster asked, leaning far too close. "So large and green. I think my bedspread is that exact color."

Was that supposed to be a compliment? A come-on? Either way, his words jolted me from my panicked stupor. I pulsed *lux lucis* into the baby spores on my arms, chest, and face, willing them to die. They halted, their frenetic division stilling as if I had frozen them. It should have wiped them out. I shoved more *lux lucis* into the spores, and the fuzzy bodies finally exploded into harmless glitter.

Better, except the tentacles still bound my wrist.

"I don't think I've seen you at a Matchmaker event before. I would have remembered you," Craig said.

"I try to avoid all functions that involve plagues."

He laughed, spewing black fuzz into the air, then shook his head. "I'm afraid I don't really get the joke."

I wiped out all *atrum* critters that landed on me, but my main focus remained on shoving *lux lucis* through my hand. If I could clean all this muck off the brewmaster, there might be a normal man underneath it. Especially if I could kill the main spore.

My clean energy surged up Craig's arm, killing a swath of spores and leaving behind a gray soul peppered with *atrum*. Okay. Craig wasn't Mr. Good Guy, but he wasn't a monster. His soul had clearly been hijacked.

I prepared a second blast, but before I could release it, the tide of diseased *atrum* foamed around Craig's bicep, the individual spores dividing again and again until they spilled down his arm and tried to creep up mine. Flinching did me no good. Craig clutched my hand with deceptive strength.

If I had been here alone or with anyone other than Alex, I wouldn't have hesitated to make a scene. Driving a knee into Craig's groin or jabbing him with my pet wood sounded pretty good right about now. But I had made it this far through my date, and I would be damned if this spore-riddled man would ruin my evening or do anything to plant a suspicion in Alex's mind that I was anything other than a normal woman.

Craig leaned in, as if to whisper in my ear. I backpedaled. The wall slapped my spine, leaving me nowhere to go.

"Don't be frightened," the brewmaster said, spores frothing from his mouth.

Right. Even without my special sight, I wouldn't have trusted a strange man who didn't release my hand after a few seconds.

"I'm usually not this forward, but there's something about you," Craig said.

He leaned in again, and his wiry beard brushed my face. I clamped my mouth shut on a scream as a scourge of spores pelted my cheeks and lips. This was too much.

My hand slammed into the brewmaster's gut before I fully registered the impulse to hit him. Craig staggered back a step, but he didn't release me. Instead, he used his momentum to yank me into the shadows of the grotto beside the restroom. I planted my heels before he dragged me out of sight of the restaurant floor, sending *lux lucis* around my head and shoulders like a demented Morse code signal until I stopped feeling the telltale resistance of *atrum*.

"Feisty!" Craig said.

I tore my gaze from the buglike *atrum* crawling across his lips. Beneath my left palm, Craig's stomach flexed and the main growth convulsed around my forearm. I flinched but forced my hand to stay put. Pulling energy from my reserves, I funneled a wallop of *lux lucis* through my hand and drove it into the massive mother spore. The mound of feelers writhed and shrank.

"Wow, you're forward," Craig said.

Spores spewed from his mouth in a fountain of black vomit, falling to coat the mother spore. The disgusting feelers cannibalized the fresh *atrum*, pumping it back into the main mass. In seconds, the damage I had inflicted had been repaired.

Strategic, focused attacks weren't working. Every spore needed to be killed at once.

The question was, did I have the strength to overpower it?

An even *better* question was, *Where the hell was Niko?*

Wild-eyed, I peered over the brewmaster's shoulder. Daphne's bright soul glimmered in the middle of the bar floor, trapped amid inebriated patrons who slowed her progress to a crawl. Niko had looped back toward the foyer, only to be caught behind a party of elderly men and women. Between five couples, they pushed three walkers, drove two motorized chairs, and wielded four canes. Niko could no more shove his way through them than I could jab Craig in the nuts with my pet wood.

My eyes darted to Alex, and my heart sank to my toes. He stared at me, standing with a hand on his chair, his face puzzled, his body language hesitant. Whatever he saw in my face made up his mind, and he started across the dining room, his gaze shifting from me to the man whose fist trapped my wrist.

If he reached me before Craig let me go, my chances of eradicating the spores dropped significantly. I might be able to explain away a strange man grabbing me, but not why I continued to cling to him, too. Judging from the scowl darkening his features, whatever Alex planned to do to the brewmaster would leave a stain of new *atrum* on his soul, too.

I would not be responsible for Alex besmirching his soul.

Screw not causing a scene.

I steeled myself and pretended Craig tugged me against him, stumbling into full-frontal contact. It felt like falling into a wall of spiders.

"That's more like it, baby," the brewmaster growled.

Tilting my head back to keep it clear of his beard, I kept my eyes closed. If I looked, I would lose my nerve and my concentration. I had never tried a full-body transfer of *lux lucis*, but revulsion gave me courage. In a violent thrust, I shoved my soul into Craig.

Lux lucis gushed from me, eating through the darkness between us. The earth tilted beneath my feet, the rapid energy loss as detrimental to my health as if I had opened an artery. My knees sagged, but I didn't relent, using my hand trapped between our bodies to pulse stronger currents of *lux lucis* into the mother spore.

Craig shifted, and I opened my eyes. With the walls a tilting backdrop, it took me a second to realize the brewmaster's face falling toward mine wasn't an illusion. His puckered lips, caked with black fuzz, swam in my vision.

I ducked, wrenching free of his hold and backing up two weak-kneed steps to brace against the wall. My wrist burned, but my arm was clean. So was my stomach. The light of my soul flickered so weakly it looked as if a single huff would extinguish it, but at least no *atrum* tainted me. I checked Craig's stomach. The giant spore had been reduced to harmless glitter.

"Come into the back with me," Craig propositioned. "I'll show you mine if you show me yours."

The man thought I was checking out his crotch. Save me from male egos.

I ran my gaze back up the brewmaster's body. A dusting of spores spilled from his mouth. *Damn it.* The infection lived on inside him, but internal health was beyond my realm of expertise. Good thing Daphne was on hand.

I turned to check on her progress but didn't make it past the vision of Alex and Niko striding side by side through the maze of tables. Alex's intent focus paled next to Niko's contained violence, his clean norm soul made bland and ordinary in comparison to Niko's blazing power. But Alex was my date, rushing to my side because he saw me in distress; Niko was just doing his job. If it were a contest between the two men, Alex won.

Craig grabbed my wrist again, and I twisted free before his fingers fully closed around my arm. Instead of attempting to escape, I wrapped my fist around his middle finger, twisting it back toward his forearm, just as Daphne had taught me. Craig's forward momentum halted as if he had hit an invisible wall. I backed him up a step, ignoring his grunt of pain. When I thrust *lux lucis* from my fingertips to clean the lingering spores caught in the knuckles of his fingers, the energy moved like taffy from my body and my head went light.

I was tapped out, but I couldn't walk away. Not with Alex barreling down on me.

6

BEER MAKES ME HOPPY

O ver Craig's shoulder, I watched Niko deftly maneuver Alex into the path of a server. My polite date did a dance with the short woman, helping her stabilize the tray of coffees she carried before she dropped them. Niko plowed past them.

The brewmaster shook his head, blinking rapidly as if coming out of a daze. He glanced down at his hand, which I held at a torturous angle, and backpedaled. I released him.

"I'm sorry. I don't know what came over me," he babbled.

Like I had suspected, under all the evil fungus, he wasn't a horrible person.

Craig attempted to stumble around me, and I pivoted to block him. Niko beat me, swinging into Craig's path and taking his hand in a politician's handshake.

"Quite a beer you've brought us tonight," Niko said, subtly pulling Craig away from me. Flares of bright *lux lucis* rolled from Niko up the brewmaster's arm, eradicating lingering spores.

I sagged back against the wall.

"Are you okay?" Alex demanded, looming over me between one blink and the next. His hands patted the air around me, as if he wanted to physically check me but didn't feel right touching me. "What was that? Did that man—"

Keep it simple.

"He thought I was his wife. Apparently he's had a bit much of his own brew."

Alex shifted to put himself between me and the brewmaster, twisting to glare at Craig's back. I peered around Alex, catching Niko's questioning glance. I nodded to let him know I was okay, though the motion was jerky. My hand shook when I patted Alex's tense arm to draw his attention back to me.

"It's okay. Really," I said.

Daphne whisked around Alex and grabbed my shoulders. "Oh my goodness, girl. I was coming to your rescue, but it looks like that was unnecessary." She tossed Alex an admiring smile that made his eyes glaze.

I ground my teeth and suppressed my flash of jealousy. If Daphne had directed that radiant expression in my direction, I probably would have reacted the same.

"Here. You look like you could use a hug." Daphne bent and squeezed me tight, whispering, "You just single-handedly prevented me from calling in a quarantine crew. Eradicating that man's internal infection is going to be a snap now, thanks to you."

She pressed her fingers to my neck just below my hairline. A jolt of energy spiked down my body, stiffening me from head to toe. Daphne's arms constricted around me, holding me upright and not letting go for the full three seconds it took my limbs to loosen again.

"A little ME gift of thanks," she whispered before stepping back. "Now go enjoy your hunk."

My soul glowed with vibrant health marginally paler than full strength. I stared at my hands in wonder, then rubbed my neck. My fingers rasped against a round paper stuck to my skin.

"Leave it," Daphne mouthed. She gave Alex's arm a pat. "Take care."

"Who was that?" Alex asked.

"Just a Good Samaritan, I guess," I said.

Daphne slid into the boisterous bar crowd, honing in on Niko and Craig. Niko must have escorted the brewmaster away from us while Daphne took care of me. When the medical enforcer reached the men, she greeted Craig like a long-lost friend, clutching his forearm with one hand. The brewmaster never noticed her other hand tweaking the back of his shirt collar and gently tapping a tiny paper circle against his skin. The moment the paper made contact, it went supernova. A bolt of *lux lucis* sank into Craig, disappearing beneath his skin. Unlike me, he appeared unaffected, but I thought I detected a slight brightening of his overall soul. It looked like Daphne had the lingering infection well under control.

Alex slid his fingers lightly down my arm and grasped my hand, drawing my attention back to him.

"You're sure you're okay?" he asked, searching my face.

The hum of *lux lucis* and fading adrenaline gave me the false sense of floating, but my fingers were rock steady in Alex's. I had done it. I had saved my region from a horrid outbreak without ruining my date. I had balanced my secret world and my relationship. I had just proved that being an enforcer and having a normal life could be done. Maybe not easily, not yet at least, but with practice, I could make this work.

And I was more than happy to get busy practicing.

I tightened my fingers around Alex's and glanced up at him through my lashes, feeling the glow of elation spread across my face. "I'm more than okay."

Alex's concerned expression cleared and he gave me a shy, close-lipped smile at odds with the heat building in his eyes.

"Want to get the cake to go?" I asked.

"You read my mind."

ABOUT THE AUTHOR

REBECCA CHASTAIN is the *USA Today* bestselling author of the Gargoyle Guardian Chronicles fantasy trilogy and the Madison Fox urban fantasy series, among other works. Inside her novels, you'll find spellbinding adventures packed with supernatural creatures, thrilling action, heartwarming characters (human and otherwise), and more than a little humor. She lives in Northern California with her wonderful husband and bossy cats.

Unlock bonus content:
Visit RebeccaChastain.com
for extras, giveaways, and so much more!

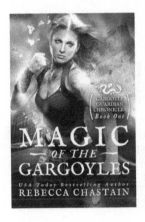 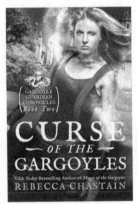 

CPSIA information can be obtained
at www.ICGtesting.com
Printed in the USA
FSHW011945031019
62687FS

9 780999 238578